4-

D1711351

The

ENDËRLAND

Chronicles

Volume I

'BOOK OF DANIEL'

To: Mary and Rick

Merry Christmas and a
Happy New Year!

Ed Marishta
London 2015

The Endërland Chronicles: Book of Daniel – 2nd edition
Cover by Erika Giselle Santiago
Copyright © 2015 Ed Marishta
ISBN13: 978-1508487944
ISBN-10: 1508487944

To my parents!

I owe you guys so much more than my respect and gratitude. You laid the foundations and started the work for me to become the man I am today, and I would not be here without your affection and support.

I love you!

CONTENTS

AUTHOR'S NOTE

The drawing of a lone wolf (or a horse, I can't remember now) staring at the moon, was the origin of the tale in these pages. It was intended as a gift to someone who was obsessed with the moon and its beauty. I challenged it and offered to do one better, to create a whole story about it, though I never dreamed - pun intended - it would turn into a book, much less be published.

I've never thought of myself as a writer, and once you've read the first few pages of "Book of Daniel", you might be inclined to agree with me. Yet, as this work born of love and dreams grew bigger and took the shape and volume it has now achieved, I decided to put it out there and share it with others who enjoy a bit of fantasy.

I would not have reached at this point, however, without the help and support of a few people close to me, who have constantly supported and encouraged me to finish this project, believing in me, even when my own lack of faith held me back. Thank you, guys; you know who you are.

Special thanks go to Erika Giselle Santiago for the amazing cover, which I'm very proud of. You are absolutely brilliant, Erika. Looking forward to collaborating with you on future projects.

I am also immeasurably grateful to my family and closest friends for being a constant source of love and joy in my life.

Above all, I thank God for inspiring and leading me to develop and complete this story, taking it to the point where it is now ready for you dear reader to enjoy.

Thank you for picking up your copy, and welcome to Endërland.

"*All that we see or seem,*
is but a dream within a dream."

Edgar Allan Poe

Chapter 1

THE REAL WORLD

September 15th was only hours away. The dawn of the new day would find Daniel officially eighteen, not that he actually cared much about it. He was at that age now when he felt too old to get excited about his birthday, and at the same time too young to dread its coming. This wasn't about him getting a year older; after all, he still had plenty of time to worry about anything like that. No, the fact of the matter was that he just wasn't overly fond of the "big day" and all that it entailed.

It had been like this for a good while now. He could hardly remember the last time he'd felt excited about his birthday, even though his dad would always find a way to make that day extra special. He had great memories of them all; some of them even stood out. His 10th birthday came to mind; his dad had taken him to Disneyland that year, and had practically gotten all the characters there to sing him Happy Birthday and pose with him for pictures and pecks on the cheek.

Daniel had never been too fond of pecks on the cheek, whether it was from people or furry animals, be they fake or real. This might have had something to do with his dad's best friend and partner, or as he knew him, Uncle Timmy. Whenever he came around, and that was quite often, Uncle Timmy would lean over, pretending to wanna kiss little Daniel on the cheek, but would, at the very last moment, opt for a little bite instead. That always made Daniel angry, especially since he always fell for it, while his father laughed out loud every time it happened. Eventually, Daniel learned to keep away from the nibbling policeman, but could never go far enough. His dad and Timmy had grown up together and were closer than brothers, hence the nickname "uncle".

The policeman, however, did redeem himself eventually; it was he who was responsible for Daniel's best birthday ever. He'd paid for both father and son to have a holiday trip for Daniel's 17th birthday. They'd spent an entire week last summer sunbathing and scuba diving in a beautiful coral reef in Corfu, Greece. With a little help from the people at the resort, his dad had practically recruited all the fish in the reef to play a part in wishing Daniel a very under-watery happy birthday. He had actually been impressed.

It was then that Daniel had really fallen in love with the sea. Swimming and diving had become his new favourite pastime. They would go seaside together as often as they could with his dad, but David never felt comfortable letting him go alone. He felt very protective of his only boy, even though he wasn't little anymore. So, Daniel had to be satisfied with a swimming pool the rest of the time. He didn't mind though, he loved swimming and was rather good at it. There was a sense of freedom he felt in the water, and even in a limited space such as a pool, he always felt he could swim forever and go far.

And yet, no matter how great a time they always had, Daniel would never feel entirely happy on his birthday. He loved his dad and appreciated everything he did for him, but try as he might, Daniel could not help but feel a little sad on his special day. He'd learned to hide this from David and had gotten better at pretending as the years went by, but deep inside he'd come to wish that they'd completely forget about the whole thing and pretend it was just another day. This way maybe he would also forget about the first ever birthday he could remember.

He had just turned five the morning his father had walked into his room, sat down on the floor with him and held him tight for a very long time. Daniel could still remember his dad's hot tears running down his spine, soaking the little t-shirt wet, and his sobs while telling him that mommy would not be there for his birthday that day. He remembered asking where she was and why she had left all day long, but he had never seen her again. David had made sure he'd still had the party and the cake, the friends, and the presents, but nothing had felt right. His mommy wasn't there, and his daddy had been so sad.

That memory haunted Daniel every year. Here he was, about to be eighteen, and he knew there would be presents, cake, and whatever else his dad had planned for the event, as he always did. But he also knew that his mother would not be there, and that despite all appearances, deep inside, his dad would be sad. And that made *him* sad too. He couldn't help it; this was how it had always been.

The noises from the laptop sitting on his bed shook Daniel free of his thoughts. He wasn't even paying attention to the movie that had been playing for almost an hour. He reached over and closed the lid, putting the computer away for the night. He didn't feel like watching anything anymore.

As he was about to switch off the light, he heard the familiar knock of his father on the door.

'Come in, dad.'

9

The door opened and David's dark wavy hair showed up first. They both had the same type of hair, healthy looking, dark, and thick, only his dad's had already begun to lose its shine and turn a lighter shade. David's smiling face followed, but the rest of his body remained hidden behind the door.

'Hey, Danny. You busy?'

'Dad, what are you up to?' Daniel could not help but smile; he knew his father all too well.

David's deep brown eyes grew even wider and brighter as he pushed the door open to reveal a small cake with a bunch of lit candles on one hand. In the other, he held a wrapped-up box with a few colourful ribbons tied around it. Walking towards his son, David began to sing the ever-dreaded 'Happy Birthday' song.

Daniel hated that song with a passion and wished someone would come up with a better alternative already, one that would actually stick. Still, he smiled and sat upright on his bed, making room for his father.

As the torturing notes finally stopped, the candles were flickering right under his nose. He breathed deeply and then attacked the little flames with all his might. All the candles went out, all but one. David blew lightly and it went out too.

'Will you never get them all at once?' he laughed.

'Never,' Daniel replied, a fake stubborn look on his young face. 'Umm, dad, you do know it's still the 14th, right?'

'Of course, son. It's just that, Timmy asked me to fill in for him tomorrow, which means I'm gonna be gone for most of it. So, I thought we'd start celebrating early and continue tomorrow evening, after I'm back. What do you say?'

This would be the first time his dad didn't organize something special for his birthday, unless, of course, this was a ruse and David had some sort of a surprise thing planned. Daniel was hoping for the former, though. He wasn't a kid anymore, and it would be a relief if there wasn't much fuss over it this year. It didn't occur to him that perhaps his dad might have finally realized how he felt about the whole thing.

'Sounds great, dad. Thanks.'

'Oh, well don't thank me just yet; you might not even like it,' replied David, putting the cake down on the bedside chair and passing the present to his son.

'I see you've had the people at the store wrap it up for you.'

'Well, you know me and presents,' he said. 'Good ideas, bad presentation.'

Daniel laughed.

The box felt kind of heavy for its size. He opened it with anticipation; despite everything, opening presents was always exciting.

The wrappings came off quickly and revealed an item that Daniel recognized right away. It was a portable air tank, small enough to contain only about 10 minutes of air under water, but very convenient and light compared to the bulky ones they needed to use whenever they went deep. Daniel jumped up from the bed, feeling like a little kid again.

'Wow, dad, you're amazing. How do you always know what to get me? Thanks, dad; I love it, really. Wow...'

'You love it? Really? Oh, I'm so glad; I wasn't sure...'

'What? Are you kidding me? When have you ever gone wrong with this stuff?'

'Oh, lots of times, trust me. Your mom would have such stories to tell if she...'

David stopped talking there and the smile on his face lost a bit of its shine. Daniel noticed but didn't let on. He hurried to speak, not wanting to ruin the moment.

'I love it, dad, thanks. Wow, I can't wait to try it.'

'Well, how about this weekend? I'm gonna be off since I'm working tomorrow. You don't have any plans, do you?'

'Me? No. I just need to ask Laura to cover for me at the library. She owes me one.'

'It's settled then; this weekend it is. Now, what about tomorrow night? What do you feel like doing?'

'Anything, dad, I don't mind.'

'We can go out for dinner if you like. Or I can cook something here and we can sit down and watch "Finding Nemo" together.'

His smile turned into a big cheeky grin as he said this.

'Dad, I'm not a kid anymore,' Daniel complained.

'I know, I know, I'm just kidding. We can watch anything you like.' David now got up from the bed. 'You used to love that movie though.'

Daniel beamed back at him.

'Still do.'

They both burst into laughter again. This felt really good, almost liberating, and for those few moments Daniel actually forgot about everything else.

Still laughing, David turned to the cake.

'Shall I cut you a slice now?'

'I'm full, dad, thanks; I'll have some tomorrow. You go ahead and have some if you want.'

'No, I'll wait for tomorrow as well. I'll go put it back in the fridge.'

David lifted the cake from the chair and collected the wrapping paper from the floor. Daniel helped.

'Ok, Danny. I'll see you tomorrow, then.'

He leaned and gave Daniel a kiss on the cheek.

'Love you, son. Sleep tight.'

'Love you too, dad. Thanks for this.'

David winked at him and made for the door.

Daniel stood there, watching his father leave the room, and a sudden feeling of sadness washed over him. It just hit him then, that despite still standing tall and strong, his father appeared tired and older. He wasn't the same man Daniel knew; age and life had marked their claim on him. Daniel's eyes began to burn from the inside and his throat suddenly grew very tight. He felt his entire face flush uncomfortably.

As David was about to close the door behind him, he called nervously.

'Dad?'

'Yeah?' came his father's reply.

Daniel suddenly couldn't continue; he felt stuck. His father pushed the door back open, waiting.

'What is it, Danny?'

'I..., I'm sorry!' was all Daniel managed to say.

'For what?'

Daniel didn't know how to continue. He stood there, trying to get the right words out, but they weren't making it easy. This was something he had meant to say for a while now, but didn't quite know when, or how.

David now appeared concerned.

'Danny, what's wrong? What are you sorry for?'

'I'm sorry that my birthday is on the same day as ..., you know...., Mom's...'

He could not say it, but he didn't have to; David understood all too well. He put the cake and the rubbish on the floor by the door and walked again towards his son. He took him in his embrace and held him tight. Daniel's tears started flowing freely now.

'That is not your fault, Danny, you know that. Not your fault.'

'I know, dad,' Daniel managed to say, pulling back from his dad's embrace, and looking down.

'I'm just..., sorry. I know you miss them a lot. And I know how difficult it's been for you, trying to appear happy for my sake every year on her anniversary.'

'Oh, Danny.' David put his hands on his son's face and with his thumbs wiped away the boy's tears. 'I *have* missed them, a lot. I still do. But they are gone, son, forever, and they're not coming back. We, however, are still here; and we have each other to take care of. Don't you think they would

13

want us to live a full and happy life, instead of mourning them all the time? And I'm not *trying* to appear happy for your sake, son, I *am* happy, because you are still here with me. You give me a reason to get out of bed every morning. I would never choose their memory over you, Danny. You hear me? Never.'

He gave his son another kiss on the forehead and made for the door again.

'Stop thinking about this and get some sleep, ok?'

'Yes, Dad...'

David was almost out of the room for the second time, when Daniel called him again.

'Dad?'

'Yes, Danny?' came the patient reply.

'Do you still dream about them?'

There was a pause before David answered again. He had not expected this conversation today. He thought about lying, about not telling his son how he dreamt of his wife and eldest son every single night. How he woke up covered in cold sweat and tears in the dark hours, gushing from the pain of losing them and missing them terribly. But somehow, he knew he shouldn't. Daniel wasn't a kid anymore and he would not be able to protect him forever from certain things. So, he decided to be truthful.

'All the time, son.'

'What's it like?' came the next merciless question.

David appeared to be thinking about it, not without some struggle. His face took on a pensive look, accentuating the still fresh wrinkles, and making him look older than he actually was.

'It's like, being with them again, I guess; reliving the very best and happiest moments I've had with them, only, a thousand times stronger.'

He now looked at his son's longing expression and understood what this was all about.

'We've talked about this before, Danny; there are plenty of people out there who never dream, or who never remember their dreams. And nobody knows why that is. But I want you to remember what I've told you; count this as a blessing. Dreams aren't always generous, son; they can also be cruel. You don't know how many times I've lost them in my dreams, over and over again. And it always hurts just like the first time. Maybe this is for the best.'

Daniel sat back on his bed. He felt tired all of a sudden, like he'd just done too many laps in the pool.

'Maybe you're right. I just..., I just don't remember them anymore, dad. Damien I could barely remember already, but now, even Mom's face is fading.'

Now it was David's turn to well up. Funny thing about being a parent; life teaches you to stand a lot of pain, to take it as it comes and become stronger, tougher. But it never teaches you how to accept the pain of the ones you love, especially your children. One more time David gulped his own emotions and remained strong in front of his son. Children should never see their parents weak.

'I tell you what; I know what we can do tomorrow. We can go through our old family photos and videos; we can make this one their year. What do you say?'

His eyes suddenly ablaze, Daniel shook his head affirmatively; this might just be his best birthday yet. For once he wasn't going to be the centre of attention for the day, and they could talk more about his mom and brother. He'd always refrained from asking his dad about them, knowing the pain those memories always caused him. But there was so much he knew his dad could tell him about them, and he wanted to know everything.

'Agreed,' he answered eagerly.

'OK then,' said David, clearly surprised at how much his son seemed to have wanted this. He almost broke down right then and there. 'It's settled, then; that is what we'll do.

15

Now, get some sleep, will you? Good night, son!'

'Good night, dad!'

The door finally closed, and Daniel was alone again. He sat there for a moment, unable to focus his thoughts on anything in particular, until he finally decided to go to sleep. It was almost 11pm and he was supposed to work the next day at the library. He put his dad's present on the floor under the bed, undid the covers, and switched off the light.

A vague image of his mother's sweet face lingered in his mind, causing him to smile slightly. He heard what his father said about dreams, but he would still give anything to see her once again, to be with her; just like it was when he was little, and she was alive and healthy. Maybe tonight would be that night.

He had never understood why he could not dream. All his life he'd listen to other people talk about their dreams, and it was always strange to him. He didn't know what they were, or how they worked; what they felt like. It made him feel weird and abnormal. So, he would make up dreams whenever the subject came up between friends. That way he wouldn't stand out so much, or so he hoped.

He was unlike any of his friends in more ways than one, not that he had many of them to begin with. Most of the guys his age were all about girls, cars, sports and other things of the sort. He liked all that stuff well enough, and yet, somehow, he never really felt comfortable hanging out with them. But this wasn't because he felt inferior or unwanted, no. He just never really cared about going out clubbing every week, booze drinking and girl chasing. Maybe he wasn't ready to grow up just yet.

So, instead, he stuck to his swimming, and reading, and hanging out with his dad. Even working in the town's public library wasn't cool for guys his age. But he didn't care; he'd come to recognize peer pressure for what it was, and it held no sway over him. Besides, the library gave him access to a world entirely different from his own, a world full of thousands of other worlds, all open and welcoming for him to explore them. And he did. What he could never visit in his dreams, he would read about, and then fantasize about.

It was while trying to understand the reason why he could not dream that he discovered this new universe of fantasy and adventure, a universe full of worlds he could enjoy being in the centre of, magical worlds where anything could happen. He grew up reading about gods and kings, treasures and dragons, elves and dwarves, and all sorts of other imaginary creatures that came to life whenever he picked up a book or watched a movie. Fantasy became a second life to him, where he could have any adventure he wanted, yet still be safe in the comfort of his own home. And the more he explored, the more he yearned for that magic.

But books and the sea were not all he was interested in; he also had a great love of the night sky and the stars. Whenever the weather was nice and the sky was clear, and that did not happen very often in good old London, he would stay up all night and study the heavens. He knew all the constellations by heart and all the stories that came with their names. He followed the news regarding new discoveries almost fanatically, and had read dozens of books and articles about the universe.

But it was the moon that fascinated him the most. He found it absolutely beautiful and enchanting, and could literally spend hours staring at it. As a little boy, he had vowed that he would one day go up there and dance on its surface, like Armstrong himself. But until then, he was happy to watch it from his bedroom window and dream about it with his eyes wide open.

He was once again adrift in his thoughts which soon began to lose all coherence and lucidity, thus helping him to slowly pass into the unconscious state of sleep. Outside, the hours raced, and the night continued to grow older. Any other night he would have slept like that until early morning, without interruption or anything at all happening. Tonight, however, was different. He was about to turn a point, and from here his life would never again be the same.

Dragging her feet down the long white marble staircase, Sam walked frustrated out of the Chicago police recruitment centre. She'd been waiting there for the last couple of hours; only to be told that she could not join the academy because of her age and health-related problems. She was furious. *What problems? What I have is a blessing, a bonus, not a problem. How many police officers do they have on the force that can stay awake and be available for work 24/7?*

'It would seem like an advantage, but it's not', the recruitment agent had told her. 'Putting your young age aside for a moment, we are not looking for robots to be on duty 24 hours a day, Miss Edison. We are looking for normal people, with normal lives and on good health. Being awake all the time does not really add to that, it takes from it. We appreciate your interest in joining the force, and I admit that I am quite impressed by some of your qualities that would have otherwise contributed to you being a fine police officer. However, the medical report is very clear, I'm afraid, and until your situation changes, we will not be able to consider you for a place in the academy.'

Sam felt so angry. She'd had such high hopes about this, and now it had all turned to ashes. So much for using her curse to help others. What else could she do? She had tried almost everything. She'd done the waitress, the maid, the receptionist, the librarian, and all sorts of other jobs she could find, but nothing had worked. She had been let go or quit from all of them at some point, and all because of her mood and bad temper. And now, she found herself clueless as to what next.

Waiting to get into the bus as it stopped in front of her, her cell phone began to ring. She took it out of her pocket and saw her mom's face on the display. She ignored the phone, putting it back in her pocket, and proceeded to pay the bus fare. Grabbing a seat towards the end of the bus, she threw her gaze outside the window, while her phone continued to ring loudly. Her mom was the persistent type.

'Are you gonna get that?' an elderly woman sitting in front of her turned around and asked, clearly annoyed.

'Back off, lady,' Sam gave her an evil look, but pressed a button on her phone to silence it anyway. The woman made a disgusted face and returned to her former position.

When the vibration finally stopped, Sam took the phone out from her pocket and checked her voicemail. Her mom had apparently given up and left her a message.

'Samantha, honey, it's mommy calling to wish you a Happy Birthday. I was hoping you would come over and we could celebrate properly this year. Daddy misses you a lot. Where are you? Please call us. Love you!'

Sam switched the phone off and put it back in her pocket. She had not seen her parents for almost a year. She'd left home for a while now, and would only visit them a couple of times every year. But every time she did, she would go through the same ordeal. They would beg her to stay and let them help her with her insomnia, but she wouldn't. They'd had their chance. She had been taken to more doctors and specialists than she could remember ever since she was five, and not one of them could do anything for her. They could not explain why she had lost the ability to sleep. She had tried countless therapies and treatments during the course of the years, but they would only make her feel worse.

Turning sixteen, she had decided that no one could help her, and she didn't want to see another specialist ever again. So, she'd made up her mind that she was going to accept her condition and live life on her own terms. Of course, her parents weren't ready to give up yet and they had not agreed with her decision, which had only led to them arguing and fighting. Sam had become very difficult to deal with, and the smallest thing would set her off and sent her on a rampage. So, for their sake, as much as her own, she had moved out and lived by herself ever since.

Being able to stay awake almost 24/7 proved of course to be a bigger problem than a blessing, despite what she kept telling herself. She tried to finish High School, but even though her grades were good, the restlessness within drove her to drop out near the end of Junior Year. What followed was a series of low paid jobs here and there that never lasted longer than a couple of months. Sam was always jumpy and easily irritated. In most cases, a row with a co-worker or a customer was the cause for her getting fired. Either that, or she would simply walk out, lacking the patience to deal with anything or anyone.

Realizing she had an attitude problem, she tried to do something about it. She tried meditation, yoga, and similar techniques. Nothing worked. At some point, someone suggested to her that she had a lot of anger inside and needed to let it out. It was then that she took up a martial arts class, where she got to punch and kick all she wanted. This appeared to calm her down a fair amount, and she got pretty good at fighting too; so, she kept that going, learning many different techniques in the process.

Money had thankfully never been an issue. Besides whatever she managed to make from working, she had access to a modest amount of money she had inherited from her late grandmother. She had been close to her Nan, and losing her when she was only fourteen had been very difficult for Sam. She used to spend a lot of time at her house, which had been just next door to theirs.

Nan had always been on her side when it came to finding a cure about her insomnia. She would always say to her: *"There's a reason for everything, my darling, including your insomnia, and one day you will find out what that is. That's when you will get your cure."*

Of course, her parents could not understand, nor accept that. They had kept the fight going. Nan had tried to comfort Sam any way she could. She would even stay awake at nights to be with her, and sleep during the days instead. Sam had loved her for that.

During the last few months of her life, Nan, as if knowing that her time was coming, had tried to prepare Sam for life on her own. She was the one who had suggested that leaving home and travelling around a lot, would probably help her cope better. She had been right, as Sam later found out.

The last thing Sam remembered about her Nan was a promise she had made, telling her that she would always be looking after her, even from beyond, when she was gone. Sam did not believe in the afterlife, but that promise had touched her. She remembered lying with her head on her Nan's lap and playing with her favourite ring.

'Don't say stuff like that, Nan. You will live for a long time.'

'It may be so, my darling, it may be so. But I still want you to know that just because you won't see me, it does not mean I am really gone. I will still be looking after you. And so that you don't forget that, I promise that this ring will be yours, when I no longer need it.'

Sam had rejoiced at the thought of owning that beautiful emerald ring, with an octagon cut shape and silver setting. It would look so perfect on her middle finger. It had been her Nan's engagement ring, though her Nan had never actually been married.

Sam didn't know much about her grandfather. Every time she would ask her Nan, she'd grow quiet and sad, with a longing and expectant look on her face, and then she would say:

'One day, child, one day you will know everything. But not just yet.'

Unfortunately, Nan had apparently forgotten her promise, because Sam never got the story, nor the ring. Her dad had told her that he didn't know anything about such promise, and Nan had been buried with it. That had been the saddest day for Sam; not only had she lost the person dearest to her, but also had her heart broken by a promise never fulfilled. She knew now there really was no life after death, and that no one would be looking after her from beyond.

The bus finally stopped in front of the church where she always got off. She loved walking past that old building; it reminded her of the church her Nan used to attend. The next stop was closer to her place, but she did not mind walking the rest of the journey. This area was generally quiet, with mostly houses left and right the streets, and a convenience store every few blocks. Not much happened here during the day, just people going about their business. The nights, however, were a different matter. Groups of young boys would hang about, and even though most of the time they were just a nuisance, somehow the streets felt less safe.

Sam had only been living here for a couple of weeks now. The place was cheap, and nobody bothered her. She didn't fear the streets. She felt confident in the ability to defend herself, but that was not all. Dealing with her share of life, she was growing increasingly tired and reckless, and did not much care about what happened to her.

It was this that drove her to make the next decision that would change her life as she knew it.

Just outside the three-storey building where she now lived, two young boys in hoodies were bothering an old beggar just for the fun of it. They kept pushing the poor guy towards each other as if he were a dodge ball, laughing hysterically, while the old man tried in vain to run away. This was common enough in her area, and, were this any other day, Sam would have just walked by and done nothing, without giving it a second thought. Today, however, she was already pissed off and needed to let off some steam.

But that was not all; there was something more to it, something Sam would understand only later. For one split second, the strangely lively eyes of the old man met hers, and she felt something she could not explain. It was not a plea for help, no, more like a weird sensation of familiarity. It was almost like they knew each other from a time long ago.

Already pumped up, she walked towards the boys with confidence.

'Hey! Let him go.'

The two boys looked back, and when they saw who it was, they ignored her. She knew them. They were about 15 and lived in that same building, just one storey above her.

'Get lost, blondie.'

She of course ignored that and moved closer. With hands in her pockets, she spoke again, this time with a hint of a threat in her voice.

'You *really* need to let him go.'

She was now standing just behind one of them, the taller one, within arm's reach. He turned very suddenly and without warning hit her very hard with the back of his hand. The strength he put to his entire arm made Sam fall back on the pavement. The other guy, shorter and skinnier, pushed the old beggar down on the pavement as well, and in just two steps was next to his friend.

'Bruh, what's wrong with you?' he yelled down at her, trying to sound older than he was. 'I told you to get lost.'

Sam put her hand on her cheek, which was now burning hot from the blow, and looked at them with such fire in her clear blue eyes. A few people started gathering around them, while more were looking out of their windows and balconies.

She stood up and faced them, looking at them straight in the eye, barely controlling her anger now.

'Listen, I suggest you take off now, if you don't wanna make a name for yourselves for getting your asses kicked by a girl.'

The bullies broke into mocking laughter.

'What?'

'Oh, you think you can kick our asses, do you?'

Sam said nothing, nor did she move a muscle. In the back of her mind, she began to recall all the instructions from her lessons and tried to calm herself down so as to have a clear head. Fighting angry would lead to her making mistakes that could cost either side dearly. But it wasn't that easy. The boys were now advancing towards her with a bullish attitude, and her anger was already getting the best of her.

She tightened her hands into fists as the tall one got one step closer. In her head, she quickly studied her position and the surroundings, already forming a strategy.

'Go on, blondie. Kick my ass.'

Sam did not wait for him to finish. She launched a strong punch right at the guy's stomach, so quickly that he was caught by surprise. As he hunched in pain, she took another hit up at his jaw, using her palm this time. She was careful to use just enough strength to bring him down, but not break his jaw and kill him. It was a classic move, and it worked every time.

As the tall kid fell down, hands covering his face, his little friend ran towards Sam with his right fist raised. She simply lifted her foot and aimed it hard at his groin. Shorty crouched in pain, and as he kneeled, Sam struck him upside down across the face with her elbow. She thought she heard a faint crack as their bones met and immediately felt guilty. The second guy fell down next to his buddy, with his hand also on his face, while everyone around them watched in silence, with the occasional applaud and cheer. Half in pain and half embarrassed, the boys just lay there without a sound.

Sam already regretted giving in to her anger, but it was done now.

'Damn you,' she scoffed, rubbing her elbow.

She then turned around and fixed herself, starting with her curly blond hair. Without looking back at her victims, she walked towards the old beggar and knelt down next to him. The man looked bad enough to make you think he would stink like sewage, but for some reason Sam did not smell anything. He had a dirty face, old and covered in long dark greasy hair. His eyes, however, looked perfectly young and shiny, and there was such pride and warmth in their gaze. Looking directly into them, she could not shake the feeling that she had seen them before.

'Are you alright? Did they hurt you?' She helped him up.

'No, they didn't,' the old man said, looking down at the two boys on the pavement. 'But looks like you hurt them. Where did you learn how to do that?'

'Yeah, well... You can learn a lot of things these days. Luckily some of them are actually useful.'

She looked towards the two guys who were now getting up and walking away stealing glances at her. Feeling bad, she tried to talk to them, 'Hey...,' but they disappeared behind the corner of the building. The spectators around them went back to their business, though some of them were still watching with smiles of approval on their faces. Nobody likes a bully.

Sam turned to the old man again.

'Do you need anything? Is there anything I can do for you?'

'Do for me? My dear girl, is there anything *I* can do for you? Looks like I owe you one.'

He didn't even sound like a beggar, not that Sam had ever had any conversations with them. Usually, they were limited to a one-sided "Can you spare some change please, God bless".

'I'm good, thanks. And you don't owe me anything, really.'

'But of course, I do; one good deed deserves another. It's the way of the world.'

Sam looked down, guilt finally catching up with her.

'I'm not so sure this was such a good deed,' she mumbled, then raised her volume. 'Anyway, I don't want anything, and what I do need, you cannot give me. So, thanks, but if you're not hurt and are okay to go on, I will go home now.'

The man reached out and touched her hand.

'Wait; don't be in such a hurry, please. Give me your hand and two more minutes of your time, and I bet I can tell you exactly what you need.'

'Excuse me?'

'I'm a seer, child, a fortune-teller. Just one look at your right hand, and I can tell you exactly what you need to know. I have never been wrong in my entire life.'

Sam took one step back in doubt.

'I'm sorry, but I don't believe in that stuff.'

The old man stood where he was.

'That's ok, you don't need to; I believe enough for both of us. I have been seeing things all my life, though I almost always keep them to myself. But I have a very good feeling about you. Please, would you let me read you? It'll be worth your while, I promise.'

He extended one hand towards Sam and just waited for her. She thought about walking away and leaving him where he stood, but something stopped her. Something in his voice, in his eyes felt sincere, pure, amicable. She felt this was real, that *he* was real.

She could not believe what she was about to do.

'This had better be good,' she said, resting her right hand unto his, palm up.

The old man smiled, then shut his bright blue eyes and placed his other hand on hers, sliding his fingers slowly throughout her palm, searching every line, every crease on it. He did that for about half a minute, without speaking, then opened his eyes and said in a low, compassionate voice.

'I see. I see you've been struggling with a serious problem for as long as you can remember, and it's affecting everything you do. I see you've been looking for a solution for a long time but have given up. And now you feel lost, like you don't know which way to go, like you have no purpose.'

Sam was actually surprised. She was expecting something more along the lines of "There's a dark shadow in your life, but some good news ahead, etc...," you know, the usual mumbo-jumbo. But this was more real, more personal than she thought it would be. This guy was good.

The old man continued.

'There's more. A broken promise seems to have broken your heart. It was someone close to you, someone you loved dearly, but they let you down. Oh, don't worry, child, things are about to change for you.'

He now looked straight into her glistening eyes, without letting go of her hand.

'Would you like me to tell you how?'

Sam was still baffled and didn't know what to think or say. Was he actually talking about her Nan? Was this guy the real deal?

'There is an answer for all of your questions, child, but it won't just come to you. You have to actually go and find it. You will need to go on a journey, no, not a spiritual one, a real one; and your first stop will be London.'

'What? London? As in England, London?'

Sam drew her hand back and changed in the face as if waking up.

'What do I wanna go to London for? If you know the answer, why can't *you* give it to me?'

'It is not that kind of answer, I'm afraid, and neither it is mine to give to you. You must find out on your own.'

'Well, that's convenient. First there's a problem I have, and then a broken promise and a broken heart. Now, a journey? Couldn't you have come up with something a bit more original and specific maybe? I think I've heard enough. Thank you very much for the séance. I'm gonna go home now. Bye.'

She turned around frustrated and started to walk towards the entrance of the building, but the old man didn't give up.

'Something specific, huh? Well, how about this? In two weeks' time, you need to be in the London Sleep Centre in England. There you will meet someone named Daniel. Stick with him and you will find the answers that you need. Happy Birthday, Sam!'

Sam stopped halfway to the doors and froze. *That was specific alright.*

'How did you...?'

She turned around to face the beggar again, but he was no longer there. *Where did he go? He was just here; he couldn't have just disappeared.* She looked around in all four directions, but the man was nowhere to be found.

Her frustration now reached a new high. Who was he and how did he know all that personal stuff about her? Was she really going to have to go to London? If so, what answers was she going to get?

Wait a minute, she thought to herself. *He mentioned a Sleep Centre. Maybe he meant that they might have a cure for me there. Maybe this Daniel is a doctor, and he can treat me.*

She hurried upstairs into her apartment and on to her computer. She googled 'London Sleep Centre' and found the website of a clinic with that same name. It was all standard stuff that she had already seen before, but there was no doctor named Daniel on their team. *That still doesn't mean anything,* she thought. *The website doesn't say everything or maybe it's just outdated.*

Over the next couple of days Sam thought about everything and considered all her options. She considered that she must have hallucinated; that the two boys had beaten *her* up instead and she had dreamed the whole thing. She considered that the guy was maybe hired by her parents to help convince her to try some new experimental therapy. However, nothing could convince her that what she experienced had been entirely fake.

In the end, she decided she had nothing to lose, so she booked an open-ended ticket for London, departing on the 27th of September. She could smell the scent of a new adventure in the air, and for the first time in a very long time, she felt ready and excited about it.

Chapter 2

I HAVE A DREAM

Underneath his closed eyelids Daniel sensed the strong light of day nagging him to wake up. Somehow it felt too early to be already morning. With some struggle and still half asleep, he opened his eyes. Nothing could have prepared him for what followed.

As his almond shaped emerald eyes kissed the first golden rays of sunshine, he got the shock of his life. Instead of the boring ceiling of his bedroom, he was staring at a clear blue sky, right on top of him. The sun was half visible, crowning on top of a series of tall mountains over the northeast horizon.

It was morning alright, but where was he? And why did he feel cold and wet?

Halfway into realizing that he was somehow floating on the sea, he lost all balance and went completely under. Unprepared, his mouth tasted the salty liquid, and he tried in vain to spit it out. He was at a loss, not quick enough to understand what was going on; everything was happening so fast. He kept going under without knowing what to do.

Lucky for him, his body recognized the circumstances it found itself in, and instinctively kicked towards the surface and the air to breathe. As his head broke the water from underneath, Daniel inhaled deeply, filling his lungs with air like he was doing it for the very first time. And in a sense, he was.

Fully awake now and struggling to stay afloat, he scanned the area around for land, and sure enough, the shore was not too far from where he was. He swam towards it, and it didn't take him long to reach. Dumbfounded, he got out of the water and just sat on the sandy beach, trying desperately to catch his breath and get his wits about. In front of him, a beautiful blue sea breathed peacefully in all its majesty, ignoring Daniel, as if he'd always been there.

But where was he? What was going on? How could he fall asleep in his bed and wake up in the middle of a foreign sea? Fear began to overcome all of his other senses. Was this bad? Would he ever be able to go back home, see his dad?

Dad!

Right then it hit him. This must be a dream, it had to; there was no other explanation for it. The last thing he remembered thinking about, before he fell asleep, was diving with his new air tank. No wonder he found himself floating on the sea, he must be having his first dream; he was sure of it now. But this felt so real! Was this what dreams were like; so beautiful, so vivid and rich in detail?

He took a long look at the scenery before him and could not believe his eyes. This place took him back to his time in Corfu with his dad; sun, sand, and sea to your heart's content, and then some. The only thing that seemed to be missing was the multitudes of people he usually found in beaches like this. Somehow, though, he was glad that he had this place all to himself.

Feeling slightly more relaxed now, he figured he was in no immediate danger, and thus slowly but surely the excitement started to kick in.

Let's see, what did he know about dreams? They usually don't make much sense, that's a given. You cannot die in a dream; he'd heard that one too. And of course, you're bound to see and do some strange things in a dream, things that usually do not happen in real life. But what kind of a dream was this going to be?

Still sitting by the big blue, he was now feeling the warmth of the sun drying out his wet clothes. Daniel smiled to himself. He was still in his pyjamas. He looked around; there was no one in sight. He decided it would be better if he stripped and hung them to dry somewhere. He wouldn't want to catch a cold. Or could he? Could he get sick in a dream?

Behind him, a pine tree forest grew green and quiet, with each tree racing the others towards the never-reaching sky. Daniel walked towards the closest ones, first taking his top off, when he noticed something odd. The pine tree next to the one he was heading towards, had something or someone hanging on it. No, not hanging, tied was more accurate.

He moved closer. Tied fast on the body of the old pine tree, hung what seemed to Daniel as a half human-half fish creature. Human because of its head, arms, and torso; fish because of the big scaly tail that replaced the lower body and legs. Underneath both armpits, where the skin began to turn into scales, he could see five pairs of gill slits that were frantically moving up and down as if gasping for air.

This was a dream alright, and here was the proof; he was seeing with his own eyes a real mermaid.

Daniel got even closer, until he was standing just beneath the poor thing. There was a faint smell of fish that made him hold his nose with his hand at first. This couldn't be good. He couldn't see its face because its head was hanging down on its chest and wasn't moving. He rose on the tips of his toes, and with a trembling hand reached for the dark red hair that covered the eyes. From the bare top, short hair and now his face, Daniel realized this was a boy. He tilted the head gently towards him and called.

'Hey. Are you alright?'

The boy opened his eyes just a little and couldn't even move them to look at Daniel. His skin was completely discoloured and cracked all over, and he looked dangerously white. With all the strength he could manage, he moved his lips to form one single word.

'Water.'

Daniel needed no time to decide what it was the boy meant; it was all too clear. He was a sea creature, and someone had tied him up here, away from the water, to die. What he needed was to get back into the sea, of course. He first looked around again to see if whoever did this might be coming back. There was no one in sight. He then studied the rope that was holding the boy to the tree. His arms were pulled back on either side of the huge trunk, and a lot of rope was used to make sure he couldn't move an inch. There were visible bruises, and his tail and fin looked badly damaged, both by the rope and the harsh bark of the tree. Thick sap ran down his back, making the situation for the merman even more unpleasant.

The rope was passed over the frail body many times in a very messy way, and since Daniel had no knife or other tool to cut it with, he would have to try and undo the knot. He dropped his pyjama top on the ground and started working. He struggled a bit with it at first, and his fingers got all sticky and dirty by the tree sap, but it proved easier than he thought. When he finally released the rope, the boy fell face down on the ground, but did not move.

Daniel turned him around face up, and then slid his hands underneath his armpits. Walking backwards, barefoot as he was, he dragged the boy towards the water and did not stop until he went in neck deep. The merboy was now completely immersed before him.

For a while nothing happened. Daniel was still holding on to the boy, not knowing what else to do. Then, suddenly, the merman's body jerked once violently, and immediately after that he felt hands pushing away from him. In the space of a few seconds the boy snaked quickly deep into the sea and out of his sight. Daniel turned where he was, but the creature was completely gone.

He stood there a few moments, waiting, and wondering, but nothing else happened. Minutes passed and eventually he guessed he would never see the boy again, so he began to head out of the water. He was happy that he had been able to save the little guy, but did he have to leave like that? It's not like he had a chance to talk to mermaids every day, after all.

He kept looking back as he dragged his feet towards the shore, and that's when he saw it. Just in front of him, about 10-12 feet into the sea, he saw what looked like a vision of his bedroom shimmering on the surface of the water. The image was barely visible, almost transparent, blending perfectly with the invisible air around it. He figured this was just about where he first was when he woke up. Heading back towards it this time, he saw that the vision grew stronger and clearer the closer he got. He was now just about to reach the spot, when the vision was disturbed by the dark red head of the merboy popping out and swimming in his direction.

Daniel stopped where he was, his attention now fully focused on the creature. The boy, who would be about 15 or 16 years old, if he was human, had almost completely regained his normal colouring, and was smiling. In just a few powerful strokes he reached Daniel and swam once very

34

quickly around him. When he came full circle, he stopped in front of Daniel and rose a bit higher, in order to be in the same level. His dark black eyes made such a beautiful contrast with his red hair and pale white tone of skin. Unlike a moment earlier, there was such life now in those eyes, that it caused Daniel to wonder if this was indeed the same merboy.

'Hi. I'm Nemo.'

His voice was light and melodic, but that wasn't what caused Daniel to chuckle.

'I'm sorry. Did you..., did you say, Nemo?' he asked, forgetting his manners for a moment.

The boy appeared embarrassed by his reaction.

'Yes, yes I did. Why is that funny? I've had this name all my life, but nobody ever laughed at it. Mother herself named me when I was born.' He now drew back looking a bit hurt. Daniel hurried to correct his mistake.

'No, no, I'm sorry; it's not funny at all. I apologize if I offended you. It's just that, well, I know someone else who goes by that name, and, well, you're a lot different, that's all. I'm Daniel.' He extended his hand above the water and Nemo shook it. He immediately changed into his happy self again as if nothing had ever happened.

'Very glad to meet you, Daniel; I mean that. If it weren't for you, I would have dried dead out there. You saved my life; thank you!'

Moving arms and legs to help himself stay afloat, Daniel replied.

'I'm just happy I happened to be there. Umm, do you mind if we move a bit closer to the shore? I'm getting a bit tired here.'

Nemo was only too eager to please.

'Oh, yes of course. Here, give me your hand.'

Daniel grabbed his cold slippery hand and with one powerful stroke of his tail Nemo took them both where the water reached knee high. Daniel sat there half immersed into water, while Nemo laid himself in front of him, cheerfully splashing his tail. The water felt so nice and unusually warm for this time of day.

'Thanks,' Daniel said, shaking the water off his longish black hair.

'Anytime,' Nemo replied. 'I'm sure I can do much more than that. After all, you did just save my life'.

'I am sure you would have done the same for me, Nemo. But, if I may ask, who put you up there?'

Nemo lowered his head as if ashamed.

'I don't have proof of this, but I believe it was my sisters.'

'Your sisters? But why would they do that?'

'They hate me; they always have. To them I'm nothing but a joke, a freak. You see, there's never been a male mermaid in our entire history. There have only been them, the females. But when my mother, the queen mermaid, laid her last egg, me, I turned out to be different from the others. They are all afraid of what this might mean, and they hate me for it. But not my mother; she loves me and protects me. She says I have a great future ahead. I don't know what she means though.'

'But if your mother is the queen, how could they touch you? Aren't they afraid?'

'They cannot, not directly. It wasn't them who tied me up that tree. But I think they set the whole thing up. They lured me to the surface with the pretence of a dare, and that's when the sky-people kidnapped me.'

'The sky-people?' Daniel asked intrigued. What kind of a dream had he ended up in?

'Yes, you know, *the sky-people*,' Nemo said as if Daniel should know perfectly what he was talking about. 'The Wingmen, the people who fly?'

Daniel kept staring blank.

36

'Don't you know who the sky-people are? Where have you been living until now, in a cave?'

'Umm, not here,' Daniel answered. 'I come from a different place, *a real* place. In fact, I'm quite sure that right now I'm in my bed sleeping and dreaming all of this.'

This made Nemo jump out of the water as high as he could with excitement, just the way Daniel had seen dolphins do at the aquarium once.

'Oh wow, you're a Visitor? Really? I can't believe this. I mean, I knew there was something different about you, but we haven't seen Visitors in a very, very long time. I didn't even think they existed anymore. Wow.'

'What's a visitor?' Daniel asked, wiping salty water from his face. Nemo realized that he had just soaked him wet from his splash.

'Sorry,' he said, making a cute guilty face. 'Visitors are people that come from another place, *your* place, I guess. Some of them visit Endërland very often and ...'

'Endërland?' Daniel interrupted.

'Yes. That's what this place, our kingdom, is called. Anyway,' he continued, 'at some point they either decide to stay here forever, or they leave and never come back again. But it's been a very long time since one has been seen here. And now, *you're* here. Oh, man, I have to tell mother. The whole kingdom will wanna know about this.'

Nemo was clearly very excited, but Daniel had no idea what this all meant.

'Umm, I don't know if I'm a Visitor or not, but I don't think I like the idea of everybody talking about me, Nemo. I'm not one who likes to be the centre of attention, if you know what I mean. Besides, I'm sure this is all just a dream, anyway. Very soon I will wake up and we'll probably never see each other again.'

37

Nemo suddenly got a very mature look on his face. Daniel for some reason thought this didn't really suit his young appearance.

'It may well be a dream to you, but I assure you, Daniel, this place is real, we are real. And if I'm right, you will be back here again.'

'Still,' Daniel insisted, 'I would prefer that you didn't tell anyone about me just yet. I would like to know this place a bit better first.'

'If that's what you want, I give you my word. I will not speak of you. But you have to meet mother. She will want to reward you for saving my life.'

Daniel wasn't sure. His timid nature usually got in the way of him meeting new people and trying new things. He tended to stick to people and places he knew well.

'Me? Meet the queen of the mermaids?'

'Actually, she's the Queen of the Seas,' Nemo corrected, 'mermaids are just its rulers. But don't worry, it won't happen today. If you come back tomorrow, with your permission, I would like to tell her about you. She is very wise and very generous; I'm sure you will enjoy meeting her.'

Certain that by morning all of this would be nothing but a vague memory, Daniel agreed. This appeared to please Nemo a great deal. He then lay back again and continued to tell Daniel more about Endërland.

He spoke about the underwater city and his mother's castle, where all the royal business and ceremonies took place. He told him of how she would soon leave the throne and the crown would pass to her successor, which still hadn't been chosen. The tradition required that the candidates compete against one another, and the one to win would become their next queen.

He told him more about the sky-people, as the mermaids called them. They looked very much like regular people, except they were much taller and slender, and of course they had big and powerful wings attached to their backs. Also, all their fingers and toes ended up in sharp claws instead of nails. Their favourite food was fish, which with the Sea-Queen's permission they were very skilful to catch.

The two people, however, were not in the best terms lately. They'd always been friendly, but recently the sky-people had become too greedy and careless about the fish they caught, thus causing a great disturbance to the mermaids, who were not happy about it one bit.

Then, of course, Daniel learned about the other group of inhabitants in the kingdom, the humans. There were many of them, most living in the great city of Endër, just a few days' travel from there. More lived in other cities and villages spread throughout Endërland. They were just regular people, living simple lives, and they loved to celebrate many things and very often.

The mermaids never really had any problem with the humans. They were good-hearted and hardworking, and they loved and respected the sea and its population. Their queen was lovely and kind, and she came often to visit and consult with his mother by the sea.

They spoke a lot and they moved a lot. Daniel wanted to see more of this place, so he got up and walked along the beach, while Nemo followed him, swimming only feet away.

Daniel still could not believe what he was experiencing. How could a dream be so alive and so beautiful? Was he really in a dream or something entirely different was happening here? And how could he find out?

Hours passed since he met the little merman, and he hadn't eaten a thing, or drank at all. Strangely enough, he felt neither hungry nor thirsty. He kept walking and talking to Nemo, seeing more of the beach, and hearing more about this place. Nemo liked to talk a lot, and he never seemed to get tired.

As the day headed towards evening and the bright sun towards the western horizon, Daniel began to grow concerned again. He thought about the vision he saw above the surface of the water. What was that about? Would he see it again if he went back to the same spot? Was he supposed to go back there if he wanted to get home again? Perhaps Nemo knew something about it.

'Nemo?' he asked. 'These Visitors you spoke of, how did they travel back and forth?'

'You mean from your world? I don't know. Nobody ever knew much about them. Why do you ask?'

'Well, thing is... I am not sure how I'm supposed to get back. I've never done this before.'

Daniel looked like a kid on his first day of school just now; shy, afraid, and ready to be told what to do and where to go.

'I guess there are people who could probably give you some answers,' Nemo suggested, 'but only mother might know who they are; you know, Visitors that have settled here. But that means that I would have to tell her about you.'

Daniel thought about it. They were hours away from the place where he found Nemo, and the sun was now already sinking behind the deep blue sea. He thought of the night that was fast approaching. What would it be like, and where would he spend it?

'If you go to see her now, how long will you be gone for?' he asked Nemo. The boy sensed some anxiety in him.

'Not long,' he answered, 'but you will be perfectly fine here. As soon as mother has told me what you need to know, I'll come find you and then we'll go see some friends of ours. They live farther down the beach. They are humans; they will take good care of you and take you anywhere you will want to go tomorrow. Ok?'

Daniel was more assured by Nemo's tone of voice, than his words. He urged him to come back soon and waved goodbye as the boy disappeared underneath the liquid glass. The sun was now almost gone, painting the sky with a vivid orange hue.

He was alone once again in a foreign place, with no one around and nothing to do but think. He sat on the sand by the water and watched the last ray of the sun sparkle far away in the west, where the ocean met the sky. Everything looked so peaceful and beautiful. He wouldn't mind living here forever; a small, nice house on the beach would be fantastic.

He remembered his dad telling him that it was his mother's dream to live by the sea. If only she could see this. His thoughts ran again towards her, and this time he found that he remembered her a lot better. He could clearly see her long black hair, beautiful green eyes, feel her soft white skin and smell her unique scent, which he had always associated with her. He felt astounded at the clarity of her image now; he remembered her just like she had been, strong, beautiful and with a huge smile on her sweet face. He was sure it was this place. He could feel it.

Night came quickly now that the sun had set, but it wasn't nearly as dark as Daniel thought it might be. The sky on top of him was unimaginably bright and full of stars, and now he could also see the moon rise from the mountains up north. The majestic sight of it caught Daniel's attention like never before. He had never seen a moon so big, so round, and bright. It instantly claimed all of the night sky as soon as it appeared. It was the most beautiful thing he had ever seen, and he felt so enchanted by it that it was as if nothing else existed around him. He forgot about Nemo, the sea, and even his mother for a moment. He could reach out with his hand and touch it; that's how close it felt to him.

Daniel smiled and silently thanked whoever had brought him to this wonderful place that seemed to offer all the things that he loved. He spent the rest of the evening staring at the bright celestial sphere rising above him, his wrists under his head as a pillow and his bare feet barely an inch from the always warm water. Eventually, his eyes closed, and sleep claimed him again. A cool breeze started to blow in from the sea, but he felt no cold, half naked as he was. Nor was he disturbed by the noises of the forest nearby at night. He slept peacefully and quietly as if he was in his own bed.

* * *

When he opened his eyes again, Daniel half expected to see stars on top of him. The only thing he saw instead was the dull white ceiling of his bedroom. It wasn't night either, it was morning, right around the usual time he woke up every day. He took a moment to shake off his sleep and focus. He was home again, which meant that everything he had experienced previously had really been just a dream.

Some dream, he thought. It was all still with him, very much real. He could still smell the ocean and the trees, feel the sand under his feet. He could clearly remember the feel of the water, the warmth of the sun, Nemo's face and voice.

Dreams, what a strange thing.

He checked the time; it was 5 past 8. He figured he had enough time to shower, have a quick bite and get ready for work. Getting out of bed, he noticed that he wasn't wearing his t-shirt. Puzzled, he looked underneath the covers and under the bed, but it wasn't anywhere. He searched the drawers, the wardrobe, the laundry bin, but nothing. He tried to recall where he could have left it, and then he remembered. In his dream, he had dropped it by the tree when he released Nemo, and he hadn't worn it again all day.

This woke him up properly. Was this for real? Was that what had actually happened? He remembered clearly falling asleep wearing the t-shirt. So where was it now?

Frustrated he decided that it must be somewhere in the house, so he just stopped looking. He couldn't have left his t-shirt inside a dream; that would be crazy. What would people say if they knew what he was thinking?

Ignoring the t-shirt, he went to the bathroom mirror. What he saw there brought on a second wave of shock. He was tanned, slightly but visibly tanned. His skin didn't burn or anything, but he could clearly see that it had turned reddish overnight.

Gobsmacked, he lifted his hands to touch his face and noticed that they were dirty. Well, sort of dirty; they looked as if they had been washed, but something had left brown sticky stains on his fingernails. In his dream he'd been trying to remove the sap from the pine tree with seawater and sand.

This couldn't be. All the signs told him that the dream last night had been real, and yet everything he knew about dreams was purely psychological or mythical. Was he in need of professional help, or something entirely out of the ordinary was happening to him? For, as far as he knew, no one had physically walked into their dreams and left their pyjamas there, or seen mermaids and flying people who didn't really exist. But, what other explanation could there be?

All that day he kept wondering and thinking about this. Yet, no matter how he rationalized it, the only plausible explanation was that he really visited this world called Endërland. He was, as Nemo had said, a Visitor. Either that, or there was something seriously wrong with him.

He, of course, spoke to no one at work about this, or any of his mates at the gym. He didn't say anything to his dad that evening either. They had a nice dinner together; saw some of the old family videos that included his mom and his older brother Damien and made a lot of jokes to make each other laugh. This, of course, was their coping mechanism trying to keep at bay the sadness and tears that the memories of their loved ones invoked.

Yet, David had not missed the fact that his son had been absentminded the whole time.

'Are you ok, Danny?' he asked as Daniel eventually announced that he was going to bed early. 'You've been a bit distracted all evening; it's as if you're someplace else. Is everything alright?'

Daniel had struggled all day with the idea of telling his father, and still hadn't decided what to do. Right now, however, he thought he could risk a little truth. He would never want to lie to his dad, but he didn't want him to think his son was losing his marbles either.

'I'm fine, dad, really. It's just..., I think I had a dream last night.' He stopped there and waited for his father's reaction. He didn't have to wait long. David was caught completely off guard.

'What? Really? A dream, dream?'

'Yes. Well, I think so. I mean, what else could it have been? I was on a beach somewhere I have never been, and everything was so beautiful. I swam in the sea, I lay on the sand, and then I woke up.'

'That was it?'

'Pretty much, yeah,' Daniel lied. He hated it, but he had no choice. He had to know for sure before he could really talk to his dad.

David took his time digesting the news.

'Wow, that's unbelievable. After all this time, you just... How do you feel?' he asked his son.

'I don't know. A bit strange, I guess. I wonder if I will be able to dream again. That's why I wanna go to bed early. You'll be ok?'

David assured him that he would be fine on his own and wished him a good night.

As he was left alone, he took another sip from his wine glass and allowed a single tear to roll down his cheek. Strangely he felt happy, fulfilled. Daniel not being able to dream had never been a big deal, but now that he could, he felt like everything was finally going to be alright for the two of them.

* * *

The sun had fully emerged from the horizon when Daniel opened his eyes again and found himself back on the same beach he had fallen asleep the previous evening. He was no longer shirtless; he was now wearing the new pair of pyjamas he'd put on before going to bed. Apparently, whatever he wore when he fell asleep, appeared in this world with him. Thinking about it, he decided he would have to make some adjustments; he couldn't go around all day wearing his pyjamas, even if this was just a dream.

He got up and stretched, feeling reinvigorated and full of energy, as if ready for a new round of adventures. The air smelled wonderfully fresh as a soft breeze blew in from the sea, bringing with it the scent that Daniel had grown to love.

He looked around for Nemo, but the merboy was nowhere to be seen. He had been gone all night. Had something gone wrong? He had said he would not be gone for too long. Not knowing what else to do, he decided to walk back towards the place where he first met Nemo. He was dying to know if the image he saw yesterday above the water was still there. It would take him a couple of hours to get there, but he had nothing better to do with his time. And he was certain Nemo would be able to find him easily.

Eventually, he thought he spotted the tree Nemo had been tied to and moved closer. Sure enough, the rope was still there, at the base of the tree. He remembered his t-shirt and looked for it, but it was not where he had left it. He decided the wind must have taken it away, so he forgot about it and turned his attention to the sea.

As he got closer to the water's edge, he spotted the vision hovering in the air not too far from him, almost translucent and invisible. It was still there, just like yesterday. He stepped into the water and swam closer. He was now right in front of it. It was like a mirage, an illusion or special effect that defied all logic, but it was there, within arm's reach. He could clearly make out the wall facing his bed, his desk with the laptop and books on, the chair where some of his clothes were resting, and a part of his wardrobe on the right side of the room. Everything just the way it looked from his bed when he was on it.

Daniel swam around it a little to the left, and the image sort of moved with him. He then swam to the right, but whichever angle he took, the image remained the same; he would always see the same thing. There was no way to get around and behind it; the vision rotated as he did.

Daniel stretched out his hand to touch it. As his fingers went through the image, he saw them as if through the mist, but felt nothing and nothing transpired. He then decided to go through it completely and see what would happen.

The moment he swam inside it, he found himself back home, waking up in his bed, in the dark. It felt very early in the night, and he was right. The clock on the wall showed half past midnight. It took him only a short moment to shake off his sleepiness and recall his last actions. He realized now that the image he went through was a way back, some kind of a portal.

This was real. Everything he had experienced was real and not just a dream like he had thought. He'd managed to go back to Endërland and discovered not one, but two ways to get back home from there.

He was now more than ready to dream again.

Chapter 3

<u>MY QUEEN</u>

The cold salty water on the face did the trick alright; Daniel woke up with a start.

'Finally,' Nemo exclaimed just a few feet away from him. 'I've been calling you for ages, man. You sleep like a rock.'

Daniel yawned and then smiled at Nemo as he got up.

'Hey Nemo. Where were you? You said you wouldn't be gone long.'

'I know, I'm sorry,' said Nemo. 'Mother wouldn't let me go without me telling her the whole story, and making sure that I was alright and no longer in danger. And then she had to think about what to do next and get advice from her counsellors regarding the wingmen. And then she wanted to take time and prepare for a proper introduction with you. I came ahead to let you know.'

'What; she's coming to meet me? Now?'

That was rather unexpected. Daniel didn't think he would have to meet the Queen of the Seas so soon. What would he say to her? How does one act in front of a real queen?

'Did she say why she is coming to see me?' he asked, fishing for tips. He must have looked or sounded a bit anxious though, because Nemo replied:

'Relax. She said she wants to thank you herself for saving me and give you the information you need in person. I think she's coming. Here, come and stand on this rock. When you see her, bow down, but do not speak. Let her address you first.'

Daniel moved nervously to the place Nemo showed him; a rock that rose higher and stretched further into the sea from the rest of the shore, like a small cape. The water beneath was enough for Nemo to be immersed chest deep.

Soon they noticed movement farther in front of them. The water rose higher for a very brief moment, and then a small silver crown broke the surface, followed by long dark red hair falling down the beautiful face of what looked like a woman in her thirties. Like Nemo's, her skin was pale white and shiny like alabaster, while her eyes were a fiery red, deep and sharp.

She was nothing like Daniel had imagined. She wore armour and had a warrior's appearance, strong features, and a piercing look in her eyes. A strange looking crossbow hung on the back of her shoulder, seemingly made out of an unusual material, kind of transparent with a hint of blue. Daniel thought he was seeing a Greek goddess gliding towards him.

There were four other mermaids following the queen, all clad in similar armour. He bowed low on one knee and remained like that until he heard the queen stop right in front of him and speak.

'Arise, Visitor.'

Daniel got up and faced her. She was mesmerizing from up close. The features that he had come to find in Nemo, were present in her as well. But, while Nemo was still a boy,

48

uncertainty and innocence still predominant on his fresh face, she radiated strength and wisdom beyond her youthful looks. Her stare was authoritative, yet gentle. And there was something there that Daniel could not read, some sort of realization that only she was aware of.

She took a long look at him and then spoke again.

'I am Eleanor, third Queen of the Seas of Endërland and Lady of the mermaids. My son has told me how you saved his life, and I am here to personally convey my gratitude, Visitor. For what you have done, my people and I will always be at your service, the sea will always be your home, and the mermaids your family. You have but to name your reward, young one, and I will see it done.'

Daniel felt overwhelmed. Her voice was so powerful and her presence even more so. But he didn't want anything. He lowered his head respectfully and spoke.

'My lady, I have done nothing to deserve a reward and even less so, your service. In fact, it is I who offer you my services, for whatever they're worth. Order me, and I shall obey.'

He could barely believe the words that had just come out of his mouth; he had never spoken like that before. He must have picked up a thing or two from all the fantasy books he had read after all.

The queen appeared pleased by his reply. She drew just a bit closer and spoke this time with a softer voice.

'You speak like royalty. Tell me, Visitor; are you a prince or a king in your world?'

Daniel chuckled at this.

'No, my lady; I was born of common people, and if there is any royalty in my blood, my father never told me about it.'

This seemed to entice the queen's interest even more.

'Your father! What about your mother? Surely *she* must be a queen.'

'Only to my father and me, my lady, and only in our memories. She is no longer with us; she died when I was a little boy.'

His voice faltered at the last words, while his eyes touched the ground. Thus, he failed to see a strange light in the queen's eyes, and the sorrow that shadowed Nemo's.

'I am sure she would be very proud to see that her son has grown up to be such a fine young man. But, tell me; is there nothing that this queen can do for you? My son told me that you seek the counsel of other Visitors that have settled here from long ago; is that so?'

'That's true, my lady. It is only my second day here, and there are a lot of things that I need to know and understand. Nemo told me that they might be able to help me, but not many know who they are.'

'I'm afraid I do not have that knowledge either, Visitor, but I can point you in the direction of one who does. And since you require nothing of me for saving my son's life, I decree that his life is yours, until his debt is properly paid. He will accompany you wherever you need to go and help you do whatever you need to do.'

Daniel had no idea what she meant; how would the merboy be able to accompany him on land? By the look on Nemo's face, however, this was good news, at least for him. He looked as happy and excited as he'd ever seen him. He swam swiftly towards his mother, looking at her straight in her fiery eyes, like a little child who had just been promised his favourite toy.

'You mean; I can go? Really?'

'Yes, Nemo; the day has finally come, my love. It's either now or never.'

Nemo gave a joyful shout and jumped as high as he could out of the water. He then dived deep down where Daniel could not see him. Three of the mermaids accompanying the queen chased after him, save for the fourth one, who with an indifferent look on her face remained where she was. He figured they were congratulating Nemo, but he still didn't understand what for.

The queen read the confusion on his young face and decided to explain.

'It is our tradition that upon reaching a certain age, each one of my mermaids has the choice to walk upon land and experience the life outside the sea for a time. If they decide to stay there forever, their wish is granted, and they become one of the people of the land. And if they decide to come back, they remain mermaids for the rest of their life and devote themselves to the sea. My son's time for this has come for quite a while, but I have been reluctant to let him go, until now. I feel this is the right time for him to take this journey, and something tells me that both your paths go together from here. Will you accept this, Visitor?'

Daniel looked at her sovereign face and then at Nemo, who just resurfaced, still looking pretty excited and goofy. How could he refuse? Did he dare reject the queen's request, or spoil this for Nemo, who clearly wanted it?

And he just realized that *he* wanted this as well. He wouldn't have to be on his own while searching for the other Visitors; Nemo would show him the way and accompany him wherever he would need to go. This was indeed good news. He bowed to the queen once again and spoke.

'It would be my pleasure, my lady.'

'Very well, then,' the queen smiled and then turned to her only son.

'Nemo. Forgive me for not having a proper ceremony for this occasion, but I would delay our Visitor no longer. Come to me, son.'

Nemo swam again towards her, full of anticipation and joy. She took him in her arms and hugged him tight. Daniel now saw the soft, maternal side of her and could not help but think of his own mother.

'This is your journey, my little one, your chance to discover who you will be. You'll have all the time you will need and all the support you can get from your sisters and me. If you decide to come back to us, there will be a place prepared for you in our kingdom. And if you decide to stay, our love and blessings will stay with you for all time.'

She gave him a kiss on the forehead, and then on the lips, where she lingered just a little, as if she was passing on something to her son. And then she let him go.

Nothing seemed to be happening at first, but soon Daniel noticed a change in the way Nemo was trying to hold himself up on the surface of the water. Until that very moment, he had been perfectly at ease staying afloat, but now he seemed to be struggling a bit. He started to swim towards the shore awkwardly and that's when Daniel noticed them. His beautiful tail was gone, and two skinny white legs had materialized instead. Nemo was still trying to use them as he would his tail, but it wasn't really working. He managed however to swim until he reached a shallow place, where he tried to stand on his new legs but failed and fell back in the water. Laughing out loud he got up again and fell again.

One of his sisters swam up to him and handed him something that Daniel couldn't make out what it was. Soon though, he understood; the queen had come prepared. Looking a bit embarrassed, Nemo struggled to wear a pair of shorts that were prepared for him. He would have looked very stupid, if Daniel didn't know this was the first time he was actually doing this. Eventually Nemo managed to wear them and tried again to walk out of the water. Daniel went to him and helped to keep him steady.

Another one of his sisters swam towards them, this time handing something to Daniel. It was a bow and a quiver full of arrows, made of the same material as the weapons that the queen and her companions were carrying, except for the tip of the arrows, which looked like it was made of silver. A beautiful golden 'D' was carved on the body of the bow and on every single arrow.

'So you can find them easily and claim them back,' she explained. 'It is my gift to you. We have never had to use them so far and I hope you never will, but something tells me you might come to need it one day. So, keep it with you, and may it never be of service.'

Daniel thanked her and bowed his head down again. Then, he shouldered the weapon, and, helping Nemo, made for dry land. Once out of the water, they both stood on the shore, facing her.

The mermaid queen had tears in her eyes.

'The Queen of Endër is the one you need to see; she has the information you seek. I will send word to her that you are coming, and she will welcome you like her own sons and tell you what you need to know. Go now and may the Great Lord lead your way.'

She waived, as did the four mermaids around her, and then the sea swallowed them back in.

* * *

'I'm walking. I'm walking,' Nemo kept shouting excitedly as he finally managed to balance himself on his two new legs and actually move. 'I can't believe I really have legs and I'm walking. This means I can run; I can breathe outside water for as long as I want, I can get to wear clothes and shoes, and do all these things that I've always dreamed of'.

'Yeah, it also means you cannot breathe under water, and you cannot swim deep into the sea, or see your family very often.'

Daniel stopped himself from talking; he shouldn't be spoiling Nemo's moment. Luckily, Nemo wasn't paying attention to what he was saying; he was much too happy to concentrate.

'She is amazing,' Daniel changed the subject, speaking of Eleanor not without a bit of envy. 'You're very lucky, Nemo, to have her as mother and queen.'

Nemo was prancing about, trying to step on every kind of surface he could see and experience the different feeling he got every time. His pale skin shone bright as the strong sunshine fell over his well-formed chest and abdomen, with his swimmer's muscles being the only thing that made him appear older than he was.

'She can be very fearsome at times. It is not easy being the Sea-Queen and she has been doing it for much longer than her predecessors. But she is also the most loved one. That's why most of the mermaids don't want to let her go.'

'Let her go where? What do you mean?'

Daniel sat down again, watching Nemo enjoy his new-found hobby and waiting for his answer. Nemo decided to try sitting as well. As he bent his knees, his body weight proved too much and he fell backwards, laughing out loud yet again. Daniel joined in the laughter and moved closer to him. Nemo eventually arranged himself in a sitting position by imitating him and then continued.

'After the queen has laid her last egg, she has only a limited time before she starts losing her power and strength, becoming like the rest of us. During this time, the successor must be found and crowned in front of all the mermaids.

After that, the old queen takes her last journey into the open sea, and she is never seen again.'

Daniel heard the sadness in Nemo's voice and saw it in his eyes. He knew exactly how the boy felt.

'For some reason though, she still reigns young and strong, and her powers have not diminished. The candidates are all ready and prepared, but the Oracle says it's not time yet. He seems to be waiting for something, and I'm glad; I don't want her to go.'

'The Oracle?'

'He's the one we all go to consult about important matters like this.'

'Ok,' said Daniel, making a mental note to ask more about this Oracle later. 'And what about these candidates? How many of them are there?'

'There are four of them, the ones that you saw earlier with mother. They are not just her companions and followers; they are all my sisters, and they all want to be the next queen. They stay with her all the time, so that they can learn everything there is to know about ruling the mermaids and the seas.'

'And who decides which one of them will be the next queen?'

'That will be decided when the competition takes place. They will all have to compete against one another in strength, bravery, and wisdom. The winner will of course earn the crown; I'm sure it's going to be Vanessa.'

'Which one was she?'

'She was the one who never smiled,' Nemo said. 'I'm sure you noticed her.'

'That, I did,' Daniel answered. 'I have a feeling she would make a terrifying queen.'

'You don't know how right you are,' Nemo commented, and stretched his legs arranging his new shorts that barely reached to his knees. They seemed to have been made from some sort of seaweed, dark green, of course, and tough, yet very light.

Daniel had the feeling that his new friend had gone somewhere dark just now, so he decided to change the subject and cheer him up again.

'You know, you might look like a man now, but you still smell like a fish,' he teased him, giving him a push and running away from him. Nemo chased after him, laughing and enjoying the new feeling that running on his new legs gave him. They played around for a while, chasing each other in and out of the water, until they got tired of it and stopped. Eventually Daniel spoke again.

'Now where do we go? How do we get to the Queen of Endër?'

'That's easy. First, we go and visit our friends that I told you about yesterday. They will help us get to Endër. Come, it's this way. Hope you can keep up,' he said, laughing and starting to run again.

It was only midday when they began to follow the coastline southwards. They stayed near water; they were both barefoot and the sand there was cool and soft. As the day grew older, it got quite hot, and carrying the bow and quiver became a tad uncomfortable. Nemo offered to carry them for him, and Daniel gratefully accepted.

They walked for a good while, stopping only here and there to check out places that seemed of interest. A few times Daniel saw wingmen flying high above them, but they were too far up for him to see them well. Still, he was excited. Apart from them, there were all sorts of birds flying in the sky, and Daniel didn't even know half of them. He could also sense the presence of animals in the forest, but he didn't get to see more than rabbits or squirrels jumping up and down the trees.

The day progressed and the sun was now well on the second half of its daily journey through the sky, when suddenly a shadow passed swiftly over them. They didn't even manage to look up, when Nemo felt something fall and break on top of his head, producing a wet and sticky mass there. It was a bird egg. Hysterical laughter followed, and in a matter of seconds three silhouettes landed in front of them. They were wingmen, three young ones by the looks of their fresh faces, and even more so, their asinine behaviour.

Two of them stood tall and slender - a bit too much for normal people - with beautiful blue and white wings starting from the back of their neck, joined to their arms and spine, and reaching all the way down to their feet. The third one, with a more silly look on his face, was shorter and of a bigger built than his friends, but still handsome to look at. Instead of blue, his wings were a combination of white and a darker shade of grey.

All three had long black hair tied back in a single braid, and piercing blue eyes. Their skin was flawless and whiter compared to that of men, and where it joined their wings, it started to first turn fluffy and eventually produce feathers, small to begin with, but longer and stronger as the wings grew. They wore little in the way of garments; some type of blue vests and trousers that, unlike Nemo's, reached down all the way to their small feet. Speaking of their feet, Daniel noticed they did not wear any shoes or sandals; the skin there was tough, like those of birds, and their toes ended up in sharp claws. Around their waist they wore belts, on which hang two sharp knives, fitted into leather sheaths to their left and right. Daniel stared amazed at the beauty of these creatures, barely believing his own eyes.

Still laughing at their brilliant practical joke, they ignored him completely and started picking on Nemo.

'Hey, fish-boy, finally got legs, huh?' spoke first one of the taller guys, who unlike the other two who didn't have a trace of hair on their fresh faces, sported a single line of hair, growing vertically just under his lower lip. The shorter one, who looked more like a human, compared to the other two, did not wait to be invited into the conversation.

'What did you do, steal them from someone? Something smells fishy to me.'

The laughter returned with a new wave. Daniel could not believe his own ears. He turned to see Nemo still cleaning himself up, not saying anything back, and didn't know if he should do something.

The bullying continued.

'So, they finally decided to kick you out then, huh? About time I'd say.'

'You're better off human, you know? I wouldn't wanna hang around a bunch of sisters that send me to die hanging on a tree either.'

Nemo stopped cleaning himself and finally looked up at them. An understanding passed between them in that short instant. Daniel half expected Nemo to jump at them in anger; after all, he was feeling rather furious himself, realizing that these three were very likely the ones who had tied Nemo up and left him there to die. But Nemo did not jump at them. Instead he lowered his head and passed through them, continuing his walk. Daniel did not understand. He really wanted to tell these guys off, and even more so, he wanted Nemo to do it. But Nemo just kept walking away.

The three bullies continued teasing Nemo, turning their back on Daniel, who still hadn't moved an inch.

'Oh, are you gonna cry now?' the tall one with the goatee teased. Daniel noticed with curiosity that the third one did not utter a word. 'Gonna swim back to mommy's arms? Oops, wait, you can't, can you?'

'No, he cannot,' Shorty replied. 'And you know what else he can't do?'

'Fly,' they both shouted at the same time and in a swift move jumped on Nemo, grabbed him by the arms, and extending their enormous wings, flew up in the air with him. The third one, who had been silent the whole time, turned to Daniel, who hurried forward to try and stop them, and pushed him back hard, throwing him down on the ground. He then arose high in the sky and flew after his friends towards the sea, while Daniel kept shouting at them to bring Nemo back down.

He could hear the boy begging for them to let him go, but they kept on laughing hysterically, flying away further above the sea. A few moments later, after apparently getting tired of carrying him, they let him fall down into the water and flew away towards mainland, shouting triumphantly.

Daniel jumped immediately in; swimming as fast as he could towards the spot where Nemo fell. Being an excellent swimmer came in handy, and he reached Nemo in no time. The boy was trying to swim back towards the shore, but he wasn't faring well. Clearly the missing tail was a big disadvantage for the ex-merman. Daniel threw one arm around his waist and swam with the help of his other arm and strong legs. In a matter of minutes, they were out of the water again.

Nemo sat on the wet sand, shaken and humiliated, tears falling down his wet face. His arms were bruised where they had grabbed him, with visible scratches from their claws. He took off the bow and quiver, and set them on the sand beside him. Daniel sat down next to him, catching his own breath.

'Are you ok, Nemo?'

Nemo wiped whatever water he could off his face, but

could not look at Daniel. He felt embarrassed.

'They are not all like that, you know?' he said. 'They are honourable people, with a great love of the sky and all things flying. Most of them are artists; they sing and dance, they make beautiful sculptures out of wood and stone, and like everyone else in our kingdom, they love to celebrate. Their queen is fierce and respectable, and they love her dearly. But these three are different, at least recently. They always make stupid pranks like today and are unkind with their words. And, I don't know why, but for some reason they always pick on me.

'I have always been afraid of them; that's another reason why most of my sisters hate me. They say I'm an embarrassment to them. Mermaids are brave and not afraid of anything. But not me. Yesterday, before you found me, Vanessa and the other three dared me to go to the surface and shoot at them, to prove that I was not afraid. I wanted so much to prove that, so I agreed, even though we are strictly forbidden to use our cross-bolts on anyone. But as soon as I broke the surface, they grabbed me and tied me up to the tree where you found me. My sisters kept watching me being dragged away and did nothing, Vanessa wouldn't let them. So, they just went back. At least they apologized today, all except for her.'

'Did you tell your mother?'

'No. They would have been in so much trouble. Besides, she wouldn't have believed me anyway; I had no way to prove it. She thinks the wingmen did this of their own accord; she's furious. She would have contacted the Sky-Queen and asked that they'd be punished, if it weren't for you.'

'Me?' Daniel asked surprised. 'What do I have to do with anything?'

'I don't know, man, but as soon as she heard that you are a Visitor, it was like none of this mattered anymore. All she wanted was to see you right away. I still don't understand it; it was like she forgot all about what they did to me.'

He stopped talking and lowered his head even more. Daniel realized that he was close to crying again, and put one hand on his shoulder.

'I'll tell you what; why don't we try and put all this behind us, just for now? You're a new person, Nemo, and have a new life ahead of you. One day we can come back and deal with all of this, and I promise you that on that day, I will be there to help you face it. But until then, what do you say we enjoy ourselves and forget about everything else, ok?'

Nemo looked at him. His face lit up a little and the sob that threatened to overtake him only seconds ago, now drew back and disappeared.

'You're right. I'm human now and we're on a mission. Besides, I have already decided that I will stay on land forever and never have to deal with my sisters again. I know I'm going to miss mother, but she will be gone eventually anyway. And when that happens, there will be no one to protect me down there.'

Daniel could not help but feel bad for his new friend. He had no idea things were this hard for him.

'Are you sure about this, Nemo? I mean, you'd be leaving behind your family, your home, everything you have ever known.'

'I am,' Nemo replied, without even thinking. He then looked at Daniel, unable to hide the sadness in his eyes. 'I don't belong in the sea, Daniel, I never have. I'm a freak.'

Daniel felt like hugging the little man. He had some idea of what it was like to feel as if you didn't belong. He did not hug Nemo, however; he wouldn't know what to do if the boy started to cry again. But he didn't have to; having gotten it out of his system, Nemo's smile now returned, though sorrow still loomed in the depth of his youthful bright eyes.

'The land is my new home now' he said, putting on a hopeful look, 'and I think it's gonna be great.'

Daniel spoke no more; he did not blame the boy. He would probably do the same himself, if he was in Nemo's shoes, so to speak.

They got up, gathered their things, and resumed their path towards the house where Nemo's friends lived. Daniel hung the bow and quiver back on his shoulder. What had just happened hovered above them like a dark cloud that threatened the sunshine for a bit, but was soon taken away by the wind.

He began once again to pay attention to the scenery around him and enjoy everything that his senses were absorbing. Despite this one bad experience, he could not help but marvel at how truly and amazingly beautiful this place was.

As the end of their journey drew near, Daniel spotted on the horizon before him a single house, built on a small cliff rising above the sea. The house seemed completely made of wood, with a rising roof and large windows on all sides. A huge garden lay in front of it, facing the woods opposite the sea.

He and Nemo slowly climbed up the cliff, making for the gate, when two huge dogs appeared in front of it. They immediately spotted the visitors and ran straight towards them. Daniel's heart began to thump like crazy inside his chest. He really did not like dogs; he'd been bitten once as a child and had grown terrified of them ever since. As they approached, he stopped walking and grabbed Nemo by the arm.

'What are we going to do, Nemo? We cannot outrun them.'

Nemo looked at him, puzzled.

'What do you mean? Outrun who, the dogs?'

Daniel shook his head affirmatively, visibly paralyzed with fear.

'Are you afraid of them? Why, I mean, what do you think they're going to do, lick you to death?'

'Ha-ha, I wish,' Daniel laughed nervously. 'No, I'm a bit more worried about their teeth. They look like they might have big sharp ones.'

Nemo seriously did not seem to understand.

'Yeah, and so? Maybe where you come from, dogs are dangerous, but here in Endërland, they are man's best friend. It's never been heard of a dog biting anyone around here, so relax and keep walking. You can stay behind me if you like. You'll see, it's going to be alright.'

Before he even finished speaking, the first of the dogs reached them and threw himself at Daniel, barking and wagging his tail with excitement. The second one was right behind and raising his huge front paws on Daniel's chest also, started to welcome him in his own way, completely ignoring Nemo.

Daniel almost fainted from fear at first, but when he saw that the animals seemed earnestly happy to see him and had no intention of hurting him, he relaxed a little. Only a little though; it would take a lot more than this to rid him of his fear of dogs. He put his hands on their furry heads and patted them lightly. The animals seemed to enjoy that and returned the favour with a good dose of saliva, by means of their long pink tongues.

Nemo, who was watching the scene with curiosity, laughed hard as Daniel recoiled, clearly disgusted.

'Wow, they're treating you like a long-lost friend. And I thought *I* was family here.'

They resumed walking towards the house, with the dogs running and jumping all around them in excitement. They passed the gate and headed towards the main door, when it opened and a young woman came out, holding a baby in her arms. Her hair, Daniel noticed, was dark red like Nemo's, her skin pale white and eyes dark black.

'Is she...?' Daniel started to ask.

'My sister,' Nemo finished his sentence.

'Just how many of them do you have?'

'No idea,' Nemo replied, shrugging. 'Sarah left us some time ago; is now married to a human, and they have a daughter. She's one of the very few who actually like me.'

He hurried towards her with arms open, and she towards him with a big smile on her face.

'Nemo. Look at you; you've got legs. Mother finally decided to let you go, huh?'

'Yes, only today; can you believe it? Oh, I've missed you, Sarah. How's little Angel? Can I hold her?'

He took the baby in his arms without waiting for an answer and started tickling and rocking her. It was then that Sarah noticed the scars on his biceps.

'What happened to you? Who did that?'

'Nothing to worry about sis; I was just fooling around with your dogs earlier.'

Sarah didn't believe him but decided to drop it for the time being and instead turned to Daniel, who walked over and presented himself.

'Hello, I'm Daniel.'

'He's a Visitor,' Nemo declared matter-of-factly. Sarah seemed pleasantly surprised.

'Really? Oh, this is such a pleasure, Daniel. I'm Sarah, Nemo's sister, as no doubt you have guessed by now. And this is my little Angel.

64

'Nemo stop rocking her so hard; she just ate and will throw up all over you.'

She was too late though. The little angel did exactly that; she threw up all over Nemo, splashing a good little portion on his face. They all laughed, Nemo the hardest. Sarah took the girl back and led the boys in.

The house looked really cosy and warm on the inside. It seemed not much different from any other house Daniel had seen back in his home world. There was a set of couches in what looked like the living room, a dining table, and chairs at the far-left corner next to the fireplace, everything made of wood. The walls seemed to be decorated with random things, while the floor was covered with huge colourful rugs. Somehow, he had expected something different, though what exactly, he could not say.

Sarah made them both some type of hot tea that Daniel had never had before; a special sea herb that her sisters gathered for her, deliciously tasting like peppermint, only much stronger and sweeter.

'A Visitor, huh?' she said as she sat down with them. 'There hasn't been one in a very long time now. So, what do you think of Endërland, Daniel?'

Daniel was not prepared to talk about his impressions of Endërland just yet; he still hadn't seen much of it after all. However, he decided to go with what he felt for the moment.

'I really like it; everything is so magical here. But it's still only my second day, and there's just so much to see and learn.'

'Which is part of the reason why we're here,' Nemo cut in, almost spilling his tea. 'We were hoping Garret would help us get to the Queen of Endër. Mother has sent word to her, and she is expecting us. Where is he, by the way?'

'He's just gone to the village nearby to discuss the preparations for the upcoming festivities; he should be back in the evening. Why do you need to see the queen?'

'She's got information that Daniel needs,' Nemo answered in short, feeling quite important. He then looked at Daniel.

'What did I tell you, people here love celebrations. You might actually be lucky and take part in this one.'

'Oh, you are really going to love it,' added Sarah. 'It's my favourite feast. There'll be great food, and drinks, and music, and dancing, and lots of games. I can hardly wait.' She sounded excited, just like a little girl, and not like the older sister of his new best friend.

They kept on talking about the coming celebrations and the people, driving the conversation from one subject to another for several hours. Daniel felt like he wanted to know everything.

Soon daylight grew dim, and Sarah lit the oil lamps around the house. Before they knew it, evening came and that's when Garret returned home. Daniel half expected him to have red hair too, but that was not the case. He was a handsome young man, seemingly in his mid-twenties, with a cheery face, kind brown eyes and short light brown hair. He warmed up to Daniel right away and kept asking question after question about his world. In return, he was more than happy to share about Endërland and their life here. Daniel admired the way he was with Sarah and little Angel; they looked like the light in his eyes, and he never seemed to get enough of them.

After a light supper, which consisted mainly of a homemade pie and lots of fruits, Sarah shared with them the story of her own pilgrimage. She told of how when her time came, she visited all of Endërland. She went all the way up to the Northern Mountains, then to the Eastern shore to visit their cousins in Tálas. She travelled through all the villages in the valley of Destiny, spent a few days in Sky-City, stayed in Endër for a while, and of course saved Arba for last, like all her sisters had done before her.

That's where she'd met Garret. He had come there to bring offerings to the Lords on behalf of his village, and they had fallen in love at first sight. Choosing not to go back to the sea had been her most difficult decision ever, but she had not regretted it. She was happy here with him, and he had promised her they would always live next to the sea, so that she would never be far away from her family.

Daniel listened as she talked about Endërland, and a greater desire arose in him to see and experience it all for himself.

'What is this place called Arba?' he asked. Until now, he had not heard of it.

'Nemo hasn't told you about it?' Garret jumped in disbelief. 'Why, it's only the most beautiful place in the whole of Endërland; the capital of our kingdom. It's where the four Lords reside in the great palace. You should definitely visit it; words cannot do it justice. I will take you there myself if needed.'

'The four Lords?' Daniel asked again, puzzled.

'Nemo, have you told him nothing at all?' Garret rebuked Nemo playfully, causing the young merman to respond with an exaggerated eyeroll. He then turned to Daniel again.

'You met the Queen of the Seas, right?'

Daniel shook his head affirmatively.

'And you are on your way to meet the Queen of Endër, or as the Lords call her, the Lady of the Land. You probably also know by now that there is a third queen; she rules the sky-people and is called the Sky-Queen, or the Lady of the Skies. Each of them, rules over their own people, however, all of us are subjects to the four Lords, who rule Endërland together, each one for a season. Autumn is the one sitting on the Silver Throne now, but his days will soon end. Winter will take over after him, and then Spring and Summer. It's a cycle that repeats itself; it has been like this since always. Endërland does not have one king or queen alone but a group of them; and they all answer to the Great Lord, the one who created Endërland and everything in it. He is the ultimate authority over us all, though we haven't seen him in a very long time, so it's really just the Lords.'

This started to feel more and more like a very complicated and confusing fairy tale world.

'Seriously?' Daniel asked. 'Winter, Spring, Summer and Autumn?'

'They are people just like you and me, Daniel; we only call them by those names because of the seasons they are in charge of.'

Daniel felt confused. First the Queen of the Seas, then the Queen of the Land; now a third queen and four other lords, who served under another great lord. Did they leave anyone out? And was he supposed to meet them all at some point?

Sarah noticed his perplexity and came to sit next to him.

'You have nothing to worry about, Daniel. Visitors have always been welcomed in Endërland and treated with the outmost honour and respect. I am sure the Queen of Endër will tell you everything you need to know. After mother, she is the wisest and most honourable woman I know; she will look after you.'

Daniel smiled a half-shy smile back at her; still feeling a bit like a little kid on his first day of school. She arranged a freckle off his forehead, something his mother used to do when he was a child and smiled sweetly.

'I'm glad Nemo brought you to us; we both are.' She looked at Garret as she said this, and he shook his head in affirmation.

Daniel smiled again. He might be in a foreign place, but somehow these people made it feel like home.

They talked some more after that, until time came for bed, and Sarah got up and arranged the living room for the two boys to sleep in. Then, with Garret and little Angel they said their goodnights and went to their own bedroom.

This was weird for Nemo; it was his first night on land, and he had never before slept like this. But as it turned out, he was far more tired than he looked, because as soon as he put his head on the soft pillow, his eyes closed, and he drifted off to a deep sleep.

Daniel smiled and decided to get some sleep himself, even though he wasn't really tired. He knew by now what was going to happen; he would wake up in his bed and would go on living his day in his own world, until time came again for him to come back to this place. And he was looking forward to it.

An idea came to him just then. Seeing as they were going to probably have to walk a lot, they would need shoes; and maybe some more appropriate clothes. He was still wearing his pyjamas, while Nemo could use a t-shirt, to avoid a nasty sunburn by walking around half-naked. So, he decided he would test a theory he had silently been working on.

* * *

When he woke up the next morning, Nemo could still be heard snoring lightly in the other bed. It was quite early, judging by the light outside the windows. Sarah and Garret were not around, so he thought they were probably still

69

asleep. He got up to stretch his legs and wash his face, and that's when he got the confirmation that his theory had been correct. Not only was he now wearing proper clothes and shoes, but he was also carrying a shoulder bag, in which there was another t-shirt and a second pair of shoes.

Since he had always appeared in this world wearing whatever he had on when he went to bed, he figured he could go to bed fully dressed and awake the same in Endërland. It was the shoulder bag he had not been too sure about, but it was still worth a try. Before getting into bed in his London home, he got dressed, put the t-shirt and shoes in the bag and put it on. Lucky for him, his dad had not gone into his room to see him that evening, or he would have thought his son had gone completely bonkers.

He took out the plain white t-shirt and sports shoes and left them by Nemo's bed. Nemo was a bit smaller than him in stature, but he was sure they would fit him just fine. He then decided to get some fresh air and so went outside to check out the garden. Sarah was already there, gathering fruit and vegetables.

'Good morning!' he greeted.

'Good morning, Daniel! How did you sleep?'

Daniel smiled. Moving daily from one world to the other seemed like he hardly ever got any sleep at all. Yet, that wasn't so. His body was fully rested and his mind as fresh as ever, even though it felt to him like he was awake twenty-four hours a day.

'Very good, thank you. Can I help you with anything?'

'Of course,' Sarah replied with delight. 'Here, take this bowl and gather some baby tomatoes over there. Only the ripest ones; they will make for a delicious salad at lunch.'

Daniel took the bowl and headed in the direction he was told. The garden was quite big, and the variation of plants being grown was vast. He was able to recognize only some of them, though. Some he had never seen before, while others seemed familiar, yet different. Like this one huge tree right in the middle of the garden, with large red fruit that looked very much like oversized cherries. Daniel had to stop for a moment and wonder about the strangeness of it all. He loved cherries and had always fantasized what they would taste like if they were the size of an apple or orange. And here, this was exactly what seemed to be going on.

'Sarah, what tree is this?' he asked her.

'That's a cherry tree, of course. You've never seen one before?'

'Oh, I have. It's just, where I come from, cherries are quite small, barely the size of my thumb, really. And, of course, they only come out early in the summer, not autumn.'

'Really? Well that's a shame; I can't imagine not having cherries all year round; or having them that small. Want to try a real one? Take a few so we can have them after breakfast.'

Daniel grabbed four of them and put them in the bowl with the baby tomatoes. Everything in the garden looked incredibly juicy and delicious, and there were so many different things to choose from.

'How do you manage to grow everything so perfect?' he asked again. 'It must require a lot of care and hard work.'

Sarah looked at him as if she didn't understand.

'Not really. The only work we do is plant the seeds; after that everything just, grows. Is it not so in your world?'

'Not exactly,' Daniel answered, helping her carry everything inside. 'We have to work very hard to make sure everything grows well and is not spoiled by bad weather or insects, or even people sometimes. They don't always turn out like this.'

'People? Why would people spoil the produce?' Sarah seemed genuinely puzzled.

'People are very different in my world,' Daniel said, not without a trace of sadness in his voice. 'They don't care much about nature, or each other. All they want is to build big houses for themselves and have lots of cars and money. A handful of them grow richer by the day, while a great many more starve to death. It's not like here, where there's plenty of everything and everyone seems happy.'

'Sounds like a dreadful place to live in,' Sarah said, looking at him with compassion. She knew close to nothing about his world, but if it was anything like what he was saying, it didn't sound great.

They went back inside the house and put the fruit and vegetables in the kitchen, where she began to clean and wash them. Daniel continued to help her prepare breakfast.

'What did you mean when you said people starve to death?' she went back to the conversation. From the look on her face, Daniel realized that she had no clear idea as to what he had been talking about.

'I mean people die of hunger,' he explained. Sarah's face didn't change.

'Hunger?' she asked again. Daniel had to stop and assure himself that she wasn't playing with him. How could she not know what hunger is? Did they have a different word here perhaps?

'You know, when you want to eat; when your body needs food, and your stomach feels empty and starts making those weird noises. That's when you are hungry. But you know what I'm talking about, right?'

Sarah's face looked even more perplexed if that were possible.

'Haven't you ever felt like that?' Daniel asked, now clearly confused.

'No,' she answered. 'Have you? I mean; ever since you got here?'

That was a good question. Daniel tried to think of a time he'd felt hungry in this world. He had spent two whole days on the beach with Nemo, without eating or drinking anything, but hadn't felt the least bit hungry or thirsty.

'No,' he replied, completely stumped. 'Why is that?'

'I don't know, but that's how it's always been in Endërland. We never really feel the need to eat, and most of the time we don't. We only do it because we enjoy it a lot. And it's always a great time when we get together around the table, especially when we have guests.'

She smiled here as she said this. Daniel was still taking it all in and realizing the implications of this, both in this world and his.

'If only this could be true in my world as well. Things would be so much different...'

They took a break from the conversation to set up the table in the kitchen. Soon, Garret got up with little Angel, and after them Nemo, who kept yawning as if he was ready for another round trip to Sleepville, open-ended ticket, of course.

As they all sat down to have breakfast, the conversation continued around Daniel's world and all the things that were different from this place. But now, as he ate, he was seeing food in a completely different way. The cherries were unbelievably tasty, and everything else just as delicious as it looked. He could eat as much or as little as he wanted, and it wouldn't have mattered. He was beginning to love this world a bit more every day.

* * *

Garret and Sarah convinced the two boys to stay there a couple more days; they loved having them around. Daniel decided he was in no hurry to meet the next queen, so he agreed to stay a while longer.

He kept going back and forth between the two worlds, living two separate lives simultaneously. By day he would wake up, make breakfast for himself and his dad, go to work and spend the rest of the day in the gym, or in his bedroom reading his books. He didn't have to worry about studying, since he had agreed with his dad to take a gap year and work until he was sure what he wanted to do. By night he would hang out with Nemo, Sarah, and Garret, learning new things about Endërland and discovering new places.

He managed to also bring along his dad's birthday present and used it to explore Nemo's sea a bit more in depth. This was an entirely different experience from what he was used to. The seas here were completely clean and untainted by human hand, with all their beauty and majesty perfectly intact.

All wildlife was absolutely friendly, in the sea or on land, as he soon also found out. Nowhere had he seen, what he knew as wild creatures in his world, hang out with what was supposed to be their prey. Whenever he would visit the forest with Garret and Nemo, he would see wolves, lions, tigers, and all sorts of wild beasts come to them just to be patted and played with. He was terrified at first, but soon learned to accept this new reality and enjoy it all. He began to think this might actually be some sort of heaven; it all seemed just too good to be true. Whatever the case, he was happy he had come to this place, and he already knew he never wanted to leave.

* * *

When the day finally came for them to depart, Garret prepared three horses for the journey, and they said their goodbyes. After he promised Sarah that he would visit them again, they set on their way north towards Endër. The journey would take them almost two full days, so they were prepared to spend a night in the forest. Daniel wasn't worried. He was starting to feel like there was nothing to fear in this world, and that was a heart-warming feeling.

The road to Endër took them through a series of small villages, where everyone they met was very friendly and invited them to their house for a visit. But they did not stop. Daniel didn't want to keep Garret away from his family any longer than he had to. The horses trotted with a light step, showing no sign of weariness, and Daniel enjoyed the ride very much. He had done some horse riding when he was a little boy, so he wasn't completely new to this.

Nemo, on the other hand, wasn't doing too great. He had barely begun to get used to walking on his own two legs, so riding a big horse on four strong ones, felt like asking a bit too much. Were it not for the horse's agility and care, Nemo would have kept on falling off. Still, he got used to it soon enough, but not before entertaining Daniel and Garret for a good while.

They did more than half of the journey on the first day. As the sun went down, they were well inside the forest of Mirë, which stretched from the sea, all the way to the borders of Endër in the north, Arba in the east, and Sky-City southwest of it. Had it not been for Garret, who knew the way very well, the boys would have gotten lost in it many times over, and would have ended up spending whole weeks trying to get out.

They camped that night in a small meadow, under the shelter of a huge and very old oak tree. It was still quite warm at night, seeing as it was still only the first half of autumn. The forest was quiet, save for the occasional animal noises on the background. Garret lit a fire, even though there was really no need for it, but somehow this made the place feel more welcoming. They sat around it and shared of the food that Sarah had packed in their bags. Daniel still couldn't get used to the fact that he was only eating out of habit.

As they ate, they noticed with astonishment that animals from deep inside the forest started coming to them, gathering by the fire. There were all kinds of them, big and small, four legged, two legged, birds too, and they all just sat around them, some even laying at their feet. Daniel felt absolutely amazed by all of this, though the other two were no less impressed.

'I have camped at this very spot many times before, but this has never happened to me,' Garret said, looking thoughtfully at Daniel. The animals seemed especially drawn to him.

'I think somehow they sense that you're not from around here,' Nemo added, plunging his hands into the beautiful mane of a fully-grown male lion that had come to sit next to him. 'They must be curious.'

Daniel was sharing some of his food with a pitch-black panther that kept purring with pleasure as he stroked its shiny fur.

'This is so unreal. I have never seen so many different animals all together. Most of them are wild where I come from and would kill each other, let alone go anywhere near people. This is incredible.'

They slept that night in the company of a horde of animals that kept growing and growing. The next day, as they resumed their journey towards Endër, the habitants of the forest trotted along and accompanied them all the way. It was such an unbelievable sight. Whoever saw it would think that a mass exodus was taking place.

By midday, however, as they reached the edge of the woods and were about to enter the borders of Endër, the animals stopped following them and remained behind. Daniel felt a bit sorry to depart from them. He looked back as he rode away, and he swore that he could feel their sadness at their departure. This had been such a strange experience.

The road from there on was much wider and more frequented; the horses now rode with a faster pace and lighter step. Every now and then they would see people coming out of the city in their horses and carriages and would always stop to greet them and have a quick chat.

Soon they joined the main road that connected Endër to most of the villages in the west and eventually led to Sky-City. Here, the travellers were much more frequent and in greater numbers. This was the only road that led to Endër and eventually to Arba, the city of the Lords. People visited the city a lot for many reasons, but most of them just went to honour the four Lords and bring them gifts. Daniel enjoyed this part of the journey especially; it somehow reminded him of the trips he would take with his dad whenever they went camping.

Soon enough, however, a little anxiety began to kick in. They were now approaching the city, and within the hour he would stand before yet another queen. He felt nervous, even more so than when he was about to meet Eleanor. Somehow, meeting the Queen of Endër sounded like a bigger deal.

They entered the wide stone gates of the city without anybody stopping them or asking them anything. Daniel was a bit surprised that there were no guards at the walls at all.

The city was built at the foot of a high hill, with a small stream running down, splitting the city in two. All the houses looked towards the very top, where one small castle stood erected, overlooking all of Endër. Every road led to this castle. That was obviously where the queen resided.

'Yes, that's the queen's castle,' Garret confirmed, 'and that's where we are headed. But we'll get off the horses here; we can walk the rest of the way. We will leave them at the inn where they will be well looked after.'

They all climbed off their horses and made for the first inn to their right, near the gates. A man came out, and after talking to Garret, he took the horses from them, leading them round the back of the inn, where he promised to clean them and feed them. Daniel noticed that Garret didn't give the man any money.

'Didn't you have to pay for that?' he asked when Garret re-joined them.

'Pay?' Garret asked back. 'What do you mean?'

'Give him money? Surely you don't expect him to just do the job without getting paid for it?'

'There is no such thing here, Daniel,' Garret answered. 'We look after one-another; we love our animals, and we love company. Food costs us nothing and work is our pleasure. Helping each other is our reward.'

'Sounds like there's a reason why you leave your world and come to ours,' Nemo said. 'I don't think I would like your world very much.'

'I don't think you would either,' said Daniel, though more to himself than to his merman friend.

They shouldered their bags and began to climb the streets towards the castle. This was unlike any city Daniel had ever been to, though he had the distinct feeling that he'd seen something like it before. The white painted houses were practically built on top of one-another; their windows were many and small, while the roofs and balconies were all covered with small red tiles. The streets were paved with little round stones, and they snaked all the way up to the top of the hill, where they all joined into one single road. That road ended up at the entrance of the castle, where once again Daniel failed to see any guards.

Inside the castle, they walked into a great courtyard filled with little gardens full of blossoming trees and innumerable kinds of flowers. There were people everywhere that played, sang, and danced, while many more seemed otherwise occupied. Children were running around following each other and making noise, and music was being played somewhere in the crowd. It sounded to Daniel like a flute, and it was very merry and melodic. Girls, all wearing long white dresses, were dancing around the young man, who appeared to be playing a small instrument, which was definitely some sort of flute.

'People gather here to prepare for the festivities; looks like it's going to be a great one this season.'

Garret approached one of the girls that was enjoying the music and spoke to her. She was beautiful, with long blonde hair and lively eyes, and was wearing a thin silver circlet on her forehead. There were a few other girls similarly dressed, and they all seemed to be overseeing the happenings in the courtyard. Daniel guessed they worked in the castle.

'I'm Íro,' the blonde girl introduced herself, her curious eyes glued on Daniel. 'Come with me, please. I will take you to the queen.'

She led them inside the castle and into the royal hall, all the while looking back and stealing glances at the two boys.

'She has been waiting for you,' she said, still looking inquisitively at Daniel. 'We expected you to arrive days ago, and she has been very anxious. I will go and inform her straight away of your arrival. Please wait here.'

The girl left and the three of them remained behind in a big room with a very high ceiling, full of large paintings on its walls, colourful flags, statues and what not. There was a long line of chairs laid out against each wall across the room, and a high throne sitting at the end, centred in the middle and very well lit.

Daniel felt nervous. This was it; he had to summon some more of that royal speech he had given the first queen, wherever that had come from.

They stood in the middle of the hall, waiting for the queen to come in at any moment, when Garret spoke.

'Well, I'm going to leave you two alone then; your business with the queen is your own. Come and find me outside when you're done.'

Daniel was about to protest, when he heard quick steps from the other side of the hall. Garret left quietly while the steps got closer. Nemo kneeled where he was and pulled Daniel from his shirt to do the same. Daniel knelt down too, lowering his head, and waiting.

A woman in a long white dress entered the hall and approached them alone. She stopped just a few feet from them and stood there, looking first at one, then the other. Her gaze focused on Daniel, who was still looking down on the marble floor.

For some unknown reason, his heart suddenly began to thump like crazy of its own accord. He could smell something familiar in the air but could not tell what it was. Then he heard her voice speak his name.

'Daniel? Daniel Adams?'

Hearing her calling him by his full name - which nobody here knew - caused him to raise his head and look at her.

Over her white dress she was wearing a royal shawl of green colour, adorned with the same emblems that Daniel had seen all over the city and the castle. Her long black hair reached down her shoulders and an elegant golden crown rested upon her head. Her face was gentle and sweet, her skin pure and perfect. Her lips dark cherry red and her eyes emerald green, just like his. There was pain and joy in those eyes, and looking at them, Daniel realized that he knew that face, he knew that voice and that scent. He knew her.

Slowly, he arose, trying hard to let out one single word. 'Mom?'

Chapter 4

INTRODUCTIONS & REUNIONS

'**M**om, is that really you?'

Daniel froze in place. His insides started to heat up, his throat tightened, and beads of sweat began forming on his forehead. For a moment, he forgot how to breathe.

The queen made one careful step towards him.

'It's me Danny, it's really me.'

This was not possible. Daniel tried desperately to find the logic that would help him make sense of all of this but felt unable to organize his thoughts. The first thing he could feel, however, was unbelief. This couldn't be real.

'This cannot be; you..., you're not real. You can't be.'

The queen made another careful step towards Daniel but stopped when she saw that he drew back from her, as if afraid.

'I promise you, Danny, I'm real. I *am* here and I am very much alive.'

'But how? How could this be? How *are* you here?'

'I will explain everything, Danny, I promise. But first come to me and let me hold you; I have waited too long for this.'

Daniel looked back at Nemo, who seemed as shocked as he was. Still, pulling himself together, the boy nodded with his head, telling him that it was ok; he could believe this.

Daniel turned to face the queen, who was still smiling at him. He struggled to command his feet. His whole being wanted to run to her, to throw his arms around her, bury his head in her chest and hold her tight for all eternity. But he did not run. Instead, he dragged his feet slowly until he was close enough to touch her.

Everything about her told him she was real. Her beautiful face had not changed one bit. Her unique sweet scent was still the same, strong as ever. She seemed smaller, no doubt because he was bigger now, but other than that, she felt exactly like he remembered her. Yet still he held back.

Slowly putting one hand on his cheek and caressing him gently, the queen called him what *she* only ever had.

'Danielito, it's really me. I'm here.'

Upon hearing that name, Daniel surrendered. He opened his arms and threw himself at her, crying like a little child.

'Mom.'

'Oh, Danny, I've missed you so much.'

Fourteen years' worth of hugs and kisses came together all at once, as mother and son fell into each other's embrace, laughing and crying simultaneously. Tears of joy and heartache fell freely and abundantly, while they locked one another inside their arms and refused to let go. Time flew around them, as they forgot about everything and everyone else in that endless moment where nothing and no one but the two of them existed.

Giving them some privacy, Nemo retreated at the back of the hall and waited. He could not help but well up with a few tears of his own and was glad that they were too preoccupied to notice. Seeing Daniel reunite with his long-lost mother, inadvertently led his thoughts to his own and the day when he would lose her to the open sea. Maybe now there was some chance that it would not be forever, that he would see her again at some point. He could only hope.

After the initial shock, Daniel was able to think clearly again and began pouring questions. The queen, however, halted him in his steps.

'Sweetheart, I know you want answers and I promise I will tell you all that I can, but right now you're gonna have to wait just a little longer. There are matters that need to be addressed. Where is your friend?'

They turned to face Nemo, whom they had forgotten all about, and saw him sitting at the far end of the hall. Daniel beckoned him to come over and introduced him.

'Mom, this is...'

'Nemo,' she finished his sentence, smiling at the red-haired boy. Daniel was not surprised. 'It's so nice to see you again. You've grown so much and turned into such a handsome young man.'

Nemo bowed in respect.

'Thank you, your majesty. Your kindness, as always, is only ever surpassed by your beauty. Mother sends her greetings.'

'And thank you, young prince. I see she has taught you well.'

She now turned to Daniel.

'Who else knows that you've come to see me?'

'Nemo's sister and her husband. Garret was the one who brought us here. He's waiting outside.'

84

'Good. I need you both to listen to me very carefully. No one must know that you are my son; this is very important. Word travels fast here, especially when it concerns Visitors, and I'm sure the Lords will have heard by now. Soon they will send for you, but we must avoid that as long as we can. Now, go and see Garret. Tell him that you will be staying with me until the celebrations and that he is welcome to stay if he wants. Then, come back to me; we have much to discuss.'

The two boys left the royal hall and went back out to find Garret in the courtyard. As Daniel anticipated, he decided he would not stay with them, but would return home to his wife and daughter. After thanking him unreservedly, they said goodbye and watched him climb down the hill on his way back home to Sarah and little Angel. Daniel would miss him; he had grown fond of his newfound brother, but he knew they would see each other again.

Back inside the castle the queen showed them the rooms where they would be staying. She told them to refresh themselves and rest, while she attended to some other pressing matters, and that soon they would get together again and talk. Daniel didn't want to be away from her; he felt as if he might lose her again, but, somehow, he knew that he had found her for good and nothing would separate them this time.

Steven Butler was what you would call a tough man, not afraid of much or many, and ruthless when it came to getting what he wanted. But once again, his knees were shaking with dread, anticipating a not so pleasant meeting with his master. He still had no good news to give him.

Born and raised in Enderland from a family of no special significance, he had been chosen by the White Lord as his personal assistant ever since he was a young boy. This had made possible gaining his allegiance and shaping up his character according to the White Lord's will and interests, and doing his master's will was all Steven Butler lived for.

But even if he ever thought of doing something else with his life, it was moments like this that reminded him that he really had no choice. There was nowhere he could hide from the White Lord, nor escape his life of servitude. So, he figured, the better he served his master and the happier he made him, the easier his life would be. There might even be some benefits. And indeed, there were; he was now the second hand of the White Lord, his most trusted man. His zeal and devotion in serving his master had made him the favourite choice for the most delicate missions, like this one. It was only when things weren't going as planned that he was reminded he was still just a servant in his lord's eyes. This was what made him dread this meeting more than any fear of punishment or reprimand from his master for his failures.

Standing in this chilling room, filled with dreadful ice sculptures he had never liked, Butler heard his master's footsteps approaching and readied himself. The big double doors behind him opened and closed swiftly, and the whole room immediately felt much fresher and brighter. Winter walked past him dressed in his kingly white robes, with his impressive ice crown on his long white hair and sat down on his royal white chair. The lord of winter clearly took his role too literally.

The only thing that broke the decorum in the room and felt out of place was an old hourglass, placed on a small table to his right, next to the throne. Winter turned it upside down every time Butler appeared before his throne, but he'd never stayed there long enough to see the sand filter through completely. And yet, this was the only object Butler ever cared about in this dreadful room.

He bowed low before his lord and did not move until told so.

'Get up,' the middle-aged man with a deep voice and the power to make his life literally a freezing hell commanded him. 'And spare me your reports; I know you've had no success whatsoever. Once again, I have done your job for you. The boy is here; he's staying with her. You will stop shadowing the others immediately and concentrate on seizing him. He is the one, he has to be. And he is mine.'

'My lord,' Butler spoke carefully. 'I have been keeping a close eye on the boy and have noticed nothing special about him whatsoever.'

'And what would you expect to see, I wonder, lightning bolts shoot out of his eyes? It's here that the boy matters; back there he is nothing, unless he's the one foretold by the old prophecy. And even if that's the case, he is too young and ignorant to know anything about it. So, stop your nonsense and do as you're told. I want you to take him into custody as soon as you go back and get me the location of that portal; his t-shirt is useless to me without that information. Then, once I've used the portal, you know what to do.'

Butler affirmed with a movement of his head. Winter continued.

'And what of our flying friends; do you have any news from them?'

'Yes, my lord. I was sent word that they now have the weapon. They are only waiting for your instructions.'

'Finally, some good news after that fiasco with the merboy. Alright then,' Winter continued, not giving any hint of contentment. 'Here's what you need to do.'

He went on to giving specific instructions that Butler would follow to the letter and have them done before the day was over. Come evening, he would leave this world behind and start his day all over again where none of his people had ever managed to go before, the Visitors' world.

Daniel checked himself in the large wall-mirror of his new room. His new clothes fitted him nicely. He could now easily pass as one of the many citizens of Endër and would have no problem blending in. Yet somehow everyone could tell he was not of this world, though he felt no different from any of them.

A knock on the door claimed his attention, and he went to answer.

'Mom.'

The queen's face shone bright as she set eyes on her long-lost son once again. She smiled and gave him a warm kiss on the cheek.

'Hello, sweetheart. May I come in?'

'Of course, mom.' Daniel backed away from the entrance and the queen walked in, locking the door behind her. Daniel noticed but said nothing.

'I just can't get used to how much you've grown,' the queen said, taking in the sight of him. 'You're a man now, and you look so much like your father.'

Daniel smiled, not knowing what to say. The queen continued to look at him as if she was afraid he might disappear at any moment.

'Nemo has kindly offered to let us have the afternoon to ourselves. There is much we need to talk about, but first there is something I want to show you.'

She went at the far end of the room, on the left side of the big double bed and began looking for something with the tip of her fingers on the surface of the flower painted wall. Stopping at the centre of a fully blossomed red rose, she applied slight pressure to the wall and took one step back. Part of the wall glided outwards silently, creating a door that led to another room very much like this one. She pushed the door open wide and walked in. Daniel followed her, puzzled.

The room was identical to the first one, down to the covers on the bed and the wall mirror.

'You cannot tell anyone about this room, Danny, not even Nemo.' His mother began.

'Why? What's it for?'

She turned and studied him for a moment, as if trying to determine just how much he knew.

'You know what happens the first time you cross over to this world, right?'

'I think so; a portal is created in the place I appear, which I can use if I want to go back anytime. Why?'

'You are not the only one who can see and use that portal, sweetheart. I believe someone may have found a way to go through it and take the place of the Visitor in the other world by doing so. If and when that happens, the Visitor is left behind, remaining here with no way back and no body to inhabit. I believe this is what's happened to your brother.'

The mentioning of his brother brought on old feelings and questions in Daniel's mind; they had never found out what really happened to him. He looked at her saddened face and felt her pain was still fresh.

'You think Damien is here?'

'I have no way of proving it but a mother's instinct. I have always felt his presence here; just like I felt yours from the moment you arrived. He's here, I know it; I just don't know where.'

89

Daniel thought of the first night he lay by the beach and fell asleep having a completely refreshed memory of his mother.

'I think I know what you mean. My first evening here I sensed your presence too. Until I got here, I was struggling to even remember your face, but that night everything became clear again, as if you had never gone.'

The queen looked at him with such hurt in her eyes. Guilt about her son's pain washed over her, but time had not yet come to talk about that.

Daniel saw what he'd just done and chided himself for being so thoughtless. He hurried to move the conversation along.

'But why didn't I feel *him* too?'

'I don't know sweetheart, maybe because my connection to him is much stronger than yours; but that's not important right now. Damien is not the only Visitor who has disappeared; there have been more, though the exact number I do not know. They are seen once or twice in the kingdom and then nothing. I think someone is either killing or capturing them, and I have my own theory on the subject. But I will not speak of that just yet.

'Back to this room; I had it built for when you got here, so that no one can find your portal and use it. But first, there is something you must do; you need to go back to where you last appeared in this world, find the portal, and go through it. Once on the other side, you'll find it's not that difficult to appear wherever you choose to in Endërland. All you have to do is think only of this room when you go to bed, and you will wake up here.'

'Will I have to do this every time I go to bed?'

'Only the one time, sweetheart. Once your portal is created here, you don't have to use it. You can go back home like you do every night in your sleep, but this way the portal will be safe and hidden from anyone, and you can use it only if and whenever you need to leave Endërland. I know it all sounds like a nuisance, Danny, but I just want to be safe. If I am right, whoever is behind these disappearances will soon come after you, and I will not lose you too.'

Having gotten his promise that he would do as she advised, they left the room, and the queen led him through the castle to the top floor, where a little surprise was waiting for them on the terrace. The girls had prepared a small banquet with sweets, fresh fruit, and delicious aromatic punch. And in the very middle, a porcelain plate with still warm white chocolate cookies, just like the ones Diane used to make when he was little. His mouth already watering at the sight of them, Daniel dug right in.

They sat on a comfortable sofa, overlooking the whole of Endër lying below their feet. It was late afternoon and soon it would be dark. Candles and oil lamps would soon be lit everywhere in the houses and streets. Here Daniel finally got the idea of just how big the city was. It stretched for miles before their eyes, bustling with life and noise even at this time of the day. There must have been tens of thousands of people living in Endër alone, and his mother was their queen.

'So, how come you are the queen?' he asked her, thus beginning 'The Talk'. Ready to finally have this conversation, Diane smiled as she mentally glanced back at her past.

'I've been visiting Endërland ever since I was little, just like Damien. It's always been in our blood, you know, my side of the family anyway. Nobody knows how and when the Great Lord built this place, but many of my ancestors have been coming here ever since anyone can remember. Most of them still live here, some in the city, others have settled in the villages outside Endër.'

'Most of them still live here? How old are they now?' Daniel interrupted.

'Time does not exist here, Danny, and we do not age; after a certain point, nobody really does. Our bodies only reflect the age we feel, and with the kind of life that we live and the good health we enjoy, we all feel pretty young. Plus, those of us who've come from our world have all died once already, so I guess we cannot die again, well, not a natural death anyway. But let me continue, and you will understand more as I do so.

'When I first started visiting, my grandfather – your great grandfather, Ari, was king. Everybody loved him. And when time came for me to become a permanent resident here, he passed the throne to me and moved to a nice little house, in a village near the mountains. He has always loved the mountains.'

'When did you know it was time for you to move here?' Daniel chose his words carefully. He tried not to sound accusatory, but he needed to know why everything happened the way it did, why she had left them.

She gazed at him for a short instant and knew that she could no longer hold back the truth.

'When we lost your brother, I'm ashamed to say that I lost my will to live. He was my firstborn, and at first it felt like someone had sucked all the air out of the world and I couldn't breathe anymore. I knew he had started to dream, and I could feel his presence whenever I was here. So, I would spend most of my days and nights asleep, looking for him. But I never found him, and things got very bad on the other side. I was abusing my body by taking too many sleeping pills for a very long time. I slept a lot, I didn't eat, and the worst of it all was that I was not able to look after you and your dad. I felt like a bad wife and mother, but the pain of losing Damien and the desperate need to find him was stronger than me. At some point, I realized that having a mother in that condition would be a lot worse for you than having no mother at all. I wasn't able to take care of you, and your dad was so focused on saving me, that you were being neglected. That's when I started thinking about leaving for good.'

She put her hand on top of his and hurried to explain herself further, fearing he would get the wrong idea, that her love for him had not been enough to cause her to stay.

'But that wasn't the only reason, my love. By the end of the first year, I realized that there was something sinister at work here, and that whoever it was that took Damien, would not stop with him. You would be next. So, I decided that the best thing for me to do, would be to come here, while I still had the chance, and do whatever I could to stop it. My body was giving up on me anyway and I didn't have much time. So, I made a choice. The last day I was awake, I kissed you goodbye and asked your dad to look after you. Then, when I got here, I was given a charmed bracelet by the Lords, which would prevent me going back even when I fell asleep. So, I never woke up again.'

'What do you mean while you had the chance?'

'We don't all end up here when we die, Danny. I guess if we die in our sleep while we're here, we get to stay. Otherwise, we go wherever people go after they die. I cheated, I had to; but I do not regret it. I knew one day you would come here, and I wanted to prepare everything for when that happened.'

She stopped for a moment and looked at him in his eyes, all the while holding his hands tight in hers. The emerald in her own eyes glistened now with an ocean full of tears of guilt and sorrow that had plagued her soul for far too long.

'I am so sorry for leaving you, my baby, for causing you all that hurt and pain. But I need you to know that I did it all out of love. I loved your brother and I love you more than anything else in both worlds. I would do anything to keep you safe.'

'What about dad?' Daniel was trying hard to fight back his own tears. 'Didn't you love him?'

'Of course, I did, sweetheart, I still do. He was my best friend, and I miss him so much, every single day. But you and Damien are the most important thing in both our lives, and I have no doubt that he would have done the same. If he knew the truth, he would agree that I did the right thing.'

'So, he doesn't know about any of this?'

'No. Unless it's absolutely necessary, we are strictly forbidden from telling anyone who is not a Visitor. He would not have understood anyway; would have thought me crazy and had me locked up probably.'

Daniel took a break from asking questions, trying in vain to claim back control over his tears. His mother observed him patiently, trying to read his mind.

The sky was now getting darker and two of the girls came to the terrace to light the lamps around them. They went back to the entrance and waited there, ready for any instructions.

All around the city, lights began to shine one after the other, competing with the stars that were lighting up the evening sky. As if on cue, the moon also joined the fight, arising from the northern horizon, big and bright just like the first time Daniel had seen it. For a single moment, he got completely lost in its captivating light, same as every other night. Everything else around him began to fade into shadow, until nothing was left but him and this unusual moon. He had to practically force himself to remember where he was and return to the conversation at hand.

94

Not without struggle, he turned again to his mother, wiped his face, and continued with his next set of questions.

'Where's the bracelet now?'

'When my body died, the bracelet was no longer necessary, and it just fell open. I gave it back to the Lords.'

'Why didn't I start to dream at the same age as you or Damien? Why did I wait until I was eighteen?'

'I have no answer to that, sweetheart; I have been wondering about it myself. Whatever the reason though, I am glad that it was so. You are now old enough to look after yourself, and this also allowed me to prepare for your arrival.'

'So, what happens now? What am I supposed to do from here?'

'You're supposed to live your life, Danny. You are only eighteen and I want you to do whatever it is that you want to do. Go to University, get a degree, get a job, find the love of your life, and get married. Build a family and grow old with them. When it is your time to leave that world behind, you can join me and the rest of our kin here if that's what you'll want. But until then, whenever you are here, we will be careful so that nobody steals your life from you or uses you for whatever purpose.'

Daniel didn't know what to think. Somehow, it seemed to him that his coming here was about more than just finding his mother and hiding away until he got old and died. Somehow, he felt he had a greater purpose, a greater destiny, or was that all the books talking? Maybe he had read too many stories. It just felt like this was not all he had come here for, and that he would find what that was out soon enough.

The queen raised a hand and caressed the hair on the side of his head.

'Are you alright sweetheart?'

Daniel did not answer right away. He was not sure what tomorrow would bring and did not think he was supposed to make any important decisions today. All he knew was that he had lost his mother a long time ago and now had found her again. So, he would enjoy this time with her and his newfound friends as long as he could and let tomorrow bring it on.

'I'm fine, mom,' he answered, giving her a hug. 'I am so happy that I found you again. Who knows, maybe we'll find Damien too. I have a very good feeling about this.'

She held tight to his embrace and replied.

'I hope so, my love, I really hope so.'

As they let go of each other, the queen wiped more tears from her eyes and took a moment to compose herself.

'Now, tell me about your dad. How is he doing?'

Daniel was glad that she asked. He loved his dad and it felt good to know that she still loved him too.

'He's great, mom; he is so good to me and really takes care of me. He can be a bit overprotective sometimes and treats me like I'm still a child, but I don't mind it. He still works with the police and is still in great shape. Still terrible at wrapping presents, though.'

They both laughed wholeheartedly.

'And he hasn't met anyone?' she asked, clearly curious.

'No, no one, mom. And he doesn't like to talk about that stuff either. I think, he's still waiting for something, I just don't know what.'

The queen didn't say anything; for a moment, she got lost in her own memories of David. Daniel did not disturb her; he now understood better the sacrifice she had had to make and what it had cost her. He wondered if he would have been strong enough to do the same, had it been his sacrifice to make, his loved ones to protect.

Eventually the queen came back to the present and got up.

'Alright then, sweetheart, I believe we've covered everything we can this evening. There's still much to talk about, but we have time. However, before we call it a night, there's someone here that has been waiting a long time to meet you. She would like to speak to you if that's alright.'

Daniel had no idea who that might be, but he didn't object. The queen called one of the two girls and said something to her. Not long after, the girl came back escorting a woman towards them. The queen made the introductions.

'Daniel, this is Veronica; she is from our world. Veronica, my son, Daniel. I will leave you two alone to talk, then. Goodnight, sweetheart. I will see you first thing tomorrow morning. The girls will help you with anything you might need. Goodnight, Veronica!'

'Goodnight, dear,' saluted the woman, sounding a lot older than she appeared.

Daniel stood up in respect as she took his mother's place on the sofa beside him. She was maybe in her late forties - early fifties. Her wavy brown hair was held back by a yellow ribbon, and it fell beautifully down her shoulders. She had a very sixties' apparel that Daniel had only seen in old movies. Her face was young, yet the look in her eyes spoke differently. She kept smiling at him, not even trying to hide her joy at seeing him there.

'Hello, darling. Oh, it's so nice to finally meet you.'

'It's nice to meet you,' Daniel replied. He was growing increasingly curious about who this woman was and what she wanted with him. 'My mom said you've been waiting to meet me?'

'A very long time, I should say, if time actually existed here. Magnificent woman your mother, isn't she? She never gave up hope of seeing you again, and she passed that hope onto me, too. We have both been waiting for you.'

'But why?' Daniel asked. 'I mean, are you family? Am I supposed to know you?'

'Oh no, darling, you don't know me. And I didn't even know your mother until I got here. But, let me tell you my story; maybe things would make more sense to you that way. Would you care to listen to it?'

Daniel answered affirmatively and she didn't wait to begin.

'A long time ago, when I was a very young girl, I met this wonderful young man. We fell in love right away and spent two wonderful years together. He often spoke to me of a world different from our own, a world where everyone was happy and lived forever. He said people there never aged, never hungered, and never died. He told me that he wanted me to join him there and build a family and a life with him.

'At first, I thought he had a wild fantasy, and because I loved him so much, it didn't bother me. But after a while I started to worry that there was something very wrong with him; I just couldn't believe him, not until I saw for myself. One night, as we fell asleep together, I woke up next to him in this place and I was astounded; everything was just the way he had described it. I knew right then and there that I wanted to be here with him, forever.

'Alas, that wasn't meant to be yet. I got news that my mother had fallen ill, and she needed me to care for her. So, I went back home. We agreed to wait until my mother had gotten better or passed away, but then something else happened. I became a mother myself, and that changed everything. I could not abandon my son, our son, and come here. So, I decided to stay. He promised that he would come back to take me when the time was right again, and he left. I stayed, raised my son, saw him get married and have his own family, until time came for me to leave that world. He came back for me when I was an old woman, tired of the years. He kept his promise and brought me here.'

She stopped for a while, her mind still swimming in her sea of memories, while Daniel formed his first question in the form of an observation.

'But you look so young?'

'I was about your age the first time I came to this place. Years went by for me back there, but here time doesn't matter. Here I look the way I feel about myself and I am not complaining about it one bit,' she said with a big grin on her face.

'Okay. I still don't understand what this has to do with me, though,' Daniel said.

'I know, darling, but I haven't finished with my story just yet. You see, my son in turn became the father of a beautiful little girl, a girl whom I loved very much. In the last years of my life she was my reason for being, my everything. Her name was Samantha, and she was very close to me. Like you, she is a Visitor, only, for some reason she can never sleep, which means that she cannot visit us either. She has had a very difficult life, and while I was alive, I tried to be there for her as much as I could. Just before I passed away, I promised her that I would always look after her, even after my death. And as a reminder of that, I promised to give her something that she really loved, this ring.'

She took from her finger a beautiful silver ring with a single diamond and showed it to him.

'Unfortunately, I failed to arrange that she receive the ring after my death, and that has been weighing heavily on my heart ever since. I know it must have hurt her that I broke that promise, and I need to make things right. That's where you come in. When I first came here, I consulted the Oracle, and he told me that a Visitor would one day come, with whom my Sam would cross paths. After talking to your mother, I came to believe that that Visitor would be you. And here you are. I have come to ask you to give her a message from me the day you will meet. I need her to know that I am very sorry for breaking my promise, and that I'm still watching over her.'

Daniel hesitated.

'But how do you know for sure that she and I will meet? What if the Oracle is wrong? What if she has passed away too? You did say you've been here for a very long time.'

'The Oracle has never been wrong, darling,' Veronica answered. 'But even if he is and you two never meet, there are still ways for you to pass my message to her. I could tell you how to find her. And I'm sure you've realized by now that time is different here from the real world. Even though it feels like I've lived a few lifetimes here, I'm sure it's only been a couple of years back there. So, what do you say?'

Daniel didn't really have to think about it. Her story did not sound any more unbelievable than the one he was living himself, and her request was small and simple. Clearly it meant a lot to her, and he could afford to do this one little thing.

'You know; I can do better than just give her your message. If we are to meet, like the Oracle has predicted, then I could give her the ring, if you still want her to have it.'

Veronica's jaw dropped.

'You can do that? It's never been heard of a Visitor taking something from here to the other world before.'

Daniel was not so sure about it now that she mentioned it. He had thought this was something that all Visitors had been able to do.

'Well, I haven't really tried this, but I have brought things from there a few times. I just figured it would be the same taking things back. I mean; it's worth a try, no?'

'It sure is, my dear.' Veronica placed the ring on his palm and closed his fingers tight around it. 'I am sure you will take good care of it.'

'I will try my best to get this to her; I promise.'

Veronica hugged him tight, thanking him a million times. She then wrote down on a piece of paper the address of her son's house, so Daniel could use it to track Sam down, and handed it to him.

Thanking him again, she got up and bade him goodnight, promising that they would see each other again. Daniel headed back to his room with the ring on his little finger and the address in his pocket. He felt good about this, almost proud. If only he could share all of this with his dad.

As the morning dawned, Steven Butler opened his eyes with an overwhelming feeling of discontent. Ever since he was sent here, he had never enjoyed a good night's sleep. He had always loved sleep; it was the only time when he felt really at peace. But now even that had been taken away from him. He was always awake and always under pressure to serve his master.

This morning, however, was slightly different. There was now a seed of hope that all this would soon be over and done with. If the boy turned out to be who the White Lord thought he was, he would be free to remain in his world and sleep all he wanted.

He got out of bed and headed to the bathroom to take a shower and shave. As he looked in the mirror, a face he had grown to hate stared back at him. The clear brown eyes of the young man whose body he had been using for years now, still felt foreign. He ignored the fact and continued with the mundane routine of the morning.

He needed to act fast today, no time to lose. He knew where the boy lived and worked, and the best chance he had of seizing him was in the evening, right after he left the gym. He just needed to call his guys back from their current posts and arrange the transport. Everything else was pretty much ready. They had the place; the clinic where he was currently posing as a janitor. Once they brought the boy there and kept him asleep, nobody would see anything suspicious. It was, after all, a sleep disorder clinic.

Confident that his plan was going to work flawlessly, Butler set out to arrange everything for that evening.

Sam was having second and third thoughts about this whole thing. She had been here for three days now and nothing the doctors were saying or doing gave her any confidence that this was any different from all the other times she had been in their hands. Yes, they told her of this new possible therapy that could give results if she agreed to try it, but that was nothing she had not heard before. And frankly she didn't really feel like letting medicine have another go at curing her insomnia. She had tried hard to get to where she was now, surrendered to the fact that her situation was permanent, and she wasn't about to risk getting her hopes up again, only to have them crushed at yet another failure.

And, of course, in her three days here, she had not met or heard of anyone named Daniel. She was not disappointed, more like angry at herself for flying halfway across the world on the words of a madman. What was she thinking? If she had told anyone what she was doing and why, they would have locked her up somewhere and thrown away the key. This was insane. These people knew no more than any other specialist she had ever seen; it was pointless. She had to go back home.

Having fought with this decision ever since she first stepped foot into the clinic, Sam finally made up her mind. She could leave this very evening, that way she wouldn't have to battle it out with the doctors and go through a meaningless debate of how she should not give up hope and trust science to do its thing. If she left now, she could still catch the tube to Heathrow and see if she could get a flight back home using her open-ended ticket. Or maybe she could hang around one or two days and see London; after all, it's not like she had plans to come back and visit anytime soon. She might as well do that now that she was here, that way this trip would not have been completely useless. Though, she might have to book a hotel somewhere. She would have stayed here, if it wasn't for the doctors and their stupid tests; after all she did pay these idiots a considerable amount of money just to check in.

Right then she thought of her Nan, and she just knew that leaving this place was the right thing to do. Nan, like her, had never placed much faith in doctors and specialists when it came to her insomnia; she had always said that her cure would come from elsewhere and at the right time. But Sam never knew what she actually meant.

She packed up her things in her suitcase, got dressed and walked out of her room. There were only a couple of people working the night shift, so she shouldn't have trouble slipping out unnoticed. The halls of the two-storey building felt lifeless this evening. There were hardly any sounds, except for the mild snoring of a man in the second room down the hall; he clearly had no trouble sleeping. Most of the rooms in the clinic were empty; she guessed there weren't a lot of people with sleeping problems like hers.

She was about to take the stairs down to the first floor when she heard what sounded like a van pulling in the driveway quietly. She went to the windows to see what was going on.

An ambulance with the lights off stopped in front of the entrance, and two men got out from the front, while a third one came out of the back doors, pulling out a wheelchair with someone in it. Sam figured this was another patient checking in, but she couldn't help but feel that something wasn't right. Why did the ambulance drive in with the lights off? And why were the men trying to be so quiet and careful?

She thought about it for a moment and decided that this was none of her business. The last time she stuck her nose where it didn't belong, she ended up on the other side of the ocean. She went back to her room quietly and hid there until the men brought the person in the wheelchair to the empty room next to hers. She waited there until it was clear that they had left, and then decided to carry on with her escape.

She opened the door silently and took a peek outside. There was no one in the hall. She closed the door behind her and tiptoed towards the stairs at the end of the hall. Just as she got there, the window to her right opened inwards and someone dropped in, right on top of her, causing both of them to fall on the floor. Sam's instincts kicked in immediately and she pushed the guy off of her, assuming an offensive position.

The young man got up and looking at her raised fists, whispered quickly.

'Wait, wait; I'm not here to hurt you. I'm looking for my friend who was just brought in here. Do you know where they put him?'

Sam eyed him suspiciously and hesitated. The geeky looking guy couldn't have been more than a couple of years older than her and was about the same height. She was sure she could take him if it came to it. Somehow though, she didn't seem to feel threatened by him.

'I don't know what you're talking about; I haven't seen anything. Now move out of my way, please.'

She made for the stairs again, but the guy stepped in front of her. She was certain she had never seen him before, yet there was something familiar about him.

'Please, lady; this is a matter of life or death. If I don't get my friend out of here, he will be gone forever.'

'This is a sleep disorder clinic; I hardly think they can do much worse than put him to sleep.'

'They can if that means he'll never wake up. Trust me, those men are not doctors, and Daniel has no sleeping problems whatsoever; well, not anymore. Won't you please help me? I think they've drugged him, and I cannot get him out of here all by myself.'

Sam stopped trying to leave. It finally happened; the reason for her coming all this way had finally materialized. She backed up one step.

'Did you just say "Daniel"? Is that the name of the guy they brought in with the ambulance?'

'Yes. Where did they put him?'

'In the room next to mine, four doors down the hall. Who is he?'

'All I can tell you is that he is very important, and right now he really needs help. Can you please help me get him out of here before they come back?'

'Where are they now?' she asked, already forming a plan in her head. This was not what she had expected when she thought she would meet this Daniel guy, but she had no choice now. She needed to see this through.

'I think they are downstairs in the cafeteria. They might be back soon, so we have to act now.'

'Do you have a car outside?'

'Of course I do, how else would I have followed them here? What are you thinking?'

'We cannot take him out by the main entrance; we'll have to lower him down the window. Then we take him to your car from the back exit. How far is your car?'

'It's just around back. Sounds perfect; let's move.'

They headed to the room, trying not to make any noise.

'I'm Freddie, by the way,' the young man introduced himself. 'What's your name?'

'Sam,' she answered as they reached the room where the men had put Daniel. They tried the door, only to find out that it was locked.

'Now what?' Freddie asked.

'I got this.' Sam opened the door to her own room, reached behind it and came back with a rusty old key in her hand. 'This building is very old, and these rooms all have the same key. That's not very smart.'

Freddie gave her an inquisitory look.

'What,' she snapped, 'there's not much to do around here, and I never sleep.'

She inserted the key and turned it, pushing the door open. Leaving the light off, they walked over by the bed where Daniel lay uncovered and unconscious, blissfully unaware of what was going on around him.

Sam took a quick look at the face of this boy who was supposed to help her find the answers to her life's questions. He had quite an attractive face, smooth spotless skin, and beautiful dark wavy hair. For some reason she felt compelled to touch it but thought better of it. A pair of fine eyebrows crowned two almond shaped eyes that finished on thick and long eyelashes, of which she felt immediately jealous. He seemed to be about the same age as her. But who was he and how was he supposed to help her with her problems?

Next to her, Freddie gave Daniel a shake and tried to wake him up. Since that didn't work, they both grabbed him by his arms and legs and transferred him to the wheelchair left by the bed. They then wheeled him out of the room all the way to the open window. Using a pair of sheets as a rope, they tied them around Daniel's chest and proceeded to slowly lower him down the second storey window.

Sam couldn't help but take in the boy's alluring scent as she held him in her arms for that one moment. She'd always had a keen nose, though when it came to boys, it often got in the way, putting her off many of her dates. But there was something so enticing, almost dizzying about the way this stranger smelled to her. *Great*, she thought to herself, *handsome and smells good. Just what I need right now.*

She forced herself to get a grip and proceeded with lowering the guy down, carefully letting him land on the pavement. Then they both climbed down the rope after him, untied him and carried him out of the clinic and into Freddie's waiting Mini Cooper.

'Nice car, Fred,' Sam complimented as they started the car and drove away as silently as they possibly could.

'Thanks, but please call me Freddie; I hate Fred.'

'No problem, Fred,' she replied, making him give her a look. 'Where are we going anyway?'

'My place for now, they will not know how to find us there. We'll be safe for a while. Listen, thank you very much for helping me with him; I couldn't have done it without you. What's your plan now? I can drop you off anywhere.'

'No, you can't; I'm sticking with you. I need to be there when he wakes up.' She motioned with her head towards Daniel still unconscious on the back seat. Freddie looked at her curiously.

'Why?'

Sam realized that there was no way to say this without sounding like a complete nut, so she just went ahead and said it.

'I cannot explain how or why, but he is the reason why I came to this clinic in the first place. I was told he might help me with something.'

She kept looking straight ahead, pretending that what she just said was not weird at all. But apparently, she didn't have to worry about that with Freddie.

'Wow. It sounds like you've had an encounter with the Oracle. I guess our meeting was not by chance after all.'

'The who?' Sam asked.

'The Oracle, Sam. He's the one who deals with everything that involves Dreamers. He helps them find their way into Endërland safely and looks after them. Daniel is a Dreamer.'

Sam actually reached with her hands to check if she might have hit her head somewhere.

'What in the world are you talking about, man?'

Freddie took his eyes off the road just long enough to see her face and realize that she really had no idea what he was talking about. He decided he needed some more info from her, however, if he was to share what he knew.

'Ok, let's backpedal just a little bit here. You don't know Daniel, right?'

'Right,' she answered.

'So, who told you to come here and look for him?'

Sam knew that this next part was the craziest bit of it all, but she also knew that it had come true, halfway at least. She could not hold back now for fear of looking like a lunatic. For that matter, this Freddie guy seemed to have a few loose screws of his own. So, she decided to say it out loud for the first time ever.

'Okay, so, about three weeks ago I ran into this beggar outside my building, who appeared to know an awful lot about me. He pretended to read my palm and discover some problems I'm dealing with. Long story short, he said, if I came here, I would meet someone named Daniel and that he would have the answers I'm looking for.'

'Yep, sounds like the Oracle. That guy can be so cryptic and mysterious sometimes, it's a wonder anyone ever understands his instructions. But he is never wrong, I guarantee you that much. And I'm glad you followed his advice; we did great together back there.'

'Have you ever met him?'

Freddie seemed to get a bit embarrassed by the question.

'No, never. I have researched and studied about him practically all of my life, and it would be a dream come true to actually meet him in person, but he only appears where he's needed.'

He stopped there for a moment as if deciding if he should go on and tell her what he knew. There was no question about it, however, Sam was meant to find out this stuff sooner or later.

'Okay, what I'm about to tell you is extremely confidential, and there is only a handful of people in the entire world who know about it and would like to keep it that way. But I'm guessing, if the Oracle has involved you in this thing, you might have a part to play, so you need to know what you're getting yourself into. So, here it goes.

'You know how when you fall in a deep sleep, you usually start dreaming?'

Sam gave him a look.

'Didn't you just find me at a sleep disorder clinic?'

'Oh right, sorry,' Freddie corrected himself quickly and then continued. 'Well, most people do anyway. What they don't realize however, is that dreams are a lot more than they appear to be. To this day, scientists still struggle to understand what they are exactly and what they mean, but no one has come even close to the truth.

'There's a whole other realm out there, Sam, existing in a completely different dimension from ours and that somehow can only be accessed through our dreams. The majority of people can perceive only a small fraction of this realm, like sensing its presence or catching glimpses of it, so to speak. This causes the images they see in their sleep, which they call dreams.

'There are, however, certain people with the ability to perceive more than just a fraction of this realm. And when that happens, their consciousness interacts with it in much the same way it does with our own, meaning, they have real experiences, just as if they were awake. Some are even able to project themselves physically onto the other side, without even meaning to do so. What they experience there though, it's usually known only to them, and that's where things get a bit more complicated. There's not just one world existing inside this realm but many, though of course, most of what we know about them is pure speculation. The only one we have proof of and have had dealings with, throughout history, is the one they call Endërland.'

He stopped narrating for just a moment, long enough to check the mirror and take another turn.

'I'm a member of a very old society that exists for one reason only: to protect the world from Dreamers gone bad. Dreamers, or Visitors as they call them in Endërland, are people who, while they are asleep, they can travel to other worlds through their dreams. In those worlds, practically everything is possible, and they can do pretty much anything. Most of the time this is a very benign and harmless thing; Dreamers go through their whole lives living in both worlds simultaneously, without causing harm to anything or anyone. Quite the opposite, a few of them are known throughout the history to have used this gift of theirs for the good of mankind, contributing either in science and culture, or causing a movement and bringing about good change. History is full of people like this that have brought ideas back from their own worlds, and helped make this one a better place, people like, Einstein, Gandhi, Mother Teresa and so on.

'However, as is usually the case, there's two sides to every coin. There have also been those during the course of time, who have tried to use this ability for their own selfish purposes, thus bringing evil into this world from whichever world they would visit in their own twisted minds. History is full of those people too, people you've most probably heard of, like Nero of Rome, Hitler, or Stalin. They are the reason why the Order of the Guardians exists. Those Dreamers who wanted to preserve this world and the people close to them who knew their truth, got together, and formed the order, and for more than two thousand years have been fighting to stop the corrupt ones from causing irreparable damage.'

Freddie finished this quick lesson on the history of Dreamers and turned to face his passenger, only to find her gawking at him.

Sam had to actually remind herself to breathe. What this guy was telling her sounded absolutely and utterly ludicrous.

'Are you being serious right now? Are you telling me that Hitler and Mother Teresa were "Dreamers" and at night they lived in another world? Wow, I am feeling so much better about myself, all of a sudden. Maybe we should turn back and have you checked by someone; this is the most stupid thing I have ever heard.'

III

'Well, you wouldn't be considered very wise if you believed everything you heard right away, and I don't expect you to. But very soon you will be convinced that this is the truth. Daniel will wake up and then he can tell you all of this for himself.'

'What makes you think I'll believe *him*?' she asked. 'And what is *your* role in all of this anyway?'

'I like to consider myself a prophet of the modern days. I know everything there is to know about the history of Dreamers, and sometimes I think I can see glimpses of the future concerning them. Like with Daniel, for example. For years now everything that's been happening around us, has led me to believe that a great Dreamer is coming; one that will have such power that he will completely change the world as we know it. There's even a prophecy about this, a very old one, which I think is about to come true. There are only a few bloodlines of Dreamers still known to us, and Daniel comes from the greatest one of them. I've been keeping an eye on him for quite some time now, and I had a vision warning me that he would be in danger today. So, I followed him all day, and as it turned out, it's a good thing I did.'

'So, he doesn't actually know you, does he?' Sam asked just to clarify. Freddie took on a guilty look.

'No, not really,' he responded. Sam sat back with a sigh.

'Great, the guy will wake up in the company of two total strangers, one of whom is a complete nutcase. I am so looking forward to this.'

Freddie did not reply. His attention was suddenly drawn to the front mirror, where an ambulance could be seen approaching fast. Sam noticed his concern and looked back.

'It's them; step on it.'

Freddie accelerated and started manoeuvring between cars, trying to gain some distance. The ambulance behind them accelerated as well and turned the sirens on. All cars currently on the road made way for it. Lucky for them, it was the middle of the night, and the streets weren't that busy.

'They're gaining on us. Go faster,' Sam shouted.

'Don't worry girly; they can never catch us in that thing.'

He turned left, leaving Euston Road, and taking Gower Street. The ambulance was right behind them. They needed to get to smaller streets, where their Mini could manoeuvre easily and lose them. Freddie took the first left out of Gower Street and then a whole series of other turns that Sam failed to keep track of. With every new turn, they gained a bit more distance from the ambulance, until after about half hour of reckless driving, they lost them completely. Freddie didn't even know where they were anymore, but that didn't matter. They kept driving until they got onto a main road again, and set on the right course for his house, which was about half hour drive to North Greenwich. Sam finally managed to relax and rest her head back.

'Dear God. What have I gotten myself into this time?'

Chapter 5

INTRODUCTIONS & REUNIONS - PART 2

aking up as daylight brightly burst through the windows did not feel as natural as every other day. Daniel's head felt clouded, heavy, as if he was rising out from under the depths of a dark and troubled sea. He opened his eyes and found that he wasn't in either of his rooms. Instead, he was in what looked more like a library, thanks to the endless books and manuscripts he saw stacked in the numerous shelves or laying all around the room.

On the couch opposite him he saw a young man sleeping. His face was turned the other direction, so he did not recognize him.

Sitting on a chair by the table in the middle of the room was someone else, a girl with long curly blonde hair, immersed in a thick hardcover book. He thought she looked very pretty and somewhat familiar. He had seen that face recently, well not quite; she looked so much like someone he had seen recently. He just could not think of whom exactly.

He coughed and that got their attention. Sam lifted her piercing blue eyes towards him, putting the book down, while Freddie got up immediately, as if he wasn't even sleeping.

'Where am I?' Daniel asked.

'You're safe,' Freddie replied first, brushing up his short brown hair with his fingers. 'You're with friends. How do you feel?'

'My head feels like it's got a twin growing up inside, but other than that, I think I'm ok. How did I get here?'

'Do you remember anything from last night?' Freddie asked, coming to sit on a chair next to him.

Daniel suddenly had a flashback of the previous evening.

'I remember getting out of the gym and walking home when I saw these two guys coming towards me. Then someone grabbed me from behind and put something against my nose that smelt funny. That's the last thing I remember. Was that you?'

'No, no,' Freddie hurried to explain. 'We don't know who they are exactly, nor why they kidnapped you. We were just lucky enough to be able to get you away from them. I'm Freddie by the way, and this is...'

'Sam,' Daniel finished his sentence, finally realizing who she looked like. 'You're Veronica's granddaughter, aren't you? What are you doing here?'

Sam, who had been listening silently until now, was taken aback.

'What? How do you know my grandmother, or me? Who are you?'

'I don't,' Daniel responded to her first question, 'but you look the spitting image of your grandmother; except for the blonde hair of course.'

Sam stood up and withdrew a step or two. She felt like she was losing it. Too many things seemed to be going on these past few weeks that she could not explain, and she had had just about enough.

'Alright, just what the heck is going on here, really? How can you possibly know who my grandmother was and what she looked like?'

'I told you,' Freddie beamed at her, referring to their prior conversation. 'He's a Dreamer.'

'A what?' Daniel asked.

'A Visitor,' Freddie clarified for him.

'And how do *you* know that?' It was Daniel's turn to freak out. 'Who are you again?'

Freddie now got up, raised his hands, and put on his best authoritative face.

'Okay, why don't we all just calm down and take it from the top. Daniel, as Sam already knows, I am part of a very old society called The Guardians, whose only purpose has always been to protect the world from Dreamers gone bad. I have been keeping an eye on you for quite some time now, and it just so happened that I was forewarned you might be in danger last night. I was watching you from a distance, when I saw the men kidnap you and take you to the clinic where Sam was staying until last night. We met and she helped me get you out of there. That was my part of the story. Now you two can tell each other the rest. Thank you!'

Having said all of that in one go, Freddie sat down again, taking one long deep breath. Sam and Daniel looked at him, then at each other, and for a moment were unsure of what to do next. Then, as if on cue, they both burst into laughter at the same time. The self-proclaimed prophet had managed to clear the air of any serious vibes, albeit not in the way he had meant to. Freddie gave them an evil look at first, but eventually joined in on the laughter as well.

'I can't believe you said all of that without breathing, Fred,' Sam said, while Freddie glared at her. 'You must have some set of lungs in you, man.'

They laughed a bit more until all three seemed to have gotten it out of their system. When they could finally breathe again, Sam turned to Daniel and said her bit.

'Well, alright then; I guess I'll go next. Looks like you already know who I am, so I'll skip the introductions. What you might not know, however, is that from the age of five I've lost the ability to sleep. At most, I may doze off with one eye open for about 10 minutes every night, but that's about it. I've been to doctors and specialists most of my life, but nobody could ever tell me why, or do anything to help me. Then, about three weeks ago, while I was minding someone else's business, I ran into a stranger who told me that if I came here, I would meet someone named Daniel and that he would help me find the answers I'm looking for. So here I am, and here you are. Your turn.'

Daniel looked at the two of them giving him their full attention now and waiting to hear his story. Up until this moment, there had always been a possibility that what he was experiencing was all in his head, that it was all something he'd made up to deal with his loss and the desire to see his mother and brother once again. Well, now he knew for sure that he wasn't crazy; this was all real.

'Well, I guess I don't have to worry about you thinking I've gone bonkers, since you already seem to know a lot about what is going on. In a way, it kinda feels good to finally be able to talk to someone about this. Here it is then.

'A couple of weeks ago, the night of my eighteenth birthday to be exact, I dreamed for the first time ever in my life; I had never had a dream before that.'

'You had your eighteenth birthday a few weeks ago?' Sam interrupted him.

'On the 15th, yes,' Daniel replied, slightly annoyed. 'Why?'

'That's the same as my birthday; we were born on the same day. What do you think that means?'

'I don't know,' Daniel answered. 'Maybe it's just a coincidence.'

'Aren't we a bit passed coincidences by now?' Sam insisted. 'I mean, we're born on the same day, you've never had a dream and I cannot sleep, which obviously means I've never had a dream either, as far as I can remember. And now I hear that there's a whole other world out there, accessible only through our dreams; c'mon guys, this cannot be just a coincidence.'

She turned now to Freddie.

'Well, Fred, you're the one with all the conspiracy theories; what do you think?'

'Honestly, Sam, I don't know what to think. You seem to have a point there, but why don't we let Daniel finish with his story before we jump into any conclusions? Go on, Daniel.'

Sam relented for the moment and did not interrupt again. Daniel continued where he'd left off.

'Anyway, in my dream I visited this place called Endërland. It's a magical place with wonderful people that live a simple and happy life, completely different from what we know here. It's like a little piece of heaven, everything there is so surreal. There's no sickness, no hunger or death there. I've been visiting this place every night in my dreams ever since, and it's just amazing.

'And then, the craziest thing happened; I ended up meeting my own mother, who died fourteen years ago, and I've spent the past few days with her. You can imagine my shock and disbelief; it took me a long while to convince myself that she was real. Apparently, she was a Visitor too, just like me, and before she died, she managed to cross over, and she's been living there ever since.

'That same night, I was also introduced to a woman called Veronica, who apparently had been waiting a long time to meet me. She told me the story of how she ended up in that place, and she also told me about you and what she promised you before she died. She said, not keeping that promise has weighed heavy on her heart ever since, and that I was her only chance at making things right. So, she gave me this for you.'

Sam watched with her eyes open wide as Daniel took off his little finger a ring, the very same ring that her Nan had promised her. She took the small piece of jewellery in her trembling hands and recognized it right away. Hot tears trailed down her flushing cheeks, as she too realized that this was indeed all real.

'She asked me to tell you that she is very sorry for not leaving you the ring like she promised, and she wants you to know that she is still looking after you.'

Daniel stopped there, realizing that Sam was no longer listening to him. With her face hidden in her palms, she walked out of the room, leaving the two of them alone. He was about to go after her, but Freddie stopped him.

'Give her some time; she will be fine. It's a lot to take all in one day. By the way, you should call your father; he must be worried.'

Daniel jumped out of the couch, realizing he had been missing since yesterday and his dad would be out of his mind.

'I'm such an idiot. Where is my jacket?'

Freddie passed him his jacket and Daniel checked the pockets for his mobile.

'It's not here; they must've taken it. Can I use your phone please?'

Freddie handed him his own mobile.

'Do not tell him where you are. We need to be safe.'

Daniel looked at him, confused. How was telling his dad where he was, going to hurt him? He didn't even know where he was anyway. He dialled his dad's number and heard it ring. David answered right away.

'Dad, it's me.'

'Danny, where are you? Are you alright? I've been going out of my mind here.'

'I'm fine, dad. I'm so sorry; I didn't mean to scare you. You didn't call anyone, did you?'

'Well, I *am* the police, Danny, if that's what you mean. I got Timmy and some of the guys looking around for you, but nothing official, no. Where are you, Danny? What's going on?'

'I'm with some friends, dad; I'm safe. But dad, something happened last night.'

'What do you mean? What happened?'

'Some people tried to kidnap me, and dad, if I come back home, I'm afraid they might try again. They were waiting for me outside the gym; they must know where I live too. I don't know what to do, dad.'

David wasn't answering. All of a sudden, he remembered some vague instructions Diane had given him before she died about moving town and changing their last name, which he had dismissed as the mumblings of a sick woman. He now felt he had made a big mistake. She had always claimed, after Damien had been kidnapped, that Daniel was not safe either, but he had not believed her. And now it was happening all over again.

'Dad? Are you still there?' Daniel's voice pulled him out of his own head.

'Yes, Danny, I'm here. Listen, are you sure you are safe where you are now?'

Freddie, who was listening to their conversation, affirmed with his head.

'Yes, dad. They won't know how to find me here.'

'Ok, son. Stay there tonight and do not go out. I want you to call me tomorrow on my mobile. I will try to come up with a plan in the meantime, ok? Until then, be safe son. I love you!'

'I love you too, dad. Talk to you soon. Bye!'

Daniel hung up and handed the phone back to Freddie.

'I didn't expect that,' he said, seating down. 'I was afraid he would have insisted I go back home right away.'

'Maybe he's thinking like a policeman; he's trying to be safe. Or maybe he knows more than you think. He was married to a Visitor after all.'

'I don't know about that,' Daniel replied. 'My mom told me that we are forbidden to tell anyone about us. She never said anything to him.'

'There are no strict rules against that, Daniel. Sometimes even non-Visitors earn the right to enter Endërland, and it's not about what they might say or do, but more about what's in their heart.'

Daniel found that very interesting to hear. He thought of Veronica, who had not been a Visitor and yet had ended up living in Endërland. Was she an exception, or other people like his dad could have the same chance as her?

'Are there a lot of non-Visitors who end up living in Endërland?' he asked.

'I don't have that answer, I'm afraid. I've only studied the history of Dreamers, the ones that we know of anyway, what they've done in this world and what they've said of the other world to people they've trusted. But what happens there, I'm afraid you have more access to than I do. You are the first Dreamer I've ever met, Daniel; you are my big chance to find out more.'

Daniel was about to ask something else but was interrupted by the door opening inwards to let Sam walk back into the room. She was trying to hide her puffy eyes by avoiding their gaze, and they did the same as to not make her feel uncomfortable, but there was no hiding the obvious. She went back to her chair, sat down again, and spoke without looking at them.

'I'm sorry about that. Everything that's been happening recently it's just too crazy, and I'm feeling a bit lost if I'm honest. I still don't know why I'm here.'

She raised her beautiful blue eyes, that Daniel found even more enchanting because of her tears, and looked at him.

'He said that you'd help me find the answers I'm looking for. How are you gonna do that? How are you going to cure me?'

Daniel wasn't sure how to even answer that. He knew he could not do anything about Sam's insomnia, just like he couldn't do anything about the fact that he hadn't had a single dream in all his life.

'Look, Sam,' he began. 'I don't know why the Oracle said what he said to you; I'm as new to this as you are. I gave my word to your grandmother that I would pass her words and ring on to you, and I did. I don't know what else I'm supposed to do for you; I'm sorry.'

'Well, that's just great,' she said, leaning back on her chair and staring at the two of them, not particularly happy. 'So, now what? What's next?'

'I don't know,' Daniel answered. 'I don't know what these people want from me, but I have a feeling they're not going to stop until they get me. I'm going to stay here tonight until I talk to my dad tomorrow and see what he's got planned. I'm sure my mom's got something to say about this as well; I've got to tell her what's happened. But I can't ask you to put yourself in danger for me any more than you already have. Maybe you should go back home, Sam.'

But going back home was the farthest thing from Sam's mind right now.

'Yeah, that's not happening anytime soon. I was told to stick with you until I got my answers, and stick with you is what I'll do, whether you like it or not. Besides, seems to me like you might need protection 24/7, and guess what, I'm your girl.'

'But you don't know what you're getting yourself into,' Daniel tried to protest.

'Oh, I think I have a better idea than you do so far, my sleeping beauty, so don't even think of trying to scare me off.'

She made a point of sounding angry with her last words, and it scared even her how easily that worked.

Daniel bit his tongue in surprise and looked at Freddie, as if asking for his support. Freddie, however, went to stand next to Sam and turned to face him.

'I'm sorry, Daniel, but I'm with Sam on this one. The Oracle clearly meant for her to be here, and I dare not go against that.'

'This is insane,' Daniel exclaimed. 'Don't you get it? It is not safe to be around me; I cannot protect you.'

'Who says I need your protection?' Sam yelled, now really angry. 'What, just because I'm a girl? I am more than capable of protecting myself, thank you very much. In fact, I might even help keep you alive. You just concentrate on finding out how to cure me and I'll take care of the rest. I am not leaving you until I've gotten what I came here for, and that's the end of it.'

Daniel tried to say more but she shunned him and went to the kitchen. Freddie couldn't help but smile.

'Damn it, she's stubborn,' Daniel scoffed. 'Well, I won't be held responsible if anything happens to her.'

'I wouldn't worry about her, mate; she's a tough one. Besides, maybe she's right; maybe she *was* sent here to help.

Which reminds me, I'm gonna have to go out for a while. I'll have to visit the Order and ask for their advice and help with this. Maybe they know something.'

'When will you be back?'

'Late afternoon, if everything goes well.' He went to his wardrobe and picked up a jacket for himself. It was the last day of September, and whatever summer London had enjoyed that year, was now well and truly over.

'Try not to kill each other until I come back, please, will you?'

Daniel smirked at him.

'What do I do until then?'

'Improvise,' Freddie said grinning and closing the door behind him.

* * *

After bloods had cooled down enough, Daniel and Sam spent the rest of the day making small talk. He was really curious about this girl who was born on the other side of the world, and yet seemed to be connected to him in ways neither of them understood yet. He kept asking her many questions, but to his dismay, Sam kept avoiding answering them like a pro. It would seem, she didn't like to talk about herself much. Plus, it was Daniel who had the more interesting bits to share, and she wanted to know it all.

Even with everything she heard though, Sam still could not believe how real all this was. Yet, she was now past the point of doubting it. It seemed just about anything was possible, and that was a comforting thought for the most part, for it gave her hope that one day she would indeed find what she was looking for. The problem, however, was that she no longer knew for sure what that was exactly.

They talked and talked until they finally got hungry, so Daniel decided to cook something quick and simple with whatever he found in Freddie's fridge.

Sam was impressed. She hadn't met many guys who cooked. In fact, none of her ex-boyfriends did, and there had been a few of them, seeing that she could never hold on to one longer than a few months.

She scowled at herself for thinking about her exes. Why would her mind go there just now?

Evening came and there was still no sign of Freddie. Daniel decided not to wait for him and went to bed; he was anxious to talk to his mother again. For some reason, he had not been able to dream the previous night. It must have been the drugs they had used to put him to sleep. Sam promised to wake him up if Freddie came back with important news, so he went ahead and slept. In no time, he found himself waking up in his other bed, on the other side of the invisible portal.

Butler braced himself to face the wrath of his master. He knew it was inevitable, just like he knew he would take it like a real man. The White Lord would not catch him being weak and beg for mercy. After all, the responsibility was all his; he should have foreseen that the Visitor would have someone guarding him. That was one mistake he was not going to make a second time. Having served his master all his life, he knew the White Lord would make sure of that. And right he was.

Sitting on his white throne, Winter was looking down at his number one man with a calm expression on his face. The hourglass on the corner table was still, its sands lifeless; the

White Lord had clearly not bothered with it today. Butler knew these were the times when he should fear him the most.

'So, it did not occur to you that he might have been under protection? Do you think I am the only one who knows just how important this boy may be?'

'Forgive me, my lord; it will not happen a second time. I will get my hands on him again, and this time no one will save him.'

Winter got up from his throne and slowly approached his servant. Butler felt the temperature in the room fall drastically and knew something bad was coming.

'Tell me, how will you get your hands on him, if you have none?'

Saying this, he grabbed Butler's left hand with his right, squeezing it hard with anger and holding it like that for what felt to Butler like an eternity. The man writhed at his master's feet in pain, screaming at the top of his lungs and unable to get away from his torturer. In an instant, the skin where Winter's icy hands touched him began to crystallize and turn first white and then slowly and gradually transparent.

When Winter finally let go of him, Butler winced in pain and began stroking his left hand with his right, hoping to keep it warm, but to no avail. Skin, flesh, and bone rapidly froze, and the ice spread over his entire hand within seconds. Butler tried to move the fingers, but they no longer responded to his commands. His hand had just turned into his very own ice sculpture.

The pain was excruciating, and he felt like crushing the hand against a wall just to get rid of the cold it brought to the very core of his body. Yet, submissively, he lifted his eyes to look at his master. Winter looked right back at him with no sign of pity or remorse; on the contrary, malice shone through every fibre of his being.

'Lucky for me, these are not the hands you will be using to capture the boy again. And this time, you will not fail me,' he scowled.

Butler bowed his head low, surrendered to his fate.

'Yes, my lord.'

'Good,' Winter ended with disgust, as he headed to his throne and sat back down.

'Now, as for our other matter, where are we with our flying little friends?'

'I have sent word to them, my lord,' Butler replied, trying very hard not to let his pain show in his trembling voice. 'I expect them to contact me with an answer very soon. However, I believe they will not do anything until after the celebrations. They care too much about that stuff and would do nothing to spoil their fun.'

Winter seemed annoyed by this but unwilling to do anything about it.

'As long as they get the job done. I guess I can keep the charade going for a while longer. Go on then, get out of my sight. And you better stay away until you have some good news to bring me.'

He signalled with his hand for Butler to leave the room, and so Butler did, hiding his frozen hand under his coat. Lucky for him, the pain was beginning to fade; otherwise he didn't know how he would manage to do anything at all. He no longer felt his hand, and it was beyond weird having a dead weight at the end of his arm. He would have to wear gloves from now on, so nobody could see what had happened to him, but he still felt lucky. This could have gone a lot worse.

Sunrise in the beautiful Endër was followed almost immediately by Nemo's knock on Daniel's door. As soon as they both left his room, he began to tell Daniel about his previous afternoon and how he had spent it helping the girls putting up decorations in the castle for the upcoming festivities. He wouldn't shut up about how beautiful all the girls were, and how he didn't know which one of them he liked more. Laughing with his friend, Daniel did not fail to realize that despite not having dreamt the previous night, it was still only the next morning here.

The queen was away dealing with royal matters, but Íro, the blonde girl they met when they first arrived at the castle, would be looking after them. Daniel noticed with amusement that Nemo acted all giddy around her. She was very young and sweet, smiling all the time at the Sea-Prince, and prompting Daniel to felt slightly envious of his younger friend.

Íro proceeded to lead them to the dining hall where the two of them sat down and had breakfast together. Daniel took the time to fill Nemo in on everything he had learned so far. He trusted his new friend, and something told him that he would have to rely on him in the near future for whatever was coming. Nemo listened to him intently, asking questions every now and again. He now knew everything that Daniel knew and wasn't too thrilled about any of it. It seemed things would be getting a lot more complicated, very soon.

The queen returned right after they'd finished their meal and sat down with them. When Daniel eventually informed her of his kidnapping, this brought a dark shadow over her beautiful face. For the first time since they had been reunited, she seemed gravely concerned.

'And you didn't recognize any of their faces?' she asked, referring to his kidnappers.

'The two who were coming towards me, I had never seen before. And the one who came behind me, I obviously didn't see. But why is that important now?'

'It probably isn't,' she answered thoughtfully, then she got up and began pacing around the area that served as a dining room for her and her guests. 'This is not good; I did not expect them to come after you so soon. They must know that you are here already, which means that you might not be safe here either.'

'But who are they mom? Who is doing all of this?'

The queen looked at both of them waiting for an explanation but wasn't sure if she should. After all, she did not have any proof for what she suspected, only assumptions. And yet, all her instincts told her that she was right.

She sat in between them, and for a moment struggled with the decision of telling them what she knew, but eventually she decided to speak.

'Endërland has always been a wonderful place to live in,' she began, 'a happy place where every living thing is good and where evil has always been absent. But lately things have been changing. It's still not very obvious, and there are only a few events that have happened recently to support this theory. The disappearance of a number of Visitors, for example, is one of them. Visitors have always been welcomed and loved in Endërland, but we haven't seen any of them for a very long time now. And the few that we remember seeing for a while, they've vanished completely, and no one knows why.

'But that's not all. Mysterious occurrences have been reported up north recently. There are numerous villages spread out from the valley of Destiny all the way up to the Northern Mountains. I've received word that people, mostly men, have disappeared all over that part of the kingdom. No one knows where they've gone, and their families are left worried and afraid, feelings they never knew until now. To make matters worse, life over there is becoming increasingly difficult and dangerous. Animals are starting to become wild and turn on each other and the people living in the area. That has never happened before. The harvest is also getting weaker with each season, and the earth is not producing as much as before. Everything is changing for the worse, and I don't think it's going to stop.

'Concerned about the future of the kingdom, I went to consult the Oracle a while back. He confirmed my fears that dark days are ahead of us. He also told me that one person alone is responsible for all of this. Evil has somehow found its way into this person's heart, and he, in turn, is corrupting all of life as we know it.'

'Did he say who this person is?' Daniel asked.

'The Oracle told me that I would know him by reading the signs correctly, and that when I did, I would have to do my own part to stop him. I have tried ever since to understand who the Oracle is talking about, and I think I know.'

She left her chair again and beckoned them to follow her. They took the spiral stairway on the east side of the castle down to the ground level, passed a number of royal chambers and entered into the official great hall where they first met. The queen led them through the long throne room, walking in the middle of the rows of chairs stacked by the walls, facing each other.

As they reached the royal throne, the queen stepped behind it, into the space between it and the wall, where a beautiful sword was hanging high, placed horizontally above its sheath. They were both masterfully crafted in steel and finished in gold. Below them hung a magnificent round shield, also finished in gold. A long spear was similarly placed on their right, whereas a bow and arrow hung to their left, thus completing the entire set. The emblem of the kingdom of Endër, the one with the horse and the tree that Daniel had seen on all the flags in the castle and around the city, was engraved in every piece.

'Wow,' Daniel exclaimed. 'They are beautiful.'

'Are these weapons?' Nemo asked. Daniel turned to him, surprised that his friend would even ask such a question. But he didn't have to think hard to understand; Endërland was a peaceful place that had never seen war, and that meant they hadn't seen many weapons either.

The queen answered Nemo's question.

'Yes, Nemo, they're weapons, just like the ones your mother has, just like the one she gave to Daniel. The Sky-Queen also has her own set. They may be different, but they are all used for the same purpose, to fight and kill, and they were all given to us as a gift by the same person.'

'The White Lord,' Nemo finished that sentence.

'Yes, the White Lord,' The queen confirmed.

'But what does this prove?' Daniel asked.

'I did not think of it at first,' the queen replied. 'It all seemed pretty innocent and generous at the time. It is, after all, a very marvellous piece of work. But then I heard that both my sisters were replicating these weapons, and many of their people are carrying them. Isn't that true Nemo?'

Nemo lowered his eyes, embarrassed.

'Both queens have produced a large quantity of these weapons and are training their people to use them. But one does beg the question, why would you need weapons in a peaceful kingdom? And that's when it dawned on me; this is a way to bring war among us. Sooner or later, someone is going to use those weapons, which means that somebody is also going to get hurt. Then, there will be reprisals and retaliations, and before we know it, all three peoples will be at war with each other.'

'But why would Winter want that? What would he have to gain from putting the three peoples at war?'

'I don't know what he's after, Danny, but whatever it is, he's got a better chance of achieving it if we're not standing together against him, if we are divided.'

She paused for a moment, thoughtful as she pondered her next words.

'I know only a little about him. He's one of the earlier Visitors that settled here. He was a great man once, honourable, strong, and brave; the Great Lord chose him as one of the residing Lords over the kingdom, after all. But he was always alone, without a family. I think his wife remained behind in the real world, and he never loved another woman. It's the saddest thing for someone to happen, living forever without someone to love.'

The queen stopped there for a moment, sadness veiling her beautiful emerald eyes. Daniel realized she was probably thinking of his father but did not know if he should speak. What could he say that would make this any better?

The queen picked up where she left off.

'Anyway, I guess that's where it must have all started. Now my sources tell me that he travels in secret up to the Northern Mountains, and that all these strange things are happening over there. The mountains are now always covered with snow and clouds, and no one who goes near the area, ever comes back. The animals that used to dwell in that region have either disappeared or moved away from there, and so have the people. Yet, despite how empty and desolate it may look, it feels like there is something brewing over there. There is a constant storm going on at the base of the mountains, which is completely unnatural and strange for our world. We have always enjoyed the best of the weather from all seasons, but this suggests the presence of constant harsh winter in the area. I'm afraid that underneath that thick dark cloud something is being done in secrecy.'

'Alright,' Daniel said. 'Let's suppose you're right and that Winter is up to something. What are we supposed to do?'

'There is nothing we can do at the moment, son. I may well be wrong about all of this, but even if I'm not, I have no way of proving anything to the other Lords and the entire kingdom. I'm afraid we're just gonna have to let things unfold for now and let him play his hand. In the meantime, we need to keep you safe back home. Here, I can protect you, but back there I was thinking you should go somewhere where nobody will think to look for you.'

'Where?'

She looked at him, anticipating the reaction that her suggestion would trigger.

'I was thinking about the village where your grandparents used to live, my birth home.'

'You want me to go to Albania?' Daniel asked, totally surprised. 'But why? I mean, can't I just hide somewhere in the UK? Dad's a police officer, after all; he can look after me. I wouldn't even know how to get to Albania.'

'Staying in the UK is not safe, sweetheart. It is very easy to find you there, and these people are obviously professionals. Getting you out of the country for a while, might give your dad a chance to focus on finding these people without worrying about your safety. Besides, you need to think of his safety as well. What if they decide to use him to get to you? They will stop at nothing, Danny; if he doesn't know where you are, they might actually leave him alone.'

Daniel sat down in one of the chairs behind him, with his head in his hands. He had not thought of this; his dad was also in danger. If they could not find him, they would probably keep a close eye on his dad, hoping that David would lead them to him. Or even worse, they might decide to use David to force him to give himself up. He could not let that happen, he had to do something. He had to make them believe that he had cut all ties with his dad. It was the only way they might leave him out of this.

Nemo sat quiet on the chair next to Daniel, listening to the conversation and feeling unable to contribute in any way so far. He looked at his troubled friend sitting beside him and took the chance to ask a question.

'I still don't understand; why do they kidnap the Visitors? What is it they want with them?'

Daniel raised his eyes towards his mother as if seconding his friend's question. The queen wished she had an answer to this one.

'I do not know, Nemo. As I understand it, Visitors always add to the life and magic of Endërland with their presence here. Maybe Winter is killing them, trying to starve the kingdom of their energy and positive influence.'

'I don't think that's it,' Daniel interrupted. 'If he had wanted me dead, I would have been by now. No, I think he wants to use me somehow. Maybe he wants to use my portal to cross over to the real world, though I don't know why anyone would want to leave this place.'

He got up and shook his head as if to clear his thoughts.

'Anyway, I can't think about that right now; I need to decide what to do about dad. How can I protect him, mom? How can I keep him safe without telling him everything? And even if I did tell him everything, would he believe me and let me go to Albania, or even go with me into hiding?'

He was standing before her now, pleading with his eyes for a helpful advice or solution. The queen saw the desperation in her son's eyes and her heart melted. She took his hands in hers and drew him closer.

'Sweetheart, I know you love your father very much, but whatever it is they want you for, I have a feeling it's a lot bigger than you and me and him altogether.'

'What are you saying?' Daniel asked, not sure he wanted to hear the answer. The queen continued with sorrowful eyes.

'I fear our whole world is in danger, Danny, and somehow, you seem to be right in the middle of everything. You might be more important than either of us imagine. Right now, you're gonna have to make a very difficult choice and just trust that your dad is capable of taking care of himself.'

Daniel broke free of her and stepped back.

'You want me to just abandon him to their mercy, and run and hide? I thought you still loved him.'

'I do, Danny, I do. But we both love you more, and your safety is more important to us than our own. Daddy knows that too, and he would agree with me.'

'I don't care,' Daniel shouted angrily. 'It might be your priority to protect me, but it's mine to protect both of you. Don't you see? If I lost either of you again, I would end up no better than Winter.'

He turned towards the exit and stormed out frustrated.

Watching him go, the queen sat distressed on her throne, feeling no longer as the ruler of a great kingdom, but as a mother who had just failed her child.

'I'll go after him,' Nemo said, and after bowing down respectfully, turned and ran after Daniel.

The queen was left alone in an immense royal hall that now felt empty and cold. She thought about what her son had just said; she saw the wisdom in his words and the love in his anger. She felt such pride, yet so much more fear and worry. Who knew how far Winter's cruelty could reach; who knew if it had any limits? How was she going to protect Daniel from him in this world or the other? She could not hide him forever.

Back in London, Daniel asked Sam and Freddie, who had finally returned, to sit down with him, and told them what his mother had suggested. They both agreed that this was the best idea, and that they should go ahead with it as soon as possible.

Understanding Daniel's fear, Freddie promised that he would ask the Order of the Guardians to keep an eye on David, and make sure that he was safe. Daniel felt much relieved to hear this; it made him feel a lot less guilty about leaving his dad behind.

While Freddie set out to arrange everything with the Order, including travel money and fake passports for all three of them, Daniel called his dad to tell him that he was going somewhere safe for a while. David began to protest, but Daniel did not change his mind.

'Come on dad, think about it; neither of us would be safe if I stayed here. I know what I'm doing and I'm with people that I trust. Unfortunately, I will not be able to contact you from where I'm going, but I want you to know that I'll be alright and I'm coming home as soon as this is over. But, dad, I will need you to be on your guard and stay alert; they might be after you now that they won't find me. Promise me you will take care of yourself and be safe, okay? I love you, dad!'

Daniel did not wait for his dad to reply but hung up and let him go. This had been the most difficult thing he'd ever had to do.

Chapter 6

BEHOLD

The house standing before them seemed like it had been built in the middle ages. Surrounded by a barely standing wooden fence, with the gate on the west side facing the main path, it was a two-storey house with six small square windows on each floor and a single chimney. It was built with stone, wood, and clay; while large stone plates, all dark brown, served as roof tiles. They seemed to be very heavy, but the house was strong and did not suffer under their weight.

The front entrance faced north, looking up a small steep hill, completely bare, only feet away. A wooden shack stood to the right, previously used to host cows and sheep. A stone courtyard that now had turned into a little jungle, stretched about 20 feet long and wide from the door of the house all the way to the main gate. A back door on the ground floor allowed access in and out of the house from the south, while on the top floor a balcony overlooked a wide and beautiful scenery. It consisted of the immediate garden below the house, a huge field farther down that ended at the brinks of the small river of Tomorrica, and finally mount Tomorr itself rising high and proud in front of them.

The trio could barely believe their eyes. This was not going to feel like hiding, more like a vacation. Daniel's grandfather and his older brother had built this house about 70 years ago. A small stone plaque by the entrance showed the exact date and the names of the two builders. Almost 25 years ago, after both his grandparents had passed away, the house had been abandoned for good, and the other family members, including his mom, had made their life in the cities or other countries. The house had been deserted ever since. Everywhere around it the grass had grown uncontrollably and turned into a little forest. It would take them some time and work to turn this place into anything resembling its former shape, but of that they had plenty.

Lucky for them, there was still electricity in the house. Daniel had found the keys right where his mother had told him he would, underneath a stone on the first step of the stairway leading to the main door. They entered the house and dropped their luggage in the first room they found. While still occupied, it appeared to have served both as a living and dining room. There was a fireplace in the middle of the wall opposite the door, and floor pillows were placed all around, covered in plastic. A table sat on the left corner, with a chair on each side, while a built-in cupboard had all sorts of serving china and tableware.

The air in the room felt heavy and mouldy, so the first thing Sam did was open all six windows to let some fresh air in. Dust and cobwebs were everywhere in the house, and they would need to do some major cleaning, if they were serious about living here for an indefinite time. They all agreed, however, to eat something and rest before they did any work.

During the following days they managed to bring the old house back to life and make it suitable enough for them to live in. A lot of work went into it, from cleaning the stone yard and the surrounding areas of the ivy and overgrown grass, to restoring the whole electricity network in the house, which was extremely old and dangerous. The water pipes were also ancient and there was only one tap, but that was more than enough for them. There was water to drink and wash, and electricity for heat and light.

While Sam took care of setting up and arranging the living conditions inside the house, the boys dealt with the more physically challenging chores around it. Firewood was going to be needed in the weeks to come. Autumn was now well into its second half, and the nights were growing chillier. They were told that cutting down healthy trees was not permitted, so they set out to gather dead wood in the forest nearby or cut down dying trees. In the course of two days they gathered enough firewood to last them for more than a month. To help with the transportation, they hired a mule from someone in the village, an old man who ran a little shop near the school with essential groceries and other goods. Anything else they could not find there; they would have to get it at the nearest town, Gramsh. By the end of the second week, the once vacant and lifeless house had been given new life and was transformed into a fairly habitable place.

Having taken care of their essential needs in the house, Sam insisted on setting up a protective grid around it just in case someone followed their trail there. Upon hearing details of her plan, Daniel tried to talk her out of it, fearing someone innocent might end up getting hurt, but to no avail. Freddie, on the other hand, was completely supportive of her decision and even gave a few pointers of his own.

The plan was to set up traps all around the house with a twofold purpose; to alert them of anyone approaching, and to slow the intruders down as much as they could. The villagers helped here; they had plenty of traps used for catching foxes that would come to prey on their chickens at night. Sam bought about a dozen of them and set them up in key points where she thought any intruders might show up.

But she wasn't done yet. If they came in large numbers, even if any of them got caught in a trap, the rest would be warned and eventually find a way into the house, unharmed. So, she went completely Rambo on them and built a whole network of mantraps, from the simplest ones, like covered holes in the ground, to the most sophisticated ones, like laser fences connected to her laptop, alerting her 24/7 of any breach of perimeter. Daniel was amazed at how well prepared she seemed to have arrived in the village, given the short time they'd had to prepare.

And yet, Sam still wasn't satisfied. By now Daniel thought that she had gone completely mental and taken this thing way too far, but the blonde ninja, as usual, ignored him and proceeded with devising an escape strategy, in case things came to the worst.

West of the old house, a dry canal branched from the riverbed and ran a foot deep and wide, previously used to carry water to the houses nearby. Sam discovered this while scouting the surrounding areas, trying to familiarize herself with the village. The villagers had used its water for many different needs in the early years, but clearly the canal had not been used for ages. With a couple of days' work however, they could get the water flowing again. Sam figured they could release the torrent back into the river about five hundred feet below their house with just a little modification.

It took them exactly three whole days and many long breaks to dig the canal back open from the start-up point, along the back of their house, and all the way down to where it joined the river again. At places, the earth proved harder to work, but in the end, they were satisfied with the results. Plenty of water came through, and what was more important, since from their house to the river was practically a straight downward line, the water ran pretty fast. This was perfect for a canoe sized raft to transport up to two people down to the river, which could then take them faster and farther down, even as far as Gramsh possibly.

Daniel had to admit that the idea was brilliant. He just didn't know if he should hope for a chance to prove that Sam's strategy worked, or that they would never have to find out.

And yet, even after all this, Sam still felt like something was missing. Being a true American at heart, she would not feel completely safe in the house without a gun. Daniel did not feel particularly fond of guns, or any other type of man-made weapon, so she went behind his back and convinced Freddie to help her purchase one.

Very discretely and promising good money, which by the way was running out real fast, they asked if the shopkeeper or someone else in the village could help them. The old man at first pretended to be offended by the offer, but the business was too good to be ignored. That very evening his son took Sam and Freddie into their house and presented them with a small collection of guns and ammunition. They had two semi-automatic rifles, one K57 machine gun, several grenades and a small handgun, which Sam immediately recognized as a very rare Beretta.

Having already decided on getting the smaller piece, especially since she could not hide a rifle or K57 from Daniel, she pretended she wasn't very happy with the choices, so as to drive the price down a bit. It was a struggle for Freddie to suppress his laughter while the "businesswoman" conducted the trade in such a professional manner, but he managed. He was actually feeling quite proud of her; Sam had made a habit out of surprising him on a daily basis ever since they'd met.

They eventually settled on 200,000 Lek for the Beretta, two extra magazines and a box of bullets, thus closing up shop for the day. On their way back to the house, Sam wouldn't even try to hide her excitement at the purchase of her new toy.

'Oh, my gosh, do you know what this is?' she almost screamed in excitement. 'This is a Beretta 93R. It fires triple-round bursts with each pull of the trigger at a cyclic rate of 1100 rounds per minute. It's got a 20-round magazine and it's perfect for lefties.' Here she raised her own left hand in the air. 'I cannot believe they've had this gun here; this is a very rare piece of work and they've stopped making it a long time ago. How lucky am I?'

Freddie rolled his eyes at her, but Sam ignored him.

'How is it you know so much about guns, anyway?'

'Well, when you have as much time to kill as I do,' here she made a gesture with the pistol, aiming somewhere in front of them, 'you find Wikipedia is your best friend. That, and I've always been fascinated with guns; I just never really had need of one, 'till now.'

'Just promise me you'll be careful with it. Please?'

Sam gave him a brazen look.

'What's the matter, Fred; am I starting to scare you?' She waved the Beretta in front of him playfully. Freddie did not seem amused.

'Ok, ok,' she caved, lowering the gun, and putting it away, hiding it underneath her clothes. Then, turning serious again, she said. 'I know what I'm doing, Freddie. Those traps are not going to keep us safe; they're only there to warn us and hopefully buy us some time. And this is only as a last resort anyway. I don't like to have to use it, but I would hate to be caught in need without it. Can you honestly promise me that it will never come to that? That they will not look for us and find us here? And if that happens, would they not do anything to get to him?'

It was the first time she'd called him Freddie, and not Fred.

Thoughtful, he looked at her, then ahead at the horizon ahead, but did not answer. It was clear that he had the same fears as she did; he wouldn't have agreed to help her otherwise. He also knew that it wasn't just Daniel they were protecting. If they ever came for him, whether they wanted him alive or dead, one thing was for sure; they had no use for the two of them.

'You cannot, can you?' Sam continued her argument. 'Well, I will stop at nothing to protect him for as long as I can. They're in for the fight of their life if they ever get this far.'

Freddie looked at her with newfound admiration. She was one of the toughest young girls he'd ever met, and she reminded him so much of someone he had known a long time ago. Beautiful and smart, yet usually quite arrogant and full of pride, there was something new about her in these last few days; something that maybe even she wasn't aware of. He'd seen it too often not to recognize it, however. It was there, in almost every little thing she did. The subtle way she cared about Daniel; the way she looked at him and spoke to and about him. The way she'd played with his hair as he slept with his head on her lap during the long bus ride from Athens. The way she would touch him seemingly casually, but with unmistakable affection. The way she took care of him, making sure he always had plenty to eat, and his clothes were always clean. All the little excuses she made just to do things with him and spend as much time as they could together. Freddie had noticed all of these but said nothing; he knew better than to interfere. Secretly though, he was rooting for the girl. She had been through a lot in her short young life and deserved a good break.

Sam, however, had gone through one or two crushes in her life, and was not entirely oblivious to the fact that she was beginning to have feelings for Daniel. She was mature enough to grasp that, whenever she thought someone was perfect, like she felt about Daniel at the moment, this meant that she was infatuated with them.

But it wasn't like she could help herself; Daniel seemed to tick all the right boxes in her checklist. Dark black longish hair? Check. Gorgeous face with just the right amount of stubble? Check. A sizzling hot torso and a nice pair of strong legs, courtesy of long hours of gym and swimming? Do you even have to ask? Check, check, check. A smile that infuriated her every time because she could feel how gooey it actually made her on the inside. Yup, check that too. And that wasn't even the best part; he was always kind and gentle in the way he spoke to both her and Freddie. He listened well, without judging or jumping into conclusions, and he never made things personal, even though she sometimes wished he did. He was helpful and caring, looking after her just as much as she looked after him. But, most importantly, when he was present, she always felt calm and in peace, never losing her cool or getting frustrated. He seemed to have the power to not only still the beast inside her, but also bring out the angel she'd kept well-hidden for years. If this wasn't enough to make a girl fall for a guy, then what is?

Sam was becoming more aware of this with each passing day, but instead of growing concerned or depressed about it, like no doubt she would have normally done, she felt happy and hopeful, despite the fact that she had practically just met the guy.

Her insomnia had not only put a strain on her daily life throughout the years; it had practically destroyed every single relationship she'd tried to have before. None of the boys she had been with had managed to cope with her mood swings and bad temper; they had all abandoned her at some point. This had made her feel even lonelier and caused her to resent practically everyone and everything.

But that all had changed when Daniel had come into her life; he was nothing like anyone she'd ever been interested in before. And she could not help but suspect that he might be feeling something towards her, too. He was just so nice with her, smiling every time he saw her and even laughing at her lame jokes. He even noticed whenever she did something different with her hair or wore something nice and pretty. Didn't that mean something? God knew she didn't want to read anything into it, but she could not ignore any of the signs either. She just hoped that they would have enough time for her to eventually find out the truth. She hated wondering.

They had been in Sotira for four weeks, when on a Saturday morning, Daniel woke Sam and Freddie up, telling them to pack some food for the day and follow him on a little excursion. Without giving them any details, he led them westward deep inside the forest, following the river up its stream, towards its spring. Mount Tomorr they kept to their left, while more hills and cliffs rose high in front of them.

It turned out, he couldn't have chosen a better day for this; the sky was completely blue, without a cloud in sight, and the sun that had just risen promised to keep them warm enough throughout the day. A wonderful fresh smell was in the air, thanks to all the florae around them, while the song of the running river kept them company all the way.

Halfway along their walk, they reached a small wooden bridge above the river, which they crossed so they could get to the other side. They then started to climb up a more difficult path leading them away from the water. By now, they could see the river with all its twists and turns from high up the hills. They went up and down a few of them for another half hour, until they reached the very last one.

Before them, a huge bare cliff appeared, rising tall towards the sky, with the odd tree growing here and there out of its vertical surface. Eagles circled the air high above, leaving and returning to their nests on the very top. The noise of the water became very loud and deep, yet they still could not see anything.

As they ventured on the edge of the hill they were on, the air grew cooler and the noise louder and clearer. Before their eyes, the top of a waterfall now appeared, with water coming out of the cliff from somewhere down in the middle. There were two parts to this waterfall, a smaller stream to their left, where the water fell from a higher source, and then a bigger one right in front of them, with a tremendous amount of water coming down in fury, forming white foam all the way down to the bottom. At the basin, a small pond was naturally created with crystal clear water, which Daniel imagined would be ice cold.

The guys looked stunned. Sam had her hand on her chest, breathing deep, while Freddie had already started taking pictures with his digital camera.

'Four weeks. Four weeks in the village and you only bring us here now?' Sam chastised him. 'What is wrong with your mom? Why didn't she tell you about this place sooner?'

'She did, actually,' Daniel answered. 'I was just waiting for the perfect day. Oh, would you stop being you for once, and just enjoy this?'

Sam smirked at him and started climbing down a narrow path towards the ravine. The guys followed her. The closer they got to the bottom, the colder the air felt and the deeper the noise of the falling water became. Fine sprinkles of icy drops fell all around them, making them shudder.

Once they had climbed all the way down, they threw their bags on the ground and improvised a small camp. Freddie started to prepare a fire, while Daniel took their drinks and put them in the cold water to keep them chilled.

Sam climbed on top of one of the big rocks right in front of the falling water and just sat there, raptured in the moment. She felt so small amid all this beauty, yet so alive; every cell in her body seeming to vibrate along with the uproar echoing through the valley. There was so much life here, and for the first time in a very long time she felt like she really wanted to live it all.

Daniel stood behind her, thoughtfully observing her. She had let her curly blonde hair down and the wind seemed to be having fun with it. She looked beautiful, paused like this, in this peaceful moment. There was none of that usual tension he had come to identify her with, no anger, no restlessness. It was like he was seeing a whole different person for the first time, and he liked this new Sam.

He didn't have much experience when it came to girls. Sure, he remembered having had his first crush on the prettiest girl in his school as a kid, but that had turned out ugly for him. He had been made to look like a fool in front of the whole class, when she had read his love letter aloud, laughing hysterically about it. So, he had never tried that again. Now, though, he felt confused. He liked Sam, she was beautiful, smart, strong, and he could sense that she liked him too. Maybe time had finally come for him to dare again?

Grabbing a drink, he went and sat down next to her, while Freddie collected firewood.

'It's really something, isn't it?' he said, taking a sip from his lemonade and staring at the waterfall. He had to speak louder in order to be heard over the sounds of the falling water.

'It's beautiful,' Sam replied, without taking her eyes away from the waterfall for even a second. She grabbed the bottle from his hands, took a long sip and handed it back to him.

Daniel smiled. This felt good, sitting next to her like this, sharing more than just a drink.

'I've lived such a small life,' she suddenly said, her eyes glued to the gurgling water before her. Daniel looked at her, not sure if he should say something. This seemed, however, like a moment for him to just listen, so, he did.

'For someone who spends more time awake than anyone alive, it really feels like I've been asleep for most of my years. Besides being angry at the world and complaining about my lot, I've done little else with my life. I've never been to places like this, and now that I'm here, it feels like I've been missing out. You know what I mean?'

It was the first time she'd ever really spoken about herself, and it made Daniel wonder why she was being so open just now. It was out of character for her to appear so vulnerable, so frail. For a moment, he felt the unexplained urge to take her in his arms, kiss her on top of her head and tell her that she was going to be alright. But he didn't.

'Sam, you're only eighteen,' he said instead. 'You've got plenty of time to go wherever you want and see anything you want.'

She smiled, still looking ahead.

'I suppose so. As the saying goes, it's never too late. Though, I think I like this place enough to stay. I could live here, you know; couldn't you? I mean if you had a proper house and all. And someone to share it with, of course.'

He turned and his eyes met hers. Behind them he saw what her words had barely hinted. Feeling his face blush rapidly, he made to look away, but found that he couldn't.

There was more than the usual in her baby blue eyes, and he felt that he just had to keep on looking.

Sam did not look away either, neither did she blink. The emerald of his eyes was captivating. She felt her heart beat faster and her face grow red hot. Her eyes then dropped down to his inviting lips, which somehow gave the impression they'd never been kissed. She felt herself move towards them without realizing it.

Daniel felt the same pull, and dropping his eyes to her velvet lips waited for them to approach. He might be ready to dare again, but he still wasn't sure about making the first move.

Sam had barely moved an inch in his direction when Freddie's voice broke the moment.

'Will someone give me a hand please?'

Daniel got up, quickly severing their eye contact, and went down to help Freddie, who was dragging a large dead tree trunk towards the fire. That would definitely keep it going for a long while.

They spent the rest of the day pretending nothing had almost happened, which was easier said than done. They explored the area around them, took lots of pictures by the water and sat at their improvised campsite eating, drinking, and telling stories. By the end, they were just resting, lying down next to the fire, and looking up at the sky.

'I guess there are places more beautiful than this in Endërland, aren't there?' Freddie said.

'This place can hold its own, believe me,' replied Daniel. Then, after a short pause he added. 'Endërland is amazing though, as far as I have seen. Here there are few places left untouched like this one, but there it's like this everywhere. And I haven't even seen the most beautiful place of it all, the city of Arba. They call it the jewel of the kingdom, their very own version of Eden. But I'll get to see it tonight.

Everyone is going there to celebrate the Day of the Kites and there will be a great feast.'

'The Day of the Kites?' Sam asked.

'The legend says that when the first ever child was born in Endërland, his father built and raised a kite to notify everyone else in the kingdom and help them find their house when they went to visit. It's a tradition that has been followed ever since, but every autumn on this day, they celebrate new life and launch thousands of kites in the sky. I can't wait to see it for myself. Wish you guys could be there to see it all with me.'

'Who knows, maybe someday we will be,' Freddie said.

'Yeah, maybe someday,' Sam repeated after him, though she didn't sound like she believed it. Ever since she had come to accept the existence of this other world, she had felt a wanting to see it for herself. She would never be a hundred per cent convinced of its existence unless she saw it with her own eyes. But that all depended on her insomnia being cured, and Sam seemed to have lost all hope of that ever happening.

Daniel felt the melancholy behind her voice but said nothing. He sincerely wished he could share his experiences in Endërland with the two of them but didn't know of any way to make that happen. He didn't particularly love being caught in two separate worlds, living two separate lives with different people around him; sometimes it all just felt too much to handle. But then he had to remind himself that he was twice blessed. He was surrounded by people that loved him in both worlds and who would do anything to protect him. How many could claim the same?

They started heading back to the village about an hour or so before it got dark. On the way back they didn't speak much but walked mostly in silence, each lost in their own thoughts. And there was much to think about, at least as far as Sam was concerned.

Upon reaching the house, she told the boys that she would go around to check the traps were ok, just so she could spend some time on her own. The lasers also had to be set, like she did every night before they went to bed.

Anything crossing into the protected grid would immediately be detected and set off the alarm in her laptop, thus, warning them of any possible intrusion. The problem with this particular system, was that any animal could set off the alarm, as it had already done so, twice, and they would still need a visual confirmation to decide if they were being attacked or just visited by a four-legged wanderer. This is why Sam had had to raise the lasers higher from the ground, so that they could only be set off by a human or a bear. They didn't have to worry much about the latter, as bears never really came this close to the village. If only that could be said of the men that were after them.

Nathaniel had a nagging feeling about this whole deal. It was one thing to play a stupid prank on the fish-boy, but why did they have to steal the arrows? What did Butler want them for, anyway? He looked at Azariel sitting calm on his branch and could not ignore the alarm bells ringing inside his head. His friend had deliberately kept him in the dark about what he intended to do.

'Tell me again why we are meeting Butler in the dead of night? And what's the deal with the arrows?'

The other wingman kept stroking his goatee and replied without even moving his eyes to look at his friend.

'Relax. I told you to wait until he gets here. Then you'll know everything.'

He gave a bored kick to the branch just below his feet and the whole tree shook lightly, causing the weakest leaves to detach and fall to the ground. A squirrel jumped scared from the tree next to theirs and kept on going. They had been waiting for a good while for the White Lord's servant, and he was losing patience quickly.

It wasn't long until they finally heard the sound of hooves approaching the edge of the woods, followed by the hoot of an owl. It was the signal they were waiting for. Azariel responded twice with the same sound. Soon their sharp and trained eyes spotted a lone horse with a rider on its back trotting in their direction. It would reach them within minutes. They got ready.

Out of the darkness of the forest, underneath their hanging feet, the hooded figure of the rider appeared and stopped. Steven Butler removed his hood, lifted his little brown eyes up and spoke without getting off his steed.

'Have you decided then?'

Nathaniel was clearly out of the loop here; he had no idea what was going on. Azariel responded without giving him a chance to find out.

'You're late. Do you think we've got nothing better to do than hang on trees in the middle of the night?'

Butler felt like yelling at the pretentious young wingman. Apart from his lord master, he allowed no one else to talk to him in that manner. He was the White Lord's number one man, after all, and that had to count for something. But he remembered that he needed these two, at least for the moment.

'My apologies,' he replied instead, slyly. 'My lord required my presence until late. I came as soon as I could. Have you made a decision? Will you do this little service for my lord? He personally asked me to assure you once again that he will honour his part of the agreement.'

Nathaniel could no longer master his curiosity.

'What agreement, Azariel? What is he talking about?'

'Keep quiet, Nathaniel; I told you I will explain everything,' the taller wingman snapped at his best friend. He then turned again to Butler.

'Tell your master that we'll do it. The three of us will be hanging by the seaside after sundown. Oh, and I also have that item you asked us to procure.'

He handed down the two arrows he had grabbed from Daniel's quiver. Butler reached up awkwardly with his right hand and took them, examining them carefully.

'Is this what I think it is?' He asked with a hint of excitement in his voice.

'They belong to the Visitor; I think that is his initial right there. We saw the Sea-Queen give the set to him as a gift.'

It was quite dark, but Nathaniel could swear he saw Butler's eyes light up. He did not like what was going on one bit but would not say anything else at the moment. This man had always troubled him. He was unlike anyone else in the kingdom, always alone and mysterious, never with a smile on his face.

'You have done very well, my friends; very well indeed. My lord Master will be most pleased about this. I am sure he will reward you extra for it.'

'As long as he keeps his word,' Azariel responded, pretending to not really care. Deep inside, however, Nathaniel knew that he was feeling quite good about himself right now.

'Alright then; when it is time, all you have to do is tell your little story. You think you can do that?'

'We can and we will,' Azariel answered for the both of them. Nathaniel started to protest again, but Azariel stopped him before he could say anything. Butler now looked at the other wingman for the first time since he got there. His face looked serene, yet there was something dark and menacing behind those small brown eyes. Nathaniel couldn't help but pull back instinctively.

'Are you sure?' Butler asked, making it a point to speak slowly and clearly.

Azariel answered with the same cockiness as before.

'It's all under control. Tell your master to start working on his part.'

Butler took his eyes off Nathaniel and forced himself to smile, or at least pretend to.

'Will do,' he said. 'Farewell.'

The wingmen watched him leave and dared not speak until they were sure he was really gone.

'In the Great Lord's name, what is going on Azariel?' Nathaniel finally burst. 'What is this deal you just agreed with the White Lord for us? What do we have to do?'

The taller wingman obsessed with his goatee sat quiet for a moment. He was now staring at Nathaniel straight in the eye as he tried desperately to understand what it was that he was involved in. After taking his own sweet time in deciding the best way to start explaining, Azariel began.

'You know that my father is one of the oldest living wingmen in the history of Endërland, right?'

'Yes, and?' Nathaniel asked.

'And that he has been the queen's right hand since the beginning of time?'

Nathaniel nodded with his head, waiting for his friend to make a point.

'He is the strongest and wisest of all our kind, and his counsel has always been heard. Why then, when time came for the clan of the Northern Mountains to have a new chieftain, my father was passed over in favour of an imbecile, a charlatan who is not worthy to even kiss my father's feet? He is the second most powerful wingman in the whole kingdom; that position was rightfully his. He should be chieftain of the northern tribe; he should actually be king.'

Without realizing it, Azariel was yelling louder and angrier than he had meant to. He saw that on the gobsmacked face of Nathaniel, who clearly had not expected *this*.

'What have you done, Azariel? What kind of deal did you make with the White Lord?'

Azariel looked at his friend intently, trying to determine whether telling him everything was the right course at this point. Nathaniel had always been soft of heart. They had grown up together, being best friends since ever. They would do anything with and for each other. He had always gone along with Azariel's little plans and games and never betrayed him, but he had also rebuked him often for going too far, according to him. Would he stand by him this time, or go against him?

Azariel decided he would take the risk and see. And if his friend wasn't on his side, well, then he'd just have to deal with him.

'The White Lord has confided in me about certain plans he has for the kingdom. And he has promised me that if I pledge my allegiance to him and help him with a few little details, he will make sure that my father gets the position he deserves. And I will be forever in his good graces.'

'What details? What do we have to do?'

'Oh, nothing big; first we have to arrange that our northern cousin gets shot by one of the Visitor's arrows, and then we just have to tell them what happened that day by the sea and to whom we think the arrows belong. That's all.'

'That's all?' Nathaniel yelled, now jumping down from the tree. 'Have you lost your mind, Azariel? Are you gonna let them kill Ghordi and start a war, all so your father can have a throne he probably doesn't even want? What is wrong with you?'

Azariel seemed to be getting angry at the reaction of his friend; he clearly had not thought this through properly. He shifted on the branch, so that he was now right on top of his friend, looking down on him.

'First off, I do not like the tone you're using with me. I am your superior in every way, Nathaniel; don't you ever forget that. Second, nobody is going to kill Ghordi; they are just going to wound him slightly, enough to call for an investigation over it. And third, war is coming, and you better believe it. It's going to happen whether or not you and I are involved, and trust me when I say this, when it all starts to come down, I would prefer to be on the side of the White Lord. You do not want him as your enemy.'

He paused for a moment and then decided to change tactics.

'You are my best friend, Nathaniel. We have done everything together ever since we were younglings. I want you on my side; I want you and your family safe.'

The mentioning of his family caught Nathaniel off guard.

'You don't need me,' he replied confused. 'I may not be able to change your mind about this, but I don't have to join you. Do I? I mean; if you really have to do this, is it necessary to drag me along with you?'

'The testimony of two witnesses will seal the deal; that's why I need you. But even if I didn't, I would still want my best friend by my side. I wouldn't want to do this or anything else without you. We stick together, remember? Brothers.'

Nathaniel's doubts were written all over his face.

'I don't like this one bit, Azariel; I don't like it at all. I don't want Ghordi to get hurt and I certainly do not want a war. I like things the way they are. I'm sorry about your father; you know I love and respect him even more than I do my own, but none of this feels right.'

'You have my word, brother; no harm will come to Ghordi. Whatever wound the arrow causes, we'll use Summer Water to heal him, and he'll be good as new in no time. And once before the Lords, we don't even have to lie or anything; only tell them what we know. I promise you; we will not have to do anything else.'

Nathaniel still didn't look convinced. Azariel was losing his patience by now and decided he had only one last card to play. He now got down from the tree and stood before his friend, still towering over him.

'Well, I guess you'll need some time to think about this, so you do that. Just know this, Nathaniel, if you betray me here, you will still go before the Lords, and they *will* hear about every single thing we have ever done. Oh yes, they will hear about how we kidnapped the fish-boy and tied him up on the tree to die; how we dropped him from the sky into the sea just for the heck of it, and how we did lots of other things together that were *your* idea, just because you've always hated the fish maids. I have a long list of misdeeds that are waiting to be confessed, my friend. I have been struggling for so long with my conscience, because I want these ugly crimes to stop, but I love my brother too much and dare not betray him. You go against me, Nathaniel, you don't just lose your best friend; you and your family lose everything. So, if I were you, I would be where I belong tomorrow, by my best friend's side.'

Azariel ended his threatening little speech, and feeling quite pleased with himself for cornering his friend, he jumped up in the air with a powerful swoosh of his wings and flew away towards Sky-City.

Nathaniel was left tongue-tied on his own. His whole life he had looked up to his best friend, had respected and loved him for being strong and fair. It seemed now, he had known him very little indeed. No one in the right mind would choose this mad path that led to sure war and death, and no friend or brother would treat people the way he just did.

What was he to do?

What choice did he have? If he did not go along with Azariel's plan, would that even matter? Just the arrow and his testimony would be enough to convince anyone. So, even if he stayed aside, he wouldn't prevent anything. On the other hand, if he spoke to someone about this, would they believe him? And would that not set off Azariel's anger?

Whichever way he rationalized it, the only choice he had was to go along with the plan and pray that the outcome would not be what the White Lord intended. For one, the arrow did not belong to the mermaids, and they could not be blamed for anything. Of course, the Visitor was innocent, but that would at least prevent a war between the mermaids and the wingmen. But then, why was Butler so happy with the arrows?

Nathaniel thought long and hard about everything but could not make up his mind. In the end, he decided to fly home as well and leave the decisions for the new day. Maybe he would see things better in the daylight.

For a place where time did not really exist, days in Endërland seemed to be going by like minutes, or at least that's how Daniel felt. He had by now managed to somehow get used to his new double life. He woke up in his own world, did his daily chores in and around the little house in Sotira, had his usual activities with Sam and Freddie throughout the day, until time came for him to go back to bed and fall asleep, only to awake again in Endërland. There, his day began anew.

Diane insisted that he should not waste his time but do something valuable with it. So, while in Sotira, Sam took it upon herself to teach him everything she knew about self-defence. It only made sense that he should learn to defend himself, seeing that there were people dead set on getting their hands on him. Of course, the added benefit to that was that the two of them would spend more time together, but Sam kept that little fact to herself. So, they spent hours every day, training in the martial art techniques that Sam had studied over the past year, even though Daniel thought that was hardly necessary. He also helped her build the escape raft and test-drive it to see if it would work as they intended it. It wasn't perfect, but it did the job.

Daniel was tempted every now and then to call his father, just to let him know that he was ok, but he knew he couldn't risk exposing himself to his kidnappers; they were surely watching David. It pained him to keep his dad away like this, but this was best for both of them. At least, he was still okay, and whoever was after Daniel had left him alone so far. Freddie kept regular contact with the Order of the Guardians, and they in turn kept an ever-watchful eye on David.

While in Endërland, Diane also made sure he was learning everything he needed to know about the history of the kingdom and familiarize himself with its people and their customs. There were few historical documents and manuscripts in the only library available in the whole kingdom, which was conveniently located in the castle.

Unlike the library where he used to work, this one wasn't very big and did not contain any books. It mostly consisted of a section on the top floor of the castle, where they stored "The Endërland Chronicles", an official publication of the kingdom throughout its history. Daniel spent hours in there every day, reading everything that had been recorded through the years, mainly by the first king of Endër, his great grandfather, Ari, and then his mother.

At first, he felt confused, as he had expected to see dates on the documents, which were more like bulletins. Instead of being dated, which was obviously not possible, since time in Endërland was not measured in months or years, they were numbered, starting from one and ending with 4769, the last one. There was no indication as to how often the bulletins were written, nor was there a visible pattern, anything that could help Daniel determine when the very first one was written and in turn how old Endërland was. It could have been a season ago or a hundred thousand as far as the records were concerned.

As for their content, Daniel would need endless seasons to sift through them all, but from what he gathered, they mainly recorded the most important things that had ever happened in Endërland, which for a kingdom without wars and conflicts wasn't much. Soon, he got tired of reading about who married whom and who begot who, or all the different celebrations and feasts that were described in unnecessary detail. There was nothing in there about the beginning, about how the kingdom and everything else in it was created by the Great Lord.

When he wasn't reading in the library or spending time with his mother, Daniel would help out with the preparations for the celebrations that were now almost finished. He and Nemo spent a lot of time with the girls in the castle, sewing up costumes, gathering flowers and making large bouquets out of them, or preparing colourful banners. They also built a kite together, painting it blue and green, and drawing the symbols of the two kingdoms of land and sea on it. It wasn't the best-looking kite ever built, but they were both very excited about it.

By the last day all the preparations were done and most of the people had already begun their journey towards Arba. Almost the entire population of Endërland got together to take part in these celebrations. The citizens of Endër and most of the villages surrounding it had already started their journey towards the city of the Lords. It would take them almost an entire day to get there on foot, and about half a day riding. Daniel and Nemo would accompany the queen in her royal carriage as she set out early morning, last of all her people.

* * *

The morning of the special day Daniel woke up and got out of his room, noticing that it wasn't as bright as usual outside. There was also a strange noise coming from everywhere around him, and that's when he looked up and saw the sky completely covered by multitudes of wingmen flying in perfect formation towards Arba. There were thousands of them, organized in quadrants of hundreds. They wore their festive clothes and flew majestically above them, almost invisible in their white-and-blues. The sky thundered with the sound of their enormous wings beating the air and their songs of celebrations. It was such a remarkable sight, and no matter how much Daniel tried to prepare himself, he could not help but gasp in awe of everything new this place presented to him.

The eventual journey to Arba was pleasant and full of anticipation for everyone, but most of all for Daniel, who was obviously experiencing this for the first time. The open royal carriage rode smoothly, whether on the stone streets of

Endër, as they were leaving it, or the well-laid main road that led to Arba. Four beautiful white stallions, wearing festive decorations with the emblem of the kingdom of Endër on each side, drew the five-people carrier with ease and a steady pace. The queen's personal coachman was sitting on the front guiding them, while joining the queen and the two boys was the beautiful Íro, who never seemed to leave his mother's side.

She and Nemo had gotten rather close during the past few days together, and Daniel could see the infatuation growing in his best friend. He thought about Sam and their own situation, and for some reason he felt kind of guilty. He no longer doubted that Sam had feelings for him, but after that moment by the waterfall, they had not tried to kiss again, or even talk about it. He liked Sam, he thought he would never meet another girl as brave and smart as her, beautiful too. She was a great friend and was risking and sacrificing a lot to help him stay safe. And knowing how she felt about him, he really wanted to return the feeling. But somehow, he held back, and he just didn't know why.

It was still early in the morning, and they were making good time; the ceremony would not start until midday. Daniel recalled what he'd read in the Chronicles about the City of the Lords. The four of them had built it from scratch. It was not really a city, even though it had been called that since always; it was more like a huge and marvellous garden located by the seaside. There on the beach, the great royal palace was built, with four separate towers that served as residence for the Lords. In between the second and third towers lay a great courtyard of stone, in the centre of which was what they called the Eternal Clock. The clock, as Daniel would later see, consisted of one single hand rotating through four quarters of a circle, with the Lords' symbols respectively carved in gold on each of them. At the moment, the hand was pointing at the golden leaf. The clock was placed on the courtyard by the Great Lord himself at the beginning, to let them know when the time was for the Silver Sceptre to be passed over to the next Lord. But that was not the only gift he had given to the city.

Daniel had also read that in the beginning, a bright star would always shine high above the palace, almost as bright as the moon itself. In time though, as the memory of the Great Lord began to fade, so did the light of that star, and it now looked just like an ordinary one. The Great Lord was not seen or heard from for a very long time, and people had begun to believe that he was nothing more than an old legend. Daniel understood the implications of that all too well; without someone to answer to, Winter or anyone else with sinister intentions would fear no one and do anything.

But the Great Lord wasn't the only one who had bestowed his gifts upon the city. The four Lords had themselves added to its magic and beauty. To begin with, Spring had created all the florae in and around the city. She had planted the surrounding wall of sequoia trees, thus creating its glorious borders and separating the city from the rest of Endërland. She had also created the amazing garden, with an endless variety of plants and flower arrangements all over the place, giving them life eternal and the ability to survive and stay fresh in every season. Daniel would never see anything more beautiful in his entire life.

Working closely with Spring, Summer had created beautiful water fountains everywhere in the city and had blessed their water with the power to heal any physical wound or hurt. They were a real sight to behold, and their water was accessible to everyone.

Autumn had given the earth the ability to turn every falling leaf from all trees inside the city into gold. People came from everywhere in the kingdom to visit the city and they collected the golden leaves to make ornaments and decorations for their homes, or gift them to others. Daniel couldn't even imagine what people in his world would do to get their hands on a city like this.

Winter's gift to the city were four giant ice statues of the Lords themselves that would never melt, all placed around the royal courtyard. They were a marvellous piece of work and one of the main attractions in the city, depicting the Lords in all their greatness and majesty. Daniel couldn't wait to see everything for himself. And the closer they got to the city, the more excited he began to feel.

The main road they were on led them straight to the Southern Gate, through which the people of Endër, the villages around the forest of Mirë, and those coming from Sky-City could enter Arba. The Northern Gate allowed access into the city to all inhabitants of the northern part of the kingdom, which included all the villages and small towns throughout the Valley of Destiny, the city of Tálas by the Northern Sea, and everyone that lived at the base of the Northern Mountains. This included the second clan of wingmen, Ghordi's people, who lived separately from their Sky-City kin.

Once again, Daniel was surprised to see that there were no actual gates or guards at the entrance of the city. Instead, the long wall of the giant Sequoia trees surrounding it, opened up where the two roads entered from the North and South, thus creating the only two ways in or out of the city. Daniel looked up at the sky-high trees as the carriage passed in between them, and suddenly felt miniscule. He had expected them to be tall, he just didn't know how tall.

Diane smiled as she watched him marvel at the beauty before him. This was it; they were now inside the famous City of the Lords.

As the open royal carriage rode past the giant gate and into the city, Daniel was met with an unprecedented symphony of sharp and bright colours, the likes of which he'd never even thought existed. Spring's gift had seemed to him like something not so grand compared to the rest of the Lords' works, but now he saw that he couldn't have been more wrong. No architect or artist from his world, living or dead, could have ever come up with such a masterpiece.

The city was indeed a huge garden filled with life, colour, and magic. He saw trees of all sorts arranged in perfect style and harmony, endless kinds of flowers eternally blossomed and fresh. He smelled their aromas filling the air, rich and appetizing at the same time.

Hundreds of smaller pathways divided from the two main roads and delved into the garden, allowing people to get lost inside it and enjoy nature's majesty like nowhere else. Beautiful water fountains were everywhere around them, adding freshness and melody to the air. Nowhere had Daniel felt life more vibrant and buzzing than in this place, and now that he got here, he never wanted to leave.

Sticking to the main road, they were now approaching the great courtyard where the four giant statues of the Lords of Arba stood visible from miles away. Everything and everyone in the vicinities looked infinitesimal compared to these magnificent ice sculptures that reflected the light of the sun, without any sign of melting from its heat. The first one to their left stood tall the statue of Autumn. Spring and Summer followed in the middle, and Winter in the end. Their towers followed the same order on the beach.

Thousands of people were gathered around the oval shaped courtyard, waiting for the ceremony to begin. To his left, the sky-people were lined up in perfect formation behind a tall ivory chair, where Daniel assumed their queen sat.

To his right, he noticed a relatively small number of mostly red-haired people standing by the sea, next to what looked like a little bay of shallow water on the eastern edge of the courtyard. A giant open seashell floated there in the centre, upon which sat proudly Eleanor, this time wearing a beautiful festive gown. Behind her the sea had turned red from the multitudes of the mermaids that had gathered to take part in the celebrations from their own element.

In the middle section, thousands of people had gathered behind the royal throne where Diane would sit. The three queens' thrones were placed at the edge of the courtyard, all facing the Silver Throne, where the reigning Lord sat. In front of it, on three lesser thrones, sat the other Lords, facing the queens and their people behind them. In the very centre of the courtyard Daniel could now see the Eternal Clock, with its one golden hand pointing at the symbol of Autumn.

As the Queen of the Land and her party of four approached the royal courtyard, the people divided and created a corridor for her to pass, bowing towards her in respect and veneration. She smiled warmly as she walked among them, looking at each of them in the eye and greeting them individually.

Daniel felt overwhelmed by the affection these people displayed towards his mother. He could not help but feel a sense of pride. Thinking of his own pain of her leaving him when he was little, it now made him feel somewhat selfish. He was clearly not the only one who needed and loved her; she was a mother to all these people, and this is where she was supposed to be. It was at this moment that he realized that, if he had ever blamed her for leaving, he had now forgiven her completely and unequivocally.

As if sensing something deep within her soul, Diane turned around and looked at him. Their eyes met for a brief but meaningful moment, and as they smiled at each other, her lips formed the words: *I love you*! Daniel replied in the same manner, and they continued their walk towards her royal throne.

They reached their destination just as the sound of a dozen trumpets filled the air, proclaiming the prompt arrival of the Lords. To their far left, Daniel saw the Sky-Queen take her place in her high seat, with a handsome young wingman standing tall and proud beside her.

'That is Séraphin, the queen's only son and heir,' Diane whispered in his ear. The two queens exchanged a quick look and bowed their heads cordially to each other.

To their far right, the Queen of the Seas sat on her floating throne, with her tail immersed into water. Her ever-present companions surrounded her, while their sisters watched and cheered in thousands from the sea.

Diane looked over and smiled at Eleanor, while taking her own place in the elegantly designed throne. Eleanor returned the gesture and then shifted her gaze to Nemo. Upon looking at her only son, her eyes brightened up at once.

Nemo waved at her, clearly happy to see his mother again. He had been thrilled to finally leave the sea and go on his long-expected journey, but he had never been away from her for so long, and Daniel knew he missed her terribly.

Nemo turned to the Queen of the Land.

'My lady, with your permission, I would take my place beside my mother.'

Diane nodded.

'Of course, Nemo, that is where you belong. Please, do let her know that I wish to meet with her after the ceremony.'

Nemo bowed down, and after giving a meaningful look to Íro and Daniel, as if to ensure them that he would be back soon, he ran in the direction of his family.

As Daniel watched him go, the crowds behind them began cheering and applauding; the Lords were now entering the courtyard one by one, heading towards their thrones.

The White Lord was first, dressed in his white royal robes, looking all humble and noble, and smiling at the crowds as if he actually meant it. He sat on the first of the three lesser thrones. Seeing him for the first time, Daniel had some difficulty believing this was the man responsible for sending him into hiding and plotting to forever change the way of life in Endërland. Looking at him, he saw a kind face, a father-like person, whom he felt he could trust and love. It was a sad thing that this was only a façade, and that the man behind it was an entirely different person.

Right behind the White Lord followed a beautiful woman with very long black wavy hair. They were arranged delightfully with lots of daisies and blended perfectly with her colourful gown. She took her seat on the second throne next to Winter. Daniel guessed she was Spring.

Next to approach was Summer. The blonde lady was wearing a long yellow dress and looking as if she was wrapped in the rays of the sun itself. She had the most radiant smile, and eyes as bright as Daniel had ever seen. She was clearly loved by the people, for the uproar grew stronger and louder as she took her place on the third throne, next to the other two rulers.

Immediately after her, the Lord of the Fall entered the courtyard, carrying the Silver Sceptre on his right hand, and taking his place on the Silver Throne without much fanfare. He had the appearance of a man in his late years, old and wise, yet you could see he was still strong and full of life.

He looked at the crowds before him and seemed to feel touched by their affection, or maybe that was how Daniel was feeling. He noticed strangely that, as soon as the Lords entered the courtyard, the atmosphere changed drastically.

The air felt fresher, if that was even possible, the sun shone brighter, and the colours all around them became even more intense and sharp. The wind died down and the sea stood still. The scent of the flowers and plants in the garden grew a lot stronger, and the sounds of nature all around them a lot clearer.

But the effect was not confined to the outside alone; to Daniel it felt as if he was truly awake, for the first time ever, and was experiencing everything exactly as it was meant to be. He felt like he could breathe better, see, and hear clearer. He felt his heart uplifted and his lips forming a big smile, completely of their own accord. It was as if happiness and joy had been injected directly into the air.

After allowing the people to cheer for a little longer, Autumn got up again and raised his arms, signalling for silence. Slowly the merriment died, and the place grew quiet.

'Citizens of Endërland; my fellow men, wingmen, and mermaids. Welcome!'

The crowds replied by throwing a strong and unified 'yeah' at his direction. He smiled heartily.

'We all know the story; the birth of the first child in the kingdom was announced to the world by raising a kite to the skies. People then got together to rejoice and celebrate this wonderful event, and this has been the tradition among us ever since. Today, in much the same way we get together in this place to celebrate all life and give thanks to our Great Lord for everything good and beautiful he has blessed us with. And we do this by symbolically raising our kites to the skies, to invite everyone to join with us. So, lift them up and let the feast begin.'

Autumn ended his short speech by raising the Silver Sceptre towards the sky with a powerful movement of his right hand, and just like that, accompanied by a great cry from the people, which echoed all the way to the Northern Mountains, a strong wind began to blow.

This was it, the part that everyone was waiting for. The kites were lifted off the ground and taken up and high as the heavens. It was an unimaginable sight to behold. All eyes were looking up at the skies, as the sun was now completely blocked from view, and the blue of the sky replaced by multitudes of colours, symbols, and patterns.

The feast had officially begun.

* * *

The celebrations went on for hours and hours. After the kites' competition, people split into smaller groups and continued celebrating, singing, and dancing, playing games, and doing everything they had prepared for the occasion. Around lunchtime, tables full of food and cool drinks were erected, and people began treating themselves and each other.

They saw and spoke to many people, most of whom Daniel didn't know, but who seemed genuinely happy to meet him. He was glad to meet with Eleanor again. It dawned on him that she had known from day one who he really was, and he felt even more grateful for her help now.

The two queens spent quite some time talking to each other, while the boys enjoyed some of the finest treats the feast had to offer. Nemo was looking especially happy, and Daniel wondered whether young Íro had something to do with it. Though she never left Diane's side, her eyes constantly travelled towards the young prince, as his did towards her.

The Lords also came down from their thrones and blended with the people. Daniel at one point noticed the White Lord and the Sky-Queen conversing warmly with each other. There was a considerable distance between them, but he could swear that underneath his white bushy eyebrows, the White Lord was looking at him intently, whenever he could manage to steal an unnoticed glance.

When their eyes eventually met for the first time, he felt a chill deep inside his spine, but he did not look away. He wanted to see inside those eyes for himself and find in there the truth that some suspected, but most were oblivious to. The eyes of the White Lord, however, were unreadable, and their contact was severed quickly.

As he followed Diane back to her throne, now re-joined by Nemo, Daniel heard his mother speak.

'My Lord Autumn. May the Great Lord's blessings be with you!'

Daniel turned swiftly to see the approaching Lord being accompanied by a second person, who immediately claimed his attention. She was a stunningly beautiful young girl, seemingly around 17 or 18, though Daniel knew better now than to trust their looks when it came to their age. She was almost as tall as him, slender and elegant in a long white dress that clung to her body tight, highlighting an amazing form. Her long black hair was left to fall free over her bare shoulders, with a single thin braid falling tastefully on her left side. She walked straight and gracefully, carrying herself with a proud and royal look. For some reason, Daniel thought of the little girl he used to have a crush on when he was in school, the one he had written the love letter to. If he saw her today, she might have looked something like this.

He felt absolutely captivated and wished he could have had more time to look at her, but Lord Autumn himself was coming to meet with them, and he obviously deserved his full and undivided attention.

He forced himself to look away from the girl and bowed down before the current ruler of Endërland, next to his mother.

'And with you, my dear Lady of the Land,' Autumn greeted her, bowing his head. This was the first time Daniel heard his mother being addressed to by that title.

Autumn's eyes turned to Daniel.

'So, I finally have the pleasure to meet with our new Visitor. I have heard much about you, son.'

Autumn extended his hand in a very human and friendly gesture and Daniel shook it, now standing up. Diane made the introductions.

'My lord, if I may, this is Daniel Adams. He has been kind enough to allow me to offer him a place at the castle, while here in Endërland.'

'It is an honour, my lord,' Daniel managed to say, trying hard not to shift his gaze from the old man to the beautiful girl standing next to him. 'Daniel Adams, at your service.'

'The honour is mine, I am sure, Daniel. May I call you Daniel?'

'Of course, my lord,' Daniel hastened to answer.

'Hadad is my name, if so you wish to call me; and my family and I are at your service. May I introduce to you my daughter, Hëna? She almost never leaves my side.'

Daniel felt shock, among other feelings he could not aptly name right then and there. He had thought she might be a helper or assistant of some sort, like Íro was to his mother.

Hëna did not shake his hand or come any closer. She just smiled courteously at him from where she was standing, bowing her head ever so slightly. Not knowing what to do, Daniel did the same, suddenly feeling very nervous looking at her pitch-black beautiful eyes.

'It has been a long time since we've had a Visitor, as I'm sure you already know,' Lord Autumn continued. 'They have always been welcomed in our kingdom and I do sorely miss news of your world. I would very much like to have the pleasure of your company tonight if you would indulge me. I would like you all to be my guests for supper.'

'It will be our honour, my lord,' the queen replied on behalf of her company.

'Good, then. I will tell my lady to prepare for your arrival. See you all after sundown.'

With that the lord of autumn greeted them and moved on towards another group of people, followed by the lovely Hëna. Daniel watched her go, the view from behind being just as beautiful, desperately hoping she would look back just once. She didn't. It was alright, though; he would see her again that very evening.

Chapter 7

THE COUNCIL

It was early in the morning when a knock on Daniel's door demanded his attention. Already awake, he had been lost in his thoughts regarding all that had transpired in the last twenty-four hours, and especially Hëna. Ever since he saw her the day before, he just couldn't stop thinking about her, about those big and beautiful black eyes, wavy long black hair resting on her delicate shoulders, and her soft white skin, spotless and shining with youth and beauty. He had been giddy with excitement, thinking he would get to see her again at her father's house, but to his dismay, she had not been present.

Instead, he was introduced to her twin brother, who Daniel decided looked nothing like her at all. To begin with, Heli was completely blond, something he had evidently taken after his mother. Also, Heli was quite big, easily the tallest person he had met in Endërland, with broad shoulders and built up muscles. Unlike serious Hëna, he always had a cheery look on his baby face, which despite his considerable size, it made him look like a young teenager. His eyes were the only thing he seemed to have in common with his sister; they were also big and dark black, yet full of a light and life that felt out of this world.

Daniel watched not without jealousy as his mother doted on him, constantly doing little things like straightening his brown leather vest, or removing his stubborn yellow hair from his forehead, as if she didn't see him very often.

Soon enough, Daniel found that he felt at ease in Heli's company. He was quite pleasant to be around and talk to. True, he did not really say much, but he was very attentive, and every now and again would ask a question or two about the other world.

Daniel had begun to limit his answers when it came to telling people in Endërland about his world. Life here was so very different from what he knew, but if Winter had his way, pretty soon that would no longer be the case. And Daniel didn't know what effect his words might have in that possible future. So, instead of talking to them about wars and hunger and other things of that sort, as he had previously done with Sarah and Garret, he tried to confine his stories to more personal experiences, or facts that he thought not too revealing.

Yet, whatever he spoke of, he found that he had their undivided attention and he thoroughly enjoyed sharing with them about his home world. If only Hëna had been there to listen also. There had been no explanation or mention of the fact that she wasn't there, and of course he hadn't asked.

Whoever was behind the door, insisted, this time with a stronger knock. He had to get up and answer. A second later he wished he hadn't. In front of him, Hëna stood as tall and beautiful as he remembered her, even though she was now wearing nothing as glamorous as the day before, and her hair was tied back in a single braid. Still, she looked breathtaking in her brown leather trousers, combined tastefully with a white long-sleeved shirt and a vest similar, if not identical to the one Heli wore the previous evening. Daniel instinctively reached for his hair, trying to straighten it down, while growing all red in the face, conscious of the fact that he was still in his pyjamas.

He gave her an awkward smile, while she stood serious before him, looking at him straight in the eyes.

'Good morning!' She greeted him with a formal tone, which Daniel didn't find very heart-warming. 'Your presence is requested in the parlour.'

She then gave him a quick look, concluding his attire was not appropriate.

'I will give you a moment to get ready.'

Before Daniel could say anything, she turned her back to him and moved a few steps from his door. Daniel sensed that whatever was going on was serious enough, so he hurried to wash up and change back into yesterday's festive clothes.

When he opened the door again, Hëna took another quick look at him, and without saying anything at all, led the way. He followed her, without knowing what to say. Somewhere deep inside him he could feel a heaviness land over his chest, bullishly claiming a dominating place. Something just did not feel right.

As they stepped into the parlour, he saw Lord Autumn and his mother sitting next to each other, immersed deep in conversation. Nemo was standing in the middle of the room, facing them with a guilty look on his face. No sign of Heli or his mother.

Hëna escorted him inside, and then she too left the room. Daniel looked first at the grim face of Autumn, and then his mother, who was trying to avoid eye contact with him.

Autumn spoke first. His tone was serene, but that did not help soothe the feeling that something was really wrong and that somehow Daniel was right in the middle of it all.

'Welcome, Daniel. I am sorry to drag you out of bed so early in the morning, but I'm afraid I have just received some very disturbing news. Something very grave has happened; something that never before in the history of our kingdom has been heard of, and I was hoping you could help shed some light over it.'

Lord Autumn paused here and looked at Diane, who sat there with a calm expression on her face, even though Daniel could see the worry behind her green eyes. He decided not to ask what had happened and let Autumn do this his way.

'I need to ask you; where were you yesterday afternoon, before you joined us here for dinner?'

This felt like an interrogation and Daniel didn't like it. What had happened that they needed to know what he did the day before?

'I spent all afternoon with Nemo in the garden, watching the celebrations. Then we went at the beach for about an hour before we came here. Nemo missed the sea.'

'Did you see or speak to anyone there?'

'There were a lot of people everywhere, but we did not speak to anyone. We swam for a while and then just rested.' He was now growing impatient and wanted to know what was going on. 'May I ask what's happened?'

Autumn ignored his question and continued with his own.

'You own a bow, a gift from the Lady of the Seas, do you not?'

'Yes, I do.'

'Have you ever used it?'

Daniel's brain was now working on full capacity, trying desperately to connect the dots.

'Of course not, I haven't even been trained with it. Can you please tell me what has happened? Why am I being asked all these questions?'

He looked at his mother again, trying to steal some sort of information from her, but she continued to avoid his gaze. Autumn pressed on with his questioning.

'Is it true that some time ago, you and Nemo had a confrontation with three young wingmen?'

Daniel recalled the incident clearly as it had happened yesterday. He still felt very angry whenever he thought of them, even though he never spoke to Nemo about it. He wanted his friend to forget all about that unpleasant experience.

'Yes. They were ...'

He was interrupted by the door opening to let Hëna in again. She went straight to her father, whispering something in his ear. He nodded and turned again to Daniel.

'Well, it appears my brother and sisters are gathered in the courtyard and are waiting for us. This matter appertains to all, I'm afraid, and I cannot keep them out of it. But, before we join them, would you allow someone to retrieve the bow and quiver from your room for us?'

Daniel agreed, surrendered to the fact that he could not do much else. He was now beginning to have some vague idea as to what might be going on and rebuked himself for having taken the weapon with him to Arba.

Autumn left the room first with his mother, and he, Nemo and Hëna followed behind them.

'This is how it begins then?' Nemo said, probably feeling as frightened as he looked.

'Looks like it,' Daniel replied.

They walked in silence the rest of the way, with Hëna trailing behind them like a prison guard. This was not how Daniel had imagined spending time with her. On top of his worry and fear over the direction things were taking, he now felt embarrassed enough, imagining what she might be thinking of him.

When they entered the oval courtyard, he felt again the same celestial presence in the air, strong as the day before. Yet, something was different this time. It felt colder, as if summer had truly gone and autumn was already turning into winter.

There were no people around this morning; everyone was on their way back home, leaving behind an empty garden.

The three Lords were sitting in the same places he had seen them yesterday, though dressed less festive now and more formal. Also on their thrones sat Eleanor, surrounded by her faithful foursome, and the Sky-Queen with Séraphin standing by her side.

Holding the ruler's sceptre in his right hand, Autumn took his place on the Silver Throne without delay, just as Diane sat on her own throne. Daniel and Nemo were led both in the middle of the courtyard, where they stood by the Eternal Clock, facing the Lords. The two boys were now the centre of everyone's attention.

It was still the early hours of the morning, but the sun shone bright in the sky, as it would in the middle of a summer's day. For some reason though, its warmth failed to reach Daniel.

'It is with a heavy heart that we are all gathered here this morning on such a short notice,' Autumn began, without standing up from his throne. 'In all of our history, there has never been a reason as grave as this for this Council to meet.'

The look in everyone's eyes seemed to agree with him. He continued.

'As most of you know by now, I was informed in the early hours of the dawn of what can only be described by one word, a crime, committed in this very citadel. Yes, an unimaginable crime. One of our beloved wingmen, a member of the Northern Tribe visiting over the festive season, was found lifeless late last night at the beach. It appears he was shot with an arrow that pierced right through his heart.'

The world suddenly felt a very small and dark place for Daniel. He knew the matter was serious but had not expected this. His heart began to race with dread, as he realized he was the one being accused of murder. He looked at the Sky-Queen and her son, whose eyes were filled with hatred and anger. He then turned to Nemo, who kept looking down as if he was guilty. His gaze travelled on to Diane's expressionless face, and then Eleanor's worried look, ending up at the High Lords in front of him. He stopped at the White Lord, who appeared genuinely shocked and outraged.

Autumn continued.

'This is the arrow that was found at the scene, and our dear Lady of the Seas was kind enough to identify it for us.'

Autumn lifted his left hand, in which he was holding a single arrow with a blood-stained silver tip and a carved 'D' on its body. Daniel had no doubt that it was one of his. Yet, for the life of him, he could not understand how it had ended up in the heart of the fallen wingman.

'This arrow belongs to the Visitor, who received it as a gift from the Lady of the Seas when they first met. Is this not true, Daniel?'

With his face burning hot and his entire body now trembling, Daniel tried to find his voice, but it failed him. A feeble '*yes*' barely came out of his lips, just as the Sky-Queen jumped out of her high ivory throne and cried: 'Justice, I want justice,' pointing a neatly polished claw towards him. Séraphin placed a hand on her shoulder, trying to comfort and calm her, but withdrew it quickly, thinking better of it.

The courtyard grew silent. Daniel could feel everyone's eyes piercing through his skin, like darts aiming for the very centre of his heart. This was insane. How could they believe he would do something like this? He knew this was all a set-up, but that didn't lessen the fear or chances of him being punished anyway. How could he prove to them that he was innocent?

Before he could even utter a word, however, he heard Nemo speak next to him.

'It wasn't Daniel, it was me. I did it.'

'No,' Daniel shouted instinctively, while at the same time Eleanor cried her son's name aloud. They both knew what he was doing.

'He didn't do anything; neither of us did,' Daniel continued without a clear idea of what else to say.

'Is this not your property, then?' Lord Autumn asked.

'It looks like one of my arrows,' Daniel answered, 'but I couldn't tell you if it really is, or how it ended up where it did. I have no quarrel with any wingman, and even if I did, I would not resort to killing him, or anyone else. It is not how I was raised.'

He stole a glance at Diane, who sat there with an inconspicuously proud look on her face.

Autumn took a moment to whisper something to Hëna, who left the courtyard immediately. He then turned to Daniel and continued with his questions.

'Isn't it true that the same day you were given this weapon, you encountered three young wingmen on the beach, south-east of the forest of Mirë? Did not an incident take place that day?'

Daniel and Nemo looked at each other but dared not speak. Clearly the whole thing was very well thought up. They had the crime, the weapon, and now the motive. How could he fight that? Embarrassed, he looked back at Diane, who continued to appear serene, much to his frustration. He had told no one, not even her about what had happened at the beach that day. Would she doubt him now; would she still believe that he and Nemo were innocent?

'The three dropped down on us,' he began, 'and started picking on Nemo, laughing at him and calling him names. It appeared to be something they did all the time. In fact, the day before, I found Nemo tied up on a pine tree out of the sea, left there to dry up and die. And he would have died if I hadn't happened to be there. I realized that day that these three were the very ones who had done this. When they were done insulting him, they grabbed him violently and flew away with him, dropping him from high up into the sea. He might have been killed by the fall, or drowned, but they were just laughing about it like it was some kind of a sick joke.'

There was anger now in Daniel's raised voice and he realized this was not going to help his case. Eleanor looked on with tears in her eyes as she heard of these new happenings concerning her son. Nemo had now lowered his head even more, not daring to look at anyone.

Autumn was about to ask something else, when before them reappeared Hëna, this time followed by two young wingmen, whom Daniel recognized right away. One of them, the tallest one with the goatee, walked in with his head down, looking guilty and ashamed, while the other, Daniel recognized as the one who had not said a word the entire time that day. He guessed; it was the 'short' one who had been shot.

The boys were led by Hëna in the middle of the yard, not two feet away from them, and bowed down before the Lords. Autumn wasted no time in continuing with his questions.

'Azariel and Nathaniel. This Council thanks you once again for bringing this matter to our attention right away. We are deeply saddened by the loss of your close friend, and will do our best to find out who is responsible. The Visitor has confirmed to us what happened at the beach the day you first met. Do you have anything else to say about that day?'

Azariel lifted his head to look at the Lords, and without daring to stroke his goatee, as he would usually do, he spoke.

'We are not proud of what we did that day, my lords, but we meant no harm to anyone, I swear. It was just a stupid prank. We sometimes do things like that to entertain ourselves, only I guess this time we went a little too far. I am deeply ashamed and sorry for having acted like a bully and caused harm to my little brother.'

Appearing genuinely remorseful, Azariel turned now to face Nemo as he spoke.

'I am so sorry, Nemo; I never meant to hurt you. I hope you can find it in your heart to forgive me one day.'

He then turned to face Eleanor and the Sky-Queen in turn to ask for their forgiveness, though neither of them replied to him. Daniel thought his acting very convincing, but he had dealt with bullies long enough in the past to be thus fooled.

'What can you tell us about yesterday?' Lord Autumn continued. 'When was the last time you saw your friend?'

'We were singing and dancing with our group until late evening. At some point, he said he was going to the beach and left. We assumed he was running after a maiden, so we did not follow. When it was time to start the journey back, he had not yet returned, so Nathaniel and I went to look for him. We looked for about an hour or so, until the night had covered everything, and almost gave up. But then, by pure chance we found him lying on the sand, his feet still touching the water. The sea appeared to have cast him ashore. He was cold and stiff and was not breathing.'

His voice faltered as if he was too troubled to speak, and he stopped.

Beside him, Nathaniel stood there as quiet as ever on the outside, not daring to face neither Nemo, nor Daniel. Inside him, however, a fierce battle was taking place. He could not believe things had turned up this way, and he was partially to blame for it. Ghordi was now dead, and an innocent man, a Visitor what's more, was being blamed for it. His queen was furious. She would make sure the mermaids paid for this, and that meant nothing good. From here on, life as he knew it in Endërland would never be the same. But he had the power to stop all of this from happening; he could tell the truth. They would believe him, they must.

As if reading his mind, Azariel turned to him and gave him a meaningful look, reminding Nathaniel of all he was promised should he decide to betray his friend. All initial courage faded right away as Nathaniel thought of his family humiliated, or worse, hurt by Azariel and those he was in league with. He would never forgive himself if anything happened to them because of him.

But that was not the only thing that kept his lips shut. He felt ashamed, having always been too weak to stand up to his best friend; Azariel had always been the strongest one, and he was no match for him. Now, this was the price to pay for his cowardice.

Sensing the tension between the two young wingmen, Lord Autumn turned now to him.

'Nathaniel, do you have anything to add on the matter?'

Torn between fear and guilt, the wingman took a moment before answering. For the sake of his family he would stay quiet for now, but in his heart, he knew that he was done with Azariel for good.

'No, my Lord Autumn, not at this time.'

He gave a defiant look to his now former friend, who understood all too well, but did not seem too bothered by it.

'Very well,' Lord Autumn continued. 'You are both excused.'

The two wingmen bowed their heads towards the Lords and queens, and made for the palace. Nathaniel walked behind, keeping his distance from Azariel. Once far enough from the courtyard and out of sight, the taller wingman turned to face him, grinning with malice.

'"Not at this time?"' he mocked. 'What do you think you're gonna do, tell them "The Truth"? And who's gonna believe you? You are nothing without me, Nathaniel, don't you ever forget that.'

'You had Ghordi killed. You lied to me and to everyone else in there. I wonder what else you are capable of.'

'You better hope you never have to find out, my friend.'

'You no longer get to call me that; your friends end up being lied to and killed, and I want none of that. You're on your own from here, Azariel. May the Great Lord have mercy on you.'

Feeling both angry and hurt, Nathaniel turned his back on Azariel and walked away from him.

'Go on, leave if you want,' Azariel called after him. 'Just remember, if you're not with me, you are against me, Nathaniel. And soon you'll find out just what that means.'

Nathaniel kept on walking, ignoring the shouts behind him. It felt good to finally stand up to his friend; he just wished he'd done it a lot sooner.

* * *

Back in the royal courtyard, Daniel was already surrendered to the fact that he was doomed. If this was anything like his own world, he was as good as guilty and should expect to be punished and maybe pay with his own life for the killing of the wingman. And Nemo would quite possibly suffer the same fate.

But he was running ahead of himself. Lord Autumn had apparently not finished with the interrogation.

'My dear Visitor. I understand that this must not be what you expected to happen when you first came to visit our world, but I am sure you comprehend the seriousness of this matter and what it means for the rest of our people from here on. This will set in motion and bring about a change, which we have all rather hoped would never come. And if we are to minimize the damage this will cause as much as we can, we must respond to this incident as firmly and as justly as possible, so that this precedent may be two-fold and we can thus bring some balance to life in our kingdom once again. So, before we decide on our next course of action, I ask you, do you have anything to say in your defence?'

Daniel could not believe it had already come to this. Nemo was standing quiet beside him, while Eleanor looked on, unable to do anything or help in any way. Diane continued to appear calm and collected as she sat there, letting everything unfold. The Sky-Queen had already put on a triumphant face, as if she was certain that the two boys would be found guilty. As for the rest of the Lords, they just sat there with no expression betraying their emotions, cold and passive, not unlike their own ice statues standing tall behind them. Daniel imagined he couldn't find a tougher crowd to convince if he had looked for it, but he had to try. He had to tell them his side of the story, and let the dice fall where they may.

'My Lords and Ladies,' he began. 'From the first moment I opened my eyes into this beautiful world, I have loved every minute of it. Every day has been and continues to be a living dream; one that I hope I will never have to wake up from. I have met many people and made many new friends, every single one of them wonderful and precious to me. I have seen many places and learned many new things, and I look forward to seeing and learning a lot more. This whole world is a little piece of heaven that I have fallen deeply and passionately in love with. But now I find myself standing here before you, accused of doing something unspeakable and unthinkable, something that is simply not true. I would never do anything, nor allow anyone to threaten your home and way of life. I guess, I'm kinda hoping that one day I will be able to call this place *my* home too.'

Daniel paused for a short moment to better sort out his thoughts and decide on how he was to continue his defence. He now appeared to have their full attention and felt a bit more optimistic about his predicament.

'Was I angry at how the three wingmen treated my new friend? Yes. Did I wish them to pay for their bullish behaviour? Absolutely. But did Nemo or I do anything about it? No, we did not. The Great Lord is our witness; that very day we decided to put this whole thing behind us and never speak of it again. And we haven't, until today.

'I do not know what happened, or who shot the young wingman and why. And I wish I knew how my arrow ended up piercing his heart. All I know is that the bow and quiver have never left my sight, except for the day of the incident. When Nemo was violently taken up in the air, he was carrying them for me. They could have easily taken one of the arrows from the quiver, though I cannot say why or even *if* they did that.'

His eyes met with the White Lord's again and were locked into a silent exchange between the two of them. Winter understood the insinuation all too well; the boy was smarter than he had counted on. Yet, he seemed unperturbed, knowing the truth would be quite hard, if not impossible to get to.

'I can offer you no proof, no witnesses that would testify of our innocence, nothing other than my word. I may be an outsider, but my word is just as good as everyone else's in this kingdom, and I can only hope that it will be enough.'

He stopped there and turned to Nemo, who gave him an approving look. The courtyard remained quiet, save for the rustling of leaves on the nearest trees as a soft breeze began blowing in from the sea.

Lord Autumn turned now to Nemo.

'Nemo, what do you have to say in your defence? It seems that you are at the centre of everything that's happened, yet you remain silent. Do you stand by the Visitor and his statement, or do you still claim to be the one responsible, as you first did?'

Nemo lifted his eyes, fearful at the prospect of them actually believing what he first said without thinking. He was having a hard time dealing with how things had turned out. A different adventure he had imagined he would experience once his turn came for his pilgrimage. He had hoped to take a long journey, visiting all of Endërland and its people, then hopefully find a nice girl and build a home with her somewhere away from the sea, where his sisters could no longer trouble him and where he would be respected and wanted. He had waited a long time for this, but now, it all seemed like it was about to end in the worst of ways.

He looked up, first at his mother sending him love from across the courtyard, and then at the Lords in front of him. With a sorrowful and trembling voice, he began to speak words that somehow sounded too mature for his young age.

'Twice I almost died at the claws of the three wingmen, my lords, and twice Daniel saved my life, without thinking or caring at all about what might happen to him. I was a stranger to him, yet he cared for me as if I was his own brother. I don't know about you, but when I see him, I see an honourable man, not a murderer. Still, if this Council so decides that he is, I will gladly take his place and receive all the punishment upon myself, so that he may go free.'

He paused for a moment and now looked Autumn straight in the eye.

'Still, I stand by what Daniel said; neither of us had anything to do with Ghordi's death.'

Nemo felt the proud look of his mother upon him, while next to him, Daniel just wanted to squeeze the smaller guy between his arms. The courtyard turned silent once again, as everyone waited for Lord Autumn to speak.

'Very well then, I think we have heard all there is to be heard for now. The Visitor and the young prince will wait at the palace to be called again, while we discuss our next step.'

He waited until Hëna escorted the two boys away from the courtyard, and then got up from the Silver Throne. He walked in the middle of the courtyard, where he could now face everyone. With his hands tied behind his back and a grave and thoughtful look on his face, which now made him appear older than before, he resumed speaking.

'My dear friends! We now face the difficult task of deciding how to respond to this most unfortunate and tragic incident. We have very few facts: the young wingman was shot down by an arrow that seems to belong to the Visitor, who appears to have had a motive for this act. Yet, both he and the young prince vehemently deny any wrongdoing and ask that we trust in their word and believe in their innocence. I must admit that I'm at a loss here. The weapon is the only real proof that we have to go by, yet that in itself is not enough to tell us who used it. I have personally spent some time with these boys, and I have nothing but praise for both of them. The Visitor may indeed be an outsider, yet he talks and behaves just like one of us. Am I not right, my dear Lady of the Land? Tell us more about him, please. You've spent more time with him than any of us has.'

Diane arose from her throne and bowed her head slightly. Winter kept his eyes glued on her.

'I have had the honour of being his host ever since he came to Endër, my Lords, and it has indeed been a privilege. I've gotten to know him a little, and if my opinion were of any value, I would say that he is innocent; they both are. I don't believe either of these boys is capable of such a vile act, whether they were born in this world, or in the other one.'

'Perhaps being too close to him has clouded your judgment, dear sister.' It was the Sky-Queen who now stood up and spoke with a harsh metallic voice. 'Perhaps you fail to see the implications of what you're saying. The weapon that killed my wingman belonged to the Visitor; I don't need any more proof than that. But, if you'd like us to believe that it wasn't him, then, what you're really saying, is that something far more sinister than simple revenge is going on here, and we are all being played. Can you explain that to us, dear sister? Is there anything you would like to share with us, that we should know?'

The tone of her voice was less sweet than her words, and she had no idea just how close to the truth those words rang. Diane thought this would be the perfect moment for her to lay open her own suspicions and theory about who should really be on trial before them today, but that time had not yet come. With a humble demeanour, she replied.

'It may be that my judgment is clouded, dear sister, just as you say. Yet, whether that is the case or not, I must speak what I feel and know to be right, and may the Great Lord be my judge. I have nothing else to say on the matter.'

She bowed down again and sat back on her throne. The Sky-Queen followed her with a cold look, unable to show any positive or negative emotion. She, however, did not sit down; she had been sitting by long enough, watching and listening to everything unfold in front of her, and now it was her turn to be heard. She moved closer to the Eternal Clock, dragging her long, elegant silver dress that matched perfectly with the grey contour of her beautiful wings, which she unfolded for a split second and closed again, as she usually did when claiming the attention of her subjects.

'A young wingman is dead, and his family is devastated; their life will never again be the same. My people have already heard about this, and they are demanding from their queen that the ones responsible be held accountable. There is no doubt in my mind that this outsider has brought his evil ways into our midst; no one born and raised in Endërland would even think of hurting his fellow man. We have all the proof we need; I don't know what else to ask for. He must be punished, and if the Sea-Prince was his accomplice, he should suffer the same fate.'

'No,' Eleanor cried in panic from her seashell throne, 'my son is innocent. He has suffered mocking and hate all his young life, yet he has never returned so much as an insult to anyone, let alone go as far as killing someone for mere revenge.'

'Maybe he finally grew tired and decided to do something about it. Or maybe his new friend was trying to show him how to finally become a man.'

Diane found both her words and tone of voice very cruel. If it weren't for the surroundings, she would have thought she was back in her home world, dealing with "real humans".

'No,' Eleanor repeated. 'I know my own son; he would never do something like that. If anyone is to be blamed for this, it's those wingmen of yours, dear sister, who have been mistreating Nemo for a long time. You say nothing of the fact that he almost died because they tied him up on that tree. If it had not been for Daniel, my son would not be here today, and in his place, we would be judging three young wingmen instead.'

'It's easy to make up stories you cannot prove,' the Sky-Queen retorted, her look and tone not very kind. 'All I know is that one of those wingmen is dead, and you provided the murder weapon.'

'Then I'll take that responsibility upon me, for choosing to give the Visitor the same kind of gift that was previously given to all three of us by our Lord Winter himself.'

Diane felt like smiling. Eleanor's words had masterfully just shifted the focus from Nemo and Daniel, to the White Lord.

'No,' it was now Lord Autumn's turn to speak up, rushing to calm things down before the situation got even more intense. The rest of the Lords looked on with clear concern.

'No fault lies with you, dear Lady of the Seas, for your choice of gift to the Visitor. We will not shift the blame to anyone, but rather try to make sure that the one responsible is held accountable. To do this we must decide if the evidence we have and everything we've heard here today is enough to determine the Visitor's guilt or innocence.'

'Brother, if I may.' For the first time that morning, Winter decided to speak. 'It seems to me that we are rushing to reach a decision about this today, and I just don't think we need to. Why not take some more time and make some effort into investigating this matter more thoroughly? Hopefully we will find some new evidence and maybe even witnesses that might help us see things clearer and make a more informed decision.'

She would have been happy to hear this under different circumstances, but knowing what she did, Diane dreaded the reason behind this "sage" advice. She knew the White Lord was after Daniel, and this sounded dangerously like he was making a play for it.

'That sounds like a wise thing to do, brother,' Autumn replied. 'However, there is one question I must ask; what would you suggest we do with the Visitor and the young prince in the mean time? If we cannot agree today that they are responsible for this act, then we have no other choice but to let them free to go.'

'Not necessarily,' Winter argued, now standing up. 'We can detain them until such time as we are ready to review this case again with new proof, and then make a final decision. After all, what's to stop the Visitor from going back to his world and never return here to face his judgment?'

It was now clear to Diane what he was trying to do. Next, Winter would offer to keep the boys somewhere safe, where he could do with them as he wished. She was not about to allow this; she did not abandon her loved ones and leave behind her entire world, so that she could lose Daniel now, just like she did Damien.

'My lords, if I may speak once again.' She stood up and did not wait for their permission. 'I can guarantee that the Visitor will do no such thing; he could not, even if he wanted to. He is bound to this world and belongs here as much as he belongs in his own. But that is not all; it seems to me we are all forgetting everything the Visitors stand for in our world. They have always brought life and added to the magic and splendour of our kingdom. Everyone that has ever visited us has been a blessing from the Great Lord himself; and I believe the same for Daniel. In my heart, I know he is an honourable young man, and if anyone doubts him, then I pray they will trust me. I will vouch for him; he will not escape.'

Silence ruled the courtyard for a short moment, as everyone seemed to ponder what Diane had just said. Winter was the first one to speak again.

'My dear Lady of the Land,' he spoke with apparent compassion and understanding in his eyes. 'You have always had our trust, and your wise counsel and kind heart has won you the love and respect of the entire kingdom and its people. However, I must apologize for feeling obligated to reveal here, what you seem to want to conceal from this respected Council, and that is the fact that the young Visitor is your son, your own flesh and blood. So, you will forgive us, if our trust is a little hard to come by in this instance; after all, a son can never do wrong in his mother's eyes.'

Diane bit her lip and lowered her eyes; she had not counted on Winter revealing this to anyone. Suddenly everyone's eyes were on her, and she felt like she was the one on trial.

'Is this true, my lady?' Autumn asked, sounding taken aback. Gathering up her courage, she looked back up and straight into his eyes.

'It is, my lord Autumn.'

'But why would you keep this from us?'

'I do beg your forgiveness, my lord, but I had my reasons for this, none of which have anything to do with why we are gathered here today. And I need you to believe me; the Visitor may be my flesh and blood, but he is a stranger to me, just like he is to all of you. He was but a toddler when I left him, and I am just getting to know the man he has become. What I said earlier about him, I did not say as his mother, but as an honest and dutiful member of this Council.'

'So, you would like us to believe, that you would not lie in order to protect your long-lost son?' The Sky-Queen's words to her cut deep and sharp.

'I would like you to believe that I would not lie, dear sister. I understand your grief and the need to blame the Visitor for what's happened, but I hold to my previous statement about him, and I speak here only as the queen of my people.'

'This Council would never accuse you of lying, my lady,' Winter continued to address her cunningly. 'We are simply concerned that your emotions might be getting in the way and preventing you from seeing clearly in this case. You and I both know that people are very different where Visitors come from; after all, we come from that very same place. This evil we are judging here today, could not have been born in Endërland, yet for the sake of truth and fairness, we are willing to consider all other possibilities. However, the boy needs to stay here, until we know for certain if he is guilty or innocent.'

He turned now to Autumn and continued with a more authoritative tone of voice.

'I say we use the bracelet on the boy; that will ensure that he remains here for as long as we need him to. Until we are ready to assemble this Council again on the matter, I would be more than happy to keep the boys under surveillance.'

'That's going a bit too far brother, don't you think?' This time it was Spring who broke her silence.

'Is it, dear sister? The way I see it, with what we know so far, these two boys are guilty more than innocent. And if I were to let them free to run around, who's to say they wouldn't hurt someone else? How would we feel if that happened?'

'Don't look now, brother,' Spring countered, 'but you're reasoning like an outsider.'

Winter's eyes lit up with a strange light underneath his bushy eyebrows, making it look as if lightning might strike at any moment. But he controlled his anger and kept himself composed. His frustration, however, was clear on his face.

'Our sister is right,' Autumn intervened. 'It is not our custom to keep prisoners.'

'That's because we've never had to deal with something like this before.'

'And we're not about to start now,' Autumn insisted, raising his tone a bit, as if growing tired of the argument. 'Until we have undeniable proof that these boys are guilty, they will be treated as innocent. The day we lose trust in one-another, will be the end of our way of life. Then, whoever brought this evil upon us, will have won.'

'Then, what do you suggest we do, brother?' Winter asked, seating back down.

Autumn headed back towards his throne, picked up the Silver Sceptre, and turned around to face them again, without sitting down. This meant he was about to make an official judgement.

'The people need an answer today about who is responsible for the crime committed, and we have to decide. We have to rely on the information we already have in order to make our decision regarding the Visitor and the Sea-Prince. And as we continue the search for the truth, if new evidence is found in the future, we will amend today's decision accordingly. But we will not pause the decision-making process here and expose these two boys to unfair treatment or risk, until we feel we have better knowledge of the facts. Agreed?'

The queens remained quiet while the rest of the Lords voiced their agreement.

'Very well then, it is now time for us to vote. Whatever we decide here today it will be undisputable unless this same Council changes its decision. Brother, guilty or innocent? What say you?'

Winter surrendered to the fact that this was how it was going to be, and without moving from his throne, he spoke coldly.

'Guilty.'

'Noted,' Autumn replied and turned to face Spring. 'Sister?'

With a soft smile on her kind face, and her eyes constantly on Diane, she answered.

'Innocent.'

'Noted,' Autumn repeated, turning now to Summer. 'Sister?'

The lovely blonde lady had been silent throughout the whole deal and looked like she would prefer to keep it that way. Unfortunately, she knew she had to speak this time, though she felt none too pleased about it.

'Guilty,' she said quickly, trying to avoid any eye contact with the queens.

'Noted,' Autumn repeated for the third time and then sat down on his high throne. He rested the Silver Sceptre on his knees, sighing.

'Alas, our job does not seem to be easy on this day. I was hoping we would be of the same mind, but it is understandable.

'I'm afraid we have a problem, my friends, for in my mind the Visitor and the Sea-Prince are innocent and that means we are still unable to make a decision about them today.'

Winter got up once again and hurriedly spoke.

'Then let us do as I suggested, brother; let us postpone the decision until we have investigated properly and have enough information. We can keep the boys somewhere safe, where no harm will come to them, and they cannot be a danger to anyone either.'

'That's not what our law says, brother,' Spring argued. 'You know very well what's to happen, should we ever fail to agree on a decision.'

Winter turned now towards her with an astonished look on his face.

'Surely you are not being serious, dear sister.'

'This is hardly the time and place for jokes, brother. We are all subject to the laws laid down by the Great Lord, and must obey them, just as we enforce them.'

'Spring is right, brother; if we cannot decide on this matter, then it is the Great Lord himself who's going to have to take up this case. I actually feel a bit relieved; this matter is too important, and I know he will make the right decision. I will agree on this though, we can use the bracelet on the Visitor to ensure he remains in this world until this case is solved.'

A barely invisible smile appeared on Diane's face as she finally felt the relief of things taking the right direction. She saw the frustration of Winter reaching a new high, and repressed her joy to hide it from his keen eyes.

'Forgive me for insisting, brother,' Winter continued to try, 'but when was the last time we ever heard from the Great Lord? When was the last time we saw him, or he spoke to us, gave us a sign that he is still here taking care of us and governing us? How long has it been, huh? Can anyone even remember? I know *I* can't.'

'You may have a point there, brother; I wish I could remember the last time I saw or heard from the Great Lord. However, that does not change the fact that we have our laws and rules to follow, and that is just what we're going to do. We are going to let the Great Lord decide the Visitor's fate.'

'And how are we going to do that, tell me, brother? How are we going to find the Great Lord, when we don't even know if he's still around?'

'It's quite simple, really; we're going to send the Visitor and the Sea-Prince to search for him.'

Winter had by now lost all patience and composure. He was pacing fast around the courtyard and speaking in a harsh tone and quick words.

'This is crazy, insanity; I still say we investigate and decide for ourselves. The Great Lord will never be found, and we will be the joke of the entire kingdom.'

Autumn now sharply arose from the Silver Throne, with the sceptre in hand and a dark shadow over his face. As he roared, the wind grew stronger and faster, blowing countless leaves from the trees around them. Thick clouds appeared in the sky from nowhere and the whole place grew darker.

'Compose yourself, brother; you forget your place. Laws were not given to us so we can choose when to follow and when to ignore them. I, for one, intend to make sure *his* instructions are followed to the letter, as long as it is my responsibility and burden to do so. When you get your turn, you may choose to defy him as you please and suffer the consequences.'

Winter gazed at the Silver Sceptre in Autumn's hand and withdrew with a deep bow and seemingly regretful smile.

'My apologies, brother; I spoke rashly. Of course, I will support the decision of the Silver Throne. I have never forgotten that I am merely a servant, appointed by the Great Lord himself. Please, forgive my passion.'

He sat back on his throne and remained quiet, at least on the outside. The wind died down, the clouds dispersed just as they had appeared, and light returned to the courtyard once more. A thousand new golden leaves were now added to the riches of the earth around them.

Autumn continued to address the Council, without sitting back down.

'Please understand, the doubts of my brother are not his alone; they are common amongst all our folk. The name of the Great Lord has long turned into legend and the people have stopped believing that he even exists. Even those who do believe, think that he has forsaken us and will never come back. I would like to challenge that belief; it seems to me that we are at a point where we need our Creator once again, so I am making this a two-purpose mission. I am sending people to look for him, and when they find him, to bring back his word to us, along with his judgment on this case. I want to see the faith of our people in the Great Lord restored.

'Please, bring the boys back before us.'

Hëna, who had been standing at a distance this whole time, left immediately towards the palace, and returned shortly with Daniel and Nemo. The boys stood nervous before the four Lords, waiting.

Autumn addressed them directly.

'My dear Visitor and Sea-Prince. This Council has been unable to come to a unanimous decision on whether you are guilty or innocent of the crime committed, so we have no other choice but to delegate your case to the Great Lord himself. Only, this has never happened before, and we have no idea how or where to find him. So, it will be your duty to search for and find him, and then submit to his judgment once you do. You will not be alone, however, nor without help and guidance; we will choose people to go with you and lead you. First, I suggest you go to Tálas, to consult with the Oracle on how to find the Great Lord. From there, you will go wherever he will direct you, and will inform us regularly of your progress.

'However, there is one thing you need to keep in mind, Daniel, if you ever want to go back to your world again. You will have only a limited time to find the Great Lord; I cannot say how long. This is because you will be given a bracelet that will prevent you from going back to your world, once you put it on, and you will not be able to take it off until this is all done. As I understand it, being in this world all the time, will cause your real body to weaken and possibly die, but as with all things concerning the Visitors and their world, we know very little. So, you see, it is in your best interest to find the Great Lord as soon as possible.'

The thought of dying caught Daniel off guard. It had crossed his mind that he might have to be punished with death for the murder of the wingman, but somehow, he thought that even if it came to that point, he might still have a chance to escape it once evening came. But now they were talking about real death; his body back in his world giving up and dying, just like his mother's had, years ago. He thought of his father never seeing him again; he thought of Sam and Freddie having to deal with his lifeless body and the aftermath. He thought of everything he would never get to do again, places he'd never go, people he'd never meet, and he felt scared. He was not ready to die.

Chapter 8

A QUEST FOR FIVE

With his right hand Daniel reached for his left wrist, touching the new object that orbited around it, not too loose, yet not too tight either. It was fairly heavy despite its small size. Daniel had never been one for wearing jewellery; the only other object he had ever worn on his wrist had been a plastic watch, which he had kept for almost four years, until it had become too old and worn out. It had been Damien's before him, and he had kept it as a reminder of his long-lost brother. Now it no longer worked, and the leather strap had been damaged years ago, but he still kept the watch with him all the time, tucked safely in his pocket.

The bracelet was unsurprisingly made of silver and gold, the finest and purest he had ever seen or touched. It was about an inch wide and completely flat and smooth, apart from two thin lines on its contours. If he looked close enough, he could make out the carved symbols of the four Lords of Endërland, repeatedly running around the bracelet like a signature of their handiwork.

Diane told him it was the very same one she had been given to wear a long time ago, and it would remain on his wrist, until the Council of the Lords decided there was no longer need for it. Until then, he would be unable to return to his world, to Sotira, where Sam and Freddie would have to deal with his unconscious body.

He wondered how long that would be; would it all be just one night, even if he spent months here, or would he sleep for a lot longer? And if so, would his body really weaken and eventually die?

The situation had definitely turned south at this point. He had been accused of committing a murder and was being sent to find his judge, a task that could literally take him all eternity, since this judge apparently did not seem to be around anymore. In the meantime, even though he was not officially a prisoner, he was denied the right to return to his world and could not go anywhere by himself.

The Council had agreed to let Daniel and Nemo go forth to find the Great Lord on the condition that they would not go unaccompanied. Autumn promised to send his best man to aid the boys, who turned out to be none other than his son, Heli. The Sky-Queen had also insisted on being involved and kept constantly informed, so she sent her own son to supervise the search and report back to them. And so it was that the three princes and Heli set off that evening from the royal palace in Arba towards Tálas, the city where the Oracle of the Great Lord lived.

With Heli upfront riding a huge snow-white stallion, quite appropriate for his size, and Daniel and Nemo following behind on separate mounts, they left Arba, passing through the Northern Gate this time. Séraphin chose not to ride with them, instead flying ahead, clearly annoyed at this babysitting duty he had no choice but to accept from his queen and mother. He had to stop and circle back quite often, since the animals could never match his speed, and this seemed to frustrate him even more. Heli, however, seemed quite amused by it, and would deliberately slow down or stop every now and then, as if to test the wingman's patience. With a joyful spirit like his, he found it hard to take Séraphin's grumpy face too seriously.

Daniel was most happy that Heli was coming along; it made this whole thing feel less like a punishment or a mission, and more like a camping trip. There was nothing official or lordly about Heli's attitude; he was just one of them, a friend coming along for the ride and leading the way through the unknown parts of Endërland.

He thought of Hëna, whom he had not seen since earlier that day, after the Council meeting had ended. He felt a weird longing for her presence, yet at the same time relief that she wasn't around. Unlike Heli, she did not give the impression of being a very cheerful person, and for that little time that Daniel spent in her presence, he'd had the uncomfortable feeling that she didn't like him very much. Well, not that exactly; it was more like he wasn't worth her attention, and for some reason that hurt even more. Still he was glad; this journey was going to be hard enough dealing with one person not particularly fond of him and Nemo, let alone two.

The moon had just crowned over the mountains when they left Arba behind and headed north. So far, this was just like any other evening he'd spent in Endërland; the full moon shone bright in the night sky, big and white as it always did in this world. He would often stay awake long after sundown to enjoy her radiant company. It was a mystery to him how it was always full and round here, every single night. Tonight, it was no different; it hovered up there with such beauty and brightness that he had to struggle to look away. He guessed it was part of the magic of this world, one of those things that were quite similar to his, and at the same time, entirely different.

He was not complaining about it one bit, though; sitting at the terrace of his mother's castle every evening had become his favourite pastime. Even Nemo had learned this by now and usually gave him his space, for which Daniel was grateful. Somehow, he felt this time belonged only to him and this unbelievably beautiful moon, and he did not feel like sharing it with anyone else.

The moon wasn't the only one that shone big and bright up there, however; the stars were endless and amazingly clear. He did not recognize this sky; all the known constellations were there, in their usual place, but there were so many more, all a lot closer than was even possible. Not a single space on the big black canvas had been left unadorned with their celestial glow.

This bountiful light made it unnecessary for them to keep torches while travelling at night; the moonlight alone was enough to see where they needed to go, and tonight it appeared to shine even brighter and closer than the usual. They could even make out the distant silhouette of Séraphin as he flew ahead of them in the dark.

Soon, however, they were going to have to camp and rest for the remainder of the night. Heli suggested that they ride for another hour or so to get some distance from Arba and set their camp by a small lake that he knew further up north. The boys agreed and followed in silence.

The trip to Tálas would take them about four days, travelling mainly along the coastline, but they did not start that way. As they left Arba, they set straight for the Valley of Destiny, leaving the seaside for a while, thus cutting short a good part of their journey. They would eventually meet the sea again farther up north. Tálas was built on the shores of the Northern Sea, and was the third biggest city in the kingdom, population wise. Despite the circumstances, Daniel was looking forward to visiting this part of Endërland for the first time.

They packed light provisions to take with them in personal bags which were loaded onto their horses; some blankets, a few extra clothes and some food and drinks that Diane had insisted they take with them. There should have been four bags altogether, including one for Séraphin, yet Daniel counted five of them: one on Nemo's horse, two on his and two more on Heli's steed. He wondered whom the other one was for but did not ask.

Nemo rode uneasy on the back of his brown mare, still feeling quite inexperienced and uncertain. Heli laughed as he saw him struggling to find the best position and hanging on too tight, not even daring to relax for fear of losing balance.

'Stop fidgeting, Nemo; Alma is a smart girl, she won't let you fall even if you tried.'

Nemo gave a nervous smile and pretended to relax a little, but that only caused Heli to laugh harder. Daniel laughed, too. He'd grown quite fond of the little guy. He actually felt protective of him, as he would over a little brother.

And right then he thought of his own brother, Damien. He hated the fact that he could not remember anything about him, and what was even worse, he could not feel anything. There was no sadness, no longing, nothing to suggest that they were related by anything else but blood. It was as if Damien was just another stranger to him, one whose path he would most probably never cross again.

They rode in silence for another hour, going up and down smooth hills, until they reached the camping spot. Séraphin, who had disappeared from almost half an hour ago, was already sitting quietly by a small fire he had started, his sizable wings wrapped around his arms and legs. The night had grown a bit chilly, and Daniel welcomed the idea of a fire.

He got off his mount and approached the wingman, who gave no sign of acknowledging him.

'We haven't been properly introduced,' he said, extending his hand. 'I'm Daniel.'

He stood there with his hand in the air waiting, but Séraphin ignored him. Daniel understood and drew away from him. Not untroubled, he walked back to his horse and began unloading the bags and removing the saddle, following Heli's lead. Nemo, who finished first, took his bag to the fireplace and sat down facing Séraphin.

'That wasn't cool, man; he was just trying to be polite.'

Séraphin still didn't move or react. He sat there with his head down and his arms and legs wrapped under his wings, appearing not to notice Nemo in front of him. This bothered Nemo.

'Ok, now you're just being rude. You're no better than your friends, you know?'

He had not even finished that sentence, when Séraphin unfolded his enormous blue and white wings and jumped on him, throwing him down on the ground. A shiny dagger appeared out of nowhere, as he held it up the boy's throat. It all happened so fast that Nemo didn't even manage to gulp.

With fire in his small bright eyes and real anger in his voice, Séraphin hissed.

'You listen to me very carefully, fish-boy. I know exactly who and what you and your friend are. You may have fooled the Council, but not me, and I will make sure you both get what you des...'

It was his turn to not be able to finish his sentence, as all of a sudden, a pair of strong hands grabbed him by his shoulders and threw him off of Nemo and with his back on the ground. Completely shocked, the Sky-Prince now found himself under Heli's strong knees and glaring gaze.

Daniel rushed beside horrified Nemo, checking to make sure he was ok and helping him up.

'That was not very cool, Séraphin,' Heli spoke with a stern voice that frightened even Daniel. His face had suddenly lost all that innocence and cheerfulness that usually characterized it, being replaced instead by a surprising harshness, which Daniel silently thought it suited him well. This was a whole other side of Heli, one that he had not anticipated he'd ever be presented to.

'Now, I know you're feeling angry and want to blame someone, but if you think that you have the right to take up the Great Lord's place and judge these two, then tell us now and save us the journey.'

Séraphin opened his eyes wide, in wonder. And he wasn't the only one.

'Go on,' Heli continued, 'you clearly think you know better than the Council of the Lords, so, why don't you? Decide right here and now if they are to be held responsible for Ghordi's death and then choose their fate. I won't stand in your way; in fact, I'll even help you. We can say to the Council that we found the Great Lord sooner than we thought and he ordered us to do it. Your mother would be *so* proud.'

Séraphin seemed to be getting the message and struggled to get free, but Heli wouldn't budge.

'Let go of me.'

'No. Not until you come to your senses and give me your word. If you're not going to be their judge, then you're going to be their ally and help them find the Great Lord.'

'Get off of me, you're crushing my wings.'

'Your word,' Heli insisted.

'Alright, you have it,' Séraphin yielded. Heli regarded him for a moment and then got off of him, helping him back up.

'I'll go along with this charade, but only so I can see them get the punishment they deserve for what they did. And I'll stay away from them as long as they stay away from me. Happy?' he snapped at Heli.

'No,' Heli answered, having regained his former composure strangely fast. 'But I'll take what I can get. Now, apologize to Nemo.'

Séraphin snorted and with a powerful flap of his wings, rose up in the air and disappeared into the night. Heli chuckled.

'He'll be back,' he said, turning to Nemo and Daniel. 'He's a good guy; he's just wrong about you. Rumour has it that his mother is very tough on him, so I guess he acts up sometimes. Are you ok, Nemo? Did he hurt you?'

'No,' Nemo replied, still shaking. 'I'm fine.'

'How do you know he's wrong?' asked Daniel, looking at his new friend with admiration. 'Why are you so sure we're innocent?'

'I just am,' Heli answered raising his shoulders, and then proceeded to bring the last two bags next to the fire. 'I couldn't say why, but I believe you; and you will have all the help I can give to prove your innocence to the rest of the kingdom. Now get some rest; you have a long day tomorrow.'

Daniel noticed that he said 'you' instead of 'we' but didn't think much of it. It had been a very long and eventful day, and he was glad for the chance to rest and forget about everything for a short while.

For the first time ever since he awoke into this new world, he went to bed knowing that he would actually sleep that night. When he'd open his eyes in the morning, he'd still be here, with Nemo, Heli and of course Séraphin. In a way, he felt relieved; he had begun to miss his dreamless nights, when he would sleep through to the morning and wake up feeling fully rested and refreshed. Now, as long as he had the bracelet on, he could do that again. He only wondered if he would dream tonight, or any of the following nights. He guessed he'd just have to wait and see.

* * *

The sun was well up high into the sky when he finally woke up, feeling rested and with a sense of satisfaction. It had been a night just like before when he didn't even know what dreams were. He had slept without so much as a vision to disturb him and he had enjoyed it.

As he yawned and rolled over in his improvised bed, he was startled by the presence of a huge brown bear lying next to him, wide-awake. Scared half to death, Daniel got up and away from the animal that barely moved its head to acknowledge him. It was then that Daniel noticed a whole crowd of animals gathered curiously in a circle around the fire. They were just sitting there, oblivious to his presence. He guessed they had been attracted by the fire and weren't afraid to come close.

Not far from him, Nemo was still sleeping, wrapped in his blanket on the opposite side of the fire that was now almost dead. No sign of Heli or Séraphin; both their belongings had been packed into their bags, but were still there, as were the horses. Daniel wondered why they had been left to sleep so long; it appeared to be almost midday.

A light breeze was blowing from the west, causing the trees around them to dance in harmony under the bright sunlight. Paying close attention, Daniel heard the sound of water splashing not far from there and remembered that they were near a lake. He could use some fresh water on his face.

Not disturbing Nemo, who looked like he was really enjoying his sleep, he began to walk in the direction of the sound. A short distance from the camp, the trees made way for a small path that, as he followed it, led to a small lake of crystal-clear water. Getting closer, he noticed a pile of clothes resting on the ground at the edge of the water. They looked like Heli's, who Daniel figured was probably taking a bath.

Sure enough, swimming in his direction from the middle of the lake, he saw a figure approaching steadily. As it drew closer to the edge of the water, Daniel was surprised to see not the blonde head of his big friend, but the dark long hair of his sister, Hëna, who proceeded to come out on dry land, naked as she was. Unable to stop himself, Daniel managed to take a peek at her elegant form, beautiful breasts, and straight long legs, before he quickly turned away from her.

'I..., I'm so sorry,' he mumbled, as his heart suddenly decided to make itself noticed with a fast and rhythmic thump. 'I had no idea you were here. I thought you were Heli.'

'I am definitely not Heli,' Hëna replied, prompting Daniel to silently agree with her. She stopped just behind him, proceeding to drain the water out of her hair, not even thinking of covering herself.

'Why are you looking the other way? Have I offended you in any way?'

'What?' The question surprised Daniel almost as much as her very presence there. 'No, of course not; it's just that, well, you're... naked.'

Hëna seemed to miss the point.

'Yes. And...?'

'And ..., it's inappropriate; well, where I come from anyway.' Daniel began to think that perhaps it was not so in this world.

'Oh..., I'm sorry,' she said, sounding sincere. 'I'm afraid I don't know much about your world. I'll get dressed.'

She picked her clothes up from the ground putting them back on, with her hair and skin still wet.

'Why is it inappropriate?' she asked walking in front of him, now wearing her brown leather trousers and white shirt that was clinging to her wet flesh, making Daniel no less uncomfortable. He was trying really hard not to stare at her. Like any boy his age, he appreciated the beauty in a girl, though he had never obsessed after their bodies, as he knew many of his friends did. But, with Hëna standing like this right in front of him, he now found himself silently agreeing with what the fuss was all about.

This, however, was not the only thing that caught him by surprise; the girl standing before him seemed entirely different from the one he met for the first time only two days ago. There was nothing of that official air he'd perceived the previous day; it was like she was another person, even more disarming, if that was possible.

'I don't know,' he finally remembered to answer, feeling the heat take over his whole body. 'It's always been like that, I guess.'

'So, people never see each other naked?'

'No, that's not what I meant. It's inappropriate for strangers to do that.'

'But we're not strangers,' she continued to pester him. Daniel began walking back towards the camp, trying to hide more than his red unwashed face as she followed behind him.

'You know what I mean,' he responded. 'Usually people only see each other like that when they are intimate. Where is Heli?' he hurried to change the subject.

'Oh, he'll be back in the evening; I'll be your guide until then.'

'You?' Daniel could not hide his shock.

'What's the matter, don't you trust me? I know this kingdom just as well as my brother does, if not better.'

'No, of course I trust you; I just thought Heli was going to be our guide, that's all.'

'He is; we both are. We do everything together; besides, you're going to need all the help you can get if you want to find the Great Lord as soon as possible, and we are your best bet.'

Daniel had no idea what she meant by that, but he was suddenly glad that she was here and was not treating him like he'd been afraid she might.

They walked back to the camp where they found Nemo awake and loading everything back onto the horses. The nightly visitors seemed to have gone back into the woods.

'Good morning, Nemo!' they both greeted him.

'Good morning, guys!' he replied, showing no sign of surprise at the sight of Hëna. 'It was nice of you to let us sleep a bit longer, Hëna; I don't think I've ever needed so much rest before. Everything is ready here; are we waiting for his royal hideousness?'

He hadn't even finished talking, when Séraphin appeared on the horizon, flying in from the south. In a matter of seconds, he landed right in front of them, looking pretty much as grumpy and cocky as ever.

'I see we are ready to move, then. Good; let's go, shall we?'

Daniel decided he must have missed something, since he seemed to be the only one surprised by the presence of Hëna there. He thanked Nemo for gathering his things and climbed onto his horse, just as Hëna and Nemo climbed on each of theirs. Séraphin rose up in the air, once again heading north.

'Any news from Arba?' Hëna called after him, before he went too far for her voice to be heard. Daniel had forgotten about the fact that he had been gone all night.

Séraphin turned around to look at Hëna, and after a moment's hesitation, answered.

'We left Arba only last night, Hëna; what news do you expect to hear?'

There was no disrespect in his voice, yet Daniel did not like his answer.

'Mermaid's Well?' The Sky-Prince continued, still hovering in the air.

'Mermaid's Well,' Hëna replied, appearing untroubled by his reply.

They rode on with a steady pace, following in the direction Séraphin flew. The trail led them away from the lake and through another series of low hills, dressed in the usual autumnal colours. Fall seemed to have matured in full upon them overnight, and the leaves falling from the trees all over were the evidence. It all looked like a beautiful landscape painting, with dominating brown and yellow. The days were still warm, however, and the rain had not visited these parts of the kingdom just yet. It still felt a bit summery, and Daniel wasn't about to complain; he had always loved summer over all seasons.

As the day wore on, Arba grew more and more distant, hiding behind the numerous hills and valleys that they crossed. They rode for long hours, without stopping for a break or refreshments; the horses were strong and the terrain fairly easy for them. They did not seem to get tired and quite enjoyed carrying the young riders.

Séraphin continued to fly ahead of them, keeping a distance, but never going too far as to lose them from sight.

Every now and then, forest creatures came out and joined them, trotting and jumping alongside them for a short while. They seemed to enjoy the company of people, as if they did not get to see them very often. The whole thing kept the journey quite entertaining and amusing; that and Nemo's continuous banter about just anything and everything he could think of. Daniel didn't mind though; he was actually glad that Nemo was providing the small talk. Hëna did not seem particularly keen on striking up a conversation, and he couldn't gather up the courage to start one either.

He kept watching her as she rode in front of them, with a grace that seemed to be a trademark of Endërland women only. She was unlike any other girl he had ever known and that included Sam. He liked Sam; if he would have a girlfriend back in his world, it would most definitely be her. He could see it happening. And yet, whereas Sam seemed to carry the weight of the world on her young shoulders, Hëna appeared relaxed and carefree. There was something magical about her that had captured Daniel from the very first moment he'd laid eyes on her. Without a warning, she had become the epicentre of his thoughts, and he was finding that harder to ignore with each passing moment.

Lost as he was in his inner musings of her, he barely heard Nemo's voice calling his name.

'Daniel, Daniel.'

Nemo was forced to shout in order to get his attention, causing Hëna to look back, wondering. The red-haired boy gave her a silly smile and did not speak until she returned to her former position. He then rode closer to Daniel, and practically whispered.

'It's a bad idea, man...'

Daniel gave him a puzzled look.

'What are you talking about?'

'You know exactly what I'm talking about; so, you better listen to me. She's definitely worth it,' Nemo nodded in Hëna's direction, 'but it will never happen. You don't know how many guys have courted her, proposed to her, and even asked her father for her hand, but she's turned them all down; every single one of them. It's like she's just not interested in that kind of stuff. No use even thinking about it, man, I'm telling you,' he finished.

Daniel felt his face grow red hot. He had no idea he had been so obvious about it; either that or Nemo had psychic powers. Yet, the embarrassment was quickly over as he pondered Nemo's words. From the first moment he saw her, he'd felt Hëna was out of his league, being as beautiful as she was and the daughter of a Lord, not to mention probably thousands of years old, which would also make her considerably more mature and experienced than him. Yet, somewhere deep inside of him there had been a hidden hope that maybe none of that really mattered, that maybe who he was would just be enough. Now, his new best friend had just killed that hope with one simple sentence: '*It will never happen*'.

He continued to ride along, trying not to think about it anymore. *At least,* he told himself, *I found out now, before I did something stupid again.* His mind recalled the humiliation he had suffered in front of his whole classroom in fourth grade, as Celina, the girl he'd had a crush on then, had read his love letter aloud. He had felt even worse after, realizing she did not love him like he did. That was not something he was looking forward to going through again.

* * *

The sun was almost at the end of its journey for the day, when they finally dismounted their horses and set up camp again to spend the night, this time near a dried up old well that everyone called the Mermaid's Well. The name came with a story apparently as old as Endërland itself.

It told of a young mermaid and her pilgrimage. She'd always had a great desire to visit the mountains, and one day, while on her way there, she had chanced upon this well. Wanting to taste its water, she had tried to bring some up, but the old wood holding the bucket had broken down and fallen inside, dragging her along. She had tried to climb back up, but the well was too deep and its walls too slimy. Her tail reappearing was all that had saved her from drowning.

Unable to climb back up, she had ended up living inside the well for many seasons. Living all alone in that confined space, she would pass her time talking to the stars she saw at night above her and singing songs they taught her. It was while she was singing one night, that her song reached the ears of a nearby passing traveller. Following her powerful voice, he found her, helping her to finally leave the well. Legend had it that they married and lived many happy seasons on land together, until she decided to go back to the sea and her family, being the only mermaid to have ever been allowed back after such a long time.

Even though so much time had passed, and the well was now dry, it was said that her song could still be heard from deep inside of it. Daniel, however, could not hear any sounds at all coming up from the deep, melodic, or otherwise. He guessed legends here in Endërland were pretty much like back in his home-world, 1% truth and 99% fiction.

As before, Séraphin was the first at the camp, fire ready. After unloading his things, Daniel went to sit by the fire, saying only a polite 'Good evening', for which he did not expect a reply, nor did he get one. Nemo joined him soon after, while Hëna set her blankets and bags on the ground near the fire, improvising a small bed. She did not sit down, however. Instead, she walked away in the twilight, saying only: 'See you later, boys.'

Again, Daniel felt like he was missing something, wondering where she was going, while Nemo and Séraphin seemed not to be bothered about it. And again, he did not ask, fearing they might get the wrong idea, or worse, the right one. He got to talking with Nemo and enjoying some more of the food they had in their packs, while Séraphin stepped away from them and began setting up his own bed.

Wingmen were amazing creatures; they had so much in common with both men and birds, that it was impossible to decide to which race they actually belonged. If you asked them, they would proudly tell you that they belonged to neither; that they were far more superior to any living race, and in a sense, they would be right. They had the best part of both and hardly any defects, apart from their unmatched pride. Besides their ability to fly hard and high as the eagles themselves, they shared their enhanced sight and sharp vision, even in the darkest night. Their sense of smell was also very strong, and they were very agile and quick in their movements.

They loved trees, especially very tall ones. Sky-City was built on the south-eastern part of the forest of Mirë, a part well known for its giant trees and beautiful landscape. They had built their nests on top of the trees, with a whole network of hanging bridges creating the infrastructure that connected everything. Of course, the word 'nests' is not the most appropriate word to use here, as they looked more like complex treehouses, varying in size, shape, and style. The wingmen were very creative and imaginative when it came to their homes, though one would be inclined to think that there is only so much you can do on top of a very tall tree.

As for their sleeping arrangements, Daniel soon found that it was actually very simple. All they required was at least two trees - or poles in their absence - standing at a near distance from each other, ideally slightly farther than the wingmen were tall. They then tied up both ends of a custom-made net on each tree, thus creating a hanging bed. Pretty much a hammock. Their huge wings then they wrapped around themselves to serve as a cover, which was ideal, as their own feathers kept them warm in colder nights.

Daniel watched as Séraphin prepared his own bed and could not help but feel amazed. The wingman's attitude had done nothing to make him feel less curious or appreciative of this magnificent race.

Besides, he understood all too well why Séraphin felt the way he did; he himself would probably behave worse if their places were reversed. Still, he felt quite uncomfortable around the winged man, and unless things somehow changed between them, he would keep his distance from him.

As Séraphin finished setting up his bed, the sun finally clocked in for the day and gave the sky over to the moon. The night drew closer, beginning to wrap everything in its dark cloak. It wasn't long after that, that the familiar silhouette of Heli appeared walking towards them, acting casual, as if he'd left them only half an hour ago.

'Hey guys, good day?' he asked, taking his place by the fire. 'Is that figs?' He reached into the small canister Nemo was holding in front of him and helped himself. 'Yum, I love figs.'

They sat there around the fire, consuming fruit from their packs and having small talk as if they'd been together all day long, while Daniel decided he could not keep quiet any longer. Having had enough mysteries for one day, he almost screamed as he asked.

'Where were you all day? How did you get here now? And where is Hëna gone?'

The boys stopped eating and talking, and turned to Daniel, suddenly realizing that he actually didn't know. Nemo looked at Heli, who with a sheepish look on his face and his mouth full of figs, raised one hand and pointed towards the moon that had just appeared over the Northern Mountains. Daniel looked in that direction and then back at Heli, still lost.

'What are you showing me?'

Heli almost swallowed the figs without chewing, before speaking as if one guilty. 'That's where I've been all day; that's where Hëna is gone for the night.'

Daniel still did not understand.

'What do you mean? Where?'

'Up there in the sky,' Heli clarified, pointing at the moon again.

Daniel looked at the bright sphere above them again, completely confused.

'You were on the moon?' he asked, not sure he got it right. Laughter broke out in the camp, as even Séraphin was unable to hold on to his grumpy mood for a moment, despite pretending he wasn't listening.

Daniel began to feel offended.

'What's so funny?'

Heli quit laughing at once and tried to turn serious.

'I'm sorry, Daniel; it's easy to forget sometimes that you're not from around here and that there's things you might not know about our world. I guess Nemo hasn't been doing a good enough job here.'

'Yeah, that's what they keep telling me,' replied Nemo, now taking a turn looking guilty. 'Sorry, Dan, I guess this is one of those things that you would call common knowledge; well for us locals anyway. You see, the reason why we never get to see Heli during the day, is because he is busy up there, giving out light and heat to all of Endërland as our sun. And during the night, Hëna takes his place in the sky as the moon. That's where she is now,' Nemo finished, pointing at the sky again and prompting Daniel to turn and take another look.

He was stumped. What Nemo said made no sense, even for a world like Endërland. How could Heli and Hëna be the sun and the moon? They were talking about a powerful star that burns hot and bright millions of miles away; how could Heli be it? He was just a man and Hëna just a girl, not some big round rock orbiting the earth. This must be just a joke; they *had* to be joking.

'Hahaha; very funny,' he said, trying not to sound too hurt. 'Go ahead, have a joke on the Visitor. I'll get you back one day.'

He expected the boys to roll down on the ground laughing out loud, but they just sat there looking all serious.

'Dan, it's the truth,' said Nemo.

'Right, "the truth". You expect me to believe that every morning Heli here is transformed from a man into a giant ball of burning fire that travels across the sky, lighting and warming up the earth, until evening comes, at which point Hëna is transformed into a big round rock that shines over the earth from dusk, 'till dawn?'

'Pretty much, yeah,' Nemo answered, insisting on keeping his poker face on. Daniel still couldn't even consider the possibility of this being true.

'Right, and I'm the Morning Star,' he said in a final effort to make them admit they were playing him.

'Actually, I see him every day,' Heli replied to this one, still sounding dead serious. 'Now, *he's* the funny one, always coming up with new jokes. I don't know where he gets them. Listen to this one he told me this morning.

'A guy tells a girl: "*Baby, your teeth are like stars.*" The girl starts going "*Aw...,*" but the guy continues, "*So yellow and far away from each other.*" Hahaha...'

Heli resumed laughing, joined by Nemo, who actually thought the joke was very funny. Séraphin pretended to be otherwise occupied, but wasn't fooling anyone, as chuckles could be heard braking through his jaws of steel.

Daniel was stuck; he didn't know what to think. The boys seemed to be serious about this; was there a chance that they were actually telling him the truth?

Why not, he thought to himself. *I have seen and heard things far less believable here; why would this be the exception?*

He looked up at the moon again, trying to imagine Hëna up there, all alone in the dark. This was beyond weird. What were the chances that the moon, which he had always loved, and the beautiful girl he was starting to have a crush on, were one and the same? How does this happen, even in a dreamworld?

Heli's voice interrupted his thoughts.

'Hëna says: "*you should see your face right now*".'

'What? She can talk to you?'

'Yes; we are twins after all. We can always hear each other's thoughts, no matter how far we are. I guess, it compensates for the fact that we can never meet.' There was sadness in his voice now.

Daniel looked at the moon again, feeling a bit exposed. It all sounded very unbelievable, but then again, this wouldn't be a dreamworld without something like this in it.

'You guys are not playing me, are you?' he gave them one last chance to admit they were fibbing. Their answer did little to convince him otherwise; he would have to eventually decide for himself whether to believe this or not, but he felt that he already did. And as he allowed himself to believe, he felt amazed yet again at this wonderful world and all the magic it was made of.

All that evening his thoughts wandered around the moon and the stars up in the night sky, and he struggled to fall asleep. When he finally dozed off, he got lost into the abyss that was the realm beyond both worlds, and where nothing and no one could reach him. Dreams would not disturb him this night either, giving his mind a much-needed chance to rest and reboot. Morning would now find him refreshed and ready for another day of travelling and new mysteries.

* * *

Three more days they rode, and when the sun rose up for the fourth one since they left Arba, the city of Tálas appeared far ahead on the horizon, still at least half a day ahead of them. They were now riding along the shoreline, with the sea breathing peacefully to their left. As far as he was concerned, Daniel had never actually seen the sea agitated here, yet another curious detail of this wondrous world.

They'd slept fewer hours that night; their bodies were now getting used to the new regime and they did not feel as tired as during the first couple of days. Daniel found it interesting that, before the bracelet, he had never really felt tired in this world, no matter what he did. He wondered what else had changed since that day.

They rode non-stop the whole day under the warm sunlight and the sweet company of the sound of waves. As always, Séraphin flew ahead of them, while Hëna rode in front of them, leading them on the ground. By now, Nemo was feeling comfortable enough riding Alma, though he had begun to complain that his backside felt numb from riding all day long.

Daniel sympathized with his younger friend, yet he felt that such trivia were unworthy of even claiming his attention, let alone sharing it with the others. No, he had more important things to occupy his mind and time with. Try as he might, he could not help but think of Autumn's warning about how much time he had before his body gave up in his world. Not even Diane could give him any answers on this. She was the only other person to ever wear the bracelet, yet she could not say how long it had taken for her body to let go. And even if she could tell him, he wasn't sure that would help; every individual was different, and they experienced the dreamworld in different ways. He could only hope that they would find this Great Lord soon enough.

As the day wore on and they got closer to Tálas, the city began to rise and take shape before them, presenting Daniel with yet another wonder like nothing he'd ever seen. It was built entirely above water, at the foot of a tall white cliff where a huge bay was formed that hosted the whole city with its hundreds of houses and buildings. On top of the cliff he could see a single house standing at its very edge, as if defying gravity and the city below.

'That's where the Oracle lives,' Hëna said, stopping to wait for them. A light breeze blew in from the sea, trying to play with her long black hair, which was tied hastily in a single braid.

Daniel and Nemo stopped where she was and looked ahead at the amazing city lying before them. It was past midday, and it would take another half hour for them to reach its outskirts. The Oracle's house, however, was an entirely different matter; they would have to go back around the cliff in order to easily climb up there, and that might take them a good two extra hours on their horses.

Daniel wanted to waste no time in meeting the Oracle, but he could not let the opportunity to visit Tálas go to waste. He might never again have the chance. Besides, Nemo was looking forward to meeting with his people, who made up more than half of the population down there. So, they agreed to visit the city first and spend a few hours there, before climbing up to see the Oracle. And so they did.

Nathaniel's father kept walking back and forth in the living room, while his mother sat next to him, pondering what their son had just shared with them. Nobody spoke for a good while and Nathaniel was getting rather nervous. He could sense his parents' disappointment with his actions, or rather lack of, and he did not blame them. He felt ashamed of what he had done and how he had handled Azariel, but there was no turning back now. The wheels had been set in motion and he needed to decide what he was going to do from here on. For that, he needed his parents' advice.

His father's light grey and blue wings twitched every few seconds behind him as the old wingman considered how to best respond to his son. Without raising his eyes from the living room floor, he spoke slowly and with half a voice, as if to himself at first.

'I will not deny that I am gravely disappointed in you, Nathaniel. I thought we raised you better than this, I thought I...' He stopped there. Then, as if a different thought crossed his mind, he shook his head and resumed speaking, this time louder.

'No, I will not take the blame for this. We've done our job right, your mother and I; others are responsible for this. This is your friend's doing, his influence has always been too strong on you.' He paused there and when he spoke again, his voice was softer. 'Still, I am glad that you've finally acknowledged this and want to set things right. Perhaps, not all is lost.'

His father's words weighed heavily on Nathaniel. His mother took his hand in hers and caressed his cheek, as she looked at him, pain veiling her gentle eyes.

'This is indeed grave news you have given us, son, even more so as you are partially responsible for what's about to happen. I never thought I would live to see this day come. You must do all that you can to make things right again. You must tell the truth.'

'Yes, but to whom?' his father asked. 'Who will listen to him? Who will believe him now? Even if he manages to get to the queen, which I highly doubt, will she take his word over that of Azariel, the son of her best adviser and friend? She has gone too far to question her own actions on the words of a young wingman with dubious reasons; she'll want to believe that she's done the right thing. No, he cannot go to the queen, not directly anyway. Someone else must be the one to get to her.'

'What about Ariel? He's an honourable man; I believe he would do the right thing, even if his own son is involved.'

'I don't know, mom. This was difficult enough telling you; I don't know if I can tell the father of my best friend that his son is plotting to send us to war with the mermaids and is doing it all for him.'

'Well, you don't have to put it in so many words, Nathaniel,' his father suggested, apparently pondering the idea. 'In any case, it's to be expected that whatever you tell him, Ariel will go to his son first, before he decides to talk to the queen. He'll want to hear it out of his own mouth; I know I would. Still, I think your mother is right, you should go to him. Tell him what you did, only what you did, and let him get to the rest of the truth on his own.'

'But Azariel will know that I've betrayed him, father. He'll come for me; he'll come for you both if he can't have me. I couldn't live with myself if anything happened to you.'

His father now sat beside him and looked into his repentant eyes for the first time that evening. He put one hand on the boy's hands and the other on his wife's, positioning himself next to her and speaking for the both of them.

'And we couldn't live with ourselves if thousands of innocent wingmen and mermaids were to die because we were too afraid to do the right thing. Understand this, Nathaniel, there is no turning back from here; someone *will* have to make sacrifices in order to stop war from happening. And if that were to be our fate, we would willingly and gladly accept it.'

He looked at his wife as he said this. She did not speak, but merely nodded in agreement, with a brave smile on her troubled face. Then they both looked at their son, who put his head down in shame and despair.

'I'm so sorry...,' was all Nathaniel managed to say, with tears rolling down his face. The thought of losing his parents was now more than a horrible prospect. He felt angry at himself for letting things come to this; whatever he did now, he risked someone getting hurt. It was only a matter of choosing the lesser evil, and though he hated it, his father was right; the sacrifice of a few was better than the loss of many. He just couldn't deal with the fact that his parents might be the ones to end up paying for his mistakes.

It was late afternoon when they finally climbed the cliff and approached the house of the Oracle. Outside it, Daniel saw the familiar face of a woman hanging her laundry out to dry. Her curly brown hair held back by a yellow ribbon was unmistakable as she moved between the white sheets with her sleeves rolled up. Whatever doubts he might have had until then about the Oracle helping them were all gone when

Daniel realized that Veronica was his wife. She would surely help him get some much-needed answers.

The horses galloped into her front yard and Veronica turned around, her eyes lighting up as she spotted Daniel.

'Daniel, darling; you came. What a wonderful surprise! Come down here and give me a big hug.'

Daniel climbed off his horse, and after passing the reins to Nemo, walked towards her. Veronica met him halfway and locked her arms tight around him, causing him to blush from head to toe. Hëna, Nemo and Séraphin got their own dose of Veronica right after him.

'We knew you'd visit us at some point but did not expect it to be so soon. It is so lovely to see you again. How was the trip? Did you enjoy it?' she asked, directing her questions mainly at Daniel.

'I did,' he answered, 'thank you. I enjoyed it very much; especially since I had such great company.'

'What? I know you're not talking about chatterbox here,' Hëna teased, pointing at Nemo. 'The guy never stops talking.'

'I do too,' Nemo responded in his own defence, sounding hurt. 'I only speak when there's something worth saying. The moment I'll have nothing to say, I promise I will shut up.'

'Yeah, that'll be the day,' Hëna replied laughing.

'Veronica,' Séraphin stepped forward, ignoring the others, and bowing ever so slightly, showing his good manners. 'Always a pleasure to see you.'

'Lovely to see you, Séraphin, as always. How is your mother?'

'She is well, thank you. She sends her regards.'

'Why, thank you; that's very kind. Please, do give her my love next time you see her.'

She looked behind them on the horizon, as if waiting for something or someone, and then opened her arms wide, nudging them towards the front door to her house.

'Why don't we go inside? It will get dark soon and my husband will be home any minute now. This will be such a nice surprise for him. He's been looking forward to meeting you, you know?'

She slipped her arm inside Daniel's and directed him towards the house.

'So, tell me, any luck getting that ring to my Sam?'

Daniel was more than happy that he had at least some good news to give that day.

'Oh, I didn't even have to look for her, you know? She found me. She looks so much like you that I knew who she was the moment I saw her.'

He went on to tell her everything as they made their way inside the house and sat down, talking like two old friends.

The Oracle returned home not long after their arrival. As had become the norm by now, he was not at all what Daniel had expected. Whenever he'd read in his books about Oracles or prophets, they were always associated with temples, powers, or celibacy. They were most often people isolated and set apart to worship and serve their gods. But as with everything else in Endërland, what was going on here was far from what Daniel thought he knew. This was no temple, just a simple house where two people lived; and the Oracle was nothing but a short man, seemingly in his early forties, dressed as commonly as everyone else and with nothing apparently special about him. What did stand out, though, to Daniel anyway, were his eyes. From the moment he saw him, Daniel could swear he had seen those eyes before, and not that long ago either. He just could not recall where.

'Darling, look, we have visitors,' Veronica exclaimed as soon as he set foot inside the door. The man proceeded to take off his shoes and place them by the door with the rest, and then walked into the living room, where the four travellers were gathered next to the fireplace.

'Hëna, Séraphin, Nemo, so good to see you all,' he greeted them, hugging them one by one, and leaving Daniel for last. 'And you must be Daniel. It's really an honour. It has been a very long time since I've had the pleasure of entertaining a Visitor. I'm the Oracle, as you might have guessed by now, but you can just call me Alfie, or Al, if you prefer.'

Now there's an unusual name for an Oracle, Daniel thought to himself, but out loud he said.

'The honour is mine, Alfie. Thank you very much for your hospitality. I know it's a bit late, but we just had to visit Tálas on our way here.'

'Yes, the city is amazing, isn't it? And don't worry about it being late; Veronica is going to prepare some dinner for us, we're going to eat and then we can talk business. I'm sure you did not come all this way just to see us. Of course, you're going to sleep here tonight, and that's non-negotiable.'

As promised, dinner was served soon. They feasted on a bountiful selection of pies, fruits, and cakes that Veronica put on the table for them, everything scrumptious to the last bit. Having been a homemaker all her life, she knew a thing or two about cooking, even though she now practiced it mostly for pleasure.

Daniel ate until he was full and could eat no more, then he sat back, watching Nemo help himself numerous times. Even Séraphin seemed to enjoy the food very much, especially the cakes. Hëna ate very little, always looking out the window, knowing that soon the sun would go down and she would have to leave.

Sure enough, daylight grew dimmer as the sun dived west into the sea, and Hëna got up from the table, thanking Alfie and Veronica for their hospitality and a delicious dinner. Saying goodnight to the rest of the guys, she walked out of the front door and left for the night. Daniel watched her go with a sense of melancholy. He was always glad to see Heli, but somehow, he could not help but feel an emptiness creep in every time she had to leave.

It wasn't long after when Heli joined them, looking blissfully happy at the sight of the table full of delicious goods. The Oracle and his wife welcomed him like an old friend and showed him to the seat Hëna had previously occupied. They all waited for him to finish eating before moving back to the fireplace, now sipping on a hot cup of tea.

Time had now come to talk business, so they let Heli tell the Oracle everything that had been going on since the celebrations, and why they had come all this way to see him. Séraphin sat there quiet, listening to Heli recount everything and making sure his face did not betray his emotions, while the Oracle took his time digesting all the new information. Daniel had to remind himself that his role as an Oracle was to simply pass on messages from the Great Lord to the people, so it was only natural that he didn't know everything.

The Oracle was silent for a short moment, before he decided to voice his thoughts aloud.

'So, it has finally begun.'

His tone reflected the sorrow that suddenly overshadowed his face. Veronica put one hand on his shoulder, trying to comfort him.

'You knew this day would come darling; it was only a matter of time.'

'That still doesn't make it any easier,' he replied.

Daniel had a feeling of déjà-vu, as once again others around him seemed to know things he didn't. This time, however, he intended to ask.

'Excuse me, but how did you know?'

The Oracle looked at him and simply said.

'Let's just say that, being the Oracle of the Great Lord, I have access to certain information that other people do not.'

'You mean, the Great Lord told you this would happen?'

'Not in so many words,' the Oracle answered, but did not elaborate. Daniel was not satisfied by his answer though.

'Does this have anything to do with all the changes that are happening in Endërland? The bad weather in the north, people and animals disappearing?'

Séraphin looked at Daniel, taken aback; this was all news to him. Heli on the other hand did not look surprised.

'It has everything to do with it,' the Oracle replied, 'and many other things happening around us that you are unaware of. Endërland is changing by the minute, and you are not going to like what it is becoming.'

'But what does this all have to do with Nemo and me? Why are we being framed for something we didn't do?'

Séraphin chuckled at the question in disbelief. The others ignored him.

'I wish I knew how you fit into all of this, Daniel, but unfortunately I don't. It could be that you were just caught in the middle of something planned a long time ago; or maybe someone has other plans for you. I'm afraid, my guess is as good as yours at this point.'

'Can't you talk to the Great Lord?' it was Nemo who spoke this time. 'Can't you ask him to show up and help us sort things out? Or at least tell us how to find him?'

The Oracle looked at the faces in front of him, expectant and hopeful. He sighed and got up from the couch, turning his back at them for a moment.

'I'm afraid, it is now my turn to give you some bad news. I have told no one of this until now; I wish I wouldn't have to, but I see no other choice.' He paused for just a moment and then turned around to face them again. 'I haven't heard from the Great Lord in a very long time. I do not know where he is, or even if he is still around. For all I know, he may have left us for good and we'll never see him again. I'm sorry, but I don't know how to help you find him.'

Nobody spoke. A cloud of desperation descended in the air above them as they began to realize that their quest had failed before it even started.

Daniel lowered his eyes on the floor, while his hand instinctively went to his bracelet. He was doomed; he would never get back home, see his father again. His body would eventually give up and he would die. And if Winter took over Endërland, he stood no chance of living for long in this world either. It was so unfair; after all, he had done nothing wrong.

'He can't have left us.' Nemo was the first to break the silence, refusing to believe the Oracle's words. 'We need him.'

'We haven't needed him for a very long time, Nemo,' the Oracle corrected him. 'He created a near perfect world here for us, so much so that we never had need of him or anything else. He's probably gone somewhere else where he is wanted.'

'But we need him now,' Nemo insisted. 'He can't just abandon us.'

'I'm not saying he has. My dear Nemo, the fact of the matter is that I simply do not know. I'm as much in the dark here as you are.'

'He could still be around, guys.' This time it was Heli who spoke, trying to inject some of his optimistic attitude to the rest of the group. 'We can't assume that he's gone forever just like that. Maybe he's retreated somewhere in the kingdom, and we just need to find him.'

'Yeah, like in his secret castle,' Séraphin said mockingly.

'Why not?' Heli replied.

'There is no castle, son of Autumn; it's just a legend, a fairy tale.'

'Actually, that's not quite true,' the Oracle intervened. 'I have it on very good authority that his castle does exist. It was the first thing he ever built when he came to Endërland; before he banished all evil in the Shadow Forest. That is where he lived in the beginning.'

'Where is it?' Nemo asked, filled with new hope. The Oracle looked at him, sad that he'd have to disappoint the young boy once again.

'I do not know. I have never been there myself, nor have I been told where it lies. I know of only one who has come from there and is still around. But alas, you have as much hope of getting the secret out of him, as you have from the Great Lord himself.'

'Why? Who is that?' Heli asked.

The Oracle exchanged looks with Veronica, knowing the kind of reaction that this next answer would provoke. She nodded her head, encouraging him to answer.

'He is the Great Lord's oldest and most faithful friend; the first being to have ever been brought into existence in Endërland, his stallion.'

He stopped speaking and just stood there staring at the faces of the young ones sitting in front of him, all stunned and speechless. He had expected this and worse.

The next words came from Séraphin.

'A horse? And just how is a horse supposed to tell us where his master's castle is? That's assuming he even knows at all.'

'I wish I had an answer for that, Sky-Prince,' said the Oracle, 'but I don't. I can tell you this, however, this is not just any horse we're talking about; this is the Great Lord's long-time companion and friend. He is no mere animal; he is a free spirit, smart as he is strong and fast. He lets no man ride him and is impossible to catch, running around the kingdom as he pleases. Something tells me that he knows the castle and he can help.'

'I guess it's just a matter of catching him, then,' Heli said standing up, as if getting ready to go after the horse right away. 'I think I know just where we might find him.'

'This is crazy,' Séraphin exploded, now losing it completely. 'You have all gone mad. First, they claim they're being framed by some great conspirator, who is apparently plotting to destroy the entire kingdom; then you want to go after the ghost of a horse who cannot be caught, hoping he will just lead you to a legendary castle that may or may not exist, and that even if it did, it will probably be impossible to find. And, if by some miracle we manage to find it, what then? We have absolutely no guaranty that the Great Lord will be there, waiting for us. This mission has turned into a joke overnight. I don't want any part in this.'

He got up and made for the door, but the voice of Daniel, who had remained silent until then, stopped him halfway.

'I don't think you have a choice, Sky-Prince.'

Séraphin turned around slowly to face Daniel, anger reddening his usually noble face. The others looked at Daniel, taken completely by surprise.

'What did you just say to me?' Séraphin demanded. Even if his face did not betray him, his menacing tone said it all. Daniel continued to speak, seating where he was, outwardly untroubled by the wingman's reaction.

'As I understand it, you were sent to follow us and keep the Council informed of our progress at all times. The choice of the direction and path we take does not lie with you, but with Nemo and me. We were the ones charged with finding the Great Lord, and that's just what we intend to do. If you turn back now, you will be disobeying the Council, and I don't think you want to do that. So, why don't you take your anger, your hate, your superiority complex, and whatever else you can manage to cram inside that bird skull of yours and just fly along as we go wherever we must?'

Without realizing it, Daniel had gotten up and was now staring down at Séraphin. He was furious. All this time he had just been sitting by, listening to Séraphin talk the way he did about him and Nemo, and though he had tried his best not to let it get to him, he could take it no more. Enough is enough, and he was done taking like a coward everything that Séraphin dished out. This stopped here.

Still, he regretted getting angry and insulting the wingman as soon as the words left his mouth. But he was not going to step back; this prince needed to know that he could not just treat them the way he did and get away with it.

Séraphin's face grew redder than raspberry sauce, and his eyes got even smaller than they usually looked. He marched in the direction of Daniel, wings rising up as if ready for flight. With a booming voice that he seemed to gather from the bottom of his lungs, he screamed.

'How dare you talk to me like that? You are nothing compared to me; less than that, you are...'

'That's enough,' the Oracle shouted, cutting Séraphin's words in the middle. 'This is my house and there will be no fighting in here.'

The boys stopped advancing towards each other, severing their eye contact, as if suddenly realizing where they were.

'Daniel, that was not a nice thing to do, talking to Séraphin that way. It is not our custom, nor a common practice to insult one-another. I had hoped for better from you.

'And as for you, Séraphin, tell me please, what did you expect? You speak of these two boys with such disgust and hatred right in front of them, and then are surprised at their reaction? Don't you see what you have become, how you have changed? Do you still doubt that things are not what they used to be?'

'Well, if things are changing, it could only be his fault,' Séraphin snapped. 'All this started to happen when he showed up.'

'Are you sure? Would you bet your life and that of your fellow wingmen on that?'

Séraphin did not answer. He wanted to say 'yes', but he couldn't. So, he drew back and did not speak again. The Oracle, who had positioned himself between them, sat back down appearing despaired.

'This is how it begins; you know? A small fight between friends and brothers, and then punches are thrown, weapons are drawn, and very soon somebody gets killed. Before you know it, we have entire wars exploding, and nothing is as it used to be. Stopping this from happening is your real mission. You need to find the Great Lord; only he can restore order to the kingdom.'

Nemo, who'd stayed back during the confrontation, now stepped forward and faced Daniel.

'What do we do, Dan? Where do we go from here?'

Daniel looked thoughtfully at the Oracle for a moment and then turned to Heli.

'Did you say you know where we might find this horse?'

Heli smiled; glad that he could share some good news at last.

'Funny thing, actually. For the last two days now, I've noticed a pitch-black horse sprinting like crazy all the way down from the Northern Mountains. It appears his general direction is the western seaside. I'll talk to Hëna, though she might have trouble locating him in the dark, but if I'm right, he should be in the area as we speak.'

'That's Lightning, alright,' the Oracle said, a smile forming on his face now, as if brought on by fond memories.

'Lightning?' Daniel asked.

'Yes. He is completely black, except for a white patch on his forehead in the shape of a lightning bolt. And he is lightning fast and tireless. This is good news indeed, Daniel; I think Lightning is coming to meet you. The Great Lord might not be gone after all.'

'So, what do we do, Daniel?' Nemo repeated the question.

Daniel looked down at his bracelet again, then at Nemo, the Oracle and finally Séraphin, on whom his eyes rested. He made two steps towards the wingman and spoke to him directly.

'I'm sorry for what I said to you in my anger; it was wrong of me. I hope you'll forgive me and continue to fly with us, because we need you.'

Séraphin just stood there, completely ignoring what he said, but Daniel didn't care. He turned to Nemo and proceeded to answer his question.

'I do not know how much time I have left, or what chance we have at finding the Great Lord, but I'm going to follow hope wherever it leads us, and I will not give up until it fails us, or we have succeeded. Are you with me?'

Nemo beamed at him and gave him a high-five.

'You bet I am. This is *our* adventure, remember? I won't let you have all the fun without me.'

'Good,' Daniel said and then turned to Heli. 'Lead the way, son of Autumn. Let's go meet Lightning.'

Chapter 9

LIGHTNING & THUNDER

Standing in the middle of the small room that served as his studio, Ariel wished he could shut his ears and block out his son's words. He had hoped against hope that somehow Nathaniel had grown angry and resentful against his son and had made everything up just to hurt him. But as he stood before Azariel, confronting him about the accusations, his worst fears came true all at once. In one single moment his whole world had come crumbling down, and he realized he had no one to blame but himself. He had been too careless with Azariel, dotting on him more than he should have, spoiling him too much. And this was the result of all his love and affection.

Azariel knelt before him, pleading with his eyes and words.

'Don't you see, father? I did this for you. You can finally have your rightful place in the kingdom; enjoy the love and respect of all wingmen as their true king. You deserve it.'

Ariel pushed his son away from him, struggling not to be overcome by disgust.

'Stop saying that,' he screamed at Azariel. 'I already have all that I want; I have never asked for more.'

'Yes, because you are too humble and noble...'

'Because I know my place and I'm happy with it. But you clearly don't. No, you are not doing this for me, Azariel; you're doing this for yourself. Pride has found its way inside your heart and it's eating you up, poisoning your mind. Whoever planted that seed, son, knew very well what they were doing.'

'No, father; I swear, I only did it for you.'

'Enough, I cannot hear you say that anymore; you have no idea what it is you're really saying. How could you think I would be alright with thousands of innocent people, *our* people dying in war; our villages and cities destroyed, our lives changed forever just so I can have a throne? What kind of a person do you think I am, to be able to live with that kind of responsibility and burden in my conscience? At what point did you take complete leave of your senses, son? When did you become so cruel and heartless, to allow for a genocide to take place, just so you can get what you want? Or are you blind and foolish not to see that that's exactly what you've brought upon us? Don't you realize what you've done? You have single-handedly destroyed our entire world and are laying it all in front of my feet. But I will not let you, no.'

He grabbed his son by his left arm and lifted him off the floor, making for the door.

'You are coming with me to the queen, and we will tell her everything. It is not too late to change things; we can still stop the worse from happening.'

Completely disappointed and angry at the reaction and treatment he was getting from his father; Azariel shook him off and stayed where he was.

'I'm not going anywhere.'

Ariel saw the look in his son's eyes and understood. He wanted to beg and plead with him to come to his senses, to be the good boy that he knew he was, and do the right thing. But he was too angry and too in a hurry to undo his son's mistake that he decided he did not need Azariel to talk to the queen.

'Fine, you stay here; the queen *will* listen to me, she always has. I will not have the kingdom torn apart and my name written in blood on the account of a fool.'

He turned and headed for the door with a broken heart. His only son, his pride and joy had brought him such pain and shame, and now he would have to let all of Endërland know that he had failed as a father. He felt completely destroyed and weak, as if all his life-force had suddenly left him.

As he reached for the door, he heard a faint sound behind him, followed immediately by a sharp pinch on his back. He stopped and searched with his left hand to find the source of the pain. To his shock, his hand met with a hard object sticking out of his back, piercing through his wings, and lodged just between his shoulders. A crazy heat began surging through his whole body and he became aware of a stronger pain inside his chest. Hot sweat began pouring uncontrollably out of every pore of his skin.

He looked behind his back and finally saw the arrow sticking out of his flesh. Stunned beyond words, he raised his eyes towards his son, only to see a crossbow in his hands and anger in his face. Burning tears began pouring as he realized what had just happened. He tried to take one step towards Azariel but found that his legs no longer obeyed his command. With his arms stretched in the direction of his son and his wings completely limp, he fell face forward, darkness overtaking him.

Azariel dropped the crossbow at his feet, terrified at the realization of what he had just done. He ran to his father, and turning him face up, tried to shake him awake, but to no avail. Ariel would not respond. There was no sign of movement or breathing in him; the only thing that seemed to be happening was the tears that somehow kept flowing from his now closed eyes. Azariel kept calling him, begging for his forgiveness, and hugging him, but he was gone.

Anger, hurt, and guilt came over him all at once in such a magnitude that he felt he was going to explode. Around his chest, he felt a strong invisible grip that threatened to crush his bones inwards, while at the same time his heart beat like it wanted to burst out and run away from him.

His mind was frantically looking for a reason to justify what had just happened and make this a bit more bearable for him. Soon, it found one. Nathaniel's face came to his mind, the one who had betrayed him to his father, and that's when hate joined the cocktail of emotions inside him. With a voice that would drown out the loudest of thunders, he held his father's lifeless body in his arms and screamed as loud as he could.

'Nathaniel....'

Under the bright light of the moon the four boys and the Oracle left the house on foot, heading towards the nearby forest down the east side of the hill; the same way they had first come from. Tálas lay behind them below the cliff, hidden under the cloak of darkness.

They continued to climb downhill onto a vast bare field, making for the forest in front of them, as per Hëna's instructions. They'd only managed to get a few hours of sleep that night, until she woke Heli up, telling him that Lightning was close. They'd all decided to come out and intercept him. According to Hëna they should be able to see him very soon.

The boys walked in silence, apart for the occasional noises that came from Nemo's stomach. The red-haired boy had eaten so much the previous evening, that he was having trouble walking properly, and would stop every few minutes to burp, something he had never in his life done before. Daniel smiled at his embarrassed face, while the others kept laughing every time, all except for Séraphin, of course.

'How do we catch him?' he asked after some time.

'Leave that to me,' Heli answered in his usual confident manner. 'I've had my good share of horse taming; I know a thing or two.'

'Horse taming?' Daniel asked again. 'I thought all animals were friendly here.'

'Well, they are. But you see, there is a special breed of horses, to which I'm guessing our Lightning belongs, that simply refuse to be mounted by anyone. I've had the opportunity of taming a couple of them, and I don't think Lightning would be much more trouble than they were.'

'I wouldn't be so sure,' the Oracle intervened. 'The breed you are talking about are not just his race; they're his family, his sons and daughters. Lightning is their father and king, and if you think that he is gonna make it as easy for you as some of them have, you got another thing coming. I think you're about to meet your match, son of Autumn.'

'Yeah, "son of Autumn",' Daniel added, making fun of the title. Heli laughed with him, not bothered by it. He then replied.

'We shall see about that.'

He refused to believe that there was anything he could fail at. Daniel liked that about him, the confidence; he wished he had a bit more of that himself. Right now, he could really use some, not knowing what each next step would bring and if he would succeed. Even though he would never admit this to the others, he did not fear just running out of time; he was also afraid of what or who he might have to face before this was all over, or that he might not be strong enough. After all, he wasn't some hero from a story, even though he certainly found himself inside one; he was just a city boy, who had never done anything remarkable in his entire life. *I mean, my dad still won't let me go to the beach on my own,* he told himself as if trying to win the argument.

'I see him,' Séraphin interrupted Daniel's inner monologue.

'Where?' Heli jumped, trying to see in the direction Séraphin was pointing. After a short while though he gave up, unsuccessfully. 'I don't see him.'

'You will in a minute,' Séraphin said, feeling all smug.

They were all staring intently ahead towards the edge of the forest where Séraphin had pointed, but they couldn't see anything. The moon illuminated the whole field in front of them with a beautiful white glow, yet they could see no sign of movement. Then, just as if appearing from nowhere, they noticed first a white mark in the shape of a lightning bolt not twenty feet ahead, followed by a shiny pair of big eyes that seemed to be observing them intently. They all halted where they were, amazed at how stealthily the large stallion had approached. Even now that he stood before them and they were beginning to make out his silhouette, they could barely hear him breathe or move.

Gasping with their mouths wide open, the four boys could not believe their eyes. The stallion standing before them was enormous, almost twice the size of a normal horse.

His legs were long and thin, but clearly firm and strong. His body was all muscle and no fat, his pitch-black skin firm and shiny, as if he was still in his prime. His long black hair fell to the right of his face and his eyes were deep and full of life. It was eerie how human they appeared to be.

As Lightning stood there, observing each one of them and deciding if they were friends or foes, Heli motioned to the others to be quiet and not move, while he slowly put one foot in front of the other towards him.

'Heli, don't,' the Oracle whispered, but Heli ignored him and kept moving.

He was getting closer and closer, approaching with a slow and steady step, all the while talking to the stallion with a soothing voice, assuring him that he meant him no harm. Eventually he got close enough to touch him on the shiny forehead, while Lightning still made no movement. Thinking that the stallion had granted permission to be touched, Heli raised his hand. That's when Lightning decided to react. As if someone had suddenly pinched him hard, he let out a high-pitched cry and rose on his hind legs, threatening to crush Heli with his front two.

Trying to avoid being kicked, Heli quickly drew backwards, stumbling as he did and breaking the fall with his hands. Séraphin moved fast behind him and pulled him away from the stallion's reach.

Half scared out of his wits; Heli laughed nervously.

'Ha-ha, you weren't kidding, Alfie; he's a feisty one, and cunning too.' He stood up again, shaking the grass off his clothes. 'I might need a bit more time here.'

'Wait, don't try anything else for now,' said the Oracle. 'Let us see what he's going to do first.'

As if taking a cue from the Oracle, Lightning calmed down again and began slowly trotting towards them. He eyed them all one by one, skipping Heli, and finally, after a moment's hesitation, decided to approach the Oracle, nudging him on the face with his large nose. Pleased, the Oracle raised his hands and began stroking him gently.

'Hello, old friend, I'm so glad you remember me. It's been a while, hasn't it?'

The others watched with wonder as the two greeted each other like friends that haven't met in a very long time. There was such joy in the Oracle's eyes and a huge smile on his face, replacing the worry of the previous evening as if wiped completely from memory.

'That's right,' he said, looking toward the boys, 'we've met before, in another time and another life. He even let me ride him once; you cannot imagine the thrill of flying against the wind faster than the wingmen themselves.'

As if recalling the same memories, Lightning aligned himself into position, motioning with his head for the Oracle to mount him. Heli watched from a distance, not without jealousy. The Oracle smiled again and stroked his long muscular neck.

'You don't know how much I would like that,' he spoke to the stallion, as if he could understand him perfectly, 'but not today, my friend. Right now, there is someone I would like you to meet.'

Keeping his hand on the stallion's neck, the Oracle walked towards Daniel, with Lightning trotting along. He let out a faint snort when they passed by Heli, otherwise completely ignoring Nemo and Séraphin. They finally stopped in front of Daniel, who was feeling as intimidated as he was amazed by this creature. He had been around horses often enough, and even though he enjoyed riding them, he wouldn't exactly call himself an aficionado. Nor were they his favourite animals; he much preferred the safer company of cats, most of the time. Yet, finding himself in front of this larger than life creature, it made him feel once again just as

247

he did when he first met Eleanor by the sea, reverence and awe being the dominating feelings among many others.

'This is Daniel,' the Oracle introduced him to the stallion. 'I think you know why he is here.'

Lightning shook his head once in response, blowing air through his nostrils. He then stretched his long neck to take a sniff at Daniel, who had to keep himself from stepping back and away from him.

'This is your moment, Daniel,' the Oracle said. 'I have a feeling that him showing up here is not a coincidence. The Great Lord may have sent him, or maybe he has felt that we need his help to find his master. If he likes you, he might lead you to him, but you have to show that you are not afraid.'

Daniel understood. He wasn't really afraid, just a bit unsure about the whole thing. Yet, his gut told him to just go with it. With confidence, he raised both his hands towards Lightning and touched his smooth black skin. The stallion seemed hesitant and doubtful at first, but then he decided to let him stroke him, appearing to enjoy the contact.

A few moments passed, and as Daniel grew more confident in his contact with Lightning, the others remained silent, bearing witness to this little miracle. Daniel could almost feel Hëna smiling down on him, and that caused him to smile in return.

Then, the unexpected happened; Lightning turned his huge body around, prompting Séraphin and Nemo to move out of the way in the process, and aligned himself next to Daniel, nudging him lightly on the head.

'This is unbelievable,' the Oracle said. 'He's inviting you to ride him. I never thought I would live to see the day. Well, what are you waiting for? Mount him.'

Daniel looked at him, half surprised and half scared.

'But he has no saddle.'

'You won't need it; he won't let you fall. Come, lift your right foot.'

Daniel climbed on top of Lightning with the help of the Oracle, and barely managed to place his hands around his neck, when the stallion sprinted off in the direction of the forest from whence he had just come. Unable to hold on anywhere else, Daniel was forced to grab Lightning's long hair right in front of him, trying not to pull. The stallion did not seem to mind that, so he held on for the rest of the ride.

And what a ride it was. The Oracle was right; this was like nothing else he had ever experienced, and that included scuba diving, which was his favourite thing. The ground moved underneath them as if they were flying over it; the trees just seemed to blend with the invisible air, and even the stars seemed like they were struggling to catch up. They reached the forest in a minute, but Lightning did not go in; instead he turned right and continued running around the edge of the field, savouring the pleasure of riding with Daniel as much as Daniel himself was.

The Oracle and the boys decided to let them enjoy themselves and returned to the house, still barely believing what they had just witnessed. The mission that had seemed doomed until then, had suddenly gotten a new seed of hope, making them feel a bit more optimistic now. The fact that Lightning had appeared and seemed willing to help made at least one legend true. Hopefully, it would not be the only one.

In Sky-City word spread of yet another crime committed by the mermaids against the wingmen, and this time the victim was none other than one of the queen's chief advisers. An emergency meeting was called by the queen to discuss how they would respond to this new incident, despite Eleanor's assurance that her mermaids had nothing to do with Ariel's untimely demise. Meanwhile the Lords from Arba urged the flying folk to remain calm and allow them to deal with the situation following the proper channels. Sky-City buzzed with angry wingmen that spoke of revenge and justice.

Inside Nathaniel's nest, his mother was preparing for him a small rucksack with few things for him to take away, while his father kept watch by the window. Nathaniel sat on a chair with a lost look on his face.

'I still don't believe Azariel would hurt his own father; something else must have happened.'

'Maybe it wasn't him,' his father replied. 'Maybe it was Butler, or another one of the White Lord's men. All I know is that mermaids have nothing to do with this; they killed him because you told him the truth, and soon they will come for you.'

'I don't want to go, dad; I don't wanna leave you,' Nathaniel said. His father moved away from the window and came to seat beside him.

'You have to, son; you have no choice. The queen will most certainly give Azariel his father's position, and when the ceremony is over, he will come for you. You have to be far away from here by then.'

'But where do I go?'

'You need to find Prince Séraphin and make him listen to you; he's our only hope at this point. He is the only one who can get to the queen with the truth, so you fly towards Tálas and find the Oracle; maybe they're still there. If not, you will have to track them down and follow them until you find them. The future of the kingdom rests in your hands, son, and that's more important than you or us right now.'

Nathaniel hated being reminded of that all the time, but his father was right. He had to accept responsibility for his own actions and do his part to make things right again; he could not afford to be afraid anymore.

He stood up slowly and faced his parents.

'I will not fail this time, father; I will make you proud. Just promise me that you will look after yourselves; I don't want anything to happen to you.'

'Don't worry about us, sweetheart,' his mother said, passing him the rucksack, 'we'll be alright.'

'We will be right here waiting for your return with good news,' his father said. 'Now fly hard and don't look back. Keep the Northern Mountains to your right at all times, and never sleep close to the ground. If you fly fast enough and take as fewer breaks as possible, you should be able to reach Tálas in just over two days.'

They hugged each other one last time and then his father opened the overhead doors for Nathaniel to fly away in the evening sky.

'May the Great Lord watch over you, my son. Remember, we love you!'

Nathaniel jumped up in the air with a powerful flap of his wings, and after hovering above them for a few seconds and saying goodbye one last time, flew away in the dark.

Having said their thanks and goodbyes to the Oracle and Veronica, the party of four set off early morning from the house on top of the cliff as soon as Heli took his place in the clear morning sky. Leading the way on the ground this time was Daniel, now riding Lightning, instead of the grey steed that had carried him all the way from Arba. The Great Lord's

stallion had initially refused to be saddled, but the Oracle had
helped calm him down and they eventually managed to adapt
for him the saddle from the other horse. This would make
riding him much more comfortable for Daniel.

'I will only give you one advice,' the Oracle had told him
before they'd left. 'Few today remember what the Great Lord
looks like, and the younger ones,' he motioned towards
Séraphin and Nemo, 'have never seen him. It may be that
you'll come face to face with him, but not recognize him. So,
I suggest that you look for the signs, and when the time is
right, you will know. Good luck, Daniel!'

As soon as they'd all mounted their horses, ready to
resume their journey, Lightning had begun trotting without
waiting for a command or a direction. The reins only served
for Daniel to hold on during the ride, as he had no idea
which way they should go, nor would Lightning be led one
direction or another. They'd climbed down the north side of
the hill and were now following the coastline towards the
western part of the Northern Mountains, which were about
ten days ahead of them, depending on how fast they rode.

There was not much on the way between them and the
Mountains, except for a few small villages and then just
endless fields, hills and woods that few had ever visited. This
part of the kingdom was little known even to Heli and Hëna,
who had never been so far north from home. What little they
knew of it, came from watching and observing from high up
in the sky.

Daniel often wondered what it was like for Heli and
Hëna when they were up there, doing what they did, but so
far, he hadn't gotten a chance to talk to either of them about
it. At night, they usually slept and rested from the day's
activities, while Heli sat by the fire and kept guard, though
they did not really anticipate any trouble. As for Hëna, she

didn't really like to talk much, and she still kept a bit of a distance from him.

The only thing that Heli told him one night, after Daniel asked him why he never slept, was that he sort of did. He explained that whenever they were up in the sky, both he and Hëna were in a sleep like state; their own bodies were at rest from any physical activity, but they were still completely alert and conscious to everything that happened around or below them. So, they never really needed any sleep once back down. Daniel, more than anyone else, could understand that part.

That was pretty much all the information he had gotten from Heli ever since their true identities were revealed to him, but there was still so much he wanted to know.

It turned out, he would get that chance sooner than he expected.

That morning, as Lightning trotted with a rhythmic pace, seemingly pretty sure of where he was going, Hëna caught up to him, leaving Nemo to ride behind them, uncharacteristically quiet and lost in his own thoughts. She was riding Starlight, the white stallion she shared with Heli, while Séraphin, who disliked horses, continued to fly ahead above them, never going too far.

'So,' Hëna began, much to his surprise, 'the Great Lord's stallion huh? Wow, who would have thought that he would ever let someone else ride him? I remember hearing stories about him; how in the beginning the Great Lord could be seen riding him around the kingdom and how even long after the Great Lord disappeared, he would still be seen running here and there, as if keeping an eye on us. But that was ages ago; he hasn't been seen or heard of in a very long time. And now, all of a sudden, here he is, real and alive, allowing you to ride him. I wonder what it is he sees in you?'

To Daniel it sounded as if she was questioning Lightning's choice and that she had some reservations about him.

'You disapprove?' he asked her without meaning to. Hëna realized she must have given him the wrong impression and hurried to explain herself.

'Oh no, I'm sorry; that's not what I meant. I want you to know that I believe in you and Nemo completely, and that my brother and I will go with you all the way. What I was trying to say is, there must be a reason why Lightning decided to let someone ride him after all this time. So many men in the past have tried to catch him without success, until he went into hiding and became no more than a legend himself.'

Hearing her speak of the past, Daniel was dying to find out just how old she was, but didn't know how to ask without sounding rude, or giving away the fact that his interest extended beyond mere curiosity.

'How ol..., I mean when were you..., umm..., how long have you been around?' he finally settled on asking, feeling his face blush all over.

Hëna saw how nervous he became all of a sudden and smiled.

'I don't know,' she answered looking straight at him, something she seldom did. Her beautiful black eyes were impossible to avoid; they captivated him, and he hurried to look away, afraid she would realize just how much he really desired to get lost inside them.

'Growing up as a child, I used to count autumns; all the times my father would take his place on the Silver Throne. But after some time, I just stopped counting and forgot all about it. It seemed pointless since it meant nothing to anyone.

'And you; how old are *you*?'

Daniel blushed even more, realizing he hadn't been all that subtle, and that now she would most probably think of him way too young compared to her. He considered increasing his true age by a year or two at least, but even if he did that, he still could not match hers. Not to mention that if the truth came out, it wouldn't help his chances with her; not that he believed he actually had any.

'I had my eighteenth birthday only recently,' he answered, half expecting her to laugh at him. But Hëna did not laugh. She continued to ride alongside him, not speaking for a while. Daniel thought this was the perfect time to ask her a question or two.

'Can I ask you something?'

'Sure,' replied Hëna, appearing curiously open to it.

'What's it like when you're up there?' Daniel went ahead with the first one. Hëna fixated her bright eyes on him for another magic moment, and then cast her gaze away on the horizon.

'I don't really know how to explain it. It's all so unbelievably beautiful and magical, with not much to do but watch whatever happens down here. I make the same journey every night; I start up north over the Mountains, travelling all over Endërland through the night, and finish down south over the sea. My job is to make sure that the kingdom is always well lit, even at night while people sleep, and that's what I do.'

'But if you're up there during the night and Heli is up there during the day, does that mean that you never get to see each other?'

As soon as the last words left his mouth, he regretted them. Hëna's face grew sombre, and she suddenly looked sad.

'For one split second every time we trade places, we get to see each other again. We smile and wave to each other from a distance, but that's it.

'We were only children when we first started doing this; we used to be inseparable before that, like twins usually are. We did everything together and wouldn't bear to be apart even for a few minutes. But then we agreed to take over for those who were doing this before us and promised each other that we would be together again when the new sun and moon were chosen. But it's been so long, and I don't know if that day will ever come. You see, I didn't join this quest just for you guys; I have my own selfish reasons for wanting to find the Great Lord. We both love doing what we do, but now it's time for someone else to take over. I want to see my little brother again, I miss him; I wanna be able to touch him and hold him in my arms and spend time with him like we used to do.'

She looked up towards the sun, and Daniel could see the tears already drowning her eyes. He rebuked himself for being the reason for it and hurried to change the subject so that he could make her think and talk about other things.

'Is it lonely when you're up there all by yourself?'

It took more than a moment for her to take that bait, but eventually she looked at him again, a smile returning on her radiant face.

'Have you ever seen me all by myself up there? I tell you; sometimes it feels that the sky is even more crowded than the earth. All those stars that have nothing better to do at night but gossip about the people down here... And when they got nothing to talk about, they just sing, all night long until daylight. I know the mermaids can sing beautifully, but I'm telling you, Daniel, you haven't heard singing until you've heard the stars.'

For the first time ever, Daniel heard her say his name aloud, and a shudder reverberated through his entire body. He listened to her as she went on and on about the stars and their singing, and their jokes and games, and he wished she would never stop. And if it wasn't too much to hope for, he wished that one day *he* would be the one she would speak that way of. The passion in her voice, the light in her eyes, everything about her enchanted him; he was falling more and more under her spell, and he knew it.

It seemed to him that things changed a lot after that day, at least as far as he was concerned. Hëna no longer rode in front of them, keeping a distance from him; she now rode between him and Nemo, actively taking part in any and all conversations, many of which she initiated herself. They spoke of many things in the days that followed, and Daniel got many of the answers he was looking for, as well as giving some of his own to both her and Nemo.

The weather began to turn colder as the days went by, and the sky replaced its clear blue with the grey of the clouds, which were now almost always present. Rain began to fall frequently, causing them to take cover whenever and wherever they could. The sea also grew noisier and more agitated, while on dry land all trees were now almost bare of any leaves, green or yellow.

What did not change at all was Séraphin's mood. If anything, he became even more withdrawn and distant with each day. He lay in his hammock in the evenings, while the boys sat by the fire eating and talking to each other. A few times Daniel thought of approaching him and attempt to make some sort of connection, but then he would recall the wingman's reaction the first time he had tried that, and would decide against it. He was uncomfortable with the situation, however, and wished there was something he could do about it. He had never had any enemies before, even though 'enemy' probably wasn't the right word here. As far as he was concerned, they were all on the same side.

Nemo, on the other hand, tried as much as he could to stay away from Séraphin, not daring to even look his way whenever they were all together in the camp. Daniel felt bad that the boy was so afraid, and without being too obvious about it, he made sure that the two of them were never alone. He doubted that Séraphin would try anything else; the wingman may have been angry and full of hate, but he was one who craved respect and honour above all else and would do nothing that could jeopardize that. Still, Daniel did not wish Nemo to feel intimidated or uncomfortable at any time because of Séraphin.

Lightning continued to lead them towards the Northern Mountains, without ever showing signs of changing course as the days chased one-another into yesterday. They abandoned the shore for a while, as it continued far to the left of the path they were on, and rode amidst endless valleys and small woods that appeared to be increasingly void of any life. They were now entering the far north part of the kingdom, and Daniel thought of all the things his mother had told him and Nemo a while back. They could still see most of the smaller animals roaming about them as they rode through the woods, but there was no sign of anything else.

At the end of the fifth day, as the moon rose above them for the first time ever looking blood red, the boys went to bed to rest and regain some energy for the following morning. Riding was becoming quite uncomfortable and tiresome for both Daniel and Nemo who were not accustomed to it, and spent more time on the horses than Heli and Hëna did. Every evening they were glad for the opportunity to stretch their legs and rest, yet morning came again, when they reluctantly mounted the horses, getting back at it.

That evening, despite feeling quite tired, Daniel somehow struggled to fall asleep. His mind was overloaded with a thousand different thoughts, each one pertaining to a problem that demanded a solution. The Great Lord, the bracelet, Winter, his mom, his dad, Damien, Sam and Freddie, Sam and Hëna; the list went on and on, and he had no clue what to do about any of it. He knew that worrying would do him no good and solve nothing; and yet, he could not help it.

Séraphin was already fast asleep in his bed, as was Nemo next to him, judging by his light snoring. Heli sat by the fire, as always, working on a little wooden figurine.

The first time Daniel had seen him carving on the piece of wood with his small knife, he had been surprised. Somehow, he had never taken Heli for an artist. The blonde wonder would not tell him what he was working on, however, and Daniel would not push. He figured he'd find out when the time was right.

As the night wore on, Daniel kept tossing and turning for a good while longer, until he finally wandered off into his dreamless sleep. He must not have slept for more than a few hours, however, because when next Heli tried to wake him up, he grunted without opening his eyes and shoved him off, turning on the other side. But Heli apparently had no intention of letting him sleep. With his powerful hands, he grabbed Daniel as he lay under his blanket and lifted him off the ground, placing him on his feet with eyes wide open.

Confused and still barely awake, Daniel frowned as he noticed that it was still quite dark all around him.

'What's going on?' he asked, unable to control his yawning. 'Why did you wake me?'

'We have visitors,' Heli replied in a low voice, hurrying to wake Nemo up. 'Hëna saw a group of large animals coming down the mountains and heading towards us in a great hurry. She says she's never seen anything like them before and does not know what they are, but they don't look friendly. We best be prepared.'

He moved on to wake Séraphin up, while Nemo joined Daniel, who quickly relayed what Heli had just said. They hurried to gather their things and load them back unto their horses, while Séraphin began to argue that this was nonsense, and that Hëna must not have seen what she thought she did.

'I'm not gonna argue with you, Séraphin,' Heli told him sharply. 'We're gonna gather our belongings and leave the camp right away. If, whatever's coming means us harm, maybe on horses we'll be able to outrun them. You can stay here if you like and do as you see fit.'

He ran over to his things and made them into a quick bundle, loading it unto Starlight, who along with Nemo's brown mare began to whine and stump the ground nervously. Lightning made no sound and did not seem to be disturbed like the other two horses. However, as soon as Daniel had loaded everything, he whinnied with a sense of urgency and shook his head, motioning for him to climb on.

'I think we need to hurry,' Daniel said to the others. 'Lightning wants us to leave right away.'

'Climb on and ride hard,' Heli told him. 'We'll be right behind you.'

Daniel did as he was told, just as Nemo climbed onto Alma. Lightning did not wait but sprinted westward as soon as his rider got hold of the reins. He was riding so fast, that Daniel could not tell if the others were following or not; he just hoped they were.

The forest flew past him, with trees and their branches only a blur on Daniel's peripheral vision. He must have been riding pretty fast, because in the space of a couple of minutes, he lost sight of the guys, and everything around him was dead quiet. Too quiet in fact, not even the usual sounds of the night could be heard.

Not without struggling, he managed to convince Lightning to stop and wait for the others. For a moment, there was no sign of them, and then through the trees, he noticed first the white stallion that Heli was riding, and sitting behind him, Nemo, who was clutching on to Heli for dear life, all the while looking back at something. No sign of Alma or Séraphin.

'Keep riding,' Heli screamed at him as they approached. 'They're too fast and too many.'

Only then did Daniel hear something like distant howls growing closer and louder by the second. They sounded like wolves, only bigger and less natural. As they drew closer, he heard other noises, which he assumed were caused by their feet trampling everything in their path. To his terror, they were spreading all around them, and he feared they would soon be surrounded.

Lightning resumed his sprint just as Heli and Nemo flew past them, heading west. He caught up in no time and they were now riding side to side.

'What are they?' Daniel asked, shouting to be heard.

'I don't know,' Heli replied in the same manner. 'I've never seen them before. There are about a dozen of them, but four stayed behind and fell on Alma. Poor thing was terrified and wouldn't move.'

Daniel looked at Nemo, who was pale and would not speak. The howls kept closing in on them. He could ride faster if he wanted, but there was no way he would leave Heli and Nemo behind to save his neck.

'Where are we headed?' he asked again, looking back, and noticing several dark shapes appearing between the trees.

'Not far from here is the village of New Sotira. If we get there, we should be safe.'

'That's where my great-grandfather lives,' Daniel remembered out loud, then he glanced back again. The shapes were growing bigger and closer. He could make out about four of them now. In this speed, they would reach them within a minute or two.

'Can't he ride any faster?' he asked Heli again, motioning at Starlight.

'He's carrying two of us; he's doing the best he can.'

'What if we carry Nemo?'

Heli turned his head and looked back at the approaching threat.

'No time; they're too fast,' he said. 'We're gonna have to stop and defend ourselves.' He pulled on the reins of his horse and stopped at a small opening between the trees. He climbed down from Starlight, and going into the extra bag that Daniel had noticed the first day, took out what appeared to be a sword in its scabbard. He unsheathed it wasting no time, speaking to Daniel as he did.

'Now it's the time to use that bow of yours, my friend. Hope your aim is as good as they say.'

He gave a meaningful smile as he said this, and then turned to Nemo.

'Nemo, do you have anything you can fight with?'

Petrified, Nemo shook his head, still sitting on the horse. Heli seemed to think for a minute. In the meantime, Daniel got off Lightning and came next to them, holding his bow already loaded. The Great Lord's stallion followed him.

'If Lightning carries Nemo away, he might have a chance of escaping,' Heli suggested.

'It's worth a try,' Daniel replied and stepped around the enormous stallion to stand by his head. He put both his hands on either side of the horse's face, looking at him straight in the eyes.

'We really need your help right now, my big friend; will you carry Nemo away from here please? For me?'

He had no idea if the horse even understood him at all, but he had no time to second-guess himself; he had to try. To their relief, Lightning shook his head once, as if agreeing, and then took a few steps aligning himself next to Starlight. Heli grabbed Nemo and easily moved him from one horse to the other, as if he was no more than a child.

'Sorry, Nemo,' he said to the shocked merman, 'this is for the best.'

The moment Nemo's hands grabbed the reins; Lightning sprinted off, without waiting to be told. Heli hit Starlight once on the back with his hand and the white steed followed Lightning, trying to keep up.

The rest happened all so quickly. As the two of them were left alone, they stood shoulder to shoulder, turning to face the danger, and not a moment too soon.

They could now see clearly what was after them.

Coming out of the trees ahead, Daniel saw what looked like four big animals walking on their two hind legs. They were completely covered in fur, their heads wolfish looking and their mouths as large as he could have imagined in his worst nightmare. Their huge torsos stood tall on their strong beefy legs, while their arms finished in something similar to human hands, only longer and armed with deadly claws. Yet, for all their monstrous appearance, there was something disturbingly human about them. The way they walked, the way they moved their head and arms, the way they appeared to be sensing things; it was all too unsettling.

Daniel immediately had an inkling as to what they were; he just couldn't bring himself to believe it.

As the first four came out of the trees, stopping not ten feet away from them, they noticed another two coming from their left. Three more appeared on their right closing in on them. Then, as they smelled something in the air and looked in the direction Nemo rode off, they ignored Daniel and Heli, and set off after the horses.

There was nothing the two boys could do for Nemo and the horses now, so they concentrated on the threat before them, hoping Lightning's speed would be enough to see Nemo to safety.

'You've really never seen these before?' Daniel asked Heli, aiming his weapon at one of the two beasts to their left. He didn't know how useful it would be, however; he'd never used the bow before.

'First time,' Heli replied, raising his sword in the direction of the biggest one in front of them. His big red eyes gleamed under the reflection of the moonlight bouncing off the sword. There was a short moment of hesitation and then, out of nowhere, Séraphin appeared dropping down on the last creature from the main group, slashing quickly with his two knives on either side of his neck, until his head hung backwards, blood gushing down like a river.

This distracted the pack for a split second, and before they could react, Séraphin rose back into the air and vanished from sight.

The two on the left began to advance faster now and Daniel did not wait but released the first arrow at the closest one. The creature must not have been very smart, or seen many arrows before, because he kept going straight without ducking, and the arrow ended up latching itself in the middle of his neck, right under his enormous jaw. It fell back, clutching its throat, and remained in that position, struggling in pain, and wrestling with death as it claimed it.

Howling wildly, the second one moved forward stepping over its companion, and continued with even more speed towards the two boys. So did the other three, though they now seemed to be more cautious after losing two of their friends.

Daniel reached for another arrow behind his back, but by the time it took him to take it out of the quiver and get it ready to fire, the werewolf was right next to him, lifting its right paw to strike, while at the same time opening its enormous mouth. Simultaneously, the biggest of the other three was almost next to Heli, when from behind them, the boys heard the unmistakable cry of the Great Lord's stallion, who rushed in, attacking the beast closer to Daniel. Raising himself up in the air, he kept kicking the werewolf ferociously hard and fast with his front two hooves, until there was nothing left of him but a pool of blood.

Behind him, Heli's white steed also emerged, putting himself between the pack leader and his master, fighting much the same way Lightning did. The big werewolf, however, was not caught by surprise, and managed to avoid the horse's kicks by stepping back and then swiftly moving to the left. It then released a powerful blow with its right hand, catching the steed on its jaw and breaking it. Just as quickly, it sank its big sharp teeth on Starlight's neck and did not let go, until the poor horse fell to the ground and stopped kicking.

Heli screamed along with his horse, and, furious at the sight of slaughter, charged ahead, sword in hand. The pack leader's teeth were still attached to Starlight's flesh, when Heli's sword came down hard on his neck and ran through it like a hot knife through butter.

As before, Séraphin dropped down from the sky behind another one of the creatures, and with a single movement sliced its throat with his two knives, leaving only one of them to deal with. The last creature turned to charge him, but Daniel fired the second arrow in its direction, hitting the right shoulder this time. The werewolf shrieked from pain and howled loudly, turning again to charge at Daniel. With a swift movement, Heli intercepted it and swung his sword, slashing the creature in the middle of its chest, and creating a large open wound that began to bleed dark red blood. Once more, Séraphin put his knives to use, this time stabbing the werewolf in the back of its neck, sliding them downward, cutting its flesh and weakening it, until it, too, fell down on the ground and stopped moving.

The forest grew quiet once again. They took a moment to catch their breath, while Heli knelt down next to Starlight, stroking the lifeless animal.

'Where's Nemo?' Daniel asked, alarmed.

'Nemo,' Heli exclaimed and got up at once. 'Séraphin, can you please fly up and see if you can spot him? Daniel and I will take Lightning and go after him, but we need to know his exact location.'

Séraphin looked as if he didn't want to do this but did not protest. He flew up and disappeared above the trees again.

Heli looked back down at Starlight, his eyes heavy with pain. Daniel went next to him and put his hand on his shoulder.

'I'm so sorry, Hel; he was a brave animal.'

'They came back for us,' said Heli. 'They must have known they were no match for these things, yet they still came back for us.' Then, sitting down once again by the fallen horse, he laid his hand on its broken body and said. 'I will come back for you, my friend. I will make sure you are laid to rest properly; I promise.'

He then got up and they both made for Lightning, when Daniel noticed something happening on the ground around them, which confirmed his theory regarding the creatures. Where the lifeless bodies of the six beasts had fallen, now lay six naked men, covered in wounds and cuts that still bled warm blood. They were ordinary people, villagers gone missing, Daniel assumed, that had somehow turned into werewolves and joined this pack. And now, they had found death at their hands. Daniel felt like he was about to throw up.

Heli noticed too and froze where he was, shocked at the sight of the dead men.

'What's going on? What is this?' he asked disturbed and frightened. 'Daniel, did we do this?'

'We had no choice,' Daniel said in a low and surrendered voice, 'they were going to kill us.'

'But these are men; how could they be men? We fought large ugly beasts; why are we seeing dead men instead of them?'

'Because they *were* the beasts. Where I come from, people make up stories about this kind of creatures, but they don't really exist. I have no idea why they would exist here in Endërland.'

'So, you knew what they were?'

'I had my suspicions; I just couldn't believe it was true; not until now.' Daniel realized what Heli was thinking and repeated. 'We had no choice, Hel, they attacked us. If we would not defend ourselves, we would have ended up dead, or worse, we would have become like them.'

'How?'

'I don't know how, or even if it would happen for sure; but that's what happens in the stories to anyone who's been bitten by a werewolf.'

'That's what they're called?' Heli asked. Daniel did not have time to answer because at that very moment Séraphin appeared among the trees above them, seemingly in a hurry.

'The fish-boy is only a couple minutes ride from you. He's climbed on top of the tallest tree, but the beasts are trying to bring it down. And they will succeed soon enough if you don't hurry up.'

Daniel noticed that he said 'you' instead of 'we' and a feeling of disgust came over him. They locked eyes for a moment, but if the wingman felt any shame, he did not show it.

'But that's not all you need to worry about,' Séraphin continued. 'The four beasts that slew Alma are headed this way and will soon reach you. I'd move soon if I were you; we may not be so lucky the second time around.'

At this point he noticed the bodies of the men and his expression changed.

'What is this? What's going on here?'

'No time to explain,' Heli answered, heading for Lightning. 'I need you to go back to Nemo and keep an eye on him until we get there. If you see that the tree is about to fall down, grab him and fly him away from there.'

Séraphin gave him a cold defiant look through his clear blue eyes and spoke only one word.

'No.'

'Séraphin, please, this is no time for holding grudges. Nemo could die if we don't help him.'

'Then he will have received his judgment. He will get no help from me either way.'

Having said his piece, Séraphin unfolded his wings and flew up once again, disappearing from view.

Heli looked at Daniel, feeling embarrassed, but did not linger to talk about it. He walked towards Lightning, but when he got near him, the stallion stepped back from him and raised himself high on his hind legs, as if to attack him. Daniel rushed to grab Heli and pull him away so he wouldn't get hurt.

'We cannot delay, Daniel; we need to get to Nemo right away. Help me please.'

Daniel could sense the desperation in his voice and see it on his face, and his respect and admiration for this wonderful man reached new highs.

'There's another way, Hel; in fact, it may be the only way to save Nemo, ourselves, and make sure that nobody else gets hurt today. But I need to ask you something first.'

'What is it?' said Heli, holding his breath. Daniel went on for the next minute or so, explaining to him the plan he'd come up with. Heli listened intently but did not seem too hopeful and convinced that Daniel's idea would work.

'How can we be sure it will work?' He asked when Daniel finished speaking. 'What if you're wrong?'

'Then we'll be in no better or worse place than we are now, and we can try to fight our way out of this again. But we have to give this a try, Hel; my gut tells me it will work.'

Heli thought about it for another moment, during which they could hear the four werewolves approaching them, and then he finally decided.

'Alright, we'll do this your way; but you better be right about this. Now, take Lightning and go; you shouldn't be here when it happens.'

He helped Daniel jump on the Great Lord's stallion and wished him good luck, while he turned now to face the fast approaching werewolves.

Daniel rode hastily in the direction that Nemo had gone earlier. A minute passed, two, three and even though Lightning was racing at his top speed, he could hear the footsteps of the beasts trailing behind him.

A very loud cracking noise, followed by the sound of trees smashing against each other, caused his heart to falter, and he bade the black stallion to hasten. In less than a minute, he arrived at the scene of the commotion and his worse fears came true.

Before him, he saw the huge oak tree that was now down, breaking other trees in the process and leaving behind a spiky trunk, less than a couple feet from the ground. The three werewolves were rummaging between the branches, obviously looking for Nemo, and nobody noticed Daniel and Lightning at first. But, as their frustration grew, one of them lifted its head and sensed them standing not too far from the scene. It let out a howl to alert its friends, and once it got their attention, they all forgot about Nemo and began running awkwardly towards Daniel, using both arms and legs.

Daniel did not wait but gave Lightning a nudge with his heel and turned around to draw them away from the place. And it worked. The werewolves set off in pursuit, determined to get at least someone to sink their teeth into.

Were he riding any other horse that night, Daniel would no doubt have become the werewolves' meal, but no creature was yet born in Endërland to match Lightning for speed. Unfortunately for Daniel, he soon found himself between the three that were following him and the other four that had previously been feasting on poor Alma.

He tried to turn to his left and leave them all behind, but they spread out before him and blocked all exits, closing in on a circle around him. It was him and Lightning against seven werewolves and it did not look very promising. So, he stopped, climbed down from Lightning, and prepared his bow, ready to shoot if necessary, and desperately hoping that Heli would come through with their plan.

The werewolves now kept closing in on him and were about to charge when something made them stop. All of a sudden, the moon and stars hid from the view, and the dark around them began to swiftly grow lighter and brighter, until night became dawn. From the eastern horizon, the sun could be seen emerging hastily, illuminating everything around them.

The werewolves stopped where they were and started to shake and howl, as if they were in terrible pain and fear. Before his very eyes, they began shedding their fur and extra skin, their bones contorting and twisting into place, all the while shrinking in size, until they were no more than mere men, no bigger than Daniel.

It took a couple of minutes, but when their transformation was finally complete, he found himself surrounded by seven men, all cowering and trying to shield themselves from the morning cold, naked as they were. When they were lucid enough to see Daniel and especially the horse he was riding on, an understanding came over them and their faces dropped with guilt and shame. The one who was closer to Daniel, went down on his knees and bowed his head.

'Forgive us, lord; we are cursed men and cannot control the beast that takes over when the moon is high.'

One by one they all went down on their knees with their heads bowed towards Daniel, and remained like that until he spoke. He wanted to tell them that he wasn't a lord, but all he could think about was Nemo.

'We will speak of this later; right now, I need to find my friend. Will you come and help me?'

The men took heart that he would ask for their help, and appearing eager, ran after him back to where the big tree had fallen.

Desperately, Daniel began searching for Nemo, remembering Séraphin saying that he had climbed at the very top. Sure enough, he found Nemo under a few thin branches, unconscious at the far end of the fallen tree. What he saw, almost made his heart stop.

Blood was dripping from Nemo's mouth, while his right arm was caught under him with the shoulder seemingly dislocated. His right leg was also twisted outward in a very painful position, but that wasn't the worst. Halfway down the lower part, the bone was broken and had cut through skin and flesh, sticking out all covered in blood. And as if that wasn't bad enough, a small tree branch had lodged itself into the left side of his chest, probably missing Nemo's heart by an inch.

Daniel's own heart faltered as he feared the worst. The boy seemed lifeless at first look, but as he got down next to him, Daniel felt a slight move of his chest and a very faint heartbeat under his palm. A ray of hope surged through him as he called upon the men to help remove the tree from on top of Nemo and clear the place around him.

He then very carefully cut the tree branch that was still attached to Nemo's body, but dared not remove it, lest the boy bled to death.

While he was doing all of this, Hëna arrived, running and holding her brother's sword in her right hand. She ignored the seven men and went straight to Daniel and Nemo.

'Is he hurt?'

'Very badly,' Daniel answered, his voice weak and trembling. 'I don't know how to help him, Hëna.'

She heard the desperation in his voice and knelt down next to him.

'Don't worry, help is on the way. Séraphin flew to New Sotira, and a group of villagers are riding towards us as we speak. They will be here in no time and then we can take him to their village. I'm sure they will have Summer water with them.'

The thought comforted Daniel and gave him hope. He just prayed that they would make it on time.

'He is the first friend I made here; you know? This is practically how we met; he was almost dying, tied to that pine tree, a minute later and it would have been too late. I don't know how he manages to get himself into these situations every time,' Daniel chuckled, not really laughing. 'It's almost like he has a knack for it. I'm just scared that one day I will fail him and won't be able to get him out. He's my best friend, Hëna; I don't know what I would do if I lost him.'

Hëna looked at him and suddenly wished she had the power to make things happen, just so that she could erase the pain from his face. But she didn't and she couldn't. Some useless words of comfort were all she could offer him.

'He will be fine, Daniel; I promise.'

Her hand rested on his shoulder and remained there for a short precious moment. She watched as Daniel tended to his friend, fixing his red hair, checking his pulse again, cleaning the blood off his face and around his wound, and something tugged inside her own chest. How could anyone believe this person would do the horrible things that they accused him of? They clearly did not see what she saw in him, or they would know how wrong they were about him, about both of them.

She had not really believed the accusations against the boys back in Arba, but she had not ruled them out either. She didn't know them after all, Daniel especially, so she could not afford to be close-minded about the possibility. But now she knew the truth, and she would give everything to make sure that they were vindicated in the eyes of all of Endërland.

She sat next to Daniel with one hand placed on Nemo's forehead, and did not get up until a few minutes later, when the villagers arrived.

The group of men coming to their aid comprised of seven of them riding on horses, all clad in similar armour and battle gear. Séraphin flew before them, leading the way. It was an unusual sight in Endërland, but one that Daniel guessed the people of this once peaceful kingdom might sadly become accustomed to.

Leading the group was a handsome man, seemingly in his early forties, with short grey hair and a neatly trimmed beard clothing a square jawline. It reminded Daniel of heroes in old movies about gladiators or Greek warriors. The man had an aura of authority about him, which suited him just fine.

As they arrived at the spot where Nemo had fallen, they dismounted their horses. Séraphin dropped beside them, saying nothing, nor looking at anyone. Daniel stared at him for a moment, then, unwilling to think about the wingman and his actions right now, he let him be and shifted his gaze to the men's leader, who began walking towards Daniel, looking at him straight in his eyes.

'Daniel Adams?' the man asked in a deep strong voice. It was the second time someone had called him by his full name in this world.

Daniel stood up and faced him, his head barely reaching up to the man's shoulders. When they were standing face-to-face, close enough for a handshake, the man smiled and spoke again.

'You have your mother's eyes. I am your great-grandfather, Ari.'

Daniel was in a state of overcoming sensation as he realized that the man standing before him was a piece of his history and past, perfectly preserved in this magical world. He tried to open his mouth but found that he didn't know what to say. So, instead he looked down at Nemo and asked.

'Can you help him? Please?'

Ari looked at him for another moment, his smile still lingering on his noble face, and then he knelt down next to Nemo to assess the boy's condition.

'Master Ari,' Daniel heard Hëna greet the man as she stepped back to let him examine Nemo. They obviously knew each other. He wondered about the title, but was too concerned with his friend to dwell on it right now. Ari studied the Sea-Prince for a moment, checking all of his wounds. He then took out from his chest a small flask containing a colourless liquid, which Daniel assumed was Summer water.

'Hold him,' the old king said to Hëna and then grabbed the broken branch sticking out of Nemo's flesh with one hand, pulling it out slowly while pouring water on the open wound with the other. Blood began to come out along with the stick, while at the same time the wound began to grow smaller and close ever so slowly, until there was nothing left but white unblemished skin.

Nemo did not open his eyes and Daniel still wouldn't allow himself to breathe.

Next, Ari moved on to Nemo's leg, setting it back into position, causing Nemo to stir and wince from the pain again. The broken bones could be seen coming out of the torn flesh, causing Daniel to cringe at the sight. Ari put them back together and poured some more water over it, watching as the flesh and skin grew again, slowly closing the wound.

And still Nemo did not wake up.

Lastly, Ari grabbed his arm in both his hands and examined it gently.

'We're lucky,' he said. 'It's not broken like his leg, but it is dislocated and it's gonna hurt bad when I put it back into place. Hold him down tight, young one.'

Hëna nodded and did as she was told. Then, with one quick move, Ari twisted Nemo's arm and forced the shoulder back into place, causing Nemo to open his eyes and scream out loud from the pain. Once in place though, the shoulder did not hurt anymore, and Nemo stopped screaming. He looked at all the people watching over him and asked.

'What happened? Where am...?' He did not finish the sentence, however. The memories rushed back to him, and he remembered everything, receiving the answer to his question in the process. He tried to move but winced as his broken leg pained him.

Ari held him down and spoke with a soft voice.

'Welcome back, little one; you need to stay down, you're still hurt. Here, drink this.'

He gave him the flask and Nemo began to drink from it like he hadn't drunk in weeks.

'This will help you get better quickly,' Ari said as he took back the flask, 'but you still need to lay down for a while.' He then turned to Daniel. 'The bones will take several days to heal properly; until then we need to keep his leg immobilized. I suggest you come and stay with us in the village during this time; he won't be able to ride in the condition he is. Plus, we have much to talk about.'

Daniel nodded with his head and simply said, 'Thank you', his voice still weak from worry. Seeing Nemo awake again, he finally allowed himself to breathe. All of the built-up tension was now being released from his body and it almost made him explode into tears. Had he been alone, he would have surely cried; *even tough men need a good cry sometimes, don't they?* But seeing as he was around other people, he tried really hard not to embarrass himself. His friend was gonna be okay, and that was a cause for celebration, after all.

Ari proceeded to immobilize Nemo's leg between two pieces of wood so that it wouldn't move during the ride, and then mounted him unto a slate that they improvised on the spot to carry him all the way to the village.

As they set out to ride to New Sotira, Daniel finally turned his attention to the seven men, who were now covering themselves with bits of clothing given to them by the villagers.

'What about them?' he asked.

'They are coming with us,' answered his great-grandfather. 'They have their own story to tell, and I for one, would listen to it.'

* * *

Hours later, having had dinner in the big hall at Ari's guesthouse, the visitors now moved to the fire chamber, sitting down on floor pillows around the room, much like at the old house in Sotira. A choice of tea or hot punch was served, as was customary in this occasion.

Ari occupied the main seat, just next to the fireplace, while Daniel sat on the other side of it. To Ari's left sat his six sons in the order which they were born, while to Daniel's right sat Nemo, with his leg bound properly now. Heli was next, and then Séraphin, wings folded behind his back. The seven former werewolves occupied the rest of the seats in the room, thus closing the circle.

Earlier that day, Ari had sent people back into the woods to find and retrieve the bodies of the fallen men and horses. The men were washed clean and dressed properly, and were then buried in a small field just outside the village. So it was that the first ever cemetery in the kingdom came to be. Messengers were sent to their respective villages to inform the families of the fate and whereabouts of their loved ones. As for the horses, they were burned where they had fallen.

For the first time in their long history, the Endërland people met with the pain and sadness of the loss of human life, and it was heart-breaking to know that this was only the beginning. These men were the first victims of Winter's madness, and if the guys did not succeed at finding the Great Lord, they would not be the last.

As for the surviving men, Daniel proposed that, since being a werewolf was an unnatural state of the human body, it could be considered a disease, and as such it might probably be cured with Summer water. So, the seven men were given some from whatever Ari and the people in the village had in store for themselves. After drinking it, all of them had fallen on the floor, going through some kind of seizure, but other than that, there had been no sign of any change in them. The fact that the night had already come, Hëna was well up in the sky, and yet they were still human, meant that Daniel had been right, and that the Summer water had worked its magic. Overcome with happiness, the men laughed and cried for a good while, thanking Daniel and the villagers, and expressing their endless gratitude. Theirs would make for yet another fascinating story to be told around the fire, as was custom among local folk.

Storytelling was one of Daniel's favourite traditions in Endërland. He had always loved stories; as a child, his mother would tell him a new one every night when she would put him to bed. After she'd died, Daniel had not bothered his dad to do the same; that had been one of the few memories he'd shared with his mother, and it just hadn't felt right to do it with someone else.

Tonight, however, as the guest of honour, it would be him who would tell his story first, and it would not be a made-up one. He was nervous, for he didn't really like to speak in front of many people. But tradition had to be observed. So, he began by recounting almost everything from day one, all that had happened before and after The Council, up until the moment his great-grandfather and his sons arrived at the place where Nemo had fallen. He left out certain things, of course, Séraphin's attitude and refusal to help Nemo being part of it, but not everything had to be shared.

When he was done, everyone raised their glasses and toasted in his honour, with Ari humorously congratulating him on his good story-telling skills.

It was Nemo's turn to share with them next. Understandably, Nemo left out even more bits from his story than Daniel had, but he also filled in some of the missing pieces from the latest events; mainly how he had stupidly thought that he would have been safer on top of a tree, thus abandoning the horses and climbing on the tallest one he could find. It was just his luck that the werewolves were unable to climb up there after him.

Another toast was raised in his honour when he finished, causing the red-haired boy to turn a darker shade. Daniel strongly suspected it was the punch, of which his friend had helped himself several times since dinner.

Next, one of the seven men offered to share with them his tale of what had happened that had led to the preceding events of the day. It was practically the same story as the rest of the thirteen men who had ended up attacking Daniel and his friends. He told of how he had been in the woods one day and had been bitten by some animal he had never seen before. He had lost consciousness and when next awakened, he'd found himself locked up in chains in a dungeon somewhere along with the other men. There, they had been kept alive and fed for many seasons, but were never allowed to go out. Every night the beast would take over, but the chains held them in place, and they were unable to go anywhere or do anything but howl in the dark. But that had all changed the previous evening, when they were suddenly released into open space, just before the moon had come out. Next thing he remembered, only seven of them were standing naked before Daniel and Lightning.

This was one of the sadder tales, as the pain of their friends' loss was still fresh. But there was also joy in it, for they had finally defeated the beast and come out of this nightmare alive and well. And now, new friendships and allegiances were formed that would likely last as long as Endërland itself.

They toasted again after the man finished, and then all turned now to Ari, whose turn had come to speak. Heli and Séraphin politely declined to share their own tales, much preferring to just sit there and listen. This was the part that Daniel had been looking forward to the most, for so many different reasons.

Ari began his tale with the first time he visited Endërland. He kept his eyes fixed on Daniel, as if this story was being told for him alone.

'I was only a little boy when I began to visit here, and for a long time it was all just a dream to me. But as I grew up, I understood that it was not so. This was a whole other world, and I seemed to be the only one who could come here. My father died in a war before I was born, so, if he ever were a Visitor, he did not make it to Endërland, and I never got the chance to meet him.

'When I was about your age, I met someone who called himself a prophet, and he told me that he knew about this world and other people who had been here before me.'

'Freddie?' Daniel interrupted, completely mystified. It couldn't be the same guy; that would make him older than Ari. Unless there was more to Freddie than he let on.

'I think he went by Alfred back then,' Ari corrected, and then continued. 'A scrawny young man, with short brown hair and a penchant for philosophy; maybe a year or two older than me.'

'Yep, definitely Freddie,' Daniel concluded. He made a mental note to get to the bottom of this the first chance he got, and then re-focused his attention on the story.

'Anyway, he introduced me to this group of people who called themselves The Guardians, and convinced me that I had a role to play in the future of both worlds. I stayed with them for a few years, all the time training to fight with guns and swords and everything else they could think off. They taught me many things, as if they were preparing me for something big and important, but nothing ever happened.

'One day I was told that my training was over and that I should go into hiding. The Order had gotten news that many people like me were going missing or being found dead, so I had to lay low for a while. That's when I started to travel around the world. I visited many places for a very long time, but finally decided to settle down in a very small and well-hidden village in Albania.'

'Sotira,' Daniel said.

'Yes. There, I met this beautiful young girl, who would become my world for the next forty years or so. And that's where your grandfather and mother were born. We didn't have the house you're staying in back then, only a humble wooden shack; but we were content. Everything else that I had been through before that, faded away as if it had never happened. Nobody ever came to look for me and I never went back. I lived the rest of my life in peace, and I died a happy man.

'Death took me in my sleep, so I got to stay here for good. The Lords offered me to be the King of the Land, and for a time I did that, even though my heart was in living a quiet and simple life with my family. So, when your mother came, I passed the reign on to her and moved out here with my new wife and sons. Our lives have been quiet and fulfilled, with not much happening, but that's the way we like it.

'But now, you come along, and bring with you a wind of change as it has never before happened in Endërland. And I can finally feel all the pieces falling into place. I may enjoy a quiet life and the beautiful silence of these mountains, but I have never forgotten what I was told, nor the reasons why I was chosen. So, when the day is upon us, and the Great Lord calls for me to serve, I will answer. I have a distinct feeling that I am about to finally get the opportunity to do what I was trained for, and I am ready, as are all my sons.'

Silence followed Ari's last ominous words, as everyone present seemed to fall into troubled thoughts of a dreaded future. Ari, however, did not allow it to go on for long. He raised one final toast, thus signalling the end of their evening together. Soon, everyone was assigned a comfortable and safe place to rest for the remainder of the night.

Daniel, however, still could not sleep. He could not help but think about everything Ari had shared, trying to understand what he had meant with his last words. And he believed he did. He could not foresee much, but one thing was certain, dark days were indeed ahead. Thankfully, it seemed he would not have to face them alone.

Chapter 10

FALLING...

Watching Azariel fly in his direction, the sun slowly setting behind him, Butler could not help but feel disgust towards the young wingman. He seemed to have fooled the rest of his kin and even his master, claiming to the former that the mermaids killed his father, and to the latter that it had been Nathaniel. Butler knew better, however; he had come to know Azariel enough to guess what had really happened, and felt nothing but disdain for the wingman. Loyal as he was to the White Lord, he would have never gone that far.

Still, he had a job to do, and whatever he thought or felt were irrelevant. He would follow his orders as long as he was comfortable doing so. And when he no longer did, well, he would just have to find a way out of all this mess.

Azariel landed in front of him, his face dark, yet proud. He folded his beautiful wings back and gave Butler an arrogant look.

'You, again. I thought I made it clear that I wanted to speak to your master.'

Butler bit his tongue to keep from cussing the impertinent wingman, and instead spoke in his usual flattery and humility.

'My lord Winter apologizes that he could not come, but he feels that we need to be prudent and lay low for a while longer. He also asked me to pass on his congratulations for inheriting your father's station. This is an opportunity that greatly improves both of our positions in realizing our common goal.'

'Yes, well, I still want to know what is being done to apprehend my father's murderer. He left his nest five days ago and I have a pretty good idea as to where he's headed. Tell your master that it is in both of our interest that he is caught before he manages to find the Sky-Prince. That would complicate things for all of us.'

'My master would like to assure you that he shares your concern and that he is dealing with this matter as we speak. Your friend has been spotted and is being followed; he will be caught before he manages to find the Sky-Prince. The situation is still under control.'

'I do not want him harmed; I want him brought before me, so I can deal with him myself. Is that understood?'

Butler could see that the new position had already boosted the wingman's ego. He continued to reply with a humble demeanour, despite feeling like what he really wanted to do was grab the boy by the neck and give him a piece of his own mind.

'If it can be helped, it will be done as you wish; you have my word. However, my lord asks that you now concentrate on your part; you must push the queen to call for battle against the mermaids. Use the voice of your people, give it strength and force the queen to bow to her people's cries. We are almost there.'

Azariel looked at Butler with a cold and empty gaze for another moment, and then turned to leave him.

'It will be done,' he simply said, before spreading his wings and taking up in the evening sky.

Poor fool, Butler thought to himself as he watched him go, and then walked back to his horse to leave the place.

On the second day after their arrival to the village, the seven now former werewolves left New Sotira for their own homes, after thanking Daniel and Ari many times, and not before pledging their allegiance and lifetime service to Daniel. Feeling somehow responsible for the death of the other men, Daniel had only accepted this as a symbolic gesture. It wasn't he who had saved them, at least, not him alone. Still, they had insisted, and so he let them.

As Ari had said, it took Nemo a good while to recover completely and be strong enough to ride again. They stayed in New Sotira six days, during which they rested as much as they could and recuperated their strength. Ari used this time to teach Daniel much of what he knew about Dreamers, the Order of the Guardians and the dream world. Daniel for his part told him everything that had taken place at the Council and what their mission was, things which he had not shared the first night. He half expected Ari to laugh at them for going after legends and fantasies, but his great-grandfather's face remained serious the entire time he spoke.

'It does appear to be a fool's mission,' he finally said, 'and I know it feels like you are seeking to find the impossible, but I believe you have made the right choice,

Daniel. I wish there was some way I could help you, or even ease your fears regarding the time you have left back in your world. Alas, I'm afraid I can do neither. What I can do, though, is pass on to you some of what was once given to me, and hope that in time it will serve you well.'

Daniel soon found out what that was. Ari spent the following days crash-training him in the use of the bow and sword. Daniel had to learn better how to defend himself, on foot, or while riding Lightning. Hëna was also there, participating in the lessons and sparring with Daniel under the tutelage of Ari and the spectating eyes of Nemo and others from the village. She and Heli had both been trained in this very place not so long ago, and that explained at least a couple of things.

Being a beginner, Daniel could not help but feel mortified whenever Hëna bested him with her moves, especially since she wasn't even trying. This would definitely not help his chances with her, he felt. Still, he did not give up; Ari was an excellent teacher, and Daniel was a quick learner. In the few days that he spent training, he learned all the basics and vowed to continue practicing with Hëna every day. Of course, he was more than happy for the extra time and exchange between the two of them, a fact that, much like Sam back in Sotira, *he* also kept to himself.

As for their friends, while Nemo sat mostly on the side, having nothing else to do but watch them spar, Séraphin always flew away for the most part of the day, without ever telling anyone where he was going, or what he was doing. Daniel and Nemo never confronted him about what happened in the woods. It was true that he had been arrogant and rude regarding the two of them, as well as refuse to help Nemo directly, but he had also saved their lives, fighting bravely and getting help from the villagers. So, Daniel was conflicted and did not really know how to feel about the wingman. He only hoped that time would do what he couldn't yet, mend things between the three of them.

* * *

At the dawn of the seventh day, they thanked Ari for his hospitality and help, and finally resumed their journey towards the Northern Mountains. Lightning led the way once again, while Hëna and Nemo followed behind him, now riding two new horses that Ari provided for them as replacements for Alma and Starlight.

Séraphin flew above them as always, but this time he seemed little concerned with watching the horizons for danger. For days now he'd been caught in a battle that had been raging on inside his heart. Endërland was changing, and he no longer needed the Oracle or anyone else telling him so to believe it. The evidence was all around him; he could see it in how the weather was changing for the worst, in how life in these parts of the kingdom was becoming increasingly sparse and frail. Danger and fear were becoming too frequently present, and that was a discomforting fact. This was not the kingdom he once knew; people were killing one-another or they were disappearing, only to turn up later transformed into wild beasts and trying to hurt others. It no longer felt safe, and that was not a welcome feeling. He hated the idea, but maybe Daniel was right after all, and whatever was happening was bigger and much more complicated than he had initially thought.

Everything that had happened recently made him think long and hard about whether Daniel and Nemo really did kill Ghordi, as well as his own attitude towards them. If it was true that they were innocent, then he would have to do a bit more than simply rethink his behaviour. Still, he was not yet ready to doubt the word of his brothers, or the conviction of his own mother, the queen, on the matter. She counted on him to uphold her will and honour, and this was his chance to finally prove to her that he was worthy of being her only son and heir. He would not let her down.

They rode on for another two days, stopping very little to rest and stretch their legs. Daniel and Hëna took every opportunity they got to keep honing their sword skills, Hëna using hers and Daniel one that Ari gave to him as a gift before departing. At night Heli took over for Hëna, and thus they continued his training for a few more hours, while Nemo and Séraphin slept.

Heli's technique was quite similar to Hëna's, but while Hëna restrained herself to match Daniel's level, Heli pushed on harder and fought tougher than she did, causing Daniel to strain a lot more. Yet, he was glad for this; he didn't feel so bad when beaten by Heli, and the further he pushed himself, the greater his skills improved. He was quite keen on matching Hëna's level, if not exceeding it.

On the third day after leaving New Sotira, the path Lightning was following brought them back by the seaside. Daniel was glad to smell the sea again and lose his gaze beyond the blue horizon. He remembered asking once if there was more land on the other side of the ocean. The answer had been that no one had ever found out, and that very few had even tried. Of those who had, none had ever returned. There were no big ships in Endërland, only small boats that were not appropriate for the deep ocean, thus whoever had attempted to cross it in the past, was assumed to have been claimed by the sea.

As for the land, the only part of the kingdom that was not surrounded by water was the northern side. That, however, was even more inaccessible, since the Northern Mountains rose crazy high and steep, stretching for miles and miles northwest to southeast. No one had ever climbed to the very top, and even the eagles would not fly that high. So, no one really knew what lay beyond them either.

Daniel found it difficult to believe that Endërland was confined between the seas and the Northern Mountains, but the people here seemed to be content with what they knew and had. Looking at the big blue sleeping peacefully to his left now, he wondered, if it ever came to it, would he choose to sail to the end of it, or climb beyond the snow-covered mountains to find out what lay out there?

* * *

They had been riding for little over an hour the morning of their fourth day, when Hëna caught up to him, appearing troubled. The wind that had now grown stronger and chillier played with her loose hair, partially covering her face. Daniel's heart still skipped a beat at the sight of her.

'There's something coming our way; they are many and they're flying fast from the southeast. A wingman is leading them towards us.'

Daniel looked to the south-eastern sky on his right but could see nothing.

'Heli?' he asked her. Hëna nodded. Daniel turned his gaze towards Séraphin, who was flying northward ahead of them, seemingly unaware of anything or anyone approaching.

'I don't think he's seen anything. How can we warn him?'

'I don't know,' Hëna replied. 'Maybe it's nothing; Heli says they're just a flock of mountain ravens, but they look much bigger in size, and they never come this far down.'

'I don't like this. If we have to protect ourselves again, I don't know how Nemo will manage. He's still weak.'

'I guess it's a shame he's human,' Hëna said. 'They wouldn't be able to get to him under water.'

Daniel silently agreed with her and looked southeast again. He thought he could now see a small black cloud appearing far in the horizon. Then, Hëna's words played back in his head, and it hit him.

'That's it,' he said, and without elaborating, started going through his bag of belongings. He found the shoulder bag he'd brought with him from home, and reached inside it to find the small air-tank that his father gave him for his birthday. 'This should keep him out of danger, at least for a while.'

He rode towards Nemo, bag in hand, and without saying anything threw the bag over Nemo's head and shoulder.

'What's going on?' Nemo asked.

'More visitors, Nemo,' Hëna replied, instead of Daniel. 'We need to be prepared for anything.'

'A flock of mountain ravens, led by a wingman, is flying fast towards us,' Daniel explained. 'In case they attack, I want you to swim away from the shore, and if you need to go under, use my air-tank. Only please use it sparingly; I don't know how much air is left in it.'

Dread materialized on Nemo's face as the prospect of another bloody battle brought back more than just unpleasant memories. Yet, despite the fear of what might happen, he felt too embarrassed to run and hide like a coward.

'I can help, Dan; I can stay and fight with you.'

Daniel understood. He knew his friend wanted to prove to himself and others that he was not a coward, but the truth was that *he* was the one who was afraid for Nemo. It occurred to him that perhaps his faith in his friend was not what it should be. Besides, he wasn't supposed to play big brother, trying to protect and save Nemo all the time, but instead give him the chance to grow up and become his own man. Today, however, was not the time for that.

'You are still weak, Nemo; your leg has not fully healed, and it may fail you. Won't you please do this just for me? I would feel much better if I know that you're safe.'

Nemo didn't seem to like this very much, but he agreed to do as Daniel asked.

They kept on riding ahead, all the time looking towards the eastern sky where they could see the small black cloud growing bigger and closer. Above them, Séraphin flew unaware of the approaching threat, still heading north. Daniel wondered why the wingman had not yet seen the birds, and wished there was a way he could alert him. He would most likely be the first one to be attacked by the flock if they indeed were hostile.

As the distance between them and the birds grew smaller, Daniel could now make out the wingman who was flying separately ahead, and the following flock, which he guessed comprised of about thirty or so ravens. They seemed to be flying hurriedly after the wingman in a disorganized group, their large black wings frantically beating the air beneath them. It would take them only minutes to reach them, and Daniel instinctively grabbed an arrow and loaded it unto the bow, ready to fire at the first sign of hostility.

They all stopped riding and got off their horses, Daniel holding his bow ready and Hëna her sword. Nemo clutched Daniel's shoulder bag and looked up with apprehension. When the approaching wingman came within hearing distance, they noticed Séraphin turning towards him and stopping in mid-air. The two exchanged a few quick words and then both turned to face the flock of ravens that were now almost on them.

'Nemo, into the water; now,' shouted Daniel. Nemo obeyed without hesitation, while Daniel aimed his bow at the ravens, which now decided to split into two groups. The first group attacked the two wingmen above them, who had already drawn their daggers. The second group dropped down towards Daniel and Hëna, their beaks aiming forward like steel darts.

Had they been a flock of normal crows, Daniel would have been less worried, but seeing the monstrous size of these things, he felt his courage waver and for a moment wishing he could go and hide with Nemo under water. The birds flying towards them were ten times the normal size. Their black wings completely blocked the sun from view, like an unannounced eclipse. They were coming down real fast, dropping like rockets from the sky, all heading towards the same target.

When they got close enough, Daniel began firing a series of arrows towards them, loading the bow as fast as he could. He hoped that despite his little-trained skills with the weapon, the arrows would find somewhere to latch themselves into the large group. He was lucky, for few of them missed; the rest caused about six or seven ravens to drop on the ground, unable to get back up. Soon though, the remaining ravens got too close for him to use the bow, so he threw it away and raised his sword, standing side by side with Hëna.

The remaining birds, still about a dozen, launched into an attack, viciously trying to hook their talons on their flesh, or strike them with their strong beaks. Daniel and Hëna began fighting them off, swinging and slashing with their swords anything that came close enough. The birds were many, coming at them from all sides, and very soon they found themselves standing back-to-back.

The ravens were huge and ferocious, and their beaks and talons hard as metal. It was difficult to get past them, but Daniel and Hëna kept on trying, bringing the oversized birds down one at a time. And still the ravens kept on coming, managing to deliver numerous cuts and scratches to both of them. One of them gave Daniel a very nasty cut on his left arm, causing it to bleed badly and soak all his clothes in red blood. His arm soon began to lose its strength and Daniel felt he could no longer lift it. He was now forced to swing his sword with only his right, which proved more difficult as the sword grew heavier by the second.

Next to them, while the other two horses had retreated from the commotion, Lightning had joined in the battle, rising on his two hind legs, and aiming at the birds that were attacking his rider. Whenever they ended up underneath his hooves, he kept on stumping on them until they were dead and stopped moving.

High above them, the battle continued just as bloody, with the two wingmen greatly outmatched. Séraphin and his new friend were quick and agile in their movements, managing to deliver deadly blows to many of their attackers. Their large wings, however, were a weakness, and eventually proved to be their undoing. The birds were too many for them, and unlike Daniel and Hëna; the two of them could not protect each-other's backs.

As the fight progressed, the two wingmen got separated, each having to fend off four or five ravens at once. Having flown for many days with little rest, Nathaniel soon felt drained of whatever energy he had left, and eventually gave up, dropping his knives and letting the ravens overtake him. The black birds violently tore at his wings, while he desperately tried to use them to cover his face, allowing himself to free-fall towards the earth. Yet, even as he fell, the ravens continued to attack him brutally, causing whatever damage they could. Resigned to the fact that he could no longer fight them, and rapidly losing consciousness, Nathaniel tried to protect his more vital parts. He wrapped himself inside his own wings as in a cocoon, and dropped towards the ground like a bullet.

It seemed he had not entirely run out of luck, however, since during the course of the fight, they had moved away from land and were now above the open sea. Thus it was that, when he finally reached the end of his free-fall, Nathaniel dived feet first into the cold water, not far from where Nemo was floating, apprehensively observing everything.

Not thinking twice about it, the ex-merman dived in after him, swimming as fast as he could. When Nemo reached him, Nathaniel had already touched bottom. Lucky for them, the water there was no more than nine or ten feet deep. Nemo grabbed the wingman with his left arm around his waist, just like Daniel had done with him before, and kicked towards the surface, using his legs and right arm to swim. This turned out to be more difficult than he had thought it would be, but he did not give up. He managed to break the surface before they both ran out of breath.

Right then, however, he wished they hadn't. As soon as they resurfaced, the ravens that were circling above, launched themselves towards them in great fury. Taking one deep breath, Nemo dived back in, dragging Nathaniel with him and going just deep enough to stay out of the ravens' reach.

Nemo knew that the birds could not get to them, and they would be safe as long as there was air in the tank. But how long was that going to last, especially now that there were two of them having to share it?

With his free hand, he searched inside Daniel's bag and found the air-tank. He put it first in his own mouth and drew one short breath to test it. To his relief, air flew inside his lungs, extending his life by another minute or so. He then put the air-tank into Nathaniel's mouth, and not a second too soon. The wounded wingman had just opened his eyes, gasping for air, and as he breathed through the nozzle, his terrified expression changed into a slightly frightened and confused one.

Nemo motioned to him to hold the air tank, while trying to come up with a plan on how to get out of this situation alive. Looking up at the relentless birds, he wished he had a crossbow with him. He had never used one, and chances were, he wouldn't be able to hit anything with it either, but he could at least try. As it were, he had no weapon to fight with or protect himself. He looked around, hoping to find something that could be of use, and that's when he saw below him one of the daggers that Nathaniel had dropped. A small blade was better than nothing at all, so he swam back down towards the bottom of the sea and retrieved the weapon.

Making sure that Nathaniel was still conscious and breathing from the air-tank, Nemo motioned for him to stay where he was, and kicked again towards the surface, knife in hand. He didn't know what he would be able to accomplish with it; he just hoped that at least he'd get a chance to see how the others were doing. Swimming in the direction of the shore, he tried to resurface at some distance from where the ravens were. But the evil birds spotted his red hair easily and rushed towards him, reaching for his flesh with their nasty claws. At least, he was drawing them away from Nathaniel, who was bound to resurface if the air-tank emptied. Nemo only had a chance to fill his lungs hastily with some much-needed air before he turned to see them approaching and diving back down. His heart was pounding like crazy.

Panic began taking over as he realized that the ravens weren't going anywhere. Swimming back to Nathaniel made no sense, as the air-tank would empty a lot quicker if they both used it. He had no choice, he would have to fight the birds off, at least that way the wingman would have a better chance at surviving. Thusly determined, he charged towards the surface one last time, holding the knife in front of him.

Just as he was about to breach the surface, concentrated on the four large ravens that were waiting for him, he suddenly saw all around him a multitude of familiar cross bolts, all rising from below and heading up. Upon exiting the water, they continued their flight until they met their targets, two or three for each raven. And just like that, the huge black birds fell from the sky one after the other, floating lifeless on the surface of the water above him. Nemo looked down to see where the cross bolts had come from, and to his delight, he saw a group of mermaids swimming in his direction, crossbows in hand. Two of them grabbed Nathaniel, who appeared to have lost conscience again.

Nemo had never been happier to see any of his sisters. He made as if to shout from joy but remembered that he was still under water. Along with the mermaids and Nathaniel, he emerged out of the water and filled his lungs with air, enjoying it just as much as that small victory.

The mermaids swam with Nathaniel to the shore, where Daniel and Hëna were fighting with the last remaining raven. Another dead one falling from the sky prompted Nemo to look up and see Séraphin fighting against two more. Two of his sisters targeted them from below and shot them down, leaving Séraphin hovering in the air, all alone for a moment. When he saw that the birds were all gone, the Sky-Prince flew down hurriedly, just as Daniel and Hëna were pulling Nathaniel out of the water.

A mixture of feelings came over Daniel as he recognized the face of the wounded wingman. For a long time, he had felt resentment and anger towards this person. He, along with his friends, was responsible not only for everything they were going through, but for sending Endërland one step closer towards war and destruction. And now, here he was, unconscious and needing their help. He didn't know how he should feel about this. This person did not deserve his help; he deserved to die.

Or, did he? Daniel realized that he didn't really know the wingman, nor why he did what he did. Yet, he was judging and condemning him in the same way Séraphin had judged and condemned him and Nemo. He was no better than the Sky-Prince.

He knelt over Nathaniel and checked his pulse. It was weak, but the wingman's heart was still beating. Then, Daniel noticed the air-tank that Nathaniel was still clutching in his hands, and his heart melted. He looked at Nemo, who was still in the water, and could not help but feel humbled and proud at the same time. His friend had apparently already forgiven the wingman, forgetting whatever had happened, and risking his own life to save him. He knew now that he would never doubt his friend's big and brave heart again.

Within seconds, Séraphin landed among them and walked straight to Nathaniel without saying a word. As he bent over to check on his friend, they noticed that his whole body was covered in cuts and bruises, scratches and blood, from the top of his head, down to his feet. His gorgeous black hair was all messy and bloodied, and his wings all torn and badly damaged. It was amazing the young prince could still stand tall and walk.

'He's unconscious, but alive,' Daniel said to him. 'He's hurt badly, though; he needs help.'

For the first time ever, Séraphin's face showed no anger or hate. There was concern there for Nathaniel, yes, but that was not all. He looked tired and almost like he was defeated. He examined Nathaniel's wounds one by one and then covered his body with his one good wing. The other one seemed to have been broken and he dared not move it yet.

Standing up, he then turned around and walked towards Nemo and the mermaids observing from the sea. Feeling too embarrassed to look at him in the eyes, with a soft and humble voice, he said to the Sea-Prince.

'Thank you for saving him, Nemo. I have been wrong about you; please forgive me, for everything.'

'And thank you,' he now addressed the mermaids. 'Your help came at a time most needed. I will always be grateful for this.'

Nemo said nothing, but simply bowed his head slightly, a feeling of accomplishment and peace washing over him.

One of the mermaids in the group, who looked like she was the oldest among them, glided forward and spoke for the rest of her sisters.

'We're happy we could be of assistance, Sky-Prince; we just wish we could have come earlier. It was only by chance that we happened to be in the area when we noticed all the commotion. Do you know what those things were?' she asked, motioning with her head towards the dead ravens all around them.

'They look like mountain ravens,' Séraphin answered, 'but I have never seen any so large or unfriendly.'

'Unfriendly,' Hëna snorted. 'There's an understatement. We almost got chopped into bits and pieces; and that's only the second time in so many days. I wonder what's next.'

'Strange things are happening indeed,' the mermaid agreed. 'Creatures never before seen, appear out of the blue, while some people disappear, and others get killed. There's talk of war in the kingdom and that has never happened before. You should be very careful, especially in these parts of Endërland; evil seems to have come this way first, for whatever reason. Which way are you headed, if I may ask?'

Séraphin now turned to look at Daniel, as if to ask for his approval first, and then answered.

'My friend is wounded badly and needs help. We are far from any village or city that I know, and the closest place I can think of where he might get the best help possible, is Dard'h.'

'The clan of your cousins?' Hëna asked. 'But that's at least six days from here.'

'Not if we go through the Shadow Forest,' Séraphin explained, knowing fully well how they would react to that suggestion.

'That is not a good idea, young Prince. That is where the Great Lord banished all evil when he first came here; to this day that evil is still there and no one who's ever gone in, has come back out. You're better off going to New Sotira.'

'That would mean turning back and losing even more precious time, and I don't think we can afford to do that,' Séraphin said, looking at Daniel again. 'We need to reach the Northern Mountains as soon as we can, and Dard'h is on our way. We just need to get there a bit sooner, that's all. There's five of us, if we count Lightning; I think we'll be alright.'

'I still think you should avoid going into the Shadow Forest; you have no idea what you may encounter there, and you will be cut off from the rest of the kingdom, with no hope of assistance from anyone, should you need it.'

'Heli agrees,' Hëna voiced her brother's opinion, 'he thinks it's a bad idea. We've never been able to see inside that forest; the trees are so high and so dense, that no light from outside can penetrate its borders. They don't call it the Shadow Forest for nothing, you know?'

'What's the alternative?' Séraphin asked, sounding desperate. 'Going around it for another six or seven days? Nathaniel might not last a day the way he is. We have to try.'

'You're forgetting one thing, Séraphin, we do not choose which way we go; we follow Lightning and Daniel.'

They both turned now to look at Daniel; Séraphin with a pleading look on his face, clearly a first for him.

In his mind, Daniel was already considering all the options. He knew that he was running out of time, but that was nothing new. And then, there was Dard'h; he wasn't particularly excited about the idea of visiting Ghordi's people. He did not imagine the mountain wingmen being any friendlier than Séraphin and his kin. Still, should he choose to risk Nathaniel dying, for fear of what might happen? He didn't know why Nathaniel had come to meet them, for all he knew, it was to make sure that they failed; yet, he could not let him die. If there was a chance that they could save his life, he'd take it.

'It seems to me that if we get to save a few days, we might have a better chance of saving Nathaniel, not to mention buying some more precious time for ourselves. I do not know what's beyond the borders of this Shadow Forest, but I'm willing to take the chance.'

Séraphin sighed with a sign of relief, while Daniel continued. 'Only, this all depends on Lightning, obviously; he's the one leading the way.'

He turned around and walked to the great black stallion who was standing not far behind them, appearing to follow the conversation closely. With one hand, Daniel stroked his long muscular neck, and spoke to him as he had done before.

'We need your help yet again, my friend. We need to know if you can lead us through the Shadow Forest, all the way to Dard'h. More than one life could be saved if we do this.'

Lightning looked at him through his big shiny eyes for a moment, as if thinking about it, and then shook his head upside down just once, in a reply that Daniel took as a 'yes'. He turned back to face the others and said.

'Well, I guess that's settled then; we're going through the Shadow Forest.'

'Thank you!' Séraphin said, bowing his head slightly in gratitude.

Hëna and Nemo did not speak.

'Very well, then,' the mermaid spoke one last time, 'I guess there is no more to be said. Safe journey, my young friends, and may the Great Lord light your way in that dark place. We take our leave now; our queen will want to hear about all of this. Good luck to you all!'

They all bowed their heads towards the company and made for the open sea when Nemo called after them.

'Wait, I didn't even ask you for your name. I would like to thank you properly someday for saving me.'

'Our queen's joy at your well-being is all the reward that we care about, young prince. However, I am known as Agnes, the Loud One.'

'Why do they call you that?'

'Perhaps one day you'll find out, Nemo, the Brave One.'

Nemo blushed at the compliment, and Daniel smiled. Agnes noticed and continued.

'Yes, I know how all the mermaids speak of you; but it will be my absolute pleasure to tell the story of your great bravery and sacrifice here today. Everyone in our kingdom will hear about it, and our queen will be most proud to have given birth to you, as I am just to have met you. Take care of yourself, young prince, and return safely.'

Not being able to think of anything else to say, Nemo simply waved and watched the mermaids disappear into the blue. He then walked out of the water, not without a sense of contentment, and joined his friends gathered around Nathaniel. The wounded wingman was still unconscious on the ground.

'I wish we had some Summer water with us,' Séraphin said as he was cleaning some of the wounds with a wet cloth. 'I don't know how else to help him.'

'The villagers in New Sotira used most of it on Nemo and the werewolves; they kept little for themselves,' Hëna reminded him. Then as if speaking for both Daniel and Nemo, she asked. 'What is he doing here anyway? Why were those things after him?'

Séraphin kept quiet for a moment, replaying the whole thing in his head.

'I do not know. The only thing he managed to tell me was that he needed to speak to me urgently and that it was very important. But there was no time; the birds were right behind him.'

'Whatever it was,' Daniel intervened, 'we'll never find out if we don't move fast. We should load him unto one of the horses and be on our way. The sooner we get to Dard'h, the greater the chances are he will survive.'

They agreed to tie Nathaniel up on Nemo's horse, with Hëna holding the reins, while Nemo would ride with Daniel. Once again, they resumed their journey towards the secret castle, this time heading towards the nearest point of entry into the Shadow Forest. No one spoke of it, but the same question was on everyone's mind: What would they encounter in the dark territories of this accursed place?

Chapter 11

ON THE RUN

$\mathcal{I}$t had been almost a week since Daniel had fallen asleep and refused to wake up, despite Sam's best efforts.

'Well, this is just grand,' she'd said to Freddie at one point. 'I can't sleep, and he can't wake up. Aren't we a pair?'

To her dismay, Freddie could not explain this any more than she could. All they knew was that Daniel's heart was still beating and his breathing appeared normal. Yet, that would not last long if he did not wake up soon.

After the first couple of days, Sam had begun to seriously worry. If Daniel did not get any nourishment in his system, his body would soon start to shut down and give up. She couldn't even entertain the thought of losing him like this. She had anticipated everything, from a siege on the little house in Sotira, to a running pursuit or a fight, and she could accept anything that might happen during a possible fend off, but losing him like this was just wrong.

Doing a quick research on the Internet on how to help keep Daniel alive, they concluded their best chance was to tube-feed him regularly. Freddie went to Gramsh to buy all that was necessary from the small town's hospital and returned the same day with enough material to last for at least two weeks. The people in Gramsh seemed to be more than happy to provide him with anything he needed, provided he flashed that green paper, of course.

303

Once back in Sotira, they fitted Daniel with the tube through his nose, and eventually managed to get some food into his stomach. It was a very delicate process and they had to be very careful while setting everything up, but once again Wikipedia, along with instructions Freddie was given in Gramsh, proved most useful.

After that, it had been mostly a matter of keeping Daniel clean and in shape. They took turns watching over him, but of course, Sam was the one who spent the most time with him. She would sit beside him for hours and hours, talking to him or exercising his arms and legs so that he did not suffer muscle atrophy from lying in bed for so long.

As she sat with him, it struck her just how much he had come to mean to her in these past few months, and for the first time in a long time, she began to feel uneasy. She looked at his handsome face, still relatively unknown to her, and played with his longish black hair, all the while wondering what it was about this one that had managed to touch her the way no one else ever had. She could think of nothing, and Daniel remained quiet, refusing to contribute to that silent conversation.

As she tried to sort out her feelings for him, she remembered the day at the waterfall and rebuked herself for not kissing him. If he never woke up, she wouldn't get that chance again. Right then and there, she decided that the moment he woke up and spoke to her, she would do it. Yet somehow, it was not the prospect of him never waking up that frightened her, but of him not kissing her back. She didn't care though, she would do what her heart demanded, and whatever happened, at least she would have peace knowing that she tried.

On the eighth evening of Daniel's sleepathon, Freddie walked into the room where they all slept, asking if she needed anything before he turned in for the night. Half aware of him even being in the room, Sam replied that she was alright, and then went back to her own thoughts. Without even commanding them, her eyes settled back on Daniel, who was breathing lightly on the mattress before her.

Earlier that day, his breathing had grown arduous, and he kept tossing and turning as if he was having a nightmare. She had tried to calm him down but had almost broken down in tears when that had failed. She hated seeing him like that but refused to leave his side anyway. She only took a few personal minutes, whenever nature called, or she had to go outside and check on the lasers and traps. Not once did she allow her guard to fall down; if they ever managed to capture Daniel a second time, it would not be because of any mistake of hers.

'He'll be alright,' she heard Freddie talking to her from his bed, 'you'll see. He's not alone in there, you know, and they won't be able to keep him for long.'

'But why take him in the first place? Why stop him from coming back? He couldn't stay away even if he wanted to.'

'Actually, that's not true. There are drugs that can induce a dreamless sleep; it wouldn't be that difficult, I imagine.'

'Yes, but why would he want that? He loves it there.'

'I'm not saying he would,' Freddie answered, 'I'm just saying ... Oh, forget about it; I don't know what I'm saying either. Things are clearly changing in Endërland, and everything I ever knew about it could just as well be history.'

Neither of them said anything for a little while, until Sam spoke again.

'Have you had any more of those dreams about him?' She referred to the dream Freddie had before Daniel was first kidnapped.

'No, none,' Freddie replied. She didn't know if that meant anything, but it changed nothing.

'Well, you know what they say; no news is good news.'

They spoke no more after that. Freddie dozed off and she went back to observing Daniel while he slept, memorizing each and every line on his beautiful face, and sinking once more into her thoughts of him.

A couple of hours into the night, while she was having one of those few precious moments when she was neither awake, nor asleep; a loud and continuous beep went off from her laptop speakers. She got up immediately and went to the nearest window that looked to the east. Even without reaching there, she heard someone scream out loud in pain, just outside the little house. One of her traps had apparently worked.

Once at the window, she looked outside and saw shadows of men moving in their direction. Freddie was at once by her side.

'They found us,' she said, hurrying towards Daniel. 'Help me with him.'

They wrapped him up in his blanket and dragged him downstairs and outside the back door. There they loaded him unto the raft that was tied fast in the canal behind the house. Holding only her gun, Sam jumped into the raft, placing Daniel's head on her lap, and cut loose the rope that held the raft to an old plum tree.

'You know what to do,' she called to Freddie, while the raft was taken away by the current. 'See you soon.'

'Good luck,' he called after her and turned hastily in the opposite direction. His job was to mislead the men and make them follow him instead of Sam and Daniel.

As the water led the raft carrying the two of them down northward, Sam prayed that no one was coming from that direction, or they wouldn't be able to get far unnoticed. But it seemed they had not completely run out of luck. They reached the river in a little over a minute without anyone spotting them, and from there, the stronger current of Tomorrica took them farther away with greater speed, first east and then turning westward towards Gramsh.

About five minutes passed and Sam was beginning to believe that they made it, when a loud and dry crack pierced the night, leaving behind a feeble echo. It appeared to come from the area around the little house they had just abandoned, and she knew exactly what it was. She immediately thought of Freddie, and fear for his life brought upon her the urge to stop the raft and run back to the house and make sure he had not been captured, or worse... But she couldn't; she was supposed to get Daniel away from there at any cost. Freddie would have done the same.

Uncontrollable anger came over her as she realized she might have seen the last of the young prophet. She had grown quite fond of the guy, even though she never allowed him to see it. She hated that she was unable to do anything about him now, and that frustrated her even more. She would have screamed out loud, if she wasn't afraid of alerting the kidnappers to their whereabouts, so she did the only thing she could do; she focused on Daniel and getting him to safety.

As they kept going, the smaller stream of Tomorrica joined the bigger river of Devoll, and their ride grew less bumpy and slower as the river grew wider and deeper. There wasn't much for Sam to do in the meantime, except make sure Daniel was all covered and comfortable. The feeding tube was still attached to him, though she had not managed to take anything to feed him with and didn't know when she would be able to find something else.

Looking at his peaceful face, she envied him; he had no idea what was going on with them and didn't have to worry. But then she remembered his troubled sleep earlier that day and realized that she had no idea what he was going through either. It was all one big crazy situation, which she never in a million years imagined she would find herself in.

If only Nan could see her now, she would surely have something to say about this.

The little canoe-like raft rode the bountiful waters of Devoll all through the night, always heading west. At places the river was so shallow, that she was forced to get off and push the raft herself, but other than that it was mostly easy sailing.

When a cluster of night-lights floated by to her far right, she figured she was now passing Gramsh. She still had a while to go; the original plan was to go as far down as Elbasan, a bigger town next to Gramsh, and then wait there for Freddie to meet them. But that had been before Daniel had fallen asleep, and before Freddie... She couldn't even think about that right now. She just knew she had to keep going and find a way to keep Daniel safe.

Busy as she was trying to figure out a solution, and aided by the darkness of the late night, she failed to notice something approaching fast in front of them and blocking their way. Before she even had a chance to react, their little raft crashed violently against a large dead trunk that had fallen into the river, throwing them overboard. The last thing she remembered was landing headfirst on hard rocks, and then it all went dark.

It was hard to believe it was barely midday as the silent group made their way between giant trees so close to each other that their tops joined high above their heads to create an impenetrable ceiling. The lack of sunlight, powerless to pierce through the thick intertwined branches, made for a cold and uninviting place, unlike any he had seen so far in Endërland. This was such a dark place, and were it not for the silver bracelet ever present on his wrist, Daniel would question whether he was still inside his dreamworld.

It had been a little more than an hour since they entered the Shadow Forest, and he was beginning to think that this wasn't the smartest decision he had ever made. Leading the way through the dark maze, following nothing but his sense of orientation, was Séraphin, on foot this time. His keen eyes could see farther than any of them, and despite deviating here and there to choose the easiest path, he maintained their course northeast, towards Dard'h.

Lightning followed, trotting in his footsteps, with Nathaniel secured fast on his back. The wounded wingman remained unconscious, despite their efforts to bring him out of his slumber. Daniel, Hëna, and Nemo followed behind on foot. The two horses that Ari had given them had been too frightened to enter the forest, so they had set them free.

Nemo and Daniel were both carrying lit torches improvised on the spot, without which they would have been unable to see farther than their own nose. Their flame gave little light and comfort in this dreadful place, but Daniel was glad to have them. He had never been too fond of the dark.

Their first few hours inside the forest went by completely uneventful. They kept on heading northeast, travelling mainly within the southern part of the huge forest. Very soon they found that cold and darkness were not the only things that set this place apart from the rest of the kingdom. As far as they could see, there was no sign of life anywhere around them; no birds flying, no squirrels going up and down the trees, no animals whatsoever. In fact, there was no sound beside that of their feet rustling through the fallen leaves and broken branches, or the occasional wind blowing here and there. Other than that, an eerie silence surrounded them, adding to the ghastliness of it all.

By the sixth hour, they were well inside the forest and knew there was no turning back now. Hëna kept looking after Nathaniel as best as she could; the young wingman had developed a high fever and his bigger wounds still kept bleeding from underneath the wraps and bandages. He would soon die if they didn't reach Dard'h in time.

Lined up behind Lightning, walking carefully on the path Séraphin chose for them, Daniel suddenly felt Nemo tagging at his elbow. He turned and saw his friend looking somewhat frightened.

'What is it, Nemo?'

'Maybe my eyes are playing a trick on me, but I swear the shadows of the trees are moving.'

'Moving?' asked Daniel.

'Yeah, it's like they're trying to get away from the light and hide behind their trees.'

Daniel looked in the distance, where the light of their torches met the trees around them. He saw nothing strange.

'It's an illusion, Nemo; the shadows move as we walk past the trees.'

'Yeah, well they're moving a bit too fast if you asked me. I don't like this.'

Daniel smiled.

'None of us like this, Nemo, it's a creepy place; but I wouldn't worry too much about shadows.'

He hadn't even finished speaking, when they felt a gust of wind blast them violently, and just like that, their torches went out and darkness engulfed them. As if scared to death, Lightning released a high-pitched cry and sprinted off as fast as he could. Séraphin called after him, and without waiting for the others, rose in the air and flew behind him, skilfully manoeuvring between trees and branches.

Left on their own, Daniel, Nemo, and Hëna stopped right where they were. They moved closer to each other, waiting for their eyes to slowly adjust to the dark, expecting the worse. They were not disappointed. They sensed movement on all sides and heard noises and sounds suggesting that a large number of people were gathering all around them. Invisible cold hands grabbed them, and using some sort of rope that felt too cold to the skin, their arms were tied to their bodies and they to each other.

This all happened in a matter of seconds. Before they could even react, a single fearsome voice of what appeared to be a person standing before their very eyes, spoke one single word.

'Walk.'

Without waiting for them to comply with the command, whoever had captured them, began to drag them forward, forcing them to put one foot in front of the other.

'Let's do as they say for now,' Hëna whispered, as if they actually had a choice. 'We need to find out what we're dealing with.'

Neither Daniel nor Nemo had a better idea, so they allowed themselves to be dragged by their invisible captors. About half an hour passed as they walked deeper into the forest, when they eventually arrived at what looked like an open court among the trees. Just enough daylight was allowed to enter from high above, making it easier now for them to see one another, and most importantly their captors. And that's when Daniel wished it was dark again.

More than two dozen creatures that had the shape and form of men but seemed to be made of dark mist, walked around them, some pulling on the ropes they had used to tie the three of them together. The ropes seemed to be made of the same substance as the creatures themselves, and it seemed to Daniel to be nothing else but shadow.

As they entered the court, heading towards the biggest redwood tree he had ever seen in his life, more shadows, seemingly belonging to the trees around them, detached and joined their friends. In no time, they found themselves surrounded by a vast multitude of shadowy creatures that kept on making dreadful whisper-like sounds.

When they finally stopped before the tall tree, the shadow that belonged to it glided upward from the ground, taking on the shape of a big man who seemed strangely as if dressed in a military uniform. All the other shadows fell silent at once, while fresh new chills went through Daniel's body.

The large shadow stood up tall before them, and in a whispery, yet booming voice, spoke.

'So, what have we here? Tourists, I see. It's been a very long time since last I've had the pleasure. Welcome, my friends; I am the General.'

At the mention of his title, all the other shadows bowed down towards him. He then moved closer to the three friends, as if trying to see them better through his hollow eyes. His face had a big round shape, but other than that, Daniel could not make out anything else; it was all just dark mist.

The General continued with a cunning kindness in his whispery voice.

'So, tell me, what business brings you into my forest? I don't usually get people coming so deep within my domain, not unless they've lost their way.'

Before any of the other two could answer, Hëna spoke first. She chose her words carefully, hoping her reply might discourage whatever sinister intentions the creatures most certainly seemed to have.

'We are on a mission from the High Council of the Lords; we were sent to find the Great Lord; his presence is needed in the kingdom.'

'Are you now?' the General asked, feigning interest and curiosity. 'Well, look no more my dears; you have found him.' The General raised his ghostly arms open wide as if to present himself. This prompted his troops to cheer for him again, which made for a strange chilling noise.

'*You're* the Great Lord?' Daniel asked, unable to hide his shock and disbelief. The General's face took on a shape that could be interpreted as a smile.

'I am, or rather used to be. The Great Lord and I were both one and the same before we came from the other world, your world, Visitor. Yes, I can smell it on you; it's still, oh, so fresh and tasty.' The General made a slurping sound that both frightened and disgusted Daniel. He continued. 'We had a different life back then, your Great Lord and I. We had it all; power, fame, riches beyond limit, and women to keep us company every night. Men worshiped and feared us, and our word was law. But, for some reason, he was never content with all of that, and somehow resented and blamed me for it. He grew tired of it all and wanted to put an end to it. It took all the strength that I could muster to finally convince him to go for a new beginning instead.

'Thus it was that we ended up here, planning to start all over again. When we did, however, he turned on me; he decided he wanted to build a world of his own, a world where he could do things his way and be happy, without me. So, he separated himself from me and imprisoned me within the borders of this accursed forest.'

'And how did he do that?' Daniel asked, not sure if he should believe a word from this creature. The General drew closer to him and stared at him intently.

'You haven't been in this world that long, have you, Visitor? With time, you find that things are possible here that you never thought could happen. I certainly didn't think *this* could happen to me; not until I found myself torn from him in a single heartbeat and abandoned here, alone and terrified. The trees have been my only friends throughout this whole time; they grew tall and dense, clothing the forest in darkness, so that I can move freely and without the light bothering me. They've taken good care of me for I don't even know how long.

'While he built an entire kingdom for himself out there, I built my own little one in here. I put whatever magic I had left into this forest and gave it its own life. There were only a handful of trees and bushes back then; now look at it, it's magnificent and endless. And it's all mine.

'With time,' he continued, 'I also learned how to multiply myself and make more of me, to keep me company. While this forest grew bigger by the day, so did the number of my young ones. It still does. And soon, there will be enough of us.'

'Enough for what?' Daniel could not help but ask.

It was impossible, but Daniel could swear he saw those hollow eyes light up for a single moment.

'Enough for my own little revolution,' the General answered, now raising his voice like he was giving a speech. 'You see, the day is coming for me to have my revenge for being imprisoned in this dark hell, cursed never to see the light of the sun, nor feel its warmth. This world will soon know the real face of its Great Lord, right before I tear it down to pieces and send it back to the abyss where it came from.'

The General yelled the last words with great anger, making even his children tremble in fear. Only Hëna seemed unperturbed.

'And how do you intend to do that?' she asked. She was hoping to buy some time while she came up with an escape plan, an idea already forming in her head. 'This forest will never grow fast enough, nor big enough; and if light bothers you as you say, you will never be able to leave it.'

'Oh, but we will, sweet girl, we will. Haven't you noticed out there? Times are changing; I know the Great Lord is no longer around. You see, even though we've been separated for ages, I have this special connection with him, and I can always feel his presence. But it's been too long since I've last felt it and that's how I know he has left this world. He's probably moved on to a new one or gone back to his old one. Better yet, he might have even died, and that means that no one can stop me from doing whatever I want to with this world. Soon, there won't be enough light left out there to bother me and mine, and that's when my moment will come.'

'What do you mean there won't be enough light?'

'Let's just say I have friends in very high places,' the General answered. 'My plan is already working, and actually even faster that I had predicted. All I have to do is wait just a little longer, and soon all the pieces will fall into place.'

Daniel had no doubt he was talking about Winter; they clearly had a deal together. Winter had the power to darken the days by blocking Heli's light, maybe that's what the General meant.

Hëna had heard all she needed to hear and decided time had come for them to leave. She whispered to Daniel standing on her right.

'When I tell you, close your eyes and don't open them until I say so.' She then turned to the General again and smiled.

'Well, we wish you good luck with your evil plan, and take our leave; we still have a long way to go.'

The General made a noise like laughter, joined by the hordes of shadows all around them. It was a nerve wrecking sound that made Daniel and Nemo tremble, but apparently not Hëna. She kept on smiling as the General spoke again.

'I'm afraid you're going nowhere, sweet girl. Desperate as your mission may be, I cannot let you run even after the slightest hope. No, you're staying here; my young ones have not feasted on human flesh for a very long time. Tonight, they party. Nice knowing you!'

The General saluted them in a military fashion and then went back to being the shadow of the massive tree. And just like that, the multitudes of shadows surrounding them, began to close in on them with incredible speed. Hëna wasted no time and shouted at Daniel and Nemo.

'Now.'

As the two boys shut their eyes tight, Hëna's skin began to glow very bright, and blinding light began to pour out from underneath her clothes and all of her body. In a matter of seconds, she was shining like a burning star, spreading powerful light all around her. The small open court now looked like a well-lit stadium. The shadows that were the closest to her, disintegrated at the first touch of light; the rest of them moved quickly and hid away behind trees in the deep of the forest.

The ropes that had been keeping them tied to each other disintegrated as well, and they were free to move again. Daniel and Nemo kept their eyes shut. From behind their eyelids, however, they could still sense the strong light, and realized what she was doing. They stayed put for another few moments, until eventually the brightness around them dimmed and Hëna told them they could now open their eyes again.

When they did, they found they needed a moment for their eyes to adjust. When eventually Daniel was able to see again, his jaw dropped. Hëna was standing before him, light still oozing out of her every pore. Her eyes were sparkling like little candle flames, her pitch-black hair looked even darker, and her skin shone like white phosphorus at night. She kept on shining enough light to keep the shadows away, but not enough to be of discomfort to either of them.

'Wow,' Nemo exclaimed first, sounding clearly excited. 'That is so cool; I didn't know you could do that.'

'Stick around, Nemo,' Hëna replied, smiling and winking at him. Her gaze then shifted on Daniel, who was still staring at her, completely awestruck.

'You're beautiful!' he finally heard the words leaving his mouth before he could stop them. Hëna smiled even more and then replied, 'Why, thank you; you're not too bad yourself'. She then burst into a sweet, delightful laughter, such as Daniel had never before heard from her. Nemo laughed too, now looking at the two of them with interest.

Realizing what he'd just said, Daniel became red all over. He felt mortified; he'd never allowed his mouth to run away from him before. Soon enough, however, he decided it was best to join the laughter and downplay the whole thing. So, he laughed along. Somewhere in the back of his mind, however, her words kept playing over and over again, '*you're not too bad yourself.*' Maybe she had meant nothing by it, but what if she had?

For the remainder of the day, he was able to think of nothing else but those words and her playful eyes as she had spoken them.

With some luck, they soon found their way back to the path they were initially following, and from there they continued their way through the forest towards Dard'h, tracing Lightning's footsteps. That proved easier than they feared, for the great stallion had almost deliberately left his trail behind, and aside from it, the forest was completely void of any other sign of life and activity.

317

Hëna continued to release enough light throughout the day, even though this began to drain her energy as the hours went by. But she could not afford to stop; the shadows kept on following them from a safe distance, never giving up their chase.

Once evening came, Heli took over leading Daniel and Nemo on their way out of the forest. Walking before them like a tall pillar of fire, he shone with a much stronger and brighter light than his sister's. His presence forced the shadows to completely disappear out of sight, so that they never saw any sign of them again.

In the early hours of the night, Hëna informed them that Lightning had already left the forest with the two wingmen, and they were now climbing their way up the hills towards Dard'h. They were about a day's walk ahead of them. Daniel and Nemo were beginning to feel quite tired but agreed not to stop until they left the Shadow Forest and were back out in the open air. So, they kept on walking without a break for the rest of the night and for the best part of the following day.

When Heli began his ascent to the skies on the third day since they'd entered the forest, they finally stepped out of the dense woods, happy like never before to see the light of day again. Before them rose tall and proud the Northern Mountains, their invisible and unreachable crest covered in snow and dark grey clouds. They stretched down east as far as the eye could see. Like most of Endërland, this was truly a sight to behold, though Daniel felt just a bit too tired to appreciate it properly.

They didn't walk long once out of the Shadow Forest; they found a small meadow that seemed perfect for them, just far enough from the edge of the woods, and set up camp to rest. It already felt like winter in this part of the kingdom, so they lit a small fire to keep warm, and then wrapped themselves in their blankets and slept.

Drained as she was of her energy, Hëna lay herself down next to the fire, and she too closed her eyes and went to sleep. Cold wind blew all around them, bringing down from the mountains more than just icy air, but the three were just too tired to notice or care.

Chapter 12

DARD'H

ëna was the first to be awakened by the noises around them. She opened her beautiful black eyes and got up, her hand immediately reaching for her sword.

'I wouldn't do that, Lightbringer.'

The words came from a bulky wingman with long white hair and large white wings half spread behind him. He stood arms crossed between two similar looking wingmen, both holding crossbows akin to the ones the mermaids used. Several more, also armed, were spread in a circle around the little camp, seemingly surrounding them.

Daniel and Nemo woke up one after the other and joined in Hëna's confusion at the sight of the armed wingmen.

'What's going on?' Daniel asked, directing his question at Hëna, rather than at their new 'friends'. The reply, however, came from the same wingman that spoke earlier.

'You must be the Visitor.' His face showed interest as he analysed Daniel standing before him, but his tone was harsh and commanding. 'What's going on is that you are coming with us; our Chieftain requests your presence. Pack your belongings; we're leaving right away.'

'What is the meaning of all this?' Hëna asked, pointing at the wingmen and their weapons. 'We are not a threat to your people.'

'My apologies, Lightbringer, but you misunderstand; we were sent to be of help and protection. Now, if you'd be so kind,' he moved aside, showing her the way. There was a hint of impatience in his voice, but the wingman knew better than to be rude to her.

The three moved quickly, packing all their belongings and shouldering their bags. Having released the horses, they were now forced to carry them on their backs all the way, and that made walking all the more arduous. The prospect of climbing uphill almost halfway up the mountains, where Dard'h was situated, now seemed even more challenging, and somehow, they doubted the armed wingmen would lend them a hand.

It was afternoon when they began climbing up the steep hill upon which the village of the wingmen was located. Sleeping for a couple of hours had not done much to restore their energy and strength, and Daniel felt even more tired than he did before.

Dragging his feet behind him, Nemo couldn't even lift his eyes off the ground. This was one of those days when he wished he was back under the sea with his mother. Heck, he'd even take his sisters' bullying over this. Still, he did not regret coming with Daniel, and was determined to go all the way. *'Until his debt is properly paid,'* his mother had said, and to that he would hold true.

The ascent was slow and difficult, but they kept on going. When they were still a good few hours from the village, Hëna departed, and Heli joined them soon after. The leader of the wingmen seemed to grow more uncomfortable in the presence of their big friend. He moved at the front of the line and stayed there until they finally arrived at Dard'h.

321

When they entered the village, they stopped in front of a small wooden shack at the far east side which had been prepared to host them. It stood a good distance from the rest of the collective houses of the Northern Tribe, and it did not match their style. It was obviously not built for them, and most likely, not by them either.

'Tomorrow, you will appear before our Chieftain who is most anxious to meet with you,' the bulky wingman told them as he prepared to leave them for the night. 'Tonight, however, you will rest here. Should you require anything, two of my wingmen will be stationed outside this door the whole time. Good night!'

He greeted them courtly and left, taking with him all but two of the armed wingmen who positioned themselves on either side of the door, like guards. This bothered Daniel even more. The northern wingmen's behaviour was unlike anything he had experienced so far in Endërland; he certainly did not feel like a guest. Still, he supposed it was to be expected; Ghordi's people were surely not very pleased with The Council's decision.

The small room inside the shack was pretty much as Daniel expected; there was a small stove in the middle, with the fire already going, and a big pile of cut wood at its feet for them to feed it. He saw three beds and a small table with water and washing amenities, but other than that, there wasn't much else. Clearly, no one ever really came in here, let alone lived in.

'Are you guys thinking what I'm thinking?' Nemo said, setting his backpack on the floor, and collapsing on the nearest bed, glad to get the weight off his feet.

'If you're thinking this is not really a guest house, then, yes,' Heli answered. He dropped his own stuff on the floor as well and went to feed the fire.

'Have you ever visited them before?' Daniel asked. He walked to one of the two remaining beds; left his bag underneath it and sat down too.

'A couple of times, yes,' Heli answered and then continued. 'I know what you're thinking, Dan, and I agree; something must be going on. They have always been a little different from the rest of their kind, but this is not how they treat their guests. Still, I wouldn't worry about it; let's wait and see what their Chieftain has to say first. In the meantime, I suggest you guys get some sleep; you both look terrible.'

Daniel and Nemo didn't even feel like responding to that; they were way too tired. They agreed that the best thing they could do right now was to rest and recover their strength. Tomorrow would come soon enough, and they could worry then about the mountain wingmen. They both lay down, happy it would be on a bed this time, and covered themselves with their blankets. As for Heli, he sat himself down by the fire, getting back to working on his wooden figurine.

* * *

Sunshine had just managed to creep in through the one window of the small shack, when a not so gentle knock on the door echoed through the silent room. Daniel woke up with a start. He opened his eyes to find Hëna sitting by the stove, staring at him.

'Good morning,' she said smiling, her eyes piercing through him with a strange light. Daniel felt slightly uncomfortable, as he usually did in her presence. He got up, his hand immediately on his stubborn hair.

'Have you been watching me all night?' he asked sheepishly.

'It's kinda hard to see through walls from up there,' she replied, her smile now turning into a grin. 'You talk in your sleep.'

'I do?' Daniel felt his cheeks grow red hot. 'Did I say anything?'

'Oh, nothing *I'd* be embarrassed about,' she said now, getting up and looking away from him, but still grinning. 'You, on the other hand...'

She stopped there, letting his imagination run wild with thoughts and theories. He followed her with his eyes, suddenly wishing he could read minds. He really enjoyed this playful side of her; he liked to think it meant something.

The second knock on the door was much stronger, and this time it woke Nemo up, too. Without waiting for a reply, the door swung open and the bulky wingman from the night before walked in, while four others waited outside.

'Good morning,' he greeted flatly, directing his words at Hëna only. 'I would like you to get ready, please; our Chieftain is expecting you.'

Hëna looked at Daniel and Nemo still rather unpresentable and answered for the three of them.

'Of course; give us a moment to refresh ourselves, please.'

The wingman nodded with his head and walked back out, closing the door behind him.

'Well, boys, time to get some answers. You ready?'

'Not really,' Nemo answered, yawning. 'I could do with some more sleep before facing more angry wingmen.'

Daniel and Hëna both smiled.

'Ready,' Daniel answered in a single word after he had finished washing his face.

They walked the distance from the small, secluded shack to the centre of the village in silence. The leader of the group walked before them with two of his men beside him;

the other two trailed behind them, their hands constantly on their weapons. On either side of them grew thick and strong trees, upon which were built numerous nests. It was nothing as artful and majestic as Sky-City, but it made an impression nonetheless, especially to Daniel, who had not yet had a chance to visit the city of the wingmen.

The centre of the village comprised of a small square among the trees, in the middle of which rose high and proud a prominent tree house. Daniel guessed it belonged to the Chieftain. Directly below it, a single throne sat on a small platform, raising it from the ground. Sitting on it, he saw a handsome looking wingman, with long blonde hair tied back neatly in a single braid. Like the rest of his tribesmen, he was slightly shorter than Séraphin and his folk, and stouter. Looking at his face, Daniel had the feeling that he should not expect any kindness from him, yet the wingman kept on smiling and putting on a cheery expression.

To his right, Daniel was surprised to see Séraphin standing. The wingman looked every bit the cold and unfriendly Sky-Prince he had seen before the Council of the Lords, and he made every attempt to avoid eye contact with the three. Daniel could not help but have a bad feeling about this. They were now truly at the mercy of the wingmen.

There was no sign of Nathaniel or Lightning so far. As they approached the square and were led before the Chieftain, Daniel began to wonder if he would ever get to see the brave stallion again.

A great number of wingmen were gathered at the square, standing at a distance from the throne of their leader. Many more sat on the branches of the surrounding trees, all looking down at the visitors being brought before them.

As they stopped only feet away from the throne, Hëna bowed her head in respect, prompting Daniel and Nemo to do the same.

'Greetings, Lord Gabriel! On behalf of my friends and myself I thank you for your kindness and hospitality. It has been a long and perilous journey, and we do appreciate the chance to rest safely with a roof over our head.'

The Chieftain bowed in return, and without losing the smile from his face, answered.

'You honour me beyond what I deserve, Lightbringer; I am no lord, but I do appreciate the courtesy. As for our kindness and hospitality, our doors will always be open to you and your brother, and you are welcome to stay with us as long as you please.

'I have to confess, however, that I had an ulterior motive when I sent for you; I was anxious to meet for myself our new Visitor and the Sea-Prince. They have become quite famed in these parts.'

Daniel lifted his eyes and looked at the blonde wingman, who was no longer smiling. He could now see the hate that had been hiding behind the smile, as well as the satisfaction that vengeance was finally at hand. Beside him, Séraphin continued to remain cold and expressionless.

The Chieftain continued.

'So, you can imagine the pleasure it brought to my people and myself, when our prince here brought us news of your arrival. It gave us a chance to make the necessary preparations.'

'Preparations?' Hëna asked, guessing what the answer would be.

'Why, for their proper trial, of course,' came the answer. 'You see, my people feel that the results of their first trial were quite..., unsatisfactory. They lost one of their own, and yet, no one was held accountable for it.'

'The Council of the Lords could not come to a decision in this matter, as I'm sure you've already been told, Lord Gabriel. So, they followed the law and passed this issue for judgment to the Great Lord. I need not assure you that his decision will more than satisfy your people and anyone else concerned.'

'I'm afraid that's just not going to do, Lightbringer. The Lords in Arba may have claimed ignorance and pretend to follow some old regulations that were never of use to anyone, but we all know that the Great Lord is long gone, and I will not have these two run free through the kingdom, laughing at the rest of us, while chasing legends.'

'WE are not pretending to be looking for anything,' replied Hëna, feeling like she was starting to lose her calm. 'We know exactly what we're doing and where we're going.'

'Of course, you do; I mean, if I wanted to find the Great Lord's long-lost castle, I too would follow a wild horse. It makes sense, doesn't it?' He directed his rhetoric question at the wingmen surrounding them, and laughter broke out in the square. Daniel did not blame them; they would not understand even if he explained it to them. After all, he still had his own doubts about the whole thing. Still, he could not help but feel his blood beginning to boil underneath his skin.

'Anyway,' the Chieftain continued, 'since you have been on the road for quite some time, it falls upon me to inform you of the latest developments in the heart of the kingdom. Your search is over, Lightbringer; you see, as of two days ago there's a new great lord and king in Endërland, the White Lord himself. And it is by his command, I'm afraid, that I must detain these two here, until he gives us permission to go ahead with their trial.'

'What?' Nemo exclaimed, without being able to stop himself.

Daniel could not believe his ears. Until now, there was always a chance that they were wrong, that Winter was not the one responsible for all that was happening in the kingdom. But now, according to Gabriel, he had come forward and declared himself great lord and king over all of Endërland. This was indeed bad news; the countdown had finally begun and there was no stopping it now.

'How do we know you're telling us the truth?' Hëna challenged. The Chieftain did not seem to take offense.

'Surely you and your brother must have observed this for yourselves, or have you been too distracted to notice?'

He gave a meaningful look to both her and Daniel. Hëna understood the insinuation all too well and became red in the face. Daniel looked at her and then turned his gaze towards Séraphin, hatred boiling inside of him as he realized the wingman had run away with his mouth.

'What of the other Lords?' Hëna asked, though what she really wanted to ask was what had happened to her father. She knew he would never go along with whatever Winter was doing.

Gabriel replied with a very diplomatic tone of voice.

'As I understand, they have pledged their allegiance to our new king and lord and will from now on serve as part of his governing body. This is the beginning of a new era, Lightbringer, and there will be many changes about.'

'So I'm beginning to see. However, I still have a little problem; I got my orders to find the Great Lord directly from the High Council, and if I'm to disobey them, I'm sorry, Lord Gabriel, but I will need a bit more than just your word.'

Gabriel smiled again, unable to hide his satisfaction.

'Lord Gabriel. I'm beginning to like the sound of that.'

He motioned to the wingman standing on his left, who came down from the platform, producing from inside his vest a rolled parchment. He handed it to Hëna, bowing his head ever so slightly, and then returned to his former position.

Hëna undid the seal and opened the parchment to read it. The letter instructed the Chieftain to detain the Visitor and Sea-Prince in the village until further notice, and was signed by His Majesty, the High King of Endërland.

Hëna took a moment to think before she spoke again. She needed to be very careful with what she said and did next; she might not be able to help Daniel and Nemo if she openly opposed Winter. She needed to buy some time, until they came up with a plan.

'Very well, then,' she finally spoke out loud. 'If this is indeed the will of the king, I shall obey. I ask only one thing, if I may, Lord Gabriel.'

'Anything, Lightbringer,' the blond wingman replied, eager to avoid any possible conflicts with her and her brother.

'I ask that I and my brother be allowed to stay with the Visitor and Sea-Prince, until their fate is decided. They were released onto our custody and remain our responsibility until the trial.'

'The shack is hardly a place worthy of your presence, Lightbringer. I would be glad to host you at my own house and treat you as my honoured guests for as long as you wish to stay.'

'Thank you, my lord, but the shack is an upgrade from the open road. It will do just fine.'

Gabriel thought about it for a moment and then decided not to pursue the matter any further.

'Very well, then; it shall be done as you ask. You may all reside in the shack until his majesty sends us word that we may proceed with the trial. That would be all,' he ended the meeting with a wave of his hand.

The armed wingmen began directing Daniel and Nemo back towards the shack and Hëna followed them, but not before giving Séraphin an angry look.

* * *

Back at the shack, Nemo could no longer hide his panic.

'What are we going to do, Dan? If they have their trial, we're as good as dead. These are Ghordi's people we're talking about. We're doomed.'

Daniel sat down by the stove, trying to relight the fire that had died during their absence.

'I somehow don't think Winter will let that happen. If he had wanted me dead, he would have had me killed a long time ago.'

'Well, he might need you, but I am quite certain that he has no use for me whatsoever. These wingmen *will* have my head, Dan.'

'Relax, Nemo,' Hëna cut in, 'It won't come to that. There won't be a trial.'

'What do you mean?' asked Nemo, now turning to her. Daniel also looked up at her, all ears.

'The first chance we get, I'm gonna break us out of here and we'll be back on our way.'

'How are you going to do that?' Daniel asked. 'You're locked in here same as we are.'

Hëna smiled at him mischievously. It made his blood boil for the second time that day, only, in the most pleasant way.

'Surely you don't think these walls can hold me in, do you?'

'I guess not,' he answered, realizing what she meant. 'Still, how are we going to continue our mission without Lightning to guide us? We won't know where to go.'

'That's why I need a little time to find out where they are keeping him and come up with a plan to free everyone at the same time. I might need Heli's help to do that. Until then, we have to be on our best behaviour and give them no reason to suspect anything.'

'What about Séraphin?' Nemo asked.

'What about him?' Daniel replied, his voice clothed in anger. 'He made his choice; we owe him nothing.'

'I agree,' Hëna said, 'Séraphin is no longer our concern. From here on, we continue without him.'

They spoke long after that about all the events that were now unravelling rapidly. The kingdom was at the brigs of war between wingmen and mermaids; Winter had crowned himself king, claiming the Silver Throne as his own as soon as the seasons had changed, and they had no idea what had happened to the other Lords and queens. Finding the Great Lord was no longer just about their innocence; and yet, it was still only a fool's errand.

Eventually, evening came and Hëna left the shack to join the stars up in the sky. Heli returned and took his place among them. They continued to talk for a while longer, discussing with him Hëna's plan, with which unsurprisingly Heli agreed. When they were finally about to get some sleep, just before midnight, the door opened and in walked Séraphin, followed by the bulky wingman. As soon as they set foot in, Heli ran towards the prince, grabbed him by the neck, and without a hint of a struggle lifted him up against the wall.

'Give me one good reason why I shouldn't break your neck, traitor.'

Daniel heard the anger in Heli's voice and could not help but get some satisfaction out of it. Ever since the audience with Gabriel, he himself had been itching to get his hands on Séraphin.

The Sky-Prince was unable to open his mouth, however, so it was the other wingman who spoke in his defence.

'He is no traitor, Lightbringer. Everything he's done and said to the Chieftain, has been to protect you all. And now, he's here to help you escape.'

Heli loosened the grip around Séraphin's neck, but only a little.

'Is this true?'

'Yes,' Séraphin managed to say with a rasping voice, prompting Heli to let him go. The wingman regained his posture and walked over to the table to grab a drink of water.

'Explain yourself,' Heli called after him.

Having soothed his throat enough, Séraphin took a seat on the bed closest to him, while the bulky wingman went back outside, shutting the door behind him. Daniel, Heli, and Nemo were still standing, looking at the Sky-Prince with expectation. But it was Daniel on whom Séraphin's eyes rested.

'When we arrived here and got Nathaniel looked after, he finally woke up and told me everything he knew. He told me how Winter had his man Butler working with Azariel to set you up. They killed Ghordi using one of the arrows they stole from you that day at the beach. The plan was not only to get custody of you apparently, but to also spark a war between the two people, and looks like they've succeeded, at least with that second part. Azariel's father found out about this from Nathaniel, so Azariel killed him, blaming this on the mermaids, too. And now, all my people are preparing to fly to battle with them to claim justice.

'Obviously using the situation as an excuse, Winter declared himself High King the moment he took his turn on the Silver Throne. He has given my people the go-ahead to fight. It all happened like you said it would, but I was too angry and stubborn to listen. Only the Great Lord can now bring an end to this madness, and that is why I'm helping you escape.

'Earlier I needed Gabriel's help in treating Nathaniel, so I had to play along and give him something. I'm sorry for fooling you, but I needed to keep Gabriel blind to my plan. I also advised Nathaniel to pretend that he doesn't even remember who he is; anyone could be a spy for the White Lord. This way he is safe from Winter, and we keep him off our scent, at least until we find the Great Lord's castle.'

'We still need Lightning for that,' Daniel reminded him.

'That's already been taken care of,' Séraphin replied. 'Nathaniel is waiting with Lightning just outside the village. If we leave now, we can reach them in less than an hour.'

Everyone was now waiting for Daniel to decide.

It had finally happened; Séraphin was now on the same page with them, though Daniel wasn't sure how to feel about it. He knew how he felt right this moment; he felt cheated. Cheated because he'd finally come to resent and hate Séraphin for all that he'd said and done, but apparently, it was all undeserved. The wingman had kept his honour and had not betrayed them. *He is a better man than I am*, Daniel told himself, feeling somewhat guilty. But none of that mattered anymore; they had to put everything that had happened behind them and get on with their mission.

He looked at Séraphin sitting before them completely disarmed and bare of his usual animosity, and walked up to him, extending his hand as a peace offering.

'I'm sorry I doubted you!'

Séraphin shook his hand, though he looked less comfortable than Daniel doing so.

'And I you.'

Daniel let go of his hand and headed to his backpack, putting it on his shoulders. He then turned around and looked at Séraphin again.

'Lead the way, my friend.'

* * *

Seeing Lightning again, Daniel realized just how much he had missed him these past few days. From day one the black stallion had been at his side, looking after him and even saving his life on more than one occasion. So, it made him wonder when, with the wounded wingman on his back, Lightning had sprinted out of the Shadow Forest and had left him behind. He did not blame him though; the shadows were dangerous creatures, and they obviously put a chill on the bones of even such a fearless animal such as Lightning. But now they were together again, and the stallion seemed to be just as happy as Daniel was to see him.

Upon proper introduction, Nathaniel bowed his head with humility, wincing from pain as he did so. The wingmen had taken good care of his wounds and he was recovering quickly, thanks for the most part to the healing powers of Summer water. But he was still quite weak and did not seem strong enough to fly. He held his mending wing awkwardly half spread behind his back, trying not to move it too much, while the biggest cuts on his body were still visible wherever his clothes did not cover him.

'I'm glad you are feeling better,' Daniel spoke first, bearing no hard feelings towards the wingman. Nathaniel lifted his head and dared to look straight in his eyes.

'Thank you! My lord Séraphin told me all that you did for me; I am forever in your debt.' He then stepped forward and kneeled before Nemo, who was standing beside Heli.

'I owe you more than my life, Nemo. Because of your bravery I still have a chance to atone for all the wrong that I did, especially against you. I promise that I'm gonna work hard to earn your forgiveness and trust.'

Not very comfortable with such scenes, Nemo looked shyly at the others before answering.

'Help us find the Great Lord and stop this war, and we're even.'

Nathaniel now looked up at Séraphin, kneeling as he was before Nemo. The Sky-Prince nodded with his head and then turned to Daniel.

'I wanted to go with you all the way and help you find the Great Lord, but as you know, I have to fly back home and try to stop my people from starting a war with the sea-folk. I am the only one who can talk to mother at this point, but I must leave now, or it will be too late. I have only one thing to ask of you; allow Nathaniel to accompany you in my stead, please. This quest belongs to all the people of Endërland, and I want a wingman to be present when the Great Lord is found.'

'Consider it done, my friend,' Daniel answered and made to climb on Lightning, but something in Séraphin's eyes told him the wingman was not yet done speaking. He moved a step closer to Daniel with his head down and continued.

'There is something else I must confess and beg your forgiveness for. When we first left Arba, my mission was to report back to the White Lord on everything regarding you, and I'm ashamed to say that so I did. While we were in New Sotira, I relayed to him all that I heard you share about your hiding place back in your world. I have put you and your friends in danger, and for that I will never forgive myself.'

Hearing of this, Daniel's heart sank. This meant that whoever was after him would soon find the little house in Sotira if they hadn't already done so. This was indeed grave news, especially since there was nothing he could do, no way to warn Sam or Freddie. He had no other option but to trust that they were able to look after themselves and would be alright.

As for Séraphin, what he'd done was real treason, and right now, Daniel wasn't too happy with the wingman. But he could see that the Sky-Prince felt awful about it, and whether he liked it or not, he understood why he'd done it. He might not be ready to forgive him right away, but he saw no point in saying it out loud. He reached for Séraphin's right hand and held it in both of his.

'What's done is done and cannot be changed. Let's just hope that everything will work out in the end. Fly fast and fly safe, Sky-Prince; hopefully, next time we will meet under happier circumstances.'

'Hopefully,' Séraphin replied and drew back, getting ready to jump up in the air, but not before turning to Nemo.

'Take good care of him, Nemo,' he said of Daniel; 'I can think of no braver man suited for the task. Your people should be proud.'

While Nemo bowed his head in thanks, Séraphin turned one last time to Heli.

'No one will look for you until morning; by then you will have gained a good distance and it will be difficult for them to find you in these mountain woods, but not impossible. Make the most of the time you have and try to stay hidden as much as you can. May the Great Lord lead your way.'

'And yours, Sky-Prince!' Heli replied. 'Fly safe.'

Séraphin said goodbye one last time and flew up into the night. The rest of the group lined up behind Lightning and began to follow him once again through unknown paths up the Northern Mountains.

They'd had their good share of walking and climbing, but Daniel was glad to be on the move again; he hated the idea of staying long in one place and losing precious time.

Finding the Great Lord was no longer just about him and Nemo; the fate of the whole kingdom depended on it.

* * *

The night kept growing colder as they continued to climb steep paths up the mountain. They tried to avoid making noise or leave any trail behind them that the wingmen from Dard'h might follow, but walking in the dark did not prove easy. The deeper they went into the woods and the higher they climbed up the mountain, the denser and thicker the clouds above them grew. There was now not a single patch of clear sky, and the moon was completely hidden from view.

They dared not light any torches for fear of giving away their position, so they had to rely on Nathaniel's sharp eyes for guidance. Very soon they began stepping on snow covered ground, which lucky for them made their surroundings more visible. The downside of that, of course was that their feet got cold and wet, and their progress much slower. But they did not stop. By daybreak they had gained enough distance from Dard'h to be confident that they were out of immediate danger. Before leaving, however, Heli advised them to stay hidden during the day and rest. Travelling only during the night would be much safer for all of them; the wingmen's eyes were sharp in the dark, but they were still more likely to be found during daylight. So, they found a small cave, well hidden from view, and set up camp there for the day. Hëna would join them soon thereafter.

The cave was located halfway up the highest peak, in the endless series of the snow-covered mountains that made up the northern borders of Endërland. The village of Dard'h was built on the foothills of a second peak to their left, low enough for it to be free of snow for the most part of the year. Why they had chosen to live that far from the rest of their

337

peers, Daniel could not say. He just knew from the Chronicles that they were only a small colony when they first settled there and had now grown to several thousands.

As he looked out of the cave at the mountainside they inhabited, he was amazed that he could not tell where their village was. The wingmen had become masters at blending with their surroundings, though it did make one wonder why they would ever need to hide, if there was never any danger to begin with.

The cave turned out to be an ideal place for them to hide and rest. Not long after daybreak and all throughout the day they saw groups of wingmen flying in pairs above them. They had obviously discovered the empty shack and were looking for them. To be safe, they decided to stay put until evening fell again, though Daniel hated this. He was cutting it real close; who knew how many days had passed since he had fallen asleep, and how much time he had left, if any at all? For all he knew, he might have already died; it's not like he would be able to sense anything from inside his dreamworld. Or would he?

As if sharing his concerns, Lightning appeared restless all day long and Daniel had to calm him down more than once. He wouldn't put it past the stallion to leave the cave and resume the journey, with or without them. Struggling a lot, he managed to get the black beauty to sit down at some point, and then sat beside him, resting his head on the stallion's muscular body.

When she returned, Hëna sat with them, her shoulder casually touching his every now and again. Nemo and Nathaniel lay down against the wall opposite them, already asleep. The wounded wingman needed all the rest he could get in order to heal. As for Nemo, well, he just seemed to really love sleeping.

They spent most of the day talking to each other like two old friends, Daniel no longer feeling so nervous around her. They had been through a lot together ever since they'd left Arba, and no longer felt like strangers. And yet, his heart would never fail to skip a beat whenever he looked into those beautiful black eyes, wondering what it would feel like. He could reach out with his hand and touch her face, her hair; he could lean over and kiss those lips, and somehow, he knew that she would not push him away. But he didn't. Instead, he chose to keep on fantasizing about it and the day when he would actually get the courage to do it. Hopefully, someday soon.

* * *

For two more nights they continued to follow Lightning, advancing from one mountain to the next into what seemed like an endless and at times pointless journey. All they ever saw around them was snow and dark clouds; life had completely abandoned these parts and it now looked like even the warmth of the sun could not reach it. It snowed constantly and the bitter cold became the norm, as if winter was born in this very place.

By the third night Lightning led them through a wide field, high as they had ever been until now. The air was cold and thin, causing them to breathe with some difficulty. As they reached the end of the field, the black stallion headed down a barely visible valley through a very narrow and slippery path.

Thinking that they were about to climb up to the next adjoining hill, Daniel got a bit frustrated that Lightning chose to take them down this path, since crossing higher up appeared much easier. But just as he was about to complain, he noticed that the path continued into something like a tunnel under where the two hills joined. If they'd continued even a couple of feet higher on the field, they would have never seen the path, nor the tunnel. Anyone who would ever venture in these parts and was looking to continue to the following hills, would have simply chosen to walk higher up the field. And even if they were looking for the path, they would not be able to find it, unless they knew exactly where it was.

Daniel's heart now began to race faster at the thought of finally arriving at their destination. The others were having similar feelings of anticipation, and as if by unspoken accord, they all hastened their pace.

The tunnel turned out to be quite short; only a few steps and they were on the other side of it, where they all stopped, staring in awe at the wonder before their eyes. The place they found themselves in was an enormous cave, inexplicably bright and covered completely in ice. A beautiful blue glow gave the whole place a moon-like shine, which Daniel especially appreciated.

On the far wall opposite them they saw the facade of a small castle, which was no doubt built inside the mountain. How deep it went they could not tell from where they were, but the courtyard in front of it seemed spacious enough to host over two hundred people. A high wall, seemingly made of ice, surrounded the courtyard. It prevented access to the castle, apart from a small iron gate, which they soon found to be locked.

'We found it,' Nemo yelled, excited and in awe. 'We found it, Dan; we found it.'

Daniel kept staring at the castle before them and didn't know if he should believe it or not.

'I do believe he's right,' Heli affirmed, 'If this is not the Great Lord's castle, then I don't know what it is. Well done, Dan; you did it.'

'*We* did it,' Daniel corrected him, not taking his eyes off the castle. He wasn't sure what to think. Its walls seemed cold and unfriendly; it looked old enough, and it gave the impression that it hadn't known life, at least not for a long time. He took two steps towards the iron gate and stopped right in front of it. 'Do you think he's in there?'

'There's only one way to find out,' Heli said, moving past him to check the gate. He gave it a push, testing it, but the gate wouldn't bulge. Ice had built up all over it, making it impossible for them to climb over.

'Guys,' Nathaniel called, while scanning the area around. 'Don't you find it strange that there's ice everywhere? This is a cave; it does not rain or snow in here, so, where did this much ice come from?'

'Maybe the water comes from the cave walls and freezes from the cold temperatures,' Daniel said thoughtfully. 'It's not that uncommon really.'

'Or maybe Winter's been here,' Nemo suggested. They all looked at each other, not sure what to say to that. Everything was possible, but if that was true, then this was bad news.'

Heli turned again to examine the gate.

'I could probably take care of the ice, but I don't know if that would help.'

'If you can take care of the ice,' Nathaniel said, getting closer to observe, 'then I'm sure with enough heat you can take care of the lock too. Have you ever tried something like that before?'

'No, but in theory it should work.'

'Then, I guess it's worth a try,' Daniel added.

Heli removed his backpack from his shoulder and handed it to him.

'Hold this for me please and give me some space. It might get a bit hot in here.'

The three boys stepped back as Heli placed his right hand where the lock was supposed to be.

Letting out a frightened sound, Lightning trotted backwards, appearing nervous. He began stomping his feet on the frozen ground, as if getting ready for a fight. Daniel walked up to him, trying to keep him calm, while watching Heli's hand gradually glow red and causing the ice over the lock to start melting. Soon, the whole gate got hot enough that all the ice on it thawed off. Then the metal of the lock began to turn first bright red and then yellow. In a manner of minutes, the heat being released from his hand left a big hole where the lock was, and the gate eventually swung open inwards.

Taking a deep breath and smiling feebly, Heli wiped the sweat from his forehead and turned to face them.

'That was easier than I thought it would be. Alright then, what are we waiting for? Daniel, you wanna go in first?'

'I think you've earned that honour, my friend. Lead on,' Daniel said, patting him on the shoulder.

'Follow me then, and better keep your weapons ready, just in case.'

Sword in hand, Heli now advanced through the open gate, while Nathaniel and Nemo followed after him. Daniel pulled on Lighting's reins, but the black stallion would not move. Shaking his big head, he refused to take a single step towards the castle, prompting Daniel to stop, too.

'Guys, wait,' he called after them, 'Lightning's afraid of something. Maybe we should...'

'Now what?' Heli called, turning around to see what the deal was. He had just entered the courtyard, when all of a sudden something sharp cut through his left thigh, causing him to fall down on the ground, screaming in pain. Blood began pouring out of the wound, and in a matter of seconds, the icy ground where he fell, turned red and soggy. Caught completely by surprise, Heli turned to see what attacked him. At that exact moment, Nathaniel and Nemo both stepped backwards out of the gate, their faces white with horror.

A loud and powerful roar echoed through the cave as from inside the courtyard a giant creature reared its triangular head high up towards the ceiling, its hollow eyes fixed on the intruder. Its shape was similar to that of a lizard, with amazingly big teeth and what seemed to be two horns, where its ears should be. As it moved slowly towards Heli, the boys could see the rest of its body. The head was attached to a gigantic horse-like torso by a thick long neck, while its long tail ended up in the shape of a blade. A line of sharp spikes ran all through its body, from the tip of its head, down to the end of its tail. It had no wings, as far as they could see.

Seeing blood dripping from its sharp tail, Heli realized that was what had wounded him. The creature was not only white as snow, but it actually appeared to be nothing but ice and snow. It was alive, yet it wasn't a living thing.

Daniel could not believe his eyes. He had read much about dragons in his books, and this thing fit most of the descriptions, yet it wasn't real; it was somebody's work. It had been manufactured for a purpose and there was only one person who could have done this.

Alarmed, he dropped Lightning's reins and everything else he was carrying on his shoulders, and drew out his bow, running towards his fallen friend.

'Heli, get out of there.'

Heli had already gotten back up to face the dragon.

'Daniel, stand back,' he called. 'This is my fight.'

'No,' Daniel shouted, firing two quick arrows at the ice beast with a speed that surprised even him. His arrows were masterfully crafted from a strong unbreakable material, finished with a silver tip, and they had never failed him before. But, as they made contact with the creature, they simply bounced back, causing no harm whatsoever.

'You can't help here,' Heli yelled. 'Guys, hold him back.'

Nemo and Nathaniel grabbed Daniel as he was darting past them to get to Heli, but they did not have to restrain him. Seeing that his arrows didn't work, Daniel stopped and tried to think.

In the meantime, the dragon had come close enough to attack Heli, and raising itself up on its hind legs threatened to crush him under its massive front paws. Heli rolled swiftly to the ground, ignoring the pain from his left thigh, and raised his arm trying to insert his blade in the underbelly of the beast. The sword glided on the hard exterior of the dragon, making a screeching sound, but causing no damage. He slid away from its hind legs, and swung his sword again, trying to cut through the left one. The sword bounced back, just like Daniel's arrows had done before.

Frustrated, Heli got back up and tried to run away from the dragon as it was turning around, but its tail swept under his feet and dropped him to the ground. Then, just as fast, the dragon aimed its blade-like tip of the tail at his heart and struck hard. Heli rolled quickly on to his left side, causing the tail to punch a hole on the ground, where he'd been only a second ago. He prepared for a second blow, and just as it came, he rolled back to his previous spot. This time, however, as the dragon's tail hit the ground next to him, he swung his sword, and as the metal struck, the thinnest part of the tail broke like glass.

There was no blood, nor any shrieking from the beast that had now managed to turn completely around, facing him again. Moving quickly, the dragon lifted its front right leg, and caught Heli on the ground between its claws. Heli screamed in pain under its immense weight and cold, while the dragon brought its large head closer, examining its prey.

Horrified at the sight of Heli being crushed, Daniel shook his friends off and ran through the gate inside the courtyard.

'Heli use your heat. It's nothing but ice; kill it with your heat.'

Daniel wasn't sure if Heli heard him or not, but he did not manage to repeat himself. The dragon swung its long tail at him and threw him flying back outside the gate. The force of the impact left Daniel gushing for air, but he didn't care. With the boys' help he got up again and began running back towards the dragon, which at that very moment released a loud roar, as if in terrible pain.

Moving backwards and away from Heli, the dragon kept on roaring as it lifted its front right leg, which Daniel saw was now halved and dripping water. Below him, Heli stood clothed completely in bright yellow fire, lifting up his sword, which was similarly covered in flames. Without looking or speaking to anyone, Heli advanced towards the dragon that seemed to have realized it could be hurt. Unable to go far from him, the dragon kept threatening him to stand back, but Heli continued to advance.

His flames grew bigger and stronger, while all the ice around him began to melt away. The dragon started to sweat as the great ball of fire cornered it against the wall of the cave. In a last attempt, it swung its tail against Heli, but the flaming sword cut through it without any resistance.

With awe and wonder in their eyes, the three boys watched as a pair of flaming wings, much like those of a wingman, grew out of the ball of fire and carried Heli up in the air. Approaching the dragon's head, while the beast was trying in vain to fight him off, Heli landed a series of blows with his fiery sword and slashed the dragon into pieces. He proceeded to slash away mercilessly, until the ice creature stopped moving and was no more. When he was done, all that was left was multiple piles of ice on the ground that continued to melt under the unbearable heat of Heli's flames.

When he was sure that the dragon was no more, Heli began to descend, reducing his flames until his naked body fell on the cold ground. The boys ran fast in his direction, dropping on their knees beside him. They noticed with horror that his chest was crushed and had turned blue under the weight of the dragon. Blood was pouring out of his mouth and right thigh. His eyes were closed, but his chest was still moving up and down as he struggled to breathe.

Daniel's heart almost stopped when he saw the state of his friend. This looked really bad.

'Nemo get some blankets please,' he spoke with a trembling voice. Nemo ran back to Lightning and their bags, returning with two blankets. They used one as a pillow under Heli's head and the other to wrap his naked and bruised body.

Daniel leaned closer to his big friend, careful not to touch his wounds.

'Heli, can you hear me? Can you open your eyes?'

Heli opened his eyes slowly and gave him a weak smile.

'Hey, Dan; I told you this was my fight.'

'Yes, it was; and you won, Heli, you killed it. Are you hurt badly? Can you move?'

'I think I've come as far as I can, my friend. I'm sorry; I can go no farther with you.'

'What are you talking about? You're gonna be ok.'

'Here,' Nathaniel drew his attention, handing him a small flask. 'It's Summer water; they gave it to me in Dard'h.'

Daniel hurriedly took it from him. Hope lifted his spirit in a heartbeat; maybe his friend would be alright after all. He poured some into Heli's mouth, who swallowed it with difficulty, and then poured some more unto his open wound. To their dismay, the water had no visible effect on the wound and Heli did not appear to be feeling any better.

'Why isn't it working?' Daniel almost screamed, scared and desperate.

'I don't know,' Nathaniel answered, 'it should work; it took much less time with me.'

'Maybe I didn't give him enough.'

He tried to make Heli drink some more, but his friend refused.

'It's alright, Dan, you tried.'

'No, I can save you,' Daniel insisted; now barely holding back his tears. The dreadful idea that Heli might not make it, was sinking into him like a rock in deep waters.

'There's nothing you can do for me, Dan, but there's still time for everyone else. Please, promise me you won't give up looking for the Great Lord. You have no idea how close you are.'

'I...,' Daniel tried to speak, but Heli had not finished.

'And promise me you will look after Hëna; she won't be the same after this.'

'I promise,' Daniel managed to say, tears chocking his every word. 'I promise.'

Heli smiled once more and then turned his head to look at the castle before them.

'We did it,' he said one last time, smiling feebly. He then spoke no more. His battered chest stopped moving up and down, and he went still.

Just as his last breath left his lungs and his eyes closed never to open again, up in the night sky, where they could not see, the light of the moon shimmered and expanded in a big quick wave throughout the sky, while the moon itself began to descend towards the earth, growing ever smaller and dimmer.

* * *

As all of Endërland was rapidly enveloped into darkness, inside the confines of the Shadow Forest, the General detached himself from his tree, stopping for a moment as if to sniff the air about. Sensing the same, the rest of the shadows gathered all around him, awaiting his orders. There were hundreds of them, all lurking around impatiently and smelling the air like a pack of starving dogs waiting for their bone.

'Do you feel it, my children? It's gone, it's really gone. We are free at last.'

The shadows exploded in a triumphant cheer and applause, though it sounded nothing like it.

'Now, we have work to do. Before anything else, we must take care of this Visitor, and I know just where to find him. You shall all pay him a visit; go, climb the mountain, and give him a kiss he will never forget. Then, you are free to feast on all the flesh you can find; it's time to rid this land of its current population. A new world order is at hand, and we will be its sole masters this time.'

Cheering maliciously and gliding above ground and between trees, the shadow armada headed speedily towards the Northern Mountains and the cave where Daniel and his friends were.

* * *

Not a minute passed since Heli gave his last breath, when Hëna appeared running through the gate, her face drenched in tears. She threw herself at her brother's dead body and hid her head in his chest; the sound of her uncontrollable sobs echoing through the cave. Time stopped all around them, and everything else went dead quiet. The only sound that could be heard was Hëna's inconsolable wailing over her brother's dead body.

She sat like that for what felt like an eternity and none of the boys dared approach her. They just stepped back, leaving the two of them alone. Daniel buried his head in his hands, as if trying to keep the images away. Not far behind him, Nemo sat down on the cold ground, weeping like a child, while next to him, Nathaniel stood with a shocked expression on his face, not even trying to fight his tears.

Daniel felt like he could shut down right then and there. He wanted to scream and shout so badly, but he couldn't. He'd grown so fond of Heli during this journey and had come to think of him as a brother and a friend. But now, he was no more, and Daniel didn't know how to process all of it. It just felt so unreal, so impossible. He refused to believe that this was happening, that Heli was really gone; yet there was no hiding from reality.

They lost track of how long they sat like that, neither of them daring to say or do something. After enough time passed, Hëna got up, wiping her face with the back of her hands.

Daniel somehow found the courage to step in front of her, head down.

'I'm so sorry, Hëna. We had no idea what was waiting for us here.'

'This isn't your fault, Daniel; he knew what he was doing.' Her words came out strained and weak, and her tears had not abated one bit. Her eyes did not meet his, however. 'We have to get inside; I have a feeling something worse is about to happen.'

'We still haven't been inside,' Nathaniel informed her in a soft compassionate voice, 'We don't know what else may be waiting for us in there.'

'We'll have to take our chances,' she said, lifting her brother's sword from the ground and heading towards the main doors. Daniel followed her, unsheathing his own sword, while Nathaniel drew out his fighting knives. Halfway to the doors, Daniel turned back and handed Nemo his bow.

'Stay with Heli please, Nemo.'

Nemo accepted the weapon without objection and stayed behind.

Once at the big doors, Hëna pushed them open and walked inside, sword first. The room appeared to be big, but it was quite dark, so she couldn't tell just how much.

'I need a torch,' she called behind her, but Daniel was already preparing one.

She had barely taken one step inside, when two men came at her, attacking simultaneously. Having no time to stop and think, she ducked as the first one swung a mace at her and slashed the second one in half with a masterful swing of her sword. He fell down on the floor and didn't move. Kneeling as she was next to his lifeless body, Hëna pointed her sword behind her as if she was sheathing it. The first man had now turned and was going for another strike, but as he approached her, he did not see her sword and ran full speed into it. The sharp metal went deep inside his guts and stopped him in the middle of his attack. Hëna then removed her sword, causing the man to wince from pain. As she got back up on her feet, the man dropped his mace and fell on the floor on top of his friend. It all happened in mere seconds.

Holding her sword up and checking her surroundings for any other threats, Hëna finally allowed herself to breathe.

Daniel and Nathaniel walked in to find her standing on top of the dead men, with an empty look on her face.

Under the light of the torch that Daniel was holding, they could finally make out clearly the two attackers, but what they saw made no sense. The men lying before them were not really men; they looked more like something between a man and a wolf. Their whole body was covered in dark grey fur, their front legs had been transformed into human arms that ended into hands with four fingers, and they walked on their back legs that looked barely human. Their heads had not changed much, and they still looked pretty much like wolfs, except for the fact that they stood, moved, and fought like men. It was clear that whoever had done this was only interested in using these creatures as fighting machines.

'Great, more monsters,' said Hëna with disgust.

'What are they?' Nathaniel asked shocked. 'I've never seen anything like this before.'

'Yeah, well, stick with us,' Hëna said in a dry and colourless tone, grabbing the torch from Daniel and moving further in to explore the room.

'This is definitely Winter's work,' Daniel said, observing the fallen wolfmen. 'The ice, the dragon, these creatures; he must have known about this place, that's why he's been trying to keep us from getting here.'

'Well, if he's been using this castle for his purposes, then what about the Great Lord? Where is he?'

'I don't know,' Daniel answered, despair and exhaustion finally catching up to him.

The room grew bigger and brighter as Hëna began to light torch after torch going forth. Soon there was enough light for them to see that they were standing in a hall big enough to host hundreds of people inside. From the door, a red carpet was laid, with tall marble pillars rising on either side, upon which were placed large golden bowls filled with burning oil. The red carpet stopped in the middle of the hall, where a single throne was raised on a platform above the ground. Even under the weak light of a few torches, they could see the throne was also made of gold. A lot of craft and care had gone into it. The rest of the hall had little in the way of ornaments or decorations. It looked like it had never actually been used and dust covered everything, except for the throne. Someone had actually sat there just recently.

'Daniel, can you bring Heli inside, please?' Hëna asked, her voice weak and trembling. 'I'm gonna check the adjoining rooms quickly to make sure there's no one else in here.'

Daniel simply nodded and headed outside. Nathaniel decided to go after Hëna in case she needed help.

Not too far from the castle, a dozen wingmen that had chanced upon their trail and followed it up to the field, were now climbing down the narrow path and heading towards the tunnel that led to the cave. They found themselves outside the castle just as Daniel and Nemo were entering the hall with Lightning carrying Heli's body.

'Stop right there,' the leader of the group shouted, drawing his crossbow, and prompting his men to do the same.

Caught by surprise, Daniel and Nemo froze in place for a moment, not knowing what to do. The wingmen began advancing faster towards them, but before they even got to the middle of the courtyard, first the ones that were in the back and then the rest of the troops began to scream.

In the faint blue light that illuminated the courtyard Daniel could make out some dark silhouettes out of the whole mess, and it was with horror that he realized what was happening.

'Nemo, we need to close the doors,' he screamed. 'Quickly.'

They moved hurriedly to shut the heavy doors, just as the wingmen slowly and painfully began to disintegrate into thin air before their very eyes. Lightning began to neigh fearfully and trot nervously behind them.

Hearing their shouts, Hëna and Nathaniel ran back into the room, weapons ready.

'What's going on?' Hëna asked.

'We need your help,' Daniel answered, alarmed. 'The shadows are outside. They will try to get in here when they're done with the wingmen.'

'What wingmen?' It was Nathaniel who asked this time.

'A group from Dard'h; I guess they found our trail and followed us here. The shadows got to them just before they could come in here. We need you, Hëna; you're the only one who can keep them off.'

'No, I'm not,' Hëna replied, a sad tone in her voice. 'I have no more light in me; it's all gone. It left me as soon as Heli died. I'm sorry, Daniel; I cannot help this time.'

'Then, what do we do?' asked Nemo, his voice trembling with fear. 'Light is the only thing that can keep them away.'

Daniel suddenly grabbed the log back from Hëna's hand and began lighting every torch in the room and setting fire to all the oil bowls on top of the pillars. The others understood what he was doing, and each grabbed a torch of their own to help. Very soon, the royal hall was lit so bright, that they needed a moment to let their eyes adjust.

They had just lit up the last torch in the big hall, when the shadows began pounding on the doors from outside. They tried to squeeze in through the cracks and from under the doors, but the room was too bright for them to survive, so they drew back. Still they kept on pounding and pounding relentlessly on the doors.

Inside, the guys breathed a momentary sigh of relief. They were safe for now, but how long was it going to last? And even if they had enough oil and torches to keep the fires going for a good while, how long could they stay in there? And what would become of their mission? Not that they knew where to go from here; they had indeed found the castle, but there was no sign of the Great Lord anywhere. Heli was dead, and unless a miracle happened, they would soon suffer the same fate.

Under the ceaseless sound of the pounding doors, everyone fell quiet and instinctively drew back to the middle of the hall, next to the throne. Daniel was the first one to say out loud what they were all thinking.

'We don't have much time; this light is not going to last forever.'

'Where do they come from?' Nathaniel asked of the shadows. He had not heard of them before.

'From the Shadow Forest; they've been stuck in there since the beginning of time.'

'But what are they?'

'It's a long story,' Daniel answered again, 'and I don't think we have enough time to tell it. We need to think of a way out of this and quickly.'

'Maybe there's a secret passage somewhere in the castle,' Nemo suggested, 'a back door out of here.'

'That's a good idea Nemo; we should start checking the entire castle right away.' Daniel felt a hint of hope revive his strength.

That hope died very soon, however, when Hëna next spoke from the steps in front of the throne, where she was now sitting.

'That won't help.'

She sounded as if she had given up.

'Why not?'

'Because they are everywhere. Heli's light was the only thing that was keeping them away, and now that he's gone, there's no stopping them. It's over, for all of us.'

'You mean; they're going to kill everyone out there? Every single person?'

'If they haven't already; it's only a matter of time.'

'Even the mermaids?' Nemo asked in a childlike voice. Hëna appeared to be thinking about it.

'They might survive; somehow I don't think the shadows can swim. Of course, they'll never be able to come ashore again even if they do.'

Everyone fell silent again, pondering the consequences of this new terror. They could not believe life in Endërland was about to end and they were locked up in here, unable to do anything about it.

'There must be something we can do,' Nathaniel said again. 'We can't just sit here and wait for everything to end.'

'If you have any ideas, I'm all ears,' Hëna replied as if she didn't really expect any.

Daniel appeared to be thinking of something.

'What happens to the sun and moon now that ...?'

He found that he could not finish that sentence. Hëna gave him an empty look.

'Someone else is supposed to take our place, but it's the Great Lord that appoints them, and as you know, he's still playing hide and seek with us.'

'Right,' Daniel remembered. 'Then I guess we really are doomed. We might as well open the doors and welcome them inside, for they will get in eventually.'

No one replied to him. They were all sitting down by now, giving in to the fact that these were their last moments alive. Daniel looked at them and then at the empty throne on his right.

355

'And we actually thought we found him. This is nothing but an empty castle with an empty chair. All that we went through, all the travelling, the running, the fighting, Heli; it was all for nothing.'

Lost in his despair, Daniel approached the throne and just slumped on it.

What happened next, no one could have foreseen. At the first contact with his body, the throne lit up entirely, as if millions of tiny lamps inside it came on all at once. The bracelet on his wrist fell open on the floor, just as a bright wave of golden light emanated from the throne and spread evenly all around them, adding to the brightness of the hall.

Before their very eyes, Heli's body, which was still resting on Lightning, began to levitate and shine increasingly bright, its light becoming one with that coming from the Golden Throne. When it reached the doors, the light went through them and outside the castle, causing a series of multiple shrieks for a brief moment, that was then followed by absolute silence. The pounding on the doors stopped at once and they could hear nothing else.

Having closed their eyes to shield them from the strong burst of light, Daniel, Hëna, Nathaniel and Nemo now opened them to find that Heli's body had disappeared.

'Where did Heli go? What did you do, Dan?' Nemo was the first to ask.

Daniel got up from the throne, confused.

'Nothing. I just..., sat here,' he answered, looking inquiringly at Hëna. Her expression was unreadable, and he couldn't tell what she was feeling. 'I don't know what happened.'

Hëna got up slowly and went to Lightning, stroking him gently and resting her head against his long neck. She said nothing, nor looked at anyone, but the fresh wave of tears down her face told them all they needed to know.

Another moment of silence went by, when all Daniel wanted to do was go to her, take her in his arms and hold her tight until all her tears were exhausted. But he held back.

Nathaniel was the next one to speak again, still completely mystified by what had just happened.

'Where did the light come from?'

Daniel looked away from Hëna, glad for the distraction.

'From here; from the throne,' he answered again, though he wasn't too sure himself.

'You must have done something.'

'I'm telling you; I just sat down.' He then looked behind them at the doors. 'Do you think they're gone?'

Nemo walked over to the doors and put his ear against them, listening for anything outside. He could hear no sounds whatsoever. Without saying anything, he unlocked the door and opened it slowly, while they approached behind him. To their relief, nothing rushed in to hurt them and they saw no shadows. But what they did see left them speechless.

The cave was now shining with the same golden light that had emanated from the throne inside the castle, and the light did not seem to stop there. They walked out of the gate, back through the tunnel and outside the cave. That's when they saw that the golden light had spread all over Endërland, conquering the darkness and wrapping everything in twilight colours.

Neither of them could believe their eyes.

'I guess it's not over yet,' Nathaniel said, staring in awe at the indescribable sight before them.

'I guess not,' Nemo agreed.

* * *

Back inside the castle, the Golden Throne kept shining bright.

'Now what?' Nemo asked the question that was in everyone's mind. 'We still have to find the Great Lord, don't we?'

'I think we already have,' Hëna answered, looking thoughtfully at Daniel.

Chapter 13

REVELATIONS & RESOLUTIONS

'He's been with us all along'.

It took them all a moment to realize who Hëna was talking about, Daniel a bit longer.

'Me?' he asked, not sure if she was joking, or the grief over her brother's death was affecting her thinking.

'*He* is the Great Lord?' Nathaniel seconded the question, disbelief evident in his voice.

Beside them, Nemo seemed to have fallen into deep thoughts, which was something that did not happen that often. Then, as if snapping out of it, a smile began forming on his young face, as he appeared to be realizing something.

'You're a Visitor,' he finally said. 'It makes sense; the Great Lord was the first ever Visitor to come to this place.'

'That doesn't prove anything,' Nathaniel argued, 'there have been many Visitors before him; that alone doesn't qualify him for being the Great Lord.'

'No, but other things do; like the fact that Lightning allowed him to be his rider, when he's never let anyone else ride him.'

'He let *you* ride him, and he carried me all the way to Dard'h.'

'Yes, but only because of him. But wait, there's more. How do you explain the fact that all the animals in the kingdom are drawn to him? I've never seen that happen with anyone before, Visitor or not. What about the Golden Throne lighting up exactly when he sat on it; was that coincidence too? His bracelet also fell open at that very same moment and he is no longer bound by its magic. Who else except for the Great Lord has the power to overcome the Council's authority?'

'Maybe the bracelet stopped working because the Council no longer exists,' Nathaniel continued to argue.

'Maybe,' Nemo granted, 'but that's not all. Daniel can take things between his world and ours, when none of the other Visitors have been known to do that; that can't be just another coincidence. This must be why Winter's been trying to capture him all this time; he knows. I'm telling you, man, these are the signs the Oracle spoke of; he *is* the Great Lord.'

'Nemo is right,' a man's voice behind them echoed through the hall. Surprised, they turned around to see the Oracle standing at the doors.

Looking at the huge hall before him with a nostalgic look on his face, he walked in, heading towards them.

'It's brighter in here than I remember.'

'You knew about this place?' Everyone turned to look at Daniel, who had been silent until now. He was confused. If the Oracle knew where the castle was all along, then why wouldn't he just tell them? Anger began building up inside of him, as he realized that the Oracle knew much more than he had let on.

'What do you mean, "Nemo is right"'? Nathaniel asked. 'Daniel really is the Great Lord?'

The Oracle approached them and put a hand on Lightning's neck, stroking him with great affection.

'Hello again, old friend; you did a great job, thank you.'

He then turned to them, smiling.

'It's good to see you again, my friends, despite the circumstances.'

Happy as he was to see him, Daniel could not understand why he hadn't told them the truth in the first place.

'You knew the entire time, didn't you? You knew about Lightning, about this castle; you knew and did not say a thing. Why? Heli might still be alive if you had told us.'

Hëna raised her eyes towards him as he mentioned her brother, her expression unreadable. Yet, she continued to remain silent. Nemo and Nathaniel lowered their heads and held their tongues. Daniel's tone of voice revealed the anger behind his words.

The Oracle's face grew sombre as his eyes met Hëna's. They appeared hollow and lost, as if all life had been sucked out of them. For a moment, nobody spoke, and then the Oracle turned to him.

'It is with a heavy heart that I come before you again. My soul weeps for Heli like it has not done so in a very long time. Believe me, I wish I had known what would happen, but I didn't. Just like I didn't know about you; I suspected, I hoped, but I couldn't tell you that, and I couldn't help you any more than I did. I told you only what you needed to know and hear, Daniel, the rest was up to you. This was your journey, and you had to find out for yourself who you are.'

Daniel looked at him, grief and anger denying him the implication behind the Oracle's words. From the moment Heli closed his eyes in his arms he had tried to hold back his tears, hoping, believing that it hadn't really happened, that he wasn't really gone. But now that he'd said it out loud, all of a sudden it all became real, and he felt the full impact of his friend's death. He felt a strong grip around his chest and found that he could no longer breathe. He was unable to say anything else, and the only thing he wanted to do was scream, scream until his lungs gave out.

So, he turned his back on them and walked out of the hall and outside the cave, stopping only when he found himself in the snow-covered field, overlooking the rest of Endërland. Nemo made to follow, but Nathaniel held him back. The Oracle hung his head in sadness, while before him, Hëna hid her tearful face in the cup of her hands, sinking back once again in her own pain and anguish.

Once outside the cave and away from everyone, Daniel finally allowed himself to cry and scream out loud like he hadn't done for a very long time.

When she finally opened her eyes, Sam found herself tucked safe under a blanket, next to a fireplace that was giving out more heat than she seemed to bear. The first thing on her mind, right after checking on the huge bump behind her head, was Daniel, and for a heartbeat she panicked, thinking she had lost him. But as she turned her head to her left, she saw him laid down on the other side of the fireplace, tucked under a blanket much like she was. He looked as peaceful as always and seemed to be fine, though she would not relax properly until she checked on him herself.

The room where they had been brought was simple and humble, old, with even older furniture and decorations all around. It reminded her of their little house back in Sotira.

As her thoughts went there, she immediately tried to think of something else; it hurt too much.

They must have been in this house for quite a while because Sam felt completely dry, even though she could not be sure whether she had landed in water or not. She was about to get up, when the wooden door creaked open and a man seemingly in his late fifties walked in, carrying firewood. Sam's hand instinctively went for the gun stacked on the back of her jeans, but the gun wasn't there. To her surprise though, it had been placed by her head, to her right. Taking a quick moment to think, she decided the man obviously wasn't a threat, so she did not touch the gun.

Seeing her awake, the man smiled as he dropped the wood in front of the fireplace. He said something in Albanian, which she of course did not understand. She smiled back apologetically and said:

'Sorry, English only I'm afraid.'

'Oh,' the man smiled even more, 'I speak English. I used to be an English teacher in my village. Are you American?'

'British', she lied, even though her accent betrayed her. 'And him?'

'He is my brother, Johnny. I'm Alyssa.'

'My name is Selim,' the man said, extending his rough hand to meet hers. 'It is nice to meet you. Are you feeling ok?'

'I have a very strong headache, but other than that I'm fine,' she said, sitting up and leaning against the wall. 'Did *you* bring us here?'

'Yes, I and my son, Eddie. We were coming back from a wedding in the other village across the river when we found you. We always cross where the river is shallow, and that is where you both were lying like fish out of water. How did you end up there?'

Sam had a quick flashback of everything that happened ever since the alarm went off on her laptop.

'It's a very long and complicated story,' she said, 'and I wouldn't even know where to start. But I am very grateful to you and your son for your help.'

'You are very welcome!'

'How long have we been here?'

'Since we found you last night; you're the first to wake up. Your brother doesn't seem to be hurt, but he's been sleeping all this time.'

Sam did not comment on that.

'It's past noon; I sent my son to the shop to buy things so we can have a nice meal; hopefully he will wake up until then.'

I wouldn't keep my hopes up, Sam thought to herself, but to Selim she said, 'That's very kind, thank you! I *am* feeling rather hungry.'

The man smiled again as he finished meddling with the fire, and then his eyes went to the gun. His smile instantly gave way to a grim expression on his face. Sam noticed and instinctively hid the gun from view.

'Like I said, it's a...'

'A long story,' Selim finished the sentence for her. 'Yes, you said so. These are difficult times we live in, yes, but the worst thing that could have happened to us, was getting our hands on those guns.'

His face grew dark, and a shadow of sadness fell upon him, obviously brought on by some painful memory.

'Did you lose someone?' Sam asked, not sure she should.

Selim looked at her, undecided, but then compelled by some reason unknown to her, he answered.

'My wife. She ... uh, killed herself less than a year ago. When our country left behind the communist regime and the people began immigrating everywhere they could, our village was left almost empty. There was no need for a school anymore, so they decided to close it. I could not get a job anywhere after that. We were very poor, neither of us working, so there was never enough. It was a difficult time, and we fought a lot. But I never thought for one minute that she would give up the way she did. I have never let a gun into the house ever since; until today.'

Sam felt bad about the man. It dawned on her that there were people out there who had more right to complain about their lot in life than she did.

'I'm very sorry,' she said. 'Believe me, I have come to hate guns myself, and I wish I didn't have to carry it around with me. But you see, there are some very bad men after my brother, and it's the only thing I have to protect him with, if they catch us.'

Selim looked at her with compassion and smiled again. It surprised her to see such a smile on a man who had so little and had gone through so much.

'It's alright,' he said. 'Let's not speak of such things anymore. You are safe here, and you can stay with us as long as you want.'

'Thank you!' Sam said and watched him as he left the room again.

She took the opportunity to get up and check on Daniel. He was fine, still lost in his dreamworld, while his body weakened bit by bit. There were already signs of it, his face had lost its colour and had grown pale white, while his lips were getting dry. Without nourishment, she knew he wouldn't last long. Yet, as long as he was alive, there was still hope that he would eventually come back to this world, to her.

* * *

Selim's son came back about an hour later with few groceries, and they began preparing lunch together. He was the youngest of five children, in his early twenties, and had chosen to stay with his father after his mother's death.

Sam had a funny feeling the moment she and the boy met; he seemed withdrawn and wary of her. As she helped them set up the dining table, she couldn't help but overhear them argue about something. The son kept mentioning the word 'Lek', which she knew meant money, but other than that she couldn't understand anything else. Had she known what was about to happen, she would have dragged Daniel out of there and left, but being still a bit shook up from last night's tumble and having no immediate plan on how to proceed from there, she was glad to have a chance to rest and think.

After lunch, Eddie left again, and she and Selim sat down having coffee and talking some more. She knew he would ask about Daniel, but she could not tell him anything; he would not believe her even if she did. All she told him was that they needed to get to the British Consulate in Tirana; she'd decided it was the only place where they would be safe from the men, until she came up with a better plan. She didn't know yet exactly how she would explain Daniel's state, but she still had time to come up with something.

Selim knew someone from the village who could take them; he would talk to the man later in the evening and they could leave the next morning if they wanted. Sam was happy with this plan. She liked Selim; he reminded her of her own dad a bit, and had the circumstances been different, she might have stayed there a bit longer. As it were, she had to take Daniel to safety and get some sustenance into his system as soon as possible.

What happened next though, she could have neither predicted, nor prevented, even though she tried. Somehow, Butler and his men had worked out how they had escaped and had followed them down the river, looking for them in all the villages in the area. To make things even easier for themselves, they'd spread word of a reward to whoever had seen the two foreigners. And that word had reached Eddie's ears.

The conversation Sam had overheard at lunch was Eddie trying to convince his father to give up the two strangers for the sake of the money, which would take them a long way. But Selim would not hear of it. He had no love of money and would not sell out his guests. So, Eddie acted on his own, contacting Butler's people and making a deal with them.

Thus it was that as evening fell, a group of six men were making their way towards the old house where Selim lived. Butler and three of his men, accompanied by an interpreter, followed Eddie through the muddy streets of the small village, where all that could be heard was the sound of their boots splashing and dogs barking.

Sam was sitting next to Daniel, exercising his arms and legs, while Selim sat by the fire, smoking on his pipe just next to Sam's improvised bed. They had already arranged for transportation to Tirana for the following day and she was beginning to hope that they were actually going to make it out of there. Then the door opened, and the room suddenly shrunk in on her.

Eddie was the first to walk inside the warm room, followed by Butler, in the body of a young man in his early twenties. He had dark long curly hair, a handsome face and neatly trimmed beard. Behind his small brown eyes, she felt the stare of someone much older than the rest of his features suggested. But the most disturbing thing for Sam was the fact that the man had a striking resemblance to Daniel.

Behind him walked in four other men, three of them carrying handguns. They positioned themselves one by the door, one by the window on the far right of the room, and the last one next to Butler. The fourth one, who never took his hands out of his pockets, simply stood by the door, waiting to see if he was needed. He was clearly a local, the interpreter, Sam guessed.

Her heart now began to race really fast as she realized they had been found, and this time it seemed unlikely that they would be able to escape. She looked at Eddie with disgust, realizing he had betrayed them. She then turned and faced Selim, feeling sorry to see his suddenly withered and ashamed face turn away from her.

Looking back at the men blocking all possible exits, she tried desperately to figure out a way out of this. Her hand went slowly behind her back, reaching for her gun, but to her panic the gun wasn't there. She instantly remembered that she had stacked it underneath her pillow, not too far from Selim's feet.

To her right, Selim shifted in his seat and said something in Albanian that was clearly directed at his son. She did not understand what it was, but by the harsh tone in his voice and the lowering of his son's eyes, she guessed Eddie didn't like it much. Their exchange did not last long, however; Butler made one step forward, took one quick look at Selim, and then concentrated his attention on Sam.

'You've made me work really hard these last few months, missy. First, you steal him from the clinic,' he said, pointing at Daniel, 'and hide him away in the middle of nowhere, where the devil himself wouldn't even think to look. Then, you turn that little house of yours into a small fortress, causing me to lose two good men with your little traps. And then, just when I think I have you, you go and pull off a brilliant escape, where, I admit, even I would have been hard-pressed for ideas. You've got style, I'll give you that, and if I wasn't so freaking tired and pissed off from chasing you around the world, I would maybe consider sitting down with you and getting to know you a bit better. Who knows, we might have even become friends.'

He smirked, looking at his men who backed him up with chuckles as he continued.

'Seeing as I'm all out of patience, and all I wanna do is get the hell out of this shithole and back into civilization, I'm gonna ask you only once to give him up without a fuss and I just might consider not shooting you down like a dog.'

'I'm afraid I can't do that,' Sam replied without even thinking. 'I have come too far and been through too much to hand him over to you just like that. Sorry, but you're gonna have to fight me for him.'

She stood between him and Daniel in a protective position, speaking with clear determination in her voice and hoping he would see she wasn't going to make it easy for him. On the inside, however, she was trembling with fear and despair, knowing there wasn't anything she could really do.

Butler smiled and reaching inside his chest for his gun, said.

'I expected as much. Unfortunately for you, blondie, I'm gonna let my bullets do the fighting for me.'

Sam's heart stopped as he slowly took out his gun and she realized this was it. She was about to close her eyes and accept her fate, feeling bad only for failing Daniel, when Eddie shouted something at his father behind her. She turned just in time to see Selim pull her gun from under her pillow and aim it at Butler.

The man beside Butler pushed him out of the way, while at the same time raising his own gun towards Selim and firing. The other two men were just as quick, only not quick enough. Sam's gun went off first, releasing three bullets one after the other and catching the first man in his chest, dropping him down at once. Unfortunately, that was the one and only time Selim managed to fire. The other two men kept on shooting at him, until he fell down forward, dropping the gun at Sam's feet.

Horrified at the sight of his father being shot dead, Eddie charged, raising his bare hands at Butler. He did not manage to get closer than two feet from him, however. A second series of bullets were fired from the same guns that killed Selim, this time dropping both Eddie at Butler's feet, as well as the translator by the door.

Kicking Eddie's now lifeless body out of the way, Butler resumed his former position with a look of rage on his face. Gazing at Selim lying face down, blood spreading from underneath him, he fired another angry shot at him, causing Sam to jump in place. His eyes then stopped on the gun that was now resting in front of Sam's feet.

'What's it gonna be, blondie?' He spoke as if he was tired and had no patience for this. 'My way, or his?' he motioned towards Selim's corpse.

Sam's hope of any escape died as she found herself surrounded by four men, three of whom were pointing guns at her. She considered every possible scenario in her head, but they all ended up with her losing. She knew Butler would not let her live, not after murdering three innocent men in front of her. Still, she looked down at her gun.

Butler saw that and gave her a wry smile.

'Really? You're actually gonna go for it?'

He motioned to his two guys to lower their weapons.

'Alright, I'll indulge you; I'll give you your fight. Here, I'm putting my gun away,' he said and slowly hid his gun back inside his chest, raising his right hand in the air. 'Just you and me; let's see if you're fast enough. If you manage to kill me, they'll let you be; they have no use for him. You can take him back; no one will ever come to look for him. I promise you!'

This was the chance Sam was waiting for; she could do this. All she had to do was bend down really fast, grab the gun, and shoot him before he got his out. She decided she would roll on to her right once she got the gun, that way she would try to escape his bullets and maybe catch him by surprise.

She threw a quick glance at the other two guys to make sure that they weren't going to intervene, and then looked back at Butler. She decided a distraction tactic might improve her chances.

'I just need you to promise me one thing,' she said, hoping he'd take the bait and think she wasn't ready yet. Butler gave her a sinister smile and asked.

'What's that?'

Before he even finished the sentence, Sam bent her knees and went down really fast, reaching for the gun with her left hand. Just as her fingers touched the still warm metal, she heard the dry and loud bang of Butler's gun. With her gun now in her hand, she continued to roll to her right, landing on her knees. She then tried to raise her left arm and point the gun at him, but a sharp pain in her stomach stopped her.

She looked down and saw her right hand clutching her belly, red-hot blood pouring out between her fingers. Shocked, she looked up at Butler, who was now standing right on top of her, his expression one of anger and spite. He raised his left arm and slapped her really hard with the back of his hand, practically spitting out the words:

'You cost me my hand.'

As she fell on the floor from the force of his slap, Sam wondered what he meant. Then, darkness began taking over, and the last thing she thought about before closing her eyes, was Daniel.

Daniel stared ahead at the scenery before him with a new eye, and finally realized just how powerful the light of the Golden Throne was. It was no longer dark outside; more like an early twilight where all the land was covered with a yellow/reddish hue, bright enough to make everything visible.

He could see all the stars in the sky shining clear and bright in what made for a magnificent view, and yet, they looked awfully lonely without the moon. All of Endërland lay before him, beautiful and calm, from the mountaintops, all the way down to the far seas. The new lighting made everything look even more spectacular than before.

He lost track of how long he'd been sitting out there, going over in his mind everything that had happened, starting with his first dream, and culminating with Heli's death and his own unexpected coronation. He'd come a long way from that very first day. He recalled the conversation with his mother, and how he had naively thought there was a bigger reason for him being here. How could he have foreseen back then that he would end up being the one responsible for the fate of the entire kingdom?

From the corner of his eye, he spotted the Oracle approaching slowly. He wiped his tears away the best he could, though he was past the point of worrying about appearing weak to him or anyone else at this point. In a few steps, the Oracle reached him and sat down next to him, laying one hand warmly on his shoulder. He was actually glad the man had come; he felt better now, calmer after releasing some of all that withheld tension, and time had finally come for some more long-awaited answers.

'How can I be the Great Lord, Alfie?' he started as soon as the Oracle sat beside him. He didn't want to waste time talking about other things, nor answer any questions about how he was feeling right now. 'I mean; I've never been here before; I have no memories of this place. The first time I came to visit Endërland was the night of my eighteenth birthday.'

The Oracle smiled. He knew there would be questions.

'Look over there,' he calmly raised his arm to point southwest of the horizon. 'That's where Arba is; that's where the five of you set out from. Do you see that big star above it?'

Daniel easily noticed the star shining right on top of Arba, brighter than any of the other stars in the sky.

'How come it's so bright?' he asked. 'I've seen it before, but I don't remember it like this.'

'That's the Great Lord's star, Daniel. When Arba was first established as the City of the Lords, that star was the Great Lord's gift to the people, so they knew that he would always be with them. With time though, as the kingdom stopped needing him and people began to forget about him, the star began to lose its power and became just like any other star in the sky, until now. The moment you sat on that throne, the star regained all its former glory, and is shining bright once again, to let the people know that the Great Lord is back.'

Daniel started to say something, but the Oracle interrupted him.

'I know you have even more questions than you did when you first came to me, but time has not come to answer them just yet. We have urgent work to do, Daniel. Endërland is at great risk, and everything that's been good and beautiful until now will soon be gone, forever. Winter has usurped the Silver Throne and has surrounded himself with an army of hideous creatures like the ones you've slain here today. The other Lords have been dethroned and imprisoned, while the wingmen are flying to war against the mermaids as we speak. If you don't accept your role in this, it will all end very soon.'

'But what can I do?' Daniel asked, still confused. 'I'm just a boy.'

'You're so much more than that, Daniel, and the sooner you realize what that means, the greater our chances are of defeating Winter. And you are not alone, we will all continue to follow you every step of the way and have your back.

'But even if you're not The One, and there is some other explanation for all of this, we must consider ourselves lucky, for the timing could not be more perfect. We need the Great Lord on our side now more than ever, all of Endërland does. Only with him we'll have a chance against Winter.'

'So, you would have me lie to everyone about who I am, or rather who I'm not, for the sake of the kingdom?'

'Sometimes what people believe is more powerful than the truth, Daniel. I know what I believe, and so do your friends; but for you the journey is still young, and you have yet a long way to go. The time will come when you will know more, and you will decide for yourself what you believe and who you will be, but until that day, I would have you trust in us and the signs, and be who you're needed.'

The Oracle gave him another pat on the shoulder, and got up, taking the path back to the cave and leaving him to his thoughts again. Daniel watched him go, feeling even more frustrated and confused than before. Somehow, he had expected more than just a little pep talk. He had expected to understand more about how all of this worked and what exactly had led him to this point. Instead, he had been left with even more questions and uncertainties.

He did not go back right away. He sat where he was, gazing at the landscape in front of him and trying in vain to piece everything together, desperate to make some sense out of it. When that failed, he finally gave up and headed back inside the cave.

As he got past the broken gate and inside the courtyard, he spotted Hëna sitting down on the steps outside the castle entrance. Her sight immediately brought to mind Heli, and he felt that foreign weight on his chest grow bigger and heavier again.

For a single moment, he actually saw him in her, and this caught him by surprise. All this time, he had thought the twins looked nothing alike, but now he could see Heli in so many little things. He was there, in the way she sat with her arms crossed and her legs half spread in front of her, like he used to do. Her fringe also fell over her eyes, as Heli's blonde locks always did. Her stare was intense just now, like his used to get for those few moments when he got really serious. And even her lips, ah, those beautiful lips, Heli would arch his a certain way whenever he was thoughtful, just like she was doing right now.

Daniel forced himself to push these thoughts aside; they were making him feel tearful again, and it wouldn't do. His own pain was nothing compared to what she was going through, and he would not presume that the loss he felt came even close to hers. Plus, he did not want to make things any harder for her. They may have found the Great Lord, but she would never see and hold her brother ever again. She might be trying hard to stay strong and in control, but Daniel could sense that she felt lost and alone without Heli.

As he reached the front steps where she was sitting, Hëna slowly got up and faced him. Without saying anything, she held out her left hand, in which she was holding something small, wrapped in a piece of soft fabric. Seeing her stand so close to him, with her eyes red and her hair unruly, Daniel felt so much like taking her in his arms and holding her tight, until all her pain and hurt were long forgotten. But he didn't think she would let him. So, he shifted his gaze down to her hand and received the small item she handed to him.

He unfolded it slowly and revealed the wooden figurine that he had seen Heli work on. He seemed to have finished it. Smaller than his palm, it was a replica of Lightning, now painted completely in black, except for the white mark in the shape of a lightning bolt on its forehead. Attached to the miniature stallion was a rider, wearing a golden crown. Daniel could swear it looked a bit like him. The details and workmanship of the little figurine were astonishing; Heli had really taken his time with it.

'It's the Great Lord,' Hëna said with a weak voice. 'Somehow, he knew, and that's why he did what he did, so that you would fulfil your destiny and we'd succeed with our mission.'

For an instant, their eyes met, and Daniel thought he was about to explode from the mass of emotions he felt just now. Without realizing it, he reached for her hand and was barely able to say.

'I'm so sorry, Hëna. I..., I wish more than anything that he was still here.'

She stood there, for the first time ever since Heli's death looking into his emerald eyes. He looked back, but was still unable to read her, and he so much wanted to know what she was thinking of him right now. Did she blame him? Did she hate him? Would she leave him now that her mission was done?

So as not to hurt him, she did not take her hand off right away, but let him hold it for a few seconds, before withdrawing it slowly.

'I know,' she only said, before walking away from him and back inside the castle, leaving him behind, in the cold of the moonless night. Daniel watched her go, and his heart sank, feeling he had lost her forever.

* * *

Back inside the hall, straining to put his thoughts of Hëna on the side, Daniel looked at the expectant faces of his friends gathered before him. He didn't know what they were thinking, or what they believed; maybe they doubted him even more than he doubted himself. But one thing he was sure the Oracle was right about, the countdown had already begun, and if they did not act now, all would be lost.

'I know you all believe that I am the Great Lord, and I don't know what to say to that. I do not feel any different; I'm still the same Daniel. However, if that's true, then we did what we set out to do. But our mission is not yet complete and there's more work to be done. We need to deal with Winter and stop him from turning this kingdom into his own playground. I will be the first to face him, if I must, but I cannot do it alone. Will you go with me?'

He looked at each of them in the eyes, trying to find there the answer he was looking for, but it was Nemo who gave it first. The red-haired boy moved one step in Daniel's direction and spoke.

'This is still our adventure, Dan. I promised I would follow you 'till the end, and I will, my lord.'

Smiling as he emphasized Daniel's new title, Nemo knelt down on one knee before him and bowed his head. He held that position, waiting for the others to join him.

Daniel was taken aback by his friend's act of reverence and did not know whether he should protest. They weren't going to start acting all official now, were they? He didn't want to be treated any differently, he wasn't interested in that. All he wanted was for this whole thing to be over and done with, so they could go back to being normal boys, just hanging by the seaside and causing trouble. Still, he guessed until that happened, he'd have to suffer some more of this nonsense and let them treat him as was the proper procedure before the Great Lord, uncomfortable as it made him feel.

Nathaniel was next to follow in Nemo's example.

'I know I speak for my prince, my queen, and the rest of my people, when I say that we will be honoured to stand beside you, whatever you decide to do, my lord. We are your loyal subjects to command as you will.'

He too knelt on one knee before Daniel and bowed his head.

'You can count me in,' the Oracle also said, kneeling beside Nathaniel. 'You will get all the help that I can give and more.'

Trotting behind him, Lightning lined himself by his side and nudged him in the face with his large nose. Daniel laughed and gave his four-legged friend a kiss on his forehead, right on top of his identifying mark.

'Thank you, my friend. I knew you wouldn't let me down.'

Only Hëna was now left to answer. Looking at her face, Daniel once again wished he knew what she was thinking. He could see the pain and heartache over the loss of her brother, but there was more behind those beautiful black eyes. How did she feel about him being the Great Lord? Would she still stand by him until the end, like she had promised, or would she abandon him now, at the end of all things? He was happy to have the guys' allegiance, but, somehow, her support meant so much more to him.

Hëna appeared to be pondering things for the briefest of moments, but then, she too knelt down next to Nemo with her head low.

'I am very happy that we found you, my lord. I will continue to follow and serve you, until Endërland is free and safe again.'

He should have felt happy, but he didn't. Her voice was cold and her words distant. He was no longer Daniel to her, no longer her friend, and whatever warmth of hope he had felt before of winning her heart, now seemed completely vanished.

Unwilling to deal with these thoughts right now, he focused on the work they had to do.

'Thank you!' he said to the four people kneeling before him. 'I don't know what qualifies me to be this Great Lord, or what I will be able to do for Endërland but knowing that you are with me gives me much hope and makes me believe that we can achieve anything. Please, stand up; I think it's time for us to make some plans.'

Everyone got back up and gave him their full attention.

'If the reports that Winter has built himself an army are true, I'm afraid we're gonna have to do the same and build our own.'

Nathaniel came forward with what seemed to be the obvious question.

'But how? I mean, we are inexperienced in these matters. I know my people are flying into battle as we speak, but for the life of me I don't know how they're gonna do it.'

'Hopefully Séraphin will have gotten to the queen in time, and we won't have to find out, Nathaniel. Still, from what I've seen, your people are quite capable with knives, and seem to have produced enough of them to arm everyone. I guess we're just going to have to use what we know and have. However, we only stand a chance against Winter if we are all united. We need to bring wingmen, mermaids, and people all together, and strike at the same time as one. If we can manage that, then I know just the person to prepare and lead our army. Does anyone have anything to write on?'

Hëna went through her belongings and produced a piece of parchment and a quill that Daniel took and began to write with. When he was done, he signed the letter, rolled it into a tube and gave it to Nathaniel.

'Do you think you're strong enough to fly, my friend?'

Nathaniel unfolded his large wings before them, the wounded one with some difficulty. He tried to mask the pain he felt but did not fully managed to.

'It's not fully healed, but I will manage,' he answered, nonetheless.

'Good. I need you to please fly to Dard'h and hand this to Gabriel in person. If he agrees, please lead them back here without wasting time. And if he doesn't, lead them here all the same.'

Nathaniel bowed his head quickly and left right away. Daniel turned around to face the other three.

'I'm gonna need a few more pieces of paper,' he said to Hëna, who handed him the rest of what she had. He took them, noticing the question in their eyes.

'If we are to bring all our people together, I'm gonna need to talk to their leaders. For that I will have to send messengers, which is why I sent Nathaniel to Dard'h. It's time to see where Gabriel's allegiance really lies.'

'In the meantime, what do we do?' Nemo asked, already feeling important and useful.

Daniel thought about it for a moment. He needed a little time to write the letters, and until he was done, there were a few things they could do.

'I would first like to get rid of those bodies; I think burning them would be best. Also, we need to search this castle and see what else may be hiding here. Who knows, maybe there are other people still here, or we may find something else that may be of use to us.'

'I'll deal with the bodies,' the Oracle offered.

'I'll take Nemo and check the rest of the castle then,' Hëna said and turned away, without waiting for an answer. 'Come, Nemo.'

Daniel watched as she went and could not help but feel guilty. He knew she needed the time to mourn her brother, they all did, but they could not afford any right now. He promised himself right then and there that he would make it up to her at some point.

* * *

As Daniel sealed the last of the letters, Nemo and Hëna walked back into the hall, to his surprise accompanying a man who looked too weak to be standing on his own two feet. Judging by his appearance, he must have been kept prisoner for a very long time. His clothes seemed old and worn out, his hair and beard had grown uncontrollably, and his skin was pale white from being out of sunlight for too long.

Seeing him, a sense of unease came over Daniel, and he felt his stomach churning. He went to meet them halfway and helped set the man down by the feet of the Golden Throne. He then took the flask Nathaniel had given him earlier and helped the man drink. The Summer water felt good and helped soothe his parched throat.

'Where did you find him?' he asked Hëna, while the man drank.

'He was being held in chains down in the dungeons,' Hëna answered, sounding disturbed. 'There were at least five skeletons around him, people, I think. They must have killed them, but, for whatever reason, I think they kept him alive.'

Daniel knelt next to the man and touched his hand. He noticed his arms had grown too skinny; his wrists were all blue and bloodied from the chains, and his nails bitten off to keep them from growing too long. Daniel felt he was going to be sick.

'Don't be afraid,' he spoke to the man with a gentle voice, 'we mean you no harm. Do you know where you are?'

The man opened his eyes just a little, struggling to adjust to the strong light in the hall, then with a coarse voice spoke slowly.

'No. I was brought here a long time ago, in the dead of night and blindfolded. I've never seen this place before today.'

'What is your name?'

The man took a while to answer, as he appeared to be thinking about it.

'I don't know,' he replied eventually, looking frustrated. 'I can't remember.'

Daniel and Hëna exchanged a look and then she asked. 'Are you a Visitor?'

'A Visitor?' the man asked, not knowing what she meant.

'Do you remember anything at all from before?' Daniel changed questions.

'I remember a man; I think he's the one who brought me here. His is the last face I've seen until today. The only other face I remember is a woman's; I actually see her in my mind all the time. She has long black hair, kind eyes and a sweet smile. But I can't remember who she is, or how I know her.'

Hearing him describe her the way he did, Daniel recalled his first evening in Endërland and the refreshed image of his mother's face. A crazy idea suddenly came to him, and his heart began to beat strong and fast. His voice trembled as he asked the next question.

'Does the name Damien mean anything to you?'

The man now opened his eyes fully and looked at him with curiosity.

'Damien,' he repeated the name, as if something clicked in his mind. 'Damien; I think that's me. Yes, that's my name; I remember now. I remember people calling me Damien; how did you know?'

Daniel almost fell on the cold stone pavement from the shock. He could not believe this; he'd found his long-lost brother when he least expected it. He started to well up once again, but he didn't care.

He gently put both hands on the man's shoulders and said.

'The woman whose face you see in your mind, Damien, is your mother, our mother, Diane. And I'm your little brother, Daniel.'

It took a moment for those words to sink in, but upon hearing the names, fragments of Damien's memories slowly began to come back to him. He felt as if he was now waking up from a deep slumber and seeing everything again, hazily at first, but clearing up slowly. The emotions that rushed back into him, accompanying those memories, shocked him to his very core. He was still too weak to contain them, so he began to sob uncontrollably.

'Daniel, is that really you? My gosh, look at you; you're a grown man now. I remember, I remember you were just a little boy running after me, always trying to get that silly watch from my wrist. How many years have passed since then?'

'Too many, brother, too many,' Daniel said, and he could speak no more. He took his brother in his arms and hugged him tight, feeling the tears travelling down his spine yet another time. He did not mind though, these were not tears of sorrow, but of joy and happiness.

He could not believe this day had finally come and he had actually found his brother. And the most wonderful thing about all this was that he did not feel like he was hugging a stranger just now, like he'd been afraid he might. Instead, this felt right, familiar even. There was something about Damien that made him think of dad all of a sudden, and he took that as a good sign and a confirmation. He might not really know the man he was hugging, but the connection he felt to him was real, and the bond stronger than blood.

'I can't believe I found you. Oh, Damien, mom will be so happy; she never gave up hope, you know. She always knew you were here.'

As the two brothers cried in each other's arms, Hëna and Nemo drew back and joined the Oracle out in the courtyard. Their hearts felt yet a bit lighter, for it seemed that the wind was indeed turning, and their luck was changing. Heli's death had brought such darkness over them and left the world so cold that it seemed impossible and unlikely they would ever feel warmth again. But now, little rays of sunshine were making it through the dark, and they desperately needed to believe that the sky would eventually clear up and joy and warmth would return to the world once again.

* * *

Once the initial shock wore off, Daniel took the time to fill Damien in on pretty much everything that had happened ever since he had gone missing. He also told him of their current situation and what their plans were. Damien, for his part, recounted as best as he could remember all he had gone through, from the first day he had begun to visit Endërland, until the moment Butler had kidnapped him and locked him in this place. But that was not before he had learned from Damien where his portal was and had taken some of his clothes. Daniel remembered his mother's caution regarding the portal and found it interesting that Butler had taken Damien's clothes.

While they spoke, Hëna, the Oracle and Nemo continued to explore the rest of the castle. Despite appearing fairly small from the outside, the castle turned out to be huge, with countless rooms having been built in the underbelly of the mountain. Yet, it seemed most of them had never even been furnished, let alone lived in.

The only area of the castle with any signs of habitation were the dungeons, but what they saw there almost scarred them for life. The whole place - apart from the far corner where Damien had been held - was like a small graveyard for animals, mainly wolves. There were bones and skulls everywhere, rotting corpses and headless torsos. The majority of them were deformed and mutated, making it hard to tell if they were animal or human. Hëna had a strong stomach, but the sight of the carnage nauseated her, and she retreated away from it. The stench of it all was too unbearable, and it was a wonder it had not spread to the rest of the castle.

It was clear now what had happened to all the animals in these parts of the kingdom, as well as where the wolfmen they killed earlier came from. This is where Winter had been experimenting with the new breed of soldiers for his army, using animals, since he knew no man would follow him. Yet, how he was able to do these things remained a mystery. The

Lords only had power when it was their season to rule and were in possession of the Silver Sceptre; and even then, their power was defined by the nature of their duties. None of them had the ability to perform such feats with the powers given to them by the Great Lord.

They were all discussing this, when in the hall entered Nathaniel, followed by Gabriel and a dozen wingmen. Unlike the first time they met, Gabriel had none of that lordly air about him now. Instead, he appeared humble and more than eager to please. Daniel saw this as a good sign. It was obvious Gabriel did not really believe Winter's claims of being the Great Lord, or he would have come with a different attitude.

Following the Oracle's advice, upon their entrance, Daniel took his place on the Golden Throne. He didn't really like the idea of acting as the man in charge, but it was vital that the wingmen, and after them the rest of Endërland, knew and believed that the Great Lord had indeed returned.

Gabriel approached the throne with his wingmen but did not kneel. Instead he looked at the Oracle standing at the right hand of Daniel and asked.

'Is it true, Far-Seer? Is he the one?'

'Have you not seen the great star over Arba, Chieftain?' the Oracle asked him in return.

'I have.'

'And you've seen it's bright outside, despite the missing moon and sun?'

'Indeed, but how is this possible?'

'The mysteries of the Great Lord are not yours to understand, Chieftain, nor are they mine to explain. You have the evidence, and you have our witness; let that be enough for you and your people.'

Gabriel lowered his eyes on the floor.

386

'Forgive me, Far-Seer; of course.' He then turned to Daniel, kneeling on one knee. His men followed his lead. 'My lord, we are overcome with joy that you have returned to us, especially at a time like this, when your presence is much needed. We come to pledge our allegiance once again to you as your loyal subjects. Command us as you will.'

Daniel bowed his head in return.

'Thank you, Chieftain; I much appreciate your loyalty and that of your people. I am indeed very happy to see you again, despite our first meeting.'

'I do beg your forgiveness, my lord; these are difficult times we're living in, and one does his best to survive.'

'One must always do the right thing, Chieftain, whether or not that threatens one's survival; otherwise, how will I know your loyalty is heart-given and true? Nevertheless,' he raised his hand to stop Gabriel from justifying himself any further, 'no one is perfect, and in the end, is what we do that really matters.

'Tell me; is there any news from your queen? Has the battle begun?'

'You'll be happy to know, my lord, that Prince Séraphin arrived just in time to stop the battle between wingmen and mermaids. I was sent word from my queen that the entire army is flying back to Sky-City. Also, your mother, the Queen of Endër, has left the city and is currently staying in New Sotira with the old king. The White Lord's men stormed her castle, but she managed to leave before they got to her.'

Daniel silently rebuked himself for not anticipating this. Of course, Winter would go after his mother, she could lead him to his portal, or at the very least be used as leverage to force him to give himself up. Luckily, she had foreseen the danger and had left just in time.

'That is great news indeed, Chieftain, thank you. Now, I will need your wingmen to deliver some messages for me.'

'Of course, my lord, my wingmen are yours to command.'

'Good. The first message will go to your queen and prince, who of course, you already know where to find. Two more letters will be delivered to the Queen of Endër and the old king in New Sotira, while the last one will go to the Sea-Queen. I want you to send a pair of wingmen to each destination; this is to ensure their own protection and delivery of the message, should they encounter any problems on the way. Once delivered, they are to return immediately with whatever reply they might have. Can you arrange that for me, Chieftain?'

As the rest of them looked at Daniel with wonder and newfound regard, Gabriel bowed his head again and hurried to answer.

'Yes, my lord, right away.'

He proceeded to call on six of his wingmen, who came forward from the rest, and split them in pairs. Daniel passed to him four sealed letters, telling him whom each one was for.

'Once you complete your mission,' Daniel now spoke to the wingmen directly, 'you will join us in the northernmost part of the Valley of Destiny; we will head there as soon as we are ready. Fly fast and remember, the fate of the entire kingdom rests upon your wings.'

The six wingmen bowed their heads once more and headed towards the exit without delay. The other six remained behind with their leader.

With Daniel's insistence, two of them accompanied Damien to one of the nearby rooms, where he could wash himself and change into a new set of clothes. The other four took turns standing guard by the entrance of the tunnel.

Standing in the wide hall, Daniel decided it was now time they sat down and talked about their next course of action. The Oracle, Hëna, Nemo, Nathaniel and Gabriel gathered around him as he now left the throne and sat on the steps in front of it. Lightning continued to observe from the entrance, where he had stationed himself like a faithful guard.

Daniel first asked the Oracle to share everything he knew about the situation in Arba so far.

'As you may know, two days ago the wingmen of Sky-City began flying towards the southern sea to battle with the mermaids, seeking justice for the alleged killing of two of their kind. What you may not know, however, is that while all of Endërland had turned its eye on the south, up north a large army secretly left the confines of the Shadow Forest, traveling incredibly and unnaturally fast all through the night. They reached the city of Arba by dawn, where Winter now has them surrounding it and guarding the gates to prevent entry or exit to anyone the White Lord has not authorized. We do not know the exact number of this army, but what we found here gives us a pretty good idea as to where it came from and what they are. The White Lord has imprisoned the other three Lords and claimed the Silver Throne as his own. He knows his season will end one day, and he obviously plans to hold on to it by force, which is where his army comes in.'

'But he must know by now that the Great Lord has returned,' Nemo spoke out loud what others were also thinking. 'He cannot still continue with his plans now, can he?'

'It is not as simple as that, young prince. I believe that the White Lord has always known who Daniel is, or at least suspected it, and that is why he's been trying to capture him all this time. But even though he failed to do that, I think he's not afraid to go against him. Somehow, the White Lord has grown very powerful, and it's possible he thinks he can defeat the Great Lord and become the absolute ruler of Endërland.'

'Can he?' Gabriel asked, looking at Daniel. The Oracle began to say something, but Daniel interrupted him, remembering something his mother had told him way back.

'That is irrelevant, Chieftain, because there is one thing Winter fears more than the Great Lord himself, and that's the united people of Endërland. This is why he's been trying so hard to set the wingmen against the mermaids, because if the people are divided, they would stand no chance against him. But I plan to bring all the people of Endërland together; the White Lord has his army; we will have ours. We will march to the gates of Arba as one and demand that he release the three Lords and give up the Silver Throne. And if war is what he wants, then war is what we'll give him.'

He stole a glimpse at Hëna, still feeling quite uncomfortable in the role he had been thrust on but found nothing of what he hoped to see in her blank eyes. She continued to sit opposite him, listening to the conversation, but not really participating. It was like she did not really want to be there.

Nemo on the other hand seemed quite excited to be part of this small council.

'Forgive me, my lord,' Gabriel spoke again, being careful with his tone of voice. 'Wouldn't it be much easier if you dealt with the White Lord yourself, without involving all the people of Endërland?'

'This plight belongs to all of us, Chieftain,' the Oracle answered instead of Daniel. 'Our lives, our homes, and everything we know and love is being threatened by one single man; do you really think we should just sit by and wait to be rescued?'

'I suppose not, Far-Seer. It's just that, even though we have crafted some weapons and trained some people to use them; we are still rather inexperienced when it comes to battle. I fear of what might happen should things go that far.'

Daniel looked at all of them now.

'I share the same fears as you do, Chieftain, but I promise you that we will face this together. I have already chosen someone who has the knowledge and training needed to lead an army into battle; he will make sure that we are well prepared and able to fight and win. Winter may have a big scary army, but they don't know war any better than we do, and they fight for a tyrant; we fight for our lives and for Endërland. That makes all the difference.

'Now, once everybody here has rested, we will leave this place and head down towards the Valley of Destiny, where we will wait for the people that will form our new army, and their leaders. Then, when we are organized and ready, we will march towards Arba.'

And with that he got up, signalling that this short meeting had just come to a close.

* * *

They had been quiet for a while, enjoying a moment of respite as Nemo helped Daniel give Lightning a much-needed bath. The stallion seemed to be enjoying the treatment. His mane had grown twice as long after being brushed, not without some difficulty.

'Do you think we're gonna end up fighting against them?' Nemo asked, breaking the silence.

'We might,' Daniel answered. He then added, 'Are you afraid?'

Nemo looked at him as if the question caught him by surprise. He appeared to think about it for a second.

'No,' he finally answered, smiling, 'I'm not. The Great Lord is on our side; what can Winter do?'

Daniel regarded him. He did not seem to be afraid; maybe he had outgrown his fear, or maybe he really believed his friend was the Great Lord. How he wished he could share the same faith and hope. He felt as if he and Nemo had somehow switched places; Nemo was the brave one now, and he was the one who was afraid.

He finally put down the piece of cloth he was using to clean Lightning's neck and flank.

'He's as good as new now. You better go get some rest, Nemo; we're gonna be moving soon.'

'What about you?' Nemo asked. 'Aren't you going to get some sleep?'

'I am, actually,' he said, remembering that he no longer had the bracelet on and could now go back to his own world. 'I'm kinda looking forward to seeing a couple of friends of mine. Save me a spot, will you; I'll be there soon.'

Nemo nodded and went inside without saying more, while Daniel remained outside with Lightning beside him, enjoying some more of his big friend's easy company.

He couldn't tell how long he stayed out there, but just when he was about to turn around and go back inside, he noticed a figure appear from the corner of his eye. Turning back to see who it was, his jaw dropped as he made out the familiar figure of Sam coming towards him through the broken gate.

Dressed as usual in her tight blue jeans and hoodie, with her blond curly hair let loose, she approached Daniel with a confused look on her face.

'Sam?' Daniel met her halfway and rushed to give her a strong hug. 'What..., how did you get here?' he asked her, bewildered.

Still in his arms, Sam looked in his deep green eyes, and without saying anything, reached up and kissed him on the lips. Caught completely off guard, Daniel just stood where he was, surrendering his mouth to hers. He was so happy to see Sam and being this close to her again brought back all the old emotions and questions in his mind. The fact that she smelled really good, and her lips felt amazing on his, didn't help either. It wasn't long though, before Hëna's image flashed in his mind, along with everything he felt about her, and he slowly drew back from Sam.

It was a very short moment, seconds really, but still long enough for Hëna to witness from the entrance of the castle where she'd just appeared. Without making herself noticed, she turned around and went back inside, leaving the two of them alone again.

'What was that for?' Daniel asked, too shy to look Sam in the eye.

'I berated myself for not kissing you that day by the waterfall, so I swore that the next time I saw you, I wouldn't chicken out,' she said with glee in her eyes, though she appeared mortified by what she'd just done. 'I didn't wanna waste the chance again, in case this dream ends too soon.'

Daniel smiled at her, not really knowing how to respond to that. He then repeated his question.

'Sam, how *did* you get here?'

Sam gave a quick look at their surroundings.

'Where is here?'

'You're in Endërland, Sam. But how? Can you sleep now?'

Right then Sam's face grew darker, and she recalled the last events of her waking life.

'They found us, Daniel, the ones who kidnapped you the first time.' She walked to the entrance of the castle and sat down on the cold steps in front of it. Daniel followed her.

'They came to the little house in Sotira at night, but I took you away in the raft, and we escaped. Freddie stayed behind to lead them on a different direction, but I think they got to him. I don't know for sure though; I only heard the gunshot in the middle of the night. I thought for a little while that we made it, but they caught up with us, and the last thing I remember is getting shot.'

She stopped talking and put her hands on her stomach, where she had been shot, but there was no sign of a wound or blood there. Daniel lowered his eyes, not daring to look at her. This was not good. Sam had tried so hard to keep him safe and had now paid dearly for it herself. Was she still alive on the other side, or was it all over for her? This was all his fault; he shouldn't have let her come along; he should have insisted she went home. If he had, none of this would have happened.

And what about him? If he went back now, he would fall right into Winter's hands and everything they were trying to accomplish would be lost forever.

He looked at Sam and their eyes met again, but this time there was just sadness there.

'Oh, Sam, I'm so sorry. I never wanted anything to happen to you.'

'Do you think I'm dead?' Sam asked matter-of-factly. To her own surprise, she wasn't worried about herself.

'I don't know,' Daniel answered, 'I don't think so. You're here; there must be a reason for that. We must find Alfie; he might be able to tell us more about this. Come with me.'

He took her by the hand and led her into the great hall.

'Who's Alfie?'

'He's the Oracle of the Great Lord, or was... It's a bit too complicated to explain.'

They'd just entered the bright hall when they saw Damien coming towards them. He was now wearing brand new clothes; had washed and cleaned himself up, and his black curly hair and beard were now neatly combed and trimmed. He looked a completely different man, handsome and already healthier.

Upon seeing him, however, Sam froze in place.

'What's *he* doing here?'

Baffled, Daniel stared at her.

'That's my brother, Damien. Do you know him?'

'Know him? I should think so; he's the one who kidnapped you the first time and who has you now. Daniel, he's the one who shot me.'

Daniel looked at his older brother, who seemed to be even more dumbfounded than he was.

'Sam, he couldn't have; he's been locked in the dungeons of this castle ever since he went missing 16 years ago. I only just found him.'

Damien approached them cautiously and went next to Daniel.

'Hëna helped me with my hair and beard,' he said. 'I came to find you so that you can see what your older brother really looks like. I must have given you a scare the way I looked before; I know I scared myself.'

He then turned to Sam, and a shy smile formed on his handsome face.

'Hello! I'm Damien.'

He extended his hand to meet hers, but she drew back even further from him, without saying anything. Daniel had already figured out what was happening.

'Sam,' he said in a soothing voice, 'it's not him. The man who shot you is using my brother's body, but he's not my brother. Do you remember what I've told you about the portals?'

Sam nodded.

'Well, I learned here that anyone can use them to travel back to our world, only, when they do, they wake up in the body of whoever created the portal in the first place. I think somebody went through Damien's, though I have no idea how he could have found it, if Damien is the only one who can see it.'

'Have I created a portal?' Sam asked.

'You must have, that's usually how it works. Do you remember where you woke up?'

'Yes, it was right outside, just before I saw you. Come, I'll show you.'

She led them outside the castle again, crossing the courtyard and through the broken gate, stopping just by the entrance of the tunnel.

'There,' she said, eyes fixed on one spot on the wall of the cave, 'can you see it? I can see part of the room from here. That's Eddie's body lying dead; you should be behind me. Oh no, they're still there, Daniel, and they're setting the whole place on fire. They want to cover their tracks. We need to do something.'

Daniel felt the panic in her voice and went close to her.

'I'm sorry, Sam, I don't see anything. It's like I...' As he was speaking, he placed one hand on her shoulder, and that's when the vision of Selim's house became visible to him too. 'Wait, I can see it. Sam, I see it; but how?'

It then came to him.

'Sam, I need you to do something for me please; take off your hoodie.'

Sam looked at him stunned for a moment but did as he said and passed her top to him. The ice inside the cave had almost all melted, but it was still quite chilly in there. Sam crossed her arms around herself to keep warm and covered, aware that Damien's eyes had not left her since the moment he first saw her.

As soon as Daniel got hold of her blouse, her portal became visible to him again.

'This is why he took your clothes, Damien,' he told his brother, who until then had remained silent. Daniel passed the blouse to him, and as soon as he handled it, Sam's portal, and the vision of what lay on the other side became visible to Damien too.

'But how did they know of this?' he asked.

'Who cares about that now?' Sam grabbed the hoodie from his hands and put it back on. 'I'm about to turn into ash over there; I can't just stand here and watch it happen.'

Daniel now turned to face her.

'You could just, stay here, you know? Whatever happens back there, you'll be safe here with the rest of us. Think about it, Sam, no more insomnia.'

'I bet,' Sam replied, outraged at the suggestion, 'I'd be sleeping for good. Oh, Daniel, don't you see? This is not about my insomnia anymore; they've got you now and I have a feeling that we won't be safe here either, as long as they do. I have to go back; I have a score to settle.'

Daniel hated to admit it, but she was right; as long as Winter was in possession of his body, he would never be completely safe and free.

'But you don't know if you'll make it out of that fire, Sam; you're wounded.'

'I'll make it, Daniel; I have to, for both of our sakes. Trust me, ok; I know what I'm doing.'

She leaned towards him and gave him another quick kiss on the lips, and then made for the portal. Just as she was about to walk into the vision, a hand grabbed her and held her in place. She turned to see Damien holding her by the wrist, but before she could scowl at him, he said.

'Sam, please don't kill him; the other me I mean. I'd like to be able to go back home someday.'

She stared at him, trying to figure out if he was joking or not, but he obviously wasn't. He really meant it.

Now, what was she to do about this? Butler had shot her and left her for dead, and she was supposed to let him live? How was that justice? And even if she agreed to that, would Butler give her that choice? She shook her head, unable to think of this just now.

'I'll try,' she simply said, vanishing from their sight and into thin air.

Chapter 14

IN THE VALLEY OF DESTINY

aving consulted with the Oracle, Daniel decided not to risk going back to his world after the news he got from Sam. He found the bracelet and put it back on, hoping it would still work, and then finally lied down and shut his eyes for some much-needed rest.

Once again, dreams did not disturb his sleep, nor did he did awake on the other side of the invisible wall that separated the two worlds. He should have felt relieved, but he didn't; time was still his enemy. He knew he was taking a big risk staying in this world, but he was counting on Winter to keep him alive for as long as he thought he had a chance to get access to his portal. And if he was wrong, well, he didn't really want to die, but this wasn't just about him anymore. If Winter had his way, there was so much more to be lost than his own life. No, he would take his chances against Winter in this world, and hope that with a little luck and a lot of help from his family and friends, things would work out for the best.

Once everyone had rested enough and was now ready to move again, they left the castle of the Great Lord and headed down towards their next destination, the Valley of Destiny. On their way down from the mountain, Daniel and Hëna rode Lightning non-stop, going as fast as the wind for what felt like a whole day's ride. Nathaniel and all the other wingmen from Dard'h flew above them, carrying Nemo and Damien in an improvised carter, while the Oracle disappeared again, saying he was needed elsewhere.

Hëna did not say a single word the entire time, and he could not find the courage to talk to her either. She sat behind him, holding on with her hands around his waist, making it all the harder for him to ignore his ever-growing desire for her. Throughout the whole ride Daniel felt her warm body brush up against his, her dizzying scent overpower his entire senses. But there were also fresh tears running down his spine, as her head casually rested against him. More than once he made to place his hand on hers and interlock his fingers with hers, but then he remembered her face and tone of voice as she pledged her allegiance to him, and he stopped himself. Rarely had he felt as lost and conflicted as he did just now, and he feared he'd never find his way out of this.

When they finally reached the Valley of Destiny, they met with the rest of Gabriel's wingmen, who had already erected the camp. Hëna locked herself inside her tent and did not come out. Daniel knew she needed the time and privacy to properly mourn her brother, so he gave instructions that she was not to be disturbed.

After their arrival, Lightning also suddenly departed from him, sprinting back northeast towards the mountains. Daniel feared he had seen the last of the stallion and his sadness doubled. He had grown so fond of his magnificent friend and could not imagine facing the end without him.

Still, he could do nothing but hope that eventually the stallion would return to him.

The location they'd picked was indeed a good choice for a gathering of troops, usually no more than two days ride from Endër or Sky-City, and less than that from New Sotira. Of course, now that there was no sun or moon, they could no longer tell whether it was day or night. Whenever the sky cleared up a bit - which was not that often - they could see the stars, but they were of no help. The whole kingdom was caught up in a state of perpetual dusk, made even gloomier by the frequent snow and cold.

They erected the camp in the northernmost part of the Valley of Destiny, an endless field that seemed to have been put there for the specific purpose of hosting a huge army. The first part of their army was already with him, a legion of well-armed wingmen from Dard'h, under the leadership of Gabriel. They had sworn their allegiance as his personal guards and had positioned themselves around his tent, surrounding him from all sides and keeping constant watch over him. Groups of them constantly patrolled the air, keeping an eye out for any possible danger or sign of movement, friendly or hostile.

They had just finished setting up the main tent where the leaders would meet, when the first messengers, the pair of wingmen who had flown to New Sotira, returned. They had spent only a few hours in the village and were sent back with the message that Ari and two of his sons, as well as the Queen of Endër, were already on their way. Ari's eldest son, Andrés, was left in charge of organizing and leading the first part of their new army. It would be comprised by men and women from New Sotira and all the surrounding villages. They would need just over a day to arrive if they rode non-stop.

Daniel was overjoyed to hear of this; he missed his mother and longed to throw his arms around her and feel like her little boy once again, if only for just a moment. Being an adult was apparently harder work than they made it look, and if he had a choice, he'd gladly go back to being a kid and have the adults worry about saving the world. Ironically enough, part of being an adult was also knowing that life did not work that way, and he had no choice but to face whatever was coming head-on.

It wasn't long after they settled when a storm hit the camp. By now the weather had turned completely against them, though this caught no one by surprise. No doubt Winter knew that the Great Lord was gathering the people around him, guessing what would follow. He would surely try anything within his power to hinder them, if not stop them altogether. Still, Daniel knew it would take a lot more than wind and snow to stop the people of Endërland from claiming back their kingdom.

Shortly after the first messengers had returned, he was notified that the second part of their new army was arriving at the camp. As he left his tent, he looked up towards the heavily clouded sky and saw the wingmen of Sky-City following their queen and prince in organized quadrants of hundreds. Watching five thousand armed wingmen landing in formation before him, Daniel's heart was uplifted with hope and joy. They still did not know the exact number of Winter's troops, but however many wolfmen he had surrounded himself with, surely, they would be no match for the valiant sons of the sky.

After their landing, the proud queen walked with her head high towards him to present herself and her people. Daniel made to kneel before her, but then remembered; despite her lordly demeanour, the Sky-Queen was now *his* subject, and just like the rest of them, she was supposed to bow to him first. And so she did, followed by Séraphin and the rest of their army behind them.

Daniel half expected to see some sign of malice or resentment in her eyes, but to his surprise and relief, he saw none. The wise queen knew her place and accepted it with humility and grace. And just like Gabriel before her, she declared her allegiance and that of her people to Daniel in the presence of everyone, followed by shouts of joy and loyalty from her wingmen.

It was agreed that a meeting would be held once all the parties had arrived, so after this brief ceremony, the Sky-Queen retreated to her tent to rest and supervise the settling of her army.

Next, in what Daniel estimated was about half a day, the convoy from New Sotira arrived, led by Diane, who as always was escorted by the ever faithful Íro. Just like the Sky-Queen had previously done, Diane knelt before her son, laying her weapons at his feet, and proclaiming her loyalty and allegiance to him. Daniel smiled as he realized his mother had armed herself with the very same weapons that Winter had gifted her. He was sure the irony would not be lost on the White Lord.

Following her lead, Ari and his two youngest sons did the same. Once again, feeling most uncomfortable, Daniel waited until his great-grandfather pledged his allegiance to him by kneeling in front of the improvised throne before he could get up and embrace him. He had not doubted that his great-grandfather would come, but now that he was here, Daniel finally felt that his plan might actually work. Ari would know how to make everything happen, and he wouldn't have to bear all the responsibility of organizing and leading these people on his young shoulders.

When the ceremonial stuff was over and done with, Diane and Daniel hurried towards each other, ignoring the eyes of everyone present in the tent. The queen hugged her younger son, happy and relieved to have him in her arms once again. She had been hoping and praying that Daniel would be safe and out of danger, but that he would turn out to be the Great Lord himself, had far exceeded her own expectations.

Yet, the surprises kept coming as Daniel now led her to his personal tent, where Damien was waiting. Daniel had made no mention of his brother in his letter and was saving the surprise for when she arrived at the camp. There, Diane was finally reunited with her eldest son, amidst tears of joy and laughter. Years of sacrifice, searching, longing, and heartache were finally recompensed as she took her firstborn in her bosom and covered him with endless hugs and kisses, making up for lost time.

Watching the two of them, Daniel finally allowed himself a brief moment of joy, taking a respite from all the recent grief and worry. His sadness over Heli's death still weighed heavy on his heart, as was his pain over Hёna's hurt, and his worry over the fate of the kingdom. But he could do nothing but hope that, whatever happened, the future would still carry plenty of moments like this.

The last to arrive at the camp were the messengers from the Queen of the Seas, with the news that Eleanor would not join them. She authorized Nemo, however, to represent her in the council. In the meantime, she would organize her mermaids and prepare them for battle. Nemo was a bit disappointed that he would not get to see her there but pleased that she had chosen him to represent her and their people in this historic and momentous gathering. Right then, he promised himself that he'd make his queen and mother proud, no matter what. He was ready for this.

The village was beginning to awake under a state of alarm as the tongues of fire claimed Selim's entire house. Butler and his men were already gone, when a single man with long greasy hair and dressed in dirty rags appeared. He entered the burning house quickly and dragged Sam's unconscious body out of there. No sooner were they out of the fire and danger, when the little house collapsed completely unto itself, making a loud cracking noise. The villagers kept gathering to witness the event.

Sam's eyes were closed, and she did not appear to be breathing. The man checked her for a pulse and when he saw that she had none, he began doing chest compressions on her to try and revive her. He did that for about half a minute and then stopped to check again for a pulse. There was nothing. He moved his hand over her abdomen, where there was still blood oozing from underneath her blouse. Lifting it, he saw the wound that the bullet had created. From his side pocket, he took out a small flask and undid its cap to pour some colourless liquid onto the wound. Reacting to it, as the blood washed away, the skin around the wound began to grow back, slowly causing the wound to close. The insides also seemed to shift, pushing the bullet towards the exit. Eventually, the wound was completely gone, as if it had never been there.

Hopeful, the man went back to doing his chest compressions on Sam. He continued doing that for about two or three more minutes, checking her pulse every now and again, but it didn't seem to be working. He was about to give up, when it suddenly happened; Sam took one deep breath, as if emerging from deep waters, and opened her baby blue eyes, greeting the evening sky above her. The man stopped pushing on her chest and put one hand underneath her head, helping her up, while with the other one he brought the small flask in front of her mouth.

'Here, drink this. You'll feel much better.'

Sam did as he said, letting the cool water soothe her aching throat and breathe life back into her insides. When she felt that she'd had enough, she pushed the flask away from her and looked at the man. A creased line formed on her forehead as she seemed to realize or remember something.

'I know you; I've seen you before.'

The man smiled.

'Yes, Sam, you have. Can you remember where?'

It took her a little longer to clear her head and remember.

'You're the homeless guy outside my building.'

The man helped her sit up, positioning himself beside her on the cool ground.

Out of their view, Selim's house continued to burn down, while the villagers tried in vain to figure out what had happened.

'Do me a favour, will you?' Sam spoke with a feeble voice. 'Don't offer to read my palm again; I couldn't take another journey to wherever it is you would send me next.'

'Hahaha...' the man laughed, 'you don't really believe in that hocus-pocus, now do you?'

Sam gave him a tired look and chuckled lightly.

'How do you feel?' The man asked.

She put her hand over her stomach, remembering her wound. As she lifted her blouse, she was surprised to see that there was nothing but smooth skin where she had previously been shot. She knew she had not dreamed it, however, and the still fresh bloodstain on her clothes proved it. She looked at the man sitting beside her.

'Did you do this?'

He looked at her with the same eyes that had drawn her to help him the first time around.

'It wasn't your time, Sam; you still have work to do. Daniel needs your help; you must get back to London. Once there, you will find Daniel in the very same place they took him before, the clinic. Butler thinks you're dead, so he's not worried about anyone rescuing him again.'

'So, that's his name,' she said, raising her tired blue eyes to look into his, as if studying him. They had the same colour as hers. 'How do you know all of this?' she asked, believing she already knew the answer.

'I know a lot of things, Sam. For example, I know why you haven't been able to sleep ever since you were little.'

Sam kept her eyes glued to his, asking through them, instead of her words.

The man continued.

'It was for your own protection. You know by now what Daniel is, right?'

Sam nodded, but again did not speak.

'You and Daniel have the same ability. Had you been able to sleep, you too would have travelled to the same place in your dreams and would most likely have fallen victim of the same person who captured Daniel's brother and others before him. Making sure you stayed out of that dreamworld was the only way to keep you safe. I'm just sorry that it cost you so much.'

Sam couldn't even blink. She finally knew, yet she felt nothing. She had partially suspected the reason when she first found out she shared the same birthday with Daniel; their similar predicament couldn't have been just a coincidence.

Then she thought of something.

'Hang on, how come Daniel can now dream, yet I'm still unable to sleep?'

'That, I do not know. Daniel is not supposed to be dreaming, but for some reason he is. I think that's because he is even more special than I thought, and for that I'm actually glad. There's a lot depending on him right now. But Sam, if Daniel does not wake up, Butler *will* kill him. You cannot let that happen; Daniel has to live.'

'He *will* live,' Sam said and got up, though a bit too fast. She felt lightheaded and almost fell back down. The man caught her by the arm and held her steady.

'You need to take care of yourself, Sam; you are still healing and will be quite weak for the next few days.'

'Don't worry about me; I'll be fine, but I need to move right away. If Butler does not feed Daniel, he won't have to kill him; he will die soon enough. I have to get to him.'

She started towards the village exit when she noticed he was not following her.

'You're not coming with me, are you?'

'No, Sam, I'm needed elsewhere. But you will be just fine, brave one; this part of your journey is almost over, and I promise you that soon you will find what you've been seeking all along.'

Sam was not sure what he meant. She thought of her reason for flying halfway across the world and smiled. She had not thought about her cure for a long time now; she no longer cared. All she wanted was for Daniel to be safe. She looked at the man one last time and said.

'You're the Oracle, aren't you?'

'I am and I'm not,' the man replied in his cryptic way. 'Who knows, maybe one day I'll introduce myself properly to you.'

'I'll hold you to it,' she said and greeted him goodbye, resuming her walk.

'Do I really have to wear this, mom?' Daniel complained as he looked at himself in the reflection of his mother's shield and saw a young king staring back at him. Diane had brought with her a brand-new pair of royal garments to go with her son's new position.

'You must, Danny,' she replied, satisfied that they fit perfectly. 'You are the Great Lord of Endërland now and need to be seen as such.'

Daniel sighed in surrender.

'At least there is no crown.'

'Yet,' Diane teased him, smiling. 'Come now, everyone's waiting for you.'

They left their tent and headed towards the main one which served as the official quarters for the Great Lord. All the leaders were now gathered inside, waiting to be formally introduced to the Great Lord and discuss their next course of action. The Oracle had once again taken his place beside Daniel's throne, while joining the improvised council this time were also Gabriel as the leader of his tribe, and Hëna. She had finally left her tent, and though there was still a weary look about her, Daniel had the feeling that she had shed the heaviest part of her burden. Still, she avoided any direct eye contact with him. Daniel tried but found it hard not to be affected by this. It was just as well that she chose to sit behind him, that way neither of them would have to deal with awkward looks.

The rest of the council members sat in a circle before him, with Diane the first on his right, followed by his great-grandfather Ari. The Oracle sat to his left, and next to him sat the proud Sky-Queen, accompanied by Séraphin, wings tucked behind his back. Gabriel followed and Nemo closed the circle, representing the mermaids.

Daniel looked at the group of people in front of him and knew that this was the moment when he had to convince them all that he was indeed their Great Lord. Only, he didn't know how; he was still trying to convince himself of that. He didn't know how he had earned that title, what gave him the right, nor had he any idea of how to prove it to himself or them. And yet, the Oracle was right, they desperately needed the Great Lord now, even if a pretender was all they could get. That would be better than nothing at all, or so at least he hoped.

When everyone had taken their place and were ready to start, it was time for him to be the Great Lord again. He was nervous. It felt beyond weird to be in front of these lords and queens and pretend that he was anything but an eighteen-year-old boy, whose experience amounted to little more than reading books and watching movies. Still, he wasn't alone; he knew Alfie would help him get through this. So, he got up from his chair and began to address his subjects.

'My dear friends. Thank you for accepting my invitation to gather here on such a short notice; I am most grateful. The last time I was standing before some of you, I was just Daniel, a Visitor; accused of a crime, for which I'm sure we now all know who is responsible. A lot has happened since that day and many things have changed. This kingdom that was once a wonderful place full of joy and life, has now become a place of fear and death. Winter has come with full power and threatens to stay forever, plunging everything into cold and darkness. Already the sun is gone and with it all the warmth and light it gave us. Endërland will not be able to survive like this for too long. Soon, all life will fade away, buried under snow and ice, and there will be nothing left of the magnificent and colourful world that we all know and love. That is why I have called you here, so that we can stop this from happening, together.'

He stopped here, measuring the mood in the room, and happily concluding that he had their undivided attention. All eyes were focused on him, watching, and listening carefully. He next looked at Alfie, who now stood up and took over.

'As you all have learned from the letter you received, we intend to build an army, as big and strong as we can, in order to face the White Lord and force him to give up the Silver Throne. We will of course try to reason with him and avoid going into battle, if possible, but I have a feeling that he will not be so easily persuaded. He has gone into too much trouble to give up the power that he now has. Perhaps having an army to back us up might cause him to reconsider, though I highly doubt it. He has surrounded himself and sealed Arba off with legions of creatures that were created for one purpose only, war. And that, I fear, can only mean one thing; he is prepared to go all the way. For this reason, we must also be prepared to fight, for without doing so, we will never be able to take back our kingdom and restore it to its former glory.'

Alfie stopped here, painfully aware that his audience felt as uncomfortable with this as they looked. He knew they had questions, so he did not delay in giving them a chance to ask them.

'Does anyone wish to speak?'

As he had anticipated, the Sky-Queen was the first one to speak. Without getting up from her chair, she bowed her head slightly towards Daniel and spoke.

'I do beg your forgiveness, my lord; you called, and my wingmen and I came to you. We have pledged to follow you into battle until our hearts stop beating, or our wings can no longer carry us, if that is your will; and to that pledge we will hold true. However, I cannot help but wonder if this is indeed the only way. You have finally returned to us; surely you, creator, and maintainer of all of Endërland have the authority and power to overcome the White Lord. Angry as I feel for allowing him to use me and my people to play his games, I do not wish to go into battle against him, knowing that even a single one of my wingmen may die.'

It was the same question Gabriel had asked before in the castle, and Daniel and the Oracle looked at each other. The Oracle made as if to speak, but guessing it was going to be the same answer he had given to the Chieftain, Daniel stopped him. He looked at the faces of the people before him and knew that he could not lie to them.

'I will not hide anything from you,' he began, his youthful eyes fixed on theirs. 'Being the Great Lord was as much a surprise to me, as it was to you all. I do not know what happened, or how I came to inherit this title, just like I do not know what power there is in me, if any at all. But I do know that if we want to save Endërland, we need to bring all our people together, and if that is the only thing I ever accomplish as your Great Lord, then that is more than I could ever wish for. I believe that being united as one is all the power we will ever need against Winter and his army.'

Everyone fell silent, pondering Daniel's words, while he fearfully expected at least the Sky-Queen to get up and storm out of the tent, furious for having been deceived. But she didn't. She bowed her head ever so slightly and spoke again with a humble voice.

'What I have seen and heard are proof enough to me that you are the Great Lord, and if bringing our people together to fight for our home is indeed the only power you have, we will still follow you and do your will. The Sky-

People are proud to be part of your army, my lord, and we will fight for you and Endërland.'

Echoes of cheers and approval sounded among the people present in the room, while the Sky-Queen leaned back in her chair and spoke no more. Daniel already felt overwhelmed; this was going much better than he had anticipated.

Diane was the one to speak next.

'My people are not trained for war and battle, my lord, but they are ready to do their part in taking back our kingdom, and they will follow you wherever you will lead them.'

Daniel smiled at her as more cheers erupted from the members of the council. He then turned his attention towards Nemo, who spoke for his queen and people.

'The mermaids of the seas will do their part in this battle, my lord; whosoever can, will start their pilgrimage today and join your army on the ground under my command; the rest will fight from the water, led by the Queen of the Seas herself.'

Nemo bowed his head like the queens before him, prompting Daniel to return the gesture. He was so proud of his best friend right now; he had come such a long way from being the frightened boy he had met on that first day, surprising and delighting everyone along the way.

Daniel continued to address the council.

'Thank you, all! I really do believe that together we can win this war. I am well aware of the difficulties in raising and organizing an army in such a short time, but I believe we have the right man for the job.'

He now turned to Ari.

'What do you say, great-grandfather, this is what you were trained for a long time ago, isn't it? Will you help us? I may be the Great Lord, and I shall be the first in line to face

Winter and his creatures on the battlefield, but I am no soldier. We will have a much better chance with you as our leading general.'

It was now Ari's turn to bow his head and speak.

'It would seem this is indeed what I was trained for, my lord, and it would be my honour to help build and lead your army into battle. You can count on me and my sons.'

Daniel bowed his head one more time and then turned to Alfie again. The Oracle took the hint.

'Very well, then. I guess there's nothing left for us to do but talk strategy and logistics.'

The meeting went on for a long while after that. There were numerous issues to be discussed, starting from procuring the weapons to arm every soldier and up to devising a strategy for taking Arba, if things went that far. The good news was that, following the Oracle's advice, his mother and Ari had long been preparing for something like this. As he learned, for quite some time New Sotira had become a secret base for producing and storing weapons, as well as training key people in the art of war. This would save them much time and effort in preparing the new army to march towards Arba. Daniel already felt much more optimistic about their predicament.

By the end of the meeting, everyone was feeling quite worn out, so they all retreated to their own tents to rest and recuperate their strength. The easy part was over and done with; the real challenges were still to come.

* * *

As time flew by, no longer bound into night or day, the weather in the valley continued to worsen. The snowfall seemed to only be getting more intense, building up all around them and making it increasingly difficult to move freely. Storm after storm hit the camp, with strong winds threatening to take away their tents and extinguish their fires. It was clear that Winter was doing his best to stop them from gathering and organizing themselves into an army that could actually threaten him.

Daniel worried that this might scare the people and bring their morale down; after all, they had always enjoyed the best of the weather in every season and never really suffered from it or anything else that nature or man could bring upon them. His fears, however, proved unfounded; somehow everyone seemed to understand that it would only get worse before it got better, and they held on.

A bit later than expected the convoy from New Sotira and the villages around arrived at the camp, bringing with them carriages filled with weapons of all sorts. There seemed to be enough there for almost everyone, wingman, mermaid or human.

The troops coming to join the new army comprised of roughly three thousand men and women gathered from all the villages nearby, with people and mermaids coming from as far as Tálas. The latter would be the first soldiers to join the battalion led by Nemo.

Among the new recruits were the seven former werewolves who had been the first to recognize Daniel as the Great Lord. Along with their fellow countrymen, they reported before Ari, who had begun sorting everyone out into different battalions and divisions.

More people continued to come from all over the kingdom, as word of mouth spread even to the most remote villages of an army gathered to end the siege of Arba and dethrone the White Lord. Soon there were about eight thousand men, wingmen, and mermaids, all armed and organized into ground and air troops. The wingmen themselves were divided into two smaller groups, one of them led by the Sky-Queen herself, and the other by Séraphin, their prince.

On the ground, Ari divided the main troops into six battalions under the command of his six sons whom he had trained himself, passing on to them all the knowledge that was once given to him. His sons in turn began giving their soldiers basic training on sword fight and self-defence.

All the joining mermaids who had chosen this perilous time for their pilgrimage formed a separate battalion. There were about seven hundred of them, all armed with what had now become the signature weapon of the sea-maidens. Most of them had never seen their prince in person, but they had heard of his latest deeds and seemed to be in awe of him whenever he was among them. And just like Daniel, Nemo felt ill at ease with his newly earned status as a hero.

The entire army was finally divided into two main units. The first one comprised of two thousand wingmen led by the Sky-Queen, Nemo's battalion of mermaids and two more battalions led by two of Ari's sons; about four thousand armed soldiers in total. These would head towards the Northern Gate of Arba, while the second group led by Daniel and Ari would knock on the city's Southern Gate. The plan was to try and enter Arba from either of the gates, hopefully at the same time, and for this they needed to separate their forces.

When Ari judged that they had gathered as many soldiers as they could at this point and had equipped everyone with some form of weapon and basic training, they decided it was finally time to head towards Arba. And so, the two armies began their march in two different directions towards the city of the Lords.

For the first time since he'd come to Endërland, Daniel had to be separated from his best friend, and though he had come to have faith in Nemo's ability to look after himself and others, he could not help but feel anxious. But he wasn't the only one; Nemo felt as nervous about this as he did.

'I don't feel right leaving you, Dan; I promised I would follow you until the end.'

Daniel felt like hugging his little friend and holding him tight for a good while, but he did not want to embarrass him in front of his battalion. Íro's beautiful eyes were also fixed on the red-hair boy, who seemed to have grown a year's worth during this past season. So, instead, he just shook his hand and gave him a friendly pat on the arm.

'Whatever debt you felt you owed me, Nemo, has long been paid. Besides, this is not the end, we will meet again, sooner than you think.'

Nemo smiled and shook his hand in the same manner, trying to appear tough. He then let go and turned to leave, but stopped after only a few steps, changing his mind. He turned back and opening his arms wide, threw himself at Daniel, and gave him a quick hug.

'It is customary to say, "May the Great Lord lead your way" on such occasions, but since you are, you know..., him, today I think I'll just say, "Good luck and see you soon, Dan."'

'See you soon, Nemo,' Daniel smiled as the young prince headed back towards his battalion, waiving at the lovely Íro one last time.

Just as the first part of their army was leaving the camp, one of the flying patrols announced that a large group of wild horses was approaching fast from the northeast. Daniel immediately thought of Lightning and ran out to see for himself. Only a moment later, he spotted the stallion leading over four hundred of his sons and daughters towards them, each one as beautiful and proud as he was.

Lightning rode straight to Daniel, whinnying with pleasure at the sight of his rider and master. Daniel almost wept from the joy of seeing his faithful friend again; he could not imagine riding any other horse into battle. He threw his arms around Lightning's long neck and gave him a well-deserved hug. He was now truly ready to face any enemy.

The rest of the horses were quickly saddled and mounted without a fuss, adding to the number of the cavalry leading the march. Daniel thought of Heli and smiled; oh, how he wished his friend could have seen this.

Behind them, the ground troops were put into formation and followed on foot.

For Daniel's unit, it was pretty much a straight wide path from where they were, all the way down to Endër. The only real difficulty so far came from the thick snow that continued to build up all around them. Every hour, those at the front of the line cutting through it would be replaced by a new batch of soldiers, to avoid them getting exhausted and slowing down the march. Riding Lightning, Daniel remained in front of the line, leading them all the way. The brave stallion never seemed to show any sign of weariness.

The Oracle rode next to him, as always never leaving his side. At times, Diane and Damien - who were now inseparable - would join them for a while, other times Séraphin would fly along, keeping them updated on their progress and everything else happening around them.

But the person whom Daniel most wanted by his side, stayed out of sight throughout the whole march. Hëna was lost somewhere among the troops, and he had no idea if she was actually with his part of the army or had followed Nemo and the Sky-Queen.

They marched with few stops for what seemed like ages to all of them but would have otherwise been two days and two nights, until they got to the borders of Endër. They avoided entering the city and continued instead marching north of it, until they joined the main road through which his mother's coach had taken them to Arba the first time around.

People continued to join their ranks as they passed near the city and the villages in the area, thus raising their numbers and spirits even higher. Almost two thousand men and women that formed part of Diane's army came out of Endër and joined their queen in the march.

Daniel's heart grew lighter the more people were added to this marching crowd that they were calling army. He was hoping beyond hope that seeing all these people gathered before him, Winter would see some sense and for their sake would back down. Yet even though he truly believed that every man had some goodness in him, he was afraid that he could not count on this when it came to the White Lord. Something else seemed to be going on with him, and he had a feeling that when the time finally came, they would not be dealing with just a man, nor even a lord.

And as he looked at the multitudes of people marching on behind him, he was suddenly afraid for their lives. What if he was leading these people to their deaths? What if the weapons they were given and the training they got weren't enough? Anyone else from his world would have called this madness, and him a mad man for leading a bunch of farmers and shepherds to fight against an army of creatures bred only for killing. How would he be able to live with the responsibility and guilt if all this failed, as it most probably would? What would his "loyal subjects" think of him then?

The closer they got to Arba, the more anxious and doubtful he became about where he was leading these people. But as the walls of the city of the Lords eventually appeared on the horizon, the Oracle, who seemed to always know what to say, put his mind at ease.

'I know you have doubts, Daniel; it's not an easy feat what we're trying to achieve. Many may die, it's true, but you must remember that the alternative is far worse. If nothing is done, everyone will die sooner or later, and that's a fact. They know that, that's why they come out to fight.'

'They come because they think the Great Lord is with them and he will protect them and grant them victory. I can't protect them, Alfie; I don't have the power.'

'Whether you have the power or not, it will be revealed in due time; until then, lead them on Daniel, and trust in their hearts and strength to protect themselves and their home.'

There was not much else he could say after that; he might not have the faith that the Oracle had in him, but there was nothing he could do about it now. There was no turning back from where they had all come. Soon they would be face to face with Winter and his creatures, and then the future of Endërland would be decided once and for all, one way or another.

Chapter 15

BATTLE

ising tall and forbidding before them, the giant ice wall hid the City of the Lords from their sight and reach. Sealing the sequoia trees inside this thick and incredibly high and slippery block of ice, Winter had effectively blocked all access routes in and out of Arba. Where the road previously entered the citadel, there now stood tall a white gate sealed shut, with only a straight vertical crease appearing where the two huge blocks of ice met.

Daniel could not help but think of Heli, he would have melted this gate open in no time. As it were, he could think of no other way to get inside the city, save for the wingmen flying over it and opening the gate from the other side. Of course, that meant they would have to deal with whoever and whatever Winter had protecting the gates, which was most likely his entire army.

The troops stopped about a mile from the white gate, with everyone falling into pre-ordained positions and waiting for instructions. Ari, Diane, and Damien rode ahead to join Daniel and the Oracle in front of the troops. Nathaniel, who was now Séraphin's second in command, accompanied his prince. The seven stood facing the ice barrier that separated them and the city. Daniel imagined that by now the other part of their army were looking at a similar picture before them.

Snow had stopped falling and the wind had died down. An eerie calm reigned all around them, with no sign of life or movement anywhere. Nothing and no one appeared at the gates to acknowledge their presence. It was as if they were too insignificant to even be noticed, let alone dealt with. Daniel had not known what to expect once before these gates, but this was even more nerve wrecking. Minutes passed since the army settled and stood there, waiting for a sign from the ice wall. Finally, Ari rode forward a few feet and called aloud.

'In the name of the Great Lord of Endërland, open these gates.'

His voice roared over the stillness, carrying his words as far down as the sea. No response came for about a minute or so, and he called again.

'In the name of the Great Lord of Endërland, open these gates.'

Again, no movement. He was about to call out for a third time, when from high above the gates, three wingmen were seen flying down in their direction. Soon enough Daniel recognized Azariel in the middle; the other two he did not know. They landed before them, tall and proud, their wings half spread, a sign of readiness for war. Apart from the two fighting knives hanging on his belt, Azariel carried no other weapon, but each of the other two held a loaded bow in their hands.

Daniel had never seen wingmen use bows before; anything but a knife was too inconvenient for them to use while in flight and their wings did not allow them to carry much. The circumstances, however, required that they adapted their fighting ways, so Ari had convinced Séraphin to equip at least part of his legion with crossbows; this way they could attack from a greater distance. They would tie an extra quiver with spare bolts to one of their long legs instead of their shoulders, and when they could no longer use the weapon, they'd just abandon it. That and a custom-made breastplate was all the armour the wingmen would have in the forthcoming battle.

Azariel looked at the seven people before him one by one, his eyes resting a bit longer on Nathaniel. An evil grin formed at the corner of his mouth, but he did not linger. He returned his gaze upon Ari, who was still a few steps ahead of his companions.

'Who is in charge of this mob?' he asked, an arrogant tone in his voice.

Ari stared him down disapprovingly and answered.

'You stand before all the people of Endërland, who have marched before these gates led by the Great Lord himself. Humble yourself, Azariel, son of Ariel, and pledge your loyalty to him.'

Azariel chuckled.

'You must be confused, old king; I see no Great Lord before me. The only Lord I know is the one sitting on the Silver Throne, behind these walls, the one who commands that you disperse and go back to your homes, lest you get what you come here seeking.'

'Then you are blind, as well as misguided, Azariel,' Séraphin spoke this time, with a harsh tone of voice, 'a traitor to your queen and people. Your master is an imposter and a murderer, and you are no better than him.'

Azariel appeared unfazed by his words. Ari continued.

'In the name of the one true Great Lord, we demand that the White Lord open the gates of Arba and release those he holds as prisoners. He is then to appear before the Great Lord and all the people of Endërland to answer for his crimes.'

'Be careful, old king, my master is the only one who does the demanding around here. He will open no gates and release no prisoners, much less appear before anyone to answer for his actions. And if you think this herd of farmers you've dragged before these walls and this fool of a pretender can threaten him, think again. I would pray that these gates stay shut if I were you, there's nothing behind them but your doom. Now, if you do not turn around and walk away, these people's blood will be on your hands, and yours alone.'

'Everyone comes here of their own accord, and they've come too far to go back. Now, I'm done exchanging words with you, call your master to show himself.'

'That's just as well, old king, I've said all that my master has commanded me to say. You have been warned and the choice is now in your hands: depart from here and you may live; stay and you will all die.'

The three wingmen stretched their wings and rose up in the air, turning their backs on the army. Only a few feet from the ground, however, Azariel stopped in mid-air and turned towards his former friend.

'Oh, Nathaniel, your father sends his regards.'

Opening his right hand, he dropped something small in Nathaniel's direction, who reached and caught it before it fell on the ground. A dreadful realization came to him, as he recognized his father's ring. Burning tears filled his eyes, and for a moment he felt lightheaded and almost fell to the ground. Struggling to retain his composure, he closed his fist around the ring, and looked up, disgust and anger churning up his insides. Azariel continued to fly away, grinning with malice.

Séraphin, who understood all too well what had just transpired, placed one hand on Nathaniel's shoulder and spoke softly.

'Do not despair just yet, brother; we don't know for sure that he's really done this.'

Head down, Nathaniel could barely make himself heard.

'I don't know him anymore; I fear he's gone where he can no longer come back from, and he blames me for it. There's not much a man like that wouldn't do.'

'Then let us stop him,' Séraphin said, 'together. Hold on to your anger, brother, the right time will come.'

Nathaniel put his father's ring on his finger and his mourning on hold, following Séraphin as they joined the rest of the group.

'What now?' Daniel asked, looking to Ari for guidance. It was Diane who answered him, gripping the hilt of her own gold-finished sword.

'We do what we came here to do, there's no turning back now.'

Séraphin added his voice to hers.

'This is about all of us, my lord; we might die in battle here today, but if we turn back now and do nothing, we will die all the same. My wingmen are ready; they will go all the way.'

'Good,' it was Ari who replied, 'because it will have to be *your* wingmen who take the first risk. This gate will not open unless from the inside, and your people are the only ones who can cross over. But once there, you are on your own and we won't be able to help you face whatever forces stand against you. Are you sure you are ready for this?'

Séraphin looked to Daniel.

'What other way is there?'

Daniel knew what he was asking and wished he had a different answer. But it was too late now to reconsider, and he had no right to make this about himself; it was their lives, their homes, their whole world these people had come here to fight for, not him. And they knew that, just like they knew they stood no chance, yet still refused to give up and turn around.

'None, I guess,' he said, barely looking at the Sky-Prince in the eye. Lightning then trotted closer to Séraphin, and he and Daniel were now face to face. Daniel extended his right hand, and the wingman shook it. 'It has been an honour and a privilege to know you, my friend; go with my blessing and make us proud yet another time.'

'The honour has been all mine, my lord. We will not fail you.'

Both he and Nathaniel bowed and headed back to their troops. Less than a minute passed and then almost three thousand wingmen - including Gabriel's legion - filled up the sky above them, flying in formations towards the city of the Lords. Only, this time, they flew not towards merriment and feasting; instead, they flew knowingly towards battle and possible death.

Those carrying crossbows were lined up first; the rest of them held up their daggers and readied themselves for battle. A sense of dread came over Daniel, as he watched them fly over the ice wall.

'I fear I've sent them to their death,' he said loud enough only for the Oracle to hear.

'They go willingly to claim back their honour and make things right again. Don't forget, it was a fellow wingman that brought about this doom, and they feel responsible for it. It has already begun, Daniel, and it can only end in blood and tears; we knew this.'

'That doesn't make it any easier to bear. What am I doing here, Alfie? If I'm the Great Lord, then where is my power?'

'It will come to you when you are ready,' the Oracle replied, just as the first sounds of the battle began to echo through all of Endërland.

In that very moment, the wind picked up again, stronger than ever, clashing with fury and rage against the wingmen's wings. At the same time, hail began to fall heavily from the skies on top of them, prompting whoever could to shield themselves. As the first lines of wingmen crossed into enemy territory, they were met with endless waves of arrows and cross bolts flying in their direction from the ground. Many fell, unable to avoid their deadly darts, while the rest continued to fly ahead towards the ground, firing their own cross bolts and targeting invisible enemies from the air. More were hurt from the huge chunks of ice that kept on falling upon them from the sky, but they kept advancing.

When at last the wave of arrows coming from the ground ceased, leaving behind hundreds of wounded or killed wingmen, those who were still flying faced a new kind of danger. Thousands of mountain ravens, the same kind that Daniel and his friends had fought by the seaside, launched a full attack against the remaining wingmen, trying to keep them from reaching the ground. They seemed to be coming from everywhere, turning the sky black like the darkest night. The wingmen, whose numbers were dropping fast, engaged into a long and brutal fight with the giant birds. Blood and feathers rained from the sky, along with a mounting number of lifeless bodies that continued to fall as the battle grew wilder and more chaotic. For every remaining wingman, there were tens of ravens that surrounded them, attacking mercilessly and tirelessly. And still the wingmen kept advancing.

Séraphin and Nathaniel, fighting side by side once again, watched with alarm as their numbers kept dropping, while it did not seem to matter how many ravens they slew. The black birds kept on coming, as numerous as snowflakes in an avalanche, filling the air with their hideous croaking and floating black feathers. Séraphin knew that they would not last long; and even if by some miracle they managed to kill all the ravens, they would still have to face the thousands of wolfmen that they knew were waiting on the ground. They needed a strategy, a plan.

'I have an idea,' Nathaniel shouted over his shoulder, caught in a battle against three ravens all at once. 'We need to find Azariel and force him to open the gates.'

'How do you know he will do it?'

'I don't; we're just gonna have to make him.'

'And how do you suppose we find him?' Séraphin asked, slashing with his knife upside the approaching beak of an enormous ugly bird.

'He will find me,' Nathaniel answered, and having killed the last of the group of ravens currently attacking him, let out a thunderous cry that drowned out all other noises.

'Azariel.'

His call seemed to draw the attention of every bird around him that was not engaged in a fight, and all at once they turned and threw themselves in his direction. Unperturbed, Nathaniel called again, this time even louder: 'Azariel.'

Within seconds, both he and Séraphin found themselves surrounded by over a hundred ravens that kept on closing the circle around them. As they braced themselves to make their last stand, another loud and angry voice echoed over all the commotion.

'Nooo..., he's mine.'

Collectively obeying his command, the ravens all scattered and dispersed, flying away from Nathaniel and Séraphin, and leaving them to face Azariel alone.

'Stand back, Prince,' Azariel howled at Séraphin, as his two companions hovered in the air behind him, bows at hand. 'This is between him and me. You're welcome to hang around and watch him die, until your turn comes'.

Séraphin looked to Nathaniel, who nodded. He then drew back and after giving his friend an encouraging smile, said.

'He's all yours.'

The air buzzed with duelling wingmen and ravens, while on the ground, the multitudes of wolfmen that anxiously awaited their turn, now looked up to watch their winged general fighting his own duel.

Azariel advanced slowly towards Nathaniel, knives in hand.

'I warned you not to go against me, Nathaniel, but you didn't listen; you just had to play the hero. Well, I bet you regret that now, don't you?'

'The only thing I regret is that I didn't do it before, Azariel; none of this would have happened if I had. No matter, this ends here, one way or the other.'

'You're right about that,' Azariel hissed, getting ever closer. 'This ends here..., with your death.' He screamed and launched himself at his former friend, aiming both knives at his heart. Nathaniel swerved in the air, avoiding the sharp metal with ease. Turning around swiftly, Azariel swung his left arm, and as he did so, his knife cut through the upper part of both of Nathaniel's wings. Numerous blue feathers fell down, with even more drops of blood racing them to the ground. Nathaniel winced from the pain but ignored it and recovered quickly. He kicked Azariel in the chest with both his feet, thus pushing himself from him and gaining a bit of distance, long enough to evaluate his wounds. The cut wasn't too deep, and no vital arteries had been damaged. He was still able to move his wings without too much pain.

He looked at Azariel who was staring at him with an evil grin on his face. Even now Nathaniel could not believe how things had gotten to this point; he did not recognize this person who was once his best friend. They had grown up together, played together, trained, and made plans for their future together; how had it come to this, that they were now enemies, trying to kill each other? In a moment of clarity, he realized that he was as much to blame for this, as Winter or Azariel himself was. He had given up on his best friend and abandoned him at the mercy of the White Lord and his lies. He had not been a good enough friend, and now it was too late to change things. Azariel was lost and so was their friendship.

All around them the battle continued brutally with both wingmen and ravens dropping from the sky like rain. Outside the gates, the ground troops could see very little of what was happening as they waited anxiously, while inside, thousands of wolfmen bred and armed for war, busied themselves slaying any wounded wingman that fell among them. Séraphin's heart began to bleed watching his brothers die one by one, while they were no closer to getting the gate open. He began to despair, thinking that he might have made a mistake leading his people into a battle they never had a chance of winning.

Then just like that, it happened; without an audible command, a good number of the ravens engaged with his wingmen split and flew with urgency towards the Northern Gate. Relief washed over Séraphin, as he realized that his mother's army had begun their attack from the North. Hopefully, this would even the odds a little.

With renewed strength and hope, the wingmen pushed on with their aerial fight against the black monstrous birds, while before him, Azariel launched his attack anew against Nathaniel. This time Nathaniel was more careful, anticipating his friend's moves. He knew how Azariel fought; they had sparred together countless times. But even though Azariel had always been stronger and faster, he had one disadvantage, he was overconfident and careless. It was this that Nathaniel intended to use against his friend; he would watch out for that right moment and make his move.

He did not have to wait long.

Having landed a number of blows and caused numerous cuts and bruises all over Nathaniel's body, Azariel seemed to be growing ever thirstier for his friend's blood. His eyes had now turned red, and frenzy seemed to have taken over him as he continued to swing and slash with both hands without resting. Blinded by his uncontrollable hate for his former friend and thinking he had him just where he wanted him, Azariel launched what he hoped would be the final blow, aiming his knives straight for Nathaniel's heart once more.

Nathaniel was badly wounded, and his muscles were beginning to fail him, but, seizing the opportunity, he called on to the last bits of energy he had left for one final move. He rolled swiftly 360 degrees in the air, letting the knives swing past him, and thus managed to get behind Azariel, grabbing him from the back and resting his own knife against his neck. Using his other arm as well as his legs, he imprisoned Azariel firmly within his own body and held him tight, using his battered wings to keep them both in the air.

Caught completely by surprise, Azariel began to wriggle, trying to get out of Nathaniel's grip. But the knife in his friend's hand pierced through the skin of his neck and caused him to stop.

'I would stay still if I were you,' Nathaniel hissed behind his ear. 'Now, order the gates open.'

As he spoke, two arrows originating from Azariel's companions, dug themselves inside his back, going in deep. Unbearable pain brought tears to his eyes and began to weaken him rapidly, but he did not let go.

Azariel chuckled, as if something funny had just happened and relaxed himself.

431

'Do not make me ask again, Azariel,' Nathaniel threatened, making the knife cut a bit deeper into Azariel's throat.

'You want the gates to open?' Azariel managed to speak, and Nathaniel eased his hand a bit. 'You got it. They can all die, for all I care.

'Open the gates,' he bellowed with a voice that had now lost its former strength. There was commotion on the ground as his orders were obeyed instantly and without question. The multitudes of wolfmen began moving to open the ice gate and be ready to march out of them.

Watching the white gate open inwards and the army of Endërland appear at the entrance, Nathaniel finally decided to release whatever energy was holding him and Azariel glued together in the air. He was too tired to keep on moving his wings, and already his limbs had started to turn numb and disobey his commands. Only, as he made to detach himself from Azariel and let him go, he found that they were still stuck together. The arrows that had pierced through his back had come out of his chest and inserted themselves into Azariel's body, one of them grazing his heart.

Nathaniel looked up at his friend, whose grin was beginning to fade fast as they began to free-fall towards the ground. In that last moment, he felt sadness come over him and regret for everything that he had allowed to happen, eventually leading to this. With one last effort, he embraced his friend once again, but this time with compassion, and whispered in his ear.

'Forgive me!'

His eyes then closed, sparing him the sight of Azariel's disgust as he tried to get out of his friend's embrace, just before they both plunged hard to the ground and certain death.

Up in the air, Séraphin was once again engaged into battle with several black ravens that were trying to tear at his wings and flesh. He saw with a braking heart his second in command go down, and his heart bled. Unable to fly to his aid, he silently said goodbye to his friend, who sacrificed his own life to give them a fighting chance. He promised himself he would honour the brave wingman properly, should they eventually win this war, and then focused on the enemy before him.

Below them, the wolfmen now moved out to meet the army of Endërland into battle, and whatever joy he felt at the opening of the gate, quickly vanished. There must have been at least six thousand troops on this side of Arba alone; his mother's army was probably facing similar numbers at the Northern Gate, without including the countless birds that seemed to be going nowhere. It did not look very promising.

Outside the gate, Daniel was thinking the same as he watched the huge number of wolfmen pouring towards them in a frenzied attack. But there was no time to sit and think, the battle was finally happening, and they had to fight or die. Taking one last look at the people beside him, he saw that they were all ready with weapons in their hands, and they were all waiting on him.

His heart faltered when he finally spotted Hëna, who had quietly positioned herself next to his brother, sword in hand. She was dressed in her battle garment and her hair was tied back in a tight single braid. Her gaze was fixed on the approaching army before her, and the focus of the battle seemed to have overcome all her recent sorrow. And still, she looked breathtakingly beautiful to him. He smiled at her as their eyes met for a single moment, and then gave a little nudge to Lightning, who began sprinting towards the approaching wolfmen. Lifting up his sword, he let out a war cry that was echoed and repeated by every single warrior as they charged behind him, heading towards certain death and eternal glory.

The distance between them and the swarming wolfmen grew smaller, and it took but seconds for the first swords to meet each other and fill the air with sparkles of fire and light. Soon, both armies were merged into one, and thus the battle for the fate of Endërland officially began.

It was weird for Sam, being back in London. She had spent the last few months of her life with Daniel and Freddie, and this place was so exclusively associated with them. So, to wander the streets of the big city alone now felt a bit depressing. Her stomach wound did not help things either; the pain was ever-present, even though it mostly irritated, rather than crippled her. But whenever she thought about it, she was glad for the pain, because she should have been dead; she *would* have been, if not for the Oracle. So, she ignored all the unpleasant feelings and thoughts that kept inviting themselves into her brain and tried instead to focus on a strategy to save Daniel.

It was true that she had the element of surprise, Butler was not expecting her, but there were still at least three of them, well-armed and dangerous. Her recent near-death experience had made her more cautious than she was by nature, but again it was not herself she was worried about. She had promised to protect Daniel, and she had failed. Fate, however, had given her a second chance, and she would not mess it up this time around.

She could not count on having help either, Freddie was gone, and she had no idea how to contact anyone from the Order, or even if they would be willing to intervene. No, she would have to do this all on her own. She knew where Daniel would be, she just had to sneak in there and take him out, much like the last time. Of course, Freddie was with her then, and it had been easy enough to carry Daniel outside. She had neither him, nor his Mini now.

Then it dawned on her; there was one other person who could help her, one who wanted Daniel safe just as much as she did, his father. She searched her brain, trying to recall Daniel's home address; she was sure he had mentioned it at some point. About a half hour later, a taxi dropped her just outside Daniel's flat.

The Lewisham neighbourhood, with two-storey houses on both sides of the street where David lived, seemed quiet tonight. She climbed up the few steps that led to the door and rang the bell. Shortly after, the hall light came on inside, and the silhouette of someone tall appeared through the glass. When the door opened, Sam was face to face with a good-looking man in his early forties, black wavy hair very much like Daniel's, and dark brown puffy eyes. She had no doubt this was David.

'Yes?' David's voice matched the tiredness in his eyes.

'Mr. Adams?'

'Yes?'

'My name's Sam. I'm a friend of Daniel.'

David gave her a weary look.

'I'm sorry, honey, but Daniel isn't here.'

'I know,' Sam interrupted him, before he continued with the story he no doubt had told many times ever since Daniel had left. 'And I know where he is. He needs our help.'

David's eyes lit up, as it appeared newfound energy surged through his entire body. He immediately led Sam in, where they talked for a good while. Sam decided she would tell him everything she knew; she didn't care much about any rules she might be breaking. Freddie wasn't around to tell her off, after all, and she had no time to come up with a whole new story that might make more sense or answer all his questions. Besides, she secretly thought that David deserved to know the truth.

After having heard everything she had to say and having asked a number of questions to better understand certain things, David got up and began pacing around the living room. Sam decided he needed the time to process everything, so she stopped talking for a while. Inside though, she was anxious to move, knowing Daniel didn't have much time.

A few minutes passed and David stopped pacing and turned to look at her.

'I'm sorry, a lot of this seems to make sense and explain a great many things, but I can't just start believing in this whole other world parallel to ours and all this Visitor business. It's all just too....'

'Crazy?' Sam finished the sentence for him. 'I know. Still, that doesn't really matter right now, does it' she continued. 'What matters is that Daniel needs our help, and he is running out of time. So, grab your gun and your car keys, and let's go.'

'My gun?' David asked doubtful.

'These guys are dangerous, Mr. Adams; they shot me and left me for dead and they will have no problem trying it a second time. We can't just go waltzing in there without some kind of protection.'

David hesitated for another moment, but then turned and sped up the stairs to his bedroom, returning less than a minute later with a small handgun. Then, heading for the door, he grabbed his keys from the hanger on the wall and they both walked out of the house without wasting any more time.

Climbing in his car, they sped off in the dark, destination Central London.

The battle had been going on for what felt like ages, with massive losses on both sides. Daniel was proud of his people. Even though they lacked experience and training, they were all fighting bravely and not backing down, despite their unnatural opponents.

Winter's wolfmen were huge. Whatever magic had turned these animals into half-human, had also given them a bad attitude, as well as a complete disregard for their own safety. Armed appropriately with only a spiked mace and then set loose, these creatures seemed to be after one thing alone, killing who and whatever crossed their path. True, they were disorganized and uncoordinated, and they did not seem to have much training either, but they did not really need it to hurt, or worse, kill someone; their bare hands did the job just fine. It looked like the only reason they were given the weapon, was so they could intimidate even more, if that were possible. Most of them used the mace for the first few blows, but once they got close enough to their enemy, they did away with it, and then it was all claws and teeth.

The army learned this the hard way early in the battle and tried as best as they could to kill the wolfmen from a distance, hurling cross bolts, arrows, or spears at them. The wolfmen numbers, however, were overwhelming, and very soon they were overrun, having to fight more than one of them at a time.

As the battle raged on for hours, Daniel's army began to diminish significantly, and the remaining soldiers were getting too exhausted from the ceaseless fighting. Daniel himself had not stopped to rest for a single moment; the wolfmen kept on coming at him from all sides. His body was covered in cuts and bruises, and a few times he'd almost let the wolfmen overtake him. But Lightning, who never left his side, always stepped in, and held them off. The brave stallion had accrued a large number of wounds, most of them aimed at his rider, but nothing seemed to slow him down. He was fearless and had managed to kill more wolfmen than any single warrior on that battlefield.

Every now and again, Daniel managed to get a glimpse of his mother and brother fighting side by side, and he couldn't help but feel anxious. He didn't want to lose them again. Diane had trained with Ari for a long time, and she was formidable in battle, but Damien was very inexperienced, and Daniel feared he would not last long. Were he not trying to concentrate in the wolfmen constantly attacking him, he would have seen Hëna fighting next to Damien, never leaving his side. It seemed, she had taken it upon herself to look after his brother and make sure he was safe.

It was not very difficult to kill the wolfmen, once they learned how; they weren't very bright or agile, and they did not protect themselves well. The problem was that there were just too many of them, and more kept on coming out of the city gates, as if the earth itself was spawning them. At this point, it was more about sheer numbers, than it was about strength or fighting skills. And even the most experienced among them did not stand a chance against too many wolfmen at the same time.

Daniel witnessed with his own eyes as his great-grandfather was surrounded by tens of wolfmen all at once, overpowering him, while his soldiers tried in vain to get them off of him. Ari did not make it easy on the creatures; he put up an amazing fight, slaying more than a dozen of them with only a few blows. But more kept on coming, and eventually, the once king of Endër fell to the ground, never to get back up again. Daniel's heart felt like it would split in half as he watched his great-grandfather go down, grief and desperation washing over him. If someone as strong and experienced as Ari did not survive, what chance did the rest of them have?

After many hours of continuous fighting and people dying, Daniel began to feel exhausted and exasperated. Their numbers kept growing smaller, while the wolfmen seemed to still be counting in thousands. The earth had turned red and seemed to be drowning in the blood of all the fallen; while everywhere they went, they stepped on corpses and severed limps. Up in the sky, the remaining wingmen continued to fight their own battle against the huge black ravens, unable to aid the ground troops.

Benefitting from a short respite, during which no wolfmen seemed to be coming his way; Daniel took the chance to look around him. His mother and brother were still alive and caught up in battle, but they and everyone else showed in their faces the same despair and fear that he felt in his bones. They could not keep this going for long; soon the wolfmen would overtake them and that would be it. There was no way out of it, they could not retreat now; they were surely going to lose.

He had no time to ponder things any longer, however; a fresh wave of wolfmen heading towards them saw that he was not engaged and advanced towards him. Daniel braced himself and raised his sword again to meet them when a loud horn sounded from inside the walls of Arba. All at once, the wolfmen stopped advancing, and those that were still engaged in battle, simply stood still. His soldiers took the chance to slay them where they stood, and to their surprise they did not defend themselves, nor fought back. They just stood there and accepted their death as if they didn't know or care. Daniel almost felt sorry for the creatures, being used by Winter, and discarded in such a manner. They had no clue as to why they were fighting or who they were fighting; they just blindly obeyed the commands of someone they didn't even know.

Both on the ground and in the sky, the armies began to regroup, with the wolfmen and ravens heading back inside the city walls. Everyone else fell into formation behind their leaders. Only then did Daniel see just how many of their people had been lost. All around him, the ground was hidden under a blanket of mutilated bodies and blood as far as the eye could see. The entire field, which was previously covered by unspoiled white snow, had now turned dark red. They would have to search the battleground for any wounded soldiers, if this truce, or whatever it was, lasted long enough.

Diane and Damien came to join him and the Oracle, just as Séraphin landed beside them, covered in blood and black feathers. Right then, the sound of a chariot coming out of the ice gate drew their attention. Turning, they saw the White Lord himself heading towards them, accompanied by Butler, who was using his one good hand to lead the two horses drawing the small chariot. It looked very much like the ones Daniel remembered seeing in old gladiator movies. The two wingmen they had seen earlier with Azariel were also flying on either side of them, like two guardian angels.

As they waited, Diane took a quick moment to check on him and make sure he was alright. While she did that, Daniel subtly checked on both of them. His mother's eyes were red; she had obviously witnessed Ari's death, just as he had. He wanted to say something, to comfort her somehow, but didn't know what. Instead, he just took both her and Damien into his embrace and hugged them tight, neither of them saying a word.

Winter's chariot finally stopped only a few yards from them, but Winter did not step out of it. Slowly and deliberately, he took a good long and wide look before him, as if assessing all the damages caused by the battle. He had a serene, almost satisfied look on his face, badly hidden under a false concerned expression. When it seemed he was done evaluating the situation, he turned to them.

'So, is this what you were hoping for, when you decided to bring these poor souls before my gates?' He motioned towards the fallen in the field.

'*Your* gates?' Diane could not help but retort, with clear disdain in her voice.

'Yes, *my* gates, my dear Lady of the Land,' Winter replied, seemingly unfazed by her tone. 'You better than anyone else here should know that regimes change all the time, and finally the time has come for just such a change in this kingdom. No more following and obeying the rule of a long-forgotten lord. We make our own future from here on, a future that need not be feared, nor fought; not as far as I'm concerned. I've always wanted the best for our kingdom, and now I am finally in the position to make it happen.'

'You have a strange way of showing your good intentions,' Diane continued to challenge him. Daniel could not be prouder of her right now; she had amazed him with her courage and skills in the battle, and even more so as she openly and bravely stood up to Winter. 'Is this how you imagined "the best" for the kingdom? The whole land has plunged into cold and darkness, and all life is fading by the minute. You've turned the animals into horrible creatures that you're using against the very people that you claim to love. You've had people murdered and imprisoned, and have now declared open war on all of Endërland. I dread to think what other "improvements" you have in mind for us.'

'Change never comes without pain and sacrifice, my lady, but it is not me who is to blame for all of this. It was not me who shut down the Lightbringers and brought about cold and darkness, nor have I murdered or imprisoned anyone. Whatever blood has been shed, has been a direct result of your actions alone. All I desire is for us to peacefully walk together into the new era. Will you not even consider that?'

'Are you really that deluded, or do you think we are fools that you can dupe with your poisonous words?'

Diane's words were as harsh as her tone of voice, and Daniel could see she had grown angry. Winter's eyes grew small and dark.

'Careful, dear lady, I will not suffer disrespect from my subjects.'

'We are not afraid of you, and we're no longer your subjects; you gave up that right when you decided to usurp the Silver Throne.'

Sensing that the conversation had taken an ugly turn, the Oracle stepped forward and smartly intervened.

'If I may, my Lord Winter, there's still the issue of the Great Lord...'

Winter now set his gaze upon him, and as he did so, darkness and malice shadowed his face. His eyes lost their bright white and blue colours, and for a split second it was as if they were empty.

'You,' he hissed, and his face and voice changed as if he was suddenly someone else. Daniel found his animosity towards the Oracle quite surprising, and once again felt as if he was missing something. Winter continued. 'Did you really think you'd keep me locked away forever? Well, I'll show you what forever really means soon enough.'

This short exchange between the two, had the others mystified. As the realization of a truth known only to the two of them became evident on his face, the Oracle took a step back, unable to hide his total shock and fear.

Seeing that he wasn't going to say anything else, Séraphin decided to speak up.

'The Oracle is right; the Great Lord is no longer missing; he has returned and is here to claim his rightful place.'

Taking his gaze off the Oracle, Winter became his old self once again and smiled defiantly, as they finally came to the point. He looked down on Daniel, who was standing next to Lightning and feeling like everyone else was fighting his battles for him. He knew that the eyes and hopes of all the people in that field were upon him; he had promised that he would deliver them, and now was his chance. But how?

'Yes,' Winter continued, 'I heard the rumours that the Great Lord has returned. Well, where is he? Why doesn't he show himself?'

Daniel literally felt everyone's eyes on him and knew it was now his turn to speak. He stepped forward and said boldly, yet without much conviction.

'I'm here. I am the Great Lord.'

Winter's chuckle was followed immediately by laughter from his two bodyguards. Only Butler continued to remain impassive and expressionless like a statue.

Daniel felt angry at this reaction, but also afraid. Hearing himself pronounce those five words, he realized that they just weren't true. He saw it on Winter's amused face, and felt it in the eyes of the people gathered around him. If he had truly been the Great Lord, none of this would have happened; no one would have had to die, and Winter would be cowering before him right now. Instead, he was laughing, as if this was just a child's innocent role-play.

'Who is fooling who now, my dear Lady of the Land? Do you really want everyone here to believe that your son is the long-lost Lord of Endërland? How very motherly of you!'

'We believe in him,' Séraphin intervened, 'and the signs cannot be refuted.'

'The signs, Sky-Prince? Which signs would those be, pray tell?' Winter asked mockingly.

'The light from the Golden Throne, the star above Arba; only the Great Lord could make that happen.'

'True,' Winter said, 'but can you prove that it was this boy who made these sings come to pass? As far as I'm concerned, the star over Arba returned when I took up the Silver Throne and declared myself Great Lord and King over Endërland. And after the Lightbringers were taken down, I couldn't just leave the kingdom in darkness, so I brought forth this light temporarily, just until the replacements for the sun and moon are chosen.'

'*You* brought forth the light?' Séraphin asked, his turn to mock the White Lord.

Winter ignored his tone.

'You would say just about anything to have your way,' Diane said, refusing to believe even for a moment that he was telling the truth.

'I could say the same for you, my lady,' Winter replied, 'however, it doesn't have to be my word against yours. The boy is here; if he is indeed the Great Lord, let him prove it, and I will step down and submit to his judgment.'

His triumphant look fell upon Daniel again, challenging him just as much as his words did. Daniel was afraid of this; he had no tricks, no power, no magic in him to prove that he was the Great Lord. He could not explain the light from the Golden Throne, nor the star above Arba. Maybe it *had* been Winter after all.

Now, more than ever, he wished he had more time at his disposal. He looked at his loved ones around him, waiting for him to show them that Winter was wrong, but he couldn't. He spotted Hëna again somewhere between the soldiers in the first row but did not have the courage to look into her eyes. He felt like a fraud; worse, he felt guilty and responsible for having given everyone false hope and leading them to certain defeat.

Winter saw the hesitation in him, and his evil grin widened.

'Well?' he asked, expectantly.

There was nothing Daniel could say or do. He lowered his head in shame and whispered.

'I can't.'

Murmurs and whispers of disappointment broke out throughout the ranks behind him, but he dared not raise his head. He had never felt like such a failure and disappointment before.

Winter shifted his gaze back to Diane.

'There goes your saviour, my lady. I hope you are as proud of him as I am.'

Diane tightened the grip around her sword and stared back at him with fire in her eyes but said nothing. No one else spoke either.

'Right,' Winter continued, raising his voice, and addressing all of them now. 'If there is nothing else to say, then this is my proposal. End this now; go back to your homes and everything will be forgiven. No more people will have to die, and no one will be punished for this rebellion. In time the doors of the citadel will reopen, the sun and moon will shine again, and life will return to normal for everyone, provided you all accept and recognize me as the only Lord and ruler over the kingdom. In return, I ask only for two things. First, the Oracle is to be handed over to me, no questions asked. Second,' he now turned to Daniel, 'you will leave our world immediately and never return. Should you fail to comply and insist on continuing this meaningless and futile battle, I guaranty that you will never see your world again. I have it on very good authority that your body is already giving up and dying. If you go back now, you might be able to save yourself, but you will never be allowed to return. You have one hour to decide.'

From somewhere inside the chariot, Winter produced an hourglass, the very same one he kept in his hall, near his throne. He turned it so that the sand began to run from one bulb into the other, and had Butler place it on the muddy ground before them. He then signalled for Butler to move, and the chariot headed back inside Arba, leaving behind the remains of an army that seemed defeated in more ways than one.

* * *

Gabriel's wingmen had raised his tent far from the commotion of the battle, and two of them were guarding the entrance when they went in. Daniel wondered what had become of the Chieftain; he had not seen him since the battle had begun. He dared not think the worst; the wingmen had been hit the hardest and suffered the greatest loss since the initial attack.

Turning to face his council, or rather those of it that were present, he now saw that Andrés, Ari's eldest son had come in his father's place. Feeling a bit awkward, Daniel went to the man and hugged him.

'I am sorry for your loss. My heart weeps for him, as if he was my own father.'

Andrés bowed his head slightly and thanked him.

Daniel looked at the rest of them, with shame burning his cheeks. He could see it in their eyes that they were waiting for some explanation, hoping for some solution, but he had none. He knew that they had questions, but he needed his own answers first. He did not feel like facing them right now, so he decided he needed to buy himself some time.

The sand continued to run through the narrow opening between the bulbs in the hourglass, which was now sitting on a table behind him.

'We have less than an hour; we need to organize a search for those wounded. Andrés, will you please see to it that they are taken away from the battlefield and looked after? Damien, will you help him, please?'

Both of them obeyed, though this was not what they had expected to hear. Next, Daniel turned to the Sky-Prince.

'Séraphin, we need to know if the battle still continues at the Northern Gate, and how the others are doing. Do you think you can send someone to find out?'

'Right away, my lord,' Séraphin answered, appearing to hesitate for the slightest moment, as if he wanted to say something. Thinking better of it, however, he followed Andrés and Damien out of the tent.

Left alone with Diane and the Oracle, Daniel turned to him now.

'Alfie.'

The Oracle was still lost in his thoughts and barely acknowledged him.

'Forgive me, Daniel; I will need a few moments on my own, if I may.'

'We're running out of time, Alfie; and I don't know what to do.'

'I know,' the Oracle simply said and excused himself, disappearing out of the tent as well.

Suddenly feeling very tired and drained of any energy, Daniel turned to Diane, sighing.

'I'm so sorry, mom; you must be so disappointed in me.'

For the first time since they had arrived before the ice wall, Diane put down her gold-finished weapons, which were now washed in blood and covered in dents and scratches. She approached and took her son in her arms, resting his head on her shoulder.

'Disappointed? No sweetheart, far from it; I couldn't be more proud of you, of the things you have done and the man you have become. Oh, Daniel, if only you could see yourself the way I see you, the way Damien sees you; he worships you. And if daddy could see you right now, he would be just as proud of you as we are.'

'But I failed you, mom; I failed them all. I'm not who you all thought I was.'

'It's not over yet, sweetheart; I still believe in you, and so do they. Look around you; no one is running away, they're all here. We all knew this would be difficult; but you know what, it's not the battle outside that worries me. The greatest battles are not fought and won out there in the battlefield, sweetheart, but in here.' She caressed his head with both hands as she said this. 'It seems to me as if you still have some fighting of your own to do. All you have to do is believe, my Danielito, and when you do, whatever you dream will come true. We will stand by you, no matter what, sweetheart. I love you!'

She kissed him on the cheek, then picked up her sword and shield and walked out of the tent, leaving him to his own thoughts.

Daniel slumped on a stool beside him, burying his face in his palms. He had hoped against hope that things would not end up here, but they had, and now he didn't know what to do. He didn't care about being caught by Winter's men; he knew he would never give them whatever they wanted from him, so they would have to kill him eventually. And he was okay with that. But he hated it that Winter had practically won, and he was powerless to do anything about it. No matter what Winter said, life in Endërland would never be the same, even if by some miracle he did manage to restore the sun and moon into the sky. But what was he to do?

The sound of feet approaching claimed his attention, and he looked up to see Hëna opening the curtains of the tent and entering without waiting to be invited. For the shortest moment he had completely forgotten about her, but now that she stood before him, tall and beautiful as ever, his feelings stirred inside of him once again. She looked worn out from the battle, with scars all over her face, and her hair no longer in a neat single braid. Yet, all Daniel could see, were her radiant eyes which he had never been able to read.

'Hëna,' he got up, surprised. He felt like smiling, unable to hide the pleasure of seeing her there, but something in her eyes stopped him. She approached him in three short steps and stopped at arms' length from him.

'What are you going to do?' she asked straight away, no courtesies. 'Do you have a plan?'

There was a slight moment of disappointment as Daniel realized she was not there for him. Of course not, she was there to find out what would happen to her world and her people. Feeling slightly hurt, he lowered his eyes and answered.

'No, not yet.'

'So, it was all for nothing?' she continued, not really asking. Daniel lifted his eyes to meet hers and almost wished he hadn't. They were cold, foreign, unfriendly.

'I'm sorry,' he whispered. 'I never wanted things to get to this point. I really thought I could help.'

'You have to go,' her words rang harsh in his ears, 'back to where you came from, back to your own world. It's the only way.'

He looked at her intently, hoping, praying for something in her eyes to tell him that she did not mean it. He did not find it.

'If you stay, we all die, Daniel. But if you leave, we have at least a chance for some kind of life. Maybe it won't be as bad as we fear. I don't know why you're even thinking about it.'

'Don't you?' he asked, looking straight in her eyes now, for the first time unafraid of what she'd see behind his. She understood and looked elsewhere. 'I stay because this is my home, too; I stay because I don't want the White Lord to win this. I stay because of you.'

She returned her gaze at him, remaining cold and indifferent.

'Well, you stay for nothing,' she said, and this time she did not look away. 'The White Lord has already won, and apparently there is nothing *you* can do about it. And this is no longer your home; nobody wants you here anymore, least of all I.'

'You don't mean that,' Daniel said, unable to hide his hurt anymore.

'Don't I?' Hëna continued, showing him no mercy. 'Ever since you came here there's been nothing but trouble. My father is a prisoner, my brother is dead; half of Endërland is lying on that field, and all in your name. Do you really think I could even look at you after all this?'

So, she did blame him for Heli's death. Something snapped inside of him as he realized she would never return his love. Instinctively, as if protecting himself from her, he took one step back. With a wounded voice and unable to look at her, he managed to say.

'If this is what you really want, then I will leave.'

'It is,' she said coldly. 'Go back to your world, Daniel, to your Sam. Forget about us.'

Caught by surprise, Daniel lifted his eyes to look at her just as she turned her back on him and walked out of the tent. How did she know about Sam? He had never shared with anyone what had happened between the two of them. And why would she mention Sam at all? If he didn't know any better, he would think that she was jealous; but of course, that would be ridiculous.

He had to force himself to stop this inner monologue and concentrate on what was actually important. The fate of Endërland rested on his hands and he couldn't be concerned with his feelings for Hëna right now. She was right, the only thing to do was to leave Endërland for good and never come back. He didn't know how he would accomplish that; perhaps if he took the bracelet with him and wore it all the time it might stop him from dreaming once again. Or perhaps he might get his hands on some of those drugs he'd heard Freddie talk about.

But he was fooling himself; he knew Winter's men were in possession of his body, and if he went back there, he would fall right into his trap. Winter would finally get what he had been seeking all this time. He had no idea if Sam had managed to get out of the burning house and back to safety, but he could not count on her help either.

In the end, it all came down to what he was willing to sacrifice in order to save Endërland and the remaining people from total and complete annihilation. He knew that if there was even a small chance that his departure or even death would spare them, he had to try; he owed them that much.

Determined, he walked out of the tent and began looking for the Oracle. He had to consult him one last time;

after all, there was also the matter of Winter's other request. He could not make that decision for Alfie too.

In the battlefield, the entire army was engaged in searching and rescuing the wounded. He turned around to scan the horizon and finally saw him, sitting on a solitary rock, with his gaze lost somewhere ahead of him. Daniel walked up to him, following his footpath on the snow, and sat down beside him. The Oracle smiled, acknowledging his presence there, but did not say anything. Unlike earlier, he now appeared calm, unfazed by the battle and all the recent happenings.

'I've got to go back, Alfie,' Daniel said after a moment had passed, his eyes tracing the horizon before them. 'I don't trust Winter and I know his men are waiting for me to wake up, but I've got no other choice. We cannot win this war and I will have no more people dying today because of me.'

The Oracle looked at him for a brief moment and then cast his gaze again over the horizon.

'You know, when the Great Lord first arrived in this place, it all looked so much different than what you see today. It was all practically barren and shapeless, nothing really existed. He created everything the way he envisioned his perfect world to be, the way he thought his own world once was, before man ruined it. And do you know how he did that? He simply thought it up, willed it into existence. Everything appeared before him just the way he wanted it to be.

'Afterwards, he wanted to make sure that this world would not go down the same path his old world did, but the only way to do that, was to purge himself from all the evil that was inside of him, so that he would not contaminate it. So, he managed to somehow split himself from that evil and locked it away somewhere where he thought it would stay hidden and trapped forever. The creature you encountered in the Shadow Forest is his evil personified, the General, one of the many identities from his former life. Evil is darkness, Daniel, and the only thing that kept it hidden away was light. This is why in his design the Great Lord assigned people to serve as the sun and moon, for it had to be people who would always keep evil at bay. But now that the sun is gone, that evil is free again to roam these lands, and boy is it mad.'

'Why didn't the Great Lord kill him in the first place?' Daniel asked.

'He didn't know how that would have affected him; they were one person you see, and even after their separation, they were still connected to each other.'

'But what does this have to do with us now?' Daniel asked again, struggling to make the connection. 'The shadows were destroyed once the golden light was released; the General is gone.'

'I fear the General is not gone, Daniel. I believe it has somehow taken over the White Lord and is using him to exact his revenge on the Great Lord and this world he created and loved. The White Lord must have wandered into the Shadow Forrest at some point; that is the only explanation I can think of as to why or how he was corrupted. All the things he has done; Winter never had that kind of power; it was always the General.'

Daniel hung his head down in despair.

'Then, we have indeed lost. If we had no chance of defeating Winter, then what hope is there in defeating this evil Great Lord himself? We're doomed, Alfie; these people are going to die, whether I leave this world or not.'

'You're right about one thing; the General will destroy this world and everyone in it, whether you go back or not.' The Oracle looked at him now, with a smile of hope and encouragement. 'But he's not going to; you can defeat him, Daniel, you are stronger than him, and he knows this. This is why he's been trying to get his hands on you all this time. If he can force you to reveal the whereabouts of your portal, or create a new one where he wants it, he can take possession of your body once and for all. Then, he would have indeed become the Great Lord over this world and will be invincible.

'But it's not only Endërland that's in danger, Daniel; if the General manages to cross over unto the other side, we don't know what he may be capable of. He might have a lot of power, and I don't even want to think of what he will do with it. Your world as you know it, might be no more. No, Daniel, no matter what happens, you can never allow him to get to your portal and take over your body. The way things are now, we have the advantage; you are the Great Lord, and you have power he does not possess.'

'But I'm not the Great Lord, Alfie; you know that. I have no power. Don't you think I would have known by now if I did? Do you think I want to let him destroy everything?'

'My dear Daniel; you still reason and think as if you were in your own world. With all that you've seen and experienced here, you still forget that this world is not bound by any laws of nature or man as you know them. In here, everything is possible.

'I'm gonna let you in on a little secret, something that no one else in this kingdom is aware of, not even you. Before you ever set foot in Endërland, people and wingmen, but no mermaids inhabited this place. They did not exist, Daniel; they only appeared in this world when you first came here. Life carried on as if everything had always been like this, as if they had always been a part of Endërland, but only I know the truth. I had my doubts at first as to whether this was you or someone else, but after all the other signs that followed, after Lightning claimed you as his rider and led you to his former master's castle, I was convinced. Nemo and the

454

mermaids are your creation, Daniel, among many other things, and that is how I know that you are the Great Lord.'

Daniel looked at him, gobsmacked. What the Oracle said sounded completely and utterly ridiculous; it made no sense. He couldn't have created the mermaids when he first got here. How would that even be possible? They had been here since the beginning of time; the mermaids already had three queens and were about to crown their fourth one; that was not something that could have happened in the space of a few months.

He felt really confused just now.

'Help me understand this, please. Someone else was the Great Lord before, and he created Endërland in the beginning. I only added to it, creating a part of it when I first got here. Is that right?'

'It was someone else who first created Endërland, yes, and I have already explained what happened to him. I thought that the kingdom would never see the Great Lord again, until you appeared, and everything began to change.'

Daniel looked at him thoughtfully. Something he had never thought about until that moment suddenly dawned on him.

'It was you, wasn't it? You were the one who first created this world; you are the Great Lord. That explains why Lightning knows you, why the General hates you so much.'

The Oracle looked at him and smiled again.

'It was me, yes. I haven't been the Great Lord in a very long time because the kingdom has had no need of him. I chose to simply be the Oracle, his voice for whosoever wanted to hear from him. That is the reason why I no longer have any power and authority over anything or anyone anymore.

'When evil began to show signs of moving and working in this world, I began to panic because I didn't know how to stop it. The only thing I could do, was to lead other Visitors here, people like you, Sam and Damien, and many others who have descended from me through different bloodlines. I was desperately hoping that one of you would have the power to take over from me.

'I have been waiting a very long time for you, Daniel, and I almost gave up hope when I realized Winter was kidnaping all Visitors. I tried to protect the rest of you by keeping you away until I thought it would be safe. But your power proved much greater than mine, and you found your way in eventually. You clearly belong in this world, Daniel, and now that you're here, it's your turn to rule.'

Daniel was lost. This was more information than he felt able to digest in such a short time. If what the Oracle said was true, it would explain a great many things which he didn't understand until that moment. It would also mean that all Visitors were related to some extent, with the Oracle being their common ancestor, including him and Sam. But what did that mean, and was it even important right now?

The more he thought about all of it, the more he felt like scratching his head. Yet, somewhere in the back of his mind some things began to make more sense. Of all the books he had read, the Greek myths involving mermaids and heroes were amongst his favourites; and this world seemed to be full of things he loved. Nemo was one of his favourite characters, and it only made sense that he would be part of a world Daniel would create for himself. As were many other things, like oversized cherries, friendly animals, the endless seas, the wonderful nature, a girl as beautiful as the moon, and so on.

He was beginning to see what the Oracle meant, and for the first time ever since he set foot in this place, he started to see everything in a new light, and allowed himself to believe that he might indeed be the Great Lord. If he had the power to create all of this, then he had the power to do a lot more, starting by saving this kingdom.

He finally got up and looked at the Oracle with a new-born hope.

'Come, Alfie. I think I know what I need to do.'

Chapter 16

WIND OF CHANGE

Nemo kept swinging his sword on all sides, afraid to stop moving his arms for even half a second. The wolfmen kept on pouring out of the city gates like an endless swarm of locusts smashing onto a dangerously outnumbered army that desperately tried to hold them back. He was scared and he could feel it deep in his bones. If so many strong and courageous wingmen could fall at the claws and teeth of the wolfmen, what chance did *he* have? And he felt angry at himself; he thought he had outgrown fear, but that did not seem to be the case. He was as afraid as he had never felt in all his young life, and that included everything he had been through since the three wingmen had tied him up on that pine tree.

But as he looked around him, he saw the same fear in the eyes of his sisters and all the other warriors. They were all of them afraid, only, none of them was running away; they all kept on fighting. Nemo understood; it wasn't about being fearless; it was about facing the danger head on and with abundant courage. He knew there were hundreds of mermaids looking up to him and taking courage from him in that very moment, and he would not let them down. So, he kept on swinging and slashing with his sword, trying desperately to remember all the recent training he had received and the moves he had learned, so that he could stay alive long enough.

Their ever-reducing army received a much-needed respite when the current wave of wolfmen coming out of the gate subsided. More inside the city wall prepared to meet them in the battlefield. Nemo desperately wished he had news from Daniel and the Southern Gate, or his mother and sisters. He had not heard anything from them in a long time and his worry was slowly turning into despair.

As if tuning in to his thoughts, a single wingman appeared to be flying low above the army, calling for him by name and title.

'Here, I'm here,' Nemo called when the wingman got close enough, raising his sword up in the air with his left arm. The right he was trying to give it a bit of rest; he knew he would need it soon enough. The wingman spotted him among the other red-haired fighters and flew straight at him, without delay.

'Prince Nemo, I'm so glad you're alive and well, my lord. I bring word from your mother; the Sea-Queen would like to see you right away.'

This messenger was not from Daniel, Nemo realized, somewhat disappointed.

'Is she alright?' he asked the wingman in a manner of urgency.

'She's been wounded, my lord,' the wingman replied, 'but it's not serious. However, she can no longer continue to lead your people in the battle, and she asks if you would take her place. What would you have me tell her?'

Nemo did not know; he had not expected this. His mother was not simply asking him to take her place in this battle; she was asking him to decide now where he belonged, on land with Daniel, Íro and all the other friends he had made during this past season, or back into the sea with her and his sisters, who no longer detested him like before. Nemo had not had time to think about this; he was not ready.

Still, if this war was lost, it would not matter much, there would be no place for him anywhere. So, he decided he would go where he was needed the most.

'Is there any news from the Southern Gate?' he asked the wingman in a hurry.

'The battle still continues there, my lord. Many have been lost, but the Great Lord still fights with us.'

'And your queen?'

'She's currently tending to some of my brothers, not far from here.'

'Lead me to her, please,' Nemo said with determination. The wingman took that as an order.

'Follow me, my lord.'

Chasing after him, Nemo decided there was no time to rebuke the wingman for treating him like the royalty that he actually was. In his own eyes he was just Nemo, the oddity, the weirdo, the rejected coward. He wouldn't have felt so uncomfortable with the wingman's reverence, were he to see himself the way everyone else saw him by now, a courageous and valiant leader, charging at the front of his proud little army; a true living hero of Endërland.

The wingman continued to fly low above the army until they reached the Sky-Queen who was about to take flight and head back to the battle once again. She spotted Nemo and stopped to let him speak to her.

'Your majesty,' Nemo bowed down to her. 'My mother has been wounded and requests from me to lead the mermaids in her stead. But I would stay here if you think this is where I am most needed.'

The tall lady with the very sharp eyes bestowed upon the young merman a warm regard, placing one hand on his shoulder. For a single exonerating moment, Nemo marvelled at this genuine affection from this queen, who it only seemed like yesterday was pointing an accusing claw at him.

'It has been my privilege to have you in my army and watch you fight like one of my own, young prince. I can think of no other more qualified to lead the mermaids in this battle, besides your mother. Go with my blessing and assurance that we will keep the fight going, until we have won this war, or none of us is left standing. Good luck, brave Nemo! May the Great Lord be with you!'

'And with you, my lady. Thank you!'

He bowed once again, stopping to bathe in this unforgettable feeling for just another moment, and then resumed to follow the wingman towards the sea, where his mother was now waiting to temporarily pass him the crown.

* * *

The Sky-Prince had just returned with news from the Northern Gate. The battle there had not stopped, and there had been great losses on either side, but the Sky-Queen and their army still kept the fight going. It seemed that Winter had concentrated most of his forces outside the Southern Gate.

More news came from the sea, where the mermaids' army, led by the fearless Eleanor, was fighting to cripple Winter's troops from the water. The beach was now covered with the lifeless bodies of hundreds of ravens and wolfmen that had fallen prey to their unfailing cross bolts, while the sea had turned red with the blood of the fallen. The queen herself had been wounded when the White Lord had interfered, using his magic to freeze the sea nearby and turn the entire area into a deadly death-trap. More brave mermaids were killed or wounded in the process.

Séraphin informed him that Eleanor had retreated back under the sea, authorizing Nemo to lead his sisters in her stead. Daniel imagined this hadn't gone down well with Vanessa, the main pretender for the Sea Throne, but he was happy about his friend. Nemo had finally accepted his rightful place among his people, ending his pilgrimage and going back to the sea. It was where he belonged.

Back on this side of the city, the ice blocks moved once again to let out the whole armada of wolfmen that soon swarmed the land before them. They did not attack, however; instead, they kept on lining up outside the white walls of the closed citadel, while their sheer numbers made for a terrifying show of force that had even the bravest of the Endërland warriors tremble to their bone. The battle had done little to lessen their numbers, while it had more than halved the forces of men, wingmen and mermaids fighting for their kingdom. Still, they stood firm and unwavering behind Daniel, who once again mounted Lightning and waited for the White Lord to show up and meet them.

He said nothing to anyone about what he planned to do; the one hour that Winter had given them was up, and this was the moment of truth. All eyes were on him, wondering, pleading, hoping, and this time, he knew he would not let them down.

Lined up at the front of his army, alongside his friends, he noticed at the last minute Hëna taking her place next to his brother once again. When their eyes briefly met, he found that there was no hate behind them, only sadness. He wished he could take that away from her once and for all, and this made him want to defeat Winter even more. It didn't matter that she didn't love him, or that she blamed him for Heli's death and everything else that had happened in Endërland since then; he felt nothing but love for her. He hurt, but he understood.

The trumpet announcing the arrival of the White Lord sounded once again, and soon the same chariot led by Butler and escorted as before by the duo of wingmen paraded in front of them. Carrying the Silver Sceptre in his right hand, Winter looked smugly at the diminished army before him. His gaze rested upon Daniel, as the chariot halted in front of him.

'You have made a decision then?' Winter asked, sounding confident and pleased with himself.

No longer afraid, and finally sure of what he was doing, Daniel nudged Lightning to go forward, where everyone could see and hear him. He turned around to take one last look at his followers and then back, facing Winter again.

'I have,' he said loud and clear. 'I cannot give you what you ask.' The sneer froze on Winter's face as Daniel boldly continued. 'What I *can* give you is a choice; send these creatures back to where they came from and give them back their freedom. Then, release the three Lords and surrender the Silver Throne and the City without any more bloodshed, and I will give you a chance to redeem yourself for all that you've done. Refuse and you'll have chosen your own doom.'

Winter's face darkened and a shadow crept over it; his eyes grew black, empty, and his voice hoarse and whispery. He laid one hand on Butler's shoulder and whispered something in his ear. Butler handed him the reins of the two horses drawing the chariot, and walked fast in the direction of the gate, disappearing inside the city. Daniel knew what he was about to do.

Winter now focused on Daniel.

'I see; so, you think you've finally sorted out your identity crisis and now believe you have the power to overthrow me. Well, I think you're bluffing; you are nothing but a foolish little boy, who has gotten in too deep...'

'You're wrong,' Daniel interrupted him, advancing forward with determination. 'I *am* the Great Lord, and my word is law. You, on the other hand, are history; you're nothing but a mistake that has fallen upon me to fix. And that is why I declare that you are no longer the Lord of Winter; I am taking from you all the power and authority that was once given to you for that purpose. From this day forth, you will be nothing but a common man, and will answer for all your crimes before those who were once your subjects.'

As Daniel spoke with a newfound thundering voice, the wind picked up blowing wildly, while the earth began to tremble and shake violently as if from a terrible earthquake. A torrent of lightning and thunders struck down from the sky, tearing at the fabric of the universe itself. People grabbed on to each other as the ground beneath their feet began to shift uncontrollably.

Before them, the Silver Sceptre began to glow red hot in Winter's hand, who let it drop to the ground as it burned him. At the same time, his magnificent crown and beautiful white robes began to melt down like snow next to fire, revealing the true face and form of the man underneath.

Deep inside the city, in the middle of the garden, the ice statues representing the four Lords began cracking and melting down too, falling to the ground and shattering into thousands of little pieces. The wind kept on blowing, taking away all the dark clouds from the sky and leaving behind a clear celestial parchment, full of shining stars and constellations.

Behind Daniel, awe and wonder materialized in the faces of all his friends and loved ones. He really was the Great Lord, and he was finally back among them.

When the last bit of cloud disappeared from the sky, the wind died down once again, and the earth stopped trembling. On the chariot before them, where the proud

White Lord once was, there now stood a man dressed in plain clothes, with dark hair and an even darker face. His empty eyes seemed to be looking directly at Daniel with an intensity that would paralyze even the bravest of men with fear. But Daniel was no longer afraid; this man could no longer harm anyone.

And yet, another sneer formed on the man's lips, as whispery words escaped his mouth.

'Nice work, kid; but if you think this changes anything, think again. I don't need the White Lord for what I have planned for all of you; I got my army, and this time I won't hold them back.'

With a swift movement, the General grabbed one of the spears placed before him and threw it hard and with incredible strength towards Daniel. The spear travelled too fast, and Daniel could see it coming towards him, sure that he would not be able to avoid it. Then, at the very last moment, he felt himself rise up in the air and moving just out of the spear's reach.

Instantly, a terrifying realization came to him of what had just happened; Lightning had raised himself on his two hind legs, thus catching the spear in his own chest. Daniel screamed as the strong animal slowly came down, bending his back legs to let him off and then laying onto one side, his eyes closing.

'No, no, no, please don't leave me,' Daniel began to cry and beg, but the spear had gone straight into the stallion's brave heart. He could feel his chest movements growing smaller with each breath, and life abandoning him. Daniel buried his head on Lightning's long neck, lying next to him and stroking him gently. His own chest hurt badly, his heart ached, and his eyes burned so much, that he could not bear it. Hot tears rolled down his face as he realized that the stallion's chest stopped moving and the animal finally was at peace.

From all over the battlefield, wherever Lightning's kin were, their cries of anguish and sorrow joined his, the echo reaching to the farthest corners of Endërland.

Realizing that Lightning was forever gone, anger rose up in Daniel, as he now stood up and turned to face the man responsible. He only saw the malicious sneer on his face before the General raised his hand towards his enemies and cried.

'Butcher them all.'

All at once the multitudes of wolfmen lining up behind him were set loose, pouring towards them like a deadly avalanche. Seeing them approach, Daniel knew that this was the end. He thought that beating Winter would work, but he had failed, and now everyone he loved would die.

They parked the car at the same spot Freddie had parked his Mini the first time around and entered the clinic from the back gate. It was after midnight and this part of the city was quiet. It helped that it was the middle of the week; weekend nights in London were much more crowded.

The building had only one entrance and Sam was sure it would be guarded. She began checking all the windows on the ground floor, hoping that one of them would be unlocked. Sure enough, the one at the far end had been left slightly open. Pushing it inwards as quietly as she could manage, she found that the window would only open enough for her to squeeze in with a bit of struggle. Being much bigger than she was, David would not be able to fit through.

'I'm gonna have to go in through the front,' he whispered, as Sam nodded from the other side of the glass.

'I'll meet you by the entrance. Be careful.'

David proceeded to walk around the building towards the front door, while she took a look at her surroundings to make sure she wasn't in any immediate danger. The room was dark and empty, with only a bedframe and a few other commodities you'd usually find in a private clinic. She went to the door and opened it silently. Peeking outside, she saw two men sitting at a table down the end of the hall, playing cards. She recognized them right away as Butler's mercenaries.

This would not be easy; she knew they had guns and she had nothing on her. They would see her coming before she even walked out of the room, and this time she would not make it. She drew back, trying to come up with a strategy, when she heard the chairs move and the two guys getting up. Peeking down the hall once again, she saw them heading towards the main entrance, and guessed that David had drawn their attention. This was the distraction she was looking for. She tiptoed behind them quickly and stopped at the reception area, now looking at the two of them from behind, engaging in a dialogue with David at the front door. Before she could even decide what to do, one of them shouted at the other, reaching for his gun.

'That's his father.'

Sam rushed towards them, having no time to stop and think. Finding herself behind the second guy, she grabbed his gun from his waist where it was holstered, the same time as David produced his and pointed it to the other man. It wouldn't have worked out better if they'd planned it. Both men raised their hands up in the air, while David walked in and relieved the first man from his weapon. The two men then got on their knees with hands tied behind their head.

'Where is my son?' David asked, his voice transformed by anger. The men remained quiet, looking down on the floor beneath them. Sam raised her hand and hit the one closest to her at the back of his head with his own gun. The man fell face forward on the floor, unconscious. She raised her hand a second time aiming at the second man, who answered hurriedly.

'He's upstairs, upstairs...'

She stopped herself for a moment and then let her hand come down hard anyway, dropping the guy on the floor next to his friend. She then ran fast up the stairs, ignoring David's calls behind her. She did not want to wait another second to find Daniel; she had wasted too much time already and she would not lose him again.

She had a feeling she would find Daniel in the same room he had been the first time. She burst in, kicking the door open, and froze at the entrance. Before her, Daniel lay on the same bed, with a pillow over his head that Butler was holding down on him. Anger blinded her into a rage, and she had to actually remind herself who the man was, so that she wouldn't have to kill him right then and there.

'Get away from him,' she screamed and threw herself at Butler, pushing him away from Daniel. Butler ended up being knocked over against the wall, still holding the pillow in his hands. He recovered quickly, however, and boiling with anger, reached for Sam, who was checking on Daniel, completely ignoring everything else. He felt cold to her touch.

Enraged, Butler grabbed her by the throat, yelling.

'You again; why aren't you dead?'

Forcing her down on the floor, he kept on squeezing her neck with such strength and anger that Sam felt powerless to fight him off. She tried in vain to force his fingers open, but he was stronger than her. The pain and agony of being strangled made her forget all about her training, and she could think of nothing she could do. Or maybe she didn't want to fight back anymore; Daniel was lying frozen on the bed next to her and she had failed to save him. Freddie was gone, too. She couldn't face the coming days knowing that it had all been for nothing, and she would have to turn to a life she hated and no longer cared for. Maybe this was for the best.

Having decided not to fight it anymore, Sam let go of Butler's fingers and prepared for the final moment. It would not be long now; she had already begun to feel numbness overtake her as her lungs frantically searched for air.

She let her eyes close, convinced that this was it, when all of a sudden, she felt the hands around her neck releasing her, and air flew back into her lungs, burning and causing her to cough violently. Tears veiled her eyes as she opened them again to see Butler lying unconscious next to her, and David lifting her off the floor and onto a chair.

'Sam, are you ok?' David asked, his face paralyzed with fear and worry. 'You ran so fast from me.'

Regaining consciousness quickly, Sam nodded, rubbing her neck with both hands.

'I'm fine,' she managed to croak, not taking her eyes off Butler. 'Did you kill him?'

'No,' David answered, 'just knocked him out. Are you sure you're alright?'

'I'm fine,' Sam repeated. 'Check on Daniel.'

David did not have to be asked twice. He turned around and in two small steps was beside his son, checking for a pulse. His hands were trembling, and his heart was beating crazy fast; all he wanted to do in that moment was to take his son into his arms and look into his emerald eyes once again. But Daniel's eyes would not open. Anguished and exhausted, David sat on the bed beside him, now lifting

Daniel towards him and holding him in his embrace, tears rolling down his face, much like the day his mother had died.

Sam almost stopped breathing for the second time that night.

'Is he...?' she asked, afraid to finish the sentence.

David did not turn to face her.

'He still has a heartbeat; it's very week and he's barely breathing, but he's still alive.'

Sam plunged deeper into her chair, feeling her emotions overtake her. She'd done it; Daniel was safe. Silent tears refused to be held back as she finally allowed herself to rest.

She was about to close her eyes and enjoy some well-earned peace, even if only for a little while, when out of the corner of her eye, she saw Butler's figure move again on the floor. Winter's number one man got up with his back towards her, while his right hand reached inside his jacket. Producing his gun, he aimed it at both father and son. This time though, he did not manage to pull the trigger; another gun went off before his did, forcing him to drop to his knees once again, and then back on the floor, dead.

Unable to believe her own actions, Sam looked down to see the gun in her hand still smoking. She had not even seen herself draw it. Realizing what she had just done, she let it fall on the floor and covered her face with her hands.

'I'm sorry, I'm sorry; I did not mean to do this. Oh no, what have I done?'

David was instantly by her side.

'Sam, you had no choice; he was going to kill us. You saved our lives.'

Unable to look at him in the eyes, Sam kept covering her face and crying in desperation. How could she tell him that she had just killed his long-lost son, his firstborn? Would he be so understanding and so quick to forgive her then, knowing she had killed one son to save the other? And what would happen when Daniel woke up and found out? Would he not hate her forever?

David did not know how to comfort her, so he went to the body of the young man lying on the floor. He turned him around face up; trying to understand why Sam was so upset but found no answer there. The black curly hair, the young-looking face, the beard, all seemed somewhat familiar to him, but he was sure he did not know this man. He went back to Sam, determined to get her out of her state.

'Sam, I need you to help me with Daniel; we need to take him to a hospital right away, or he will die.'

Hearing Daniel's name again, Sam wiped the tears from her face and got up, avoiding eye contact with David.

'Should we call an ambulance?'

'No, it will be faster if we drive him there ourselves. Can you help me carry him down to the car?'

'Of course,' Sam nodded. 'What about him?' she then asked, motioning towards the lifeless body of Butler lying on the floor.

'I will sort everything out later; but right now, Daniel is all that matters. I'm not gonna lose him too, Sam. He's all I've got.'

She understood.

Once again, Daniel was carried out of that building unconscious and in the dead of night. They climbed into David's car and drove fast through the city streets towards the nearest hospital. Time was still their enemy.

The wolfmen kept on coming towards them, wild as the waves of a raging sea and numerous as the drops of water of a stormy rain. Furious that Lightning was taken away from him, Daniel turned to face them, sword in hand. All around him, everyone else braced themselves for yet another bloody battle, and this time they all knew it would be to the death. He could see it in their eyes.

This time though, he intended to do something about it; no more people would die today, not if he could help it. He looked at the faces of the ones he loved and everyone else that had left their home and followed him there; they had been through more than enough. It was time for the Great Lord to take it from here.

But what could he do? How could he defeat a wild and endless army of wolfmen with less than two thousand people left?

It was then that he looked up to the sky and remembered all the talks he'd had with Heli and Hëna; and just like that, he knew what to do. Raising his sword towards the heavens and looking up at the stars, he called out with the strength of a thousand voices, just as the first sounds of clashing weapons began to echo through the air.

'Brothers and sisters in the sky; Endërland needs you. Come down to us; join the fight to defend your kingdom and let this war end today.'

His voice caused everyone to stop - including the wolfmen who forgot what they were commanded to do – and they all stared at him, half scared, and half confused. The people did not understand what he was trying to do, and some even began to wonder if he had lost his mind, but Hëna knew. She finally smiled in relief. Everything would be okay now.

Nothing seemed to be happening at first, but soon more and more people began to look up at the sky and point. It began sporadically; stars would first shimmer where they were, as if waking up from a deep slumber, and then they would appear to move, slowly at first. Only it was not sideways towards each other, but downwards, falling towards the earth. One by one, all the stars of the heaven began dropping down, until the whole sky above them was lit up with a golden rain of burning fire. All stared with their heads up and their mouths open in awe of this breath-taking scene that even the most elaborate fireworks could never match.

As the heavenly bodies got closer and closer to the ground, people began to see their true form and cheered. In a matter of minutes after Daniel's call, the air above them was filled with hovering warriors, all clad in shining armour to the bone, their wings of fire making them look like an army of angels from heaven. They were everywhere, thousands and thousands of them, way too many to count, and all ready to fight.

Daniel's eyes were focused on one of them in particular. From the moment the stars began reacting to his call, his attention was drawn to the shiny one above Arba, the star of the Great Lord. It was the first to come down from its place in the sky and was now floating in the air towards him. Daniel recognized the shape, the face, the hair of the man, and as the two of them were within earshot of each other, he could not help but smile and well up at the same time.

'It's so good to see you again, my friend,' he said, feeling a joy such as he had not felt ever since he'd found his mother and brother again.

With the usual cheerful look on his face, Heli smiled back at him and bowed his head.

'We've come to pledge our allegiance, my lord; the army of heaven is at your command.'

He looked exactly as Daniel remembered seeing him when he defeated the ice dragon, except for the armour he was now wearing.

'Good,' Daniel said, feeling happier than he could even express. 'Now, let's finish this.'

'Yes, my lord,' Heli replied with a grin, and rose up in the air again, his wings of fire obeying his will. At the last moment, he spotted his sister among the crowd, who smiled at him through tearful eyes. He winked at her and then turned towards Arba, followed by the rest of his friends.

Tens of thousands of flying warriors now set their sight on the hideous creatures bred by the General. Fiery arrows rained from the sky, filling the air with screeches of pain and torment, while the earth gorged on more of their blood and lifeless corpses. The wolfmen and remaining black ravens seemed to have lost their purpose, and upon feeling the danger of being overrun, began retreating inside the city, abandoning the battle. But there was no hiding from the army of the sky; wherever they went, fire rained upon them and consumed them all one by one.

Bolstered by the new reinforcements, the remaining men and wingmen of Endërland resumed the battle, now with renewed hope and strength.

Seeing that he had lost the war, the General grabbed the reins of the chariot and led the duo of horses back towards the white gate. He did not manage to get far, however, a gold-finished spear flying in his direction found itself landing on his back, striking him between his ribs and straight into his heart. The once Lord of Winter fell out of his chariot, facedown, breathing his last.

Watching from a distance, Diane breathed deeply and allowed the rest of her armour to fall to the ground. Daniel's eyes met hers from a distance, and he smiled with great pride.

As life abandoned the body he inhabited, the General was forced to leave it and flee somewhere he could find safety. But as soon as he was exposed to the light still emanating from the Golden Throne, he began to disintegrate just like the rest of the shadows before him. His last screams joined those of the remaining wolfmen, as once again they began to go through transformation, returning to their original form, no longer bound by his evil magic. Soon, thousands of wolves were seen running away from the battlefield towards the Northern Mountains and the place they once called home.

All around the city of the Lords, in and out of the ice wall that was now melting down, men, wingmen, and mermaids began cheering and shouting from joy, praising the army of the sky and the Great Lord. Winter was defeated, his army of creatures eliminated, and Arba along with the rest of Endërland was free once again.

The battle was over.

Chapter 17

A NEW WORLD

Standing in the oval-shaped courtyard, next to the Eternal Clock with its one hand now bordering between winter and spring, Daniel felt like breaking down and crying. Winter and his creatures had caused colossal damage to the glorious city. There was little left of that wondrous and colourful garden that was once full of life; everything had been trampled and stepped on mercilessly.

Summer's fountains had almost all been destroyed, but thankfully there were still a few left standing, and their water was being used to restore health to all the wounded from the battle. The earth was hidden under the remains of all the unnatural birds and animals that were being moved away to designated burning sites. Swords, spears, knives, and arrows were everywhere, and Daniel felt sick at the very sight of them.

The sky was still empty and dark, looking very strange without the usual host of stars to brighten it up. Heli and the rest of the celestial army were still busy helping out on the ground with the wounded and the fallen. The air buzzed with the flapping of their fiery wings, and those of the remaining wingmen, who worked tirelessly to restore order in the aftermath of the battle.

Their sorrows however were not over yet. As Daniel watched, a group of six wingmen, led by Séraphin and followed by hundreds more, flew in, carrying with them the body of their fallen queen. Word spread and songs were already being sung of her bravery and fierce courage. So many had fallen in the battlefield, and despite the final victory, this was indeed a sad day for all of Endërland.

The wingmen sat their queen's body down on the cold pavement of the royal courtyard, at the feet of her tall ivory throne. They improvised out of the blue a bed of beautiful flowers, which Daniel wondered where they got. Two wingmen sat on their knees opposite each other, at her head and feet. They unfolded their beautiful blue and white wings, covering her entire lifeless body, in the likeness of an image not unfamiliar to Daniel. They stayed that way for the remainder of the ceremony, which was about to begin.

With the help of the celestial army under Heli's lead, all the bodies of the fallen heroes were placed on the side, until the ceremony was over, and it was decided on the best way to honour them. When all was done, everyone gathered before the Silver Throne, waiting for the Lords to appear. Hëna and Damien had gone together into Winter's tower to release them, and were now walking behind them as Autumn, Spring, and Summer entered the royal courtyard, heading towards Daniel. There was indescribable pain and horror in their eyes as they were finally confronted with the consequences of Winter's sins.

The three approached Daniel and kneeled before him, pledging their loyalty and allegiance. After that, they stood up again and headed towards their thrones, but did not sit down. Behind him, Diane took her own place standing before her throne, with Íro as always by her side, while to his left Séraphin stood by his mother's throne. To his far-right, Eleanor appeared from the water, with her left arm and shoulder wrapped up in bandages. Nemo was by her side, now back in his merman form, his beaming eyes shifting between Daniel and the lovely Íro.

Daniel's heart was instantly uplifted upon seeing his friend again. He wanted to run towards him and give him a big hug, public or not, but it would have to wait. Everyone was here, and they were all once again waiting for him.

He turned to face the entire army gathered before him, men and wingmen grouped on the ground behind their leaders, and mermaids in the sea behind their queen and prince. Heli and his friends continued to populate the air above them, organized in their own quadrants of thousands. Their collective light made the whole city look even brighter than the sunniest day.

Everyone looked tired and worn out, but gone was from their faces the fear and dread of the impending doom. The war was over, and they had won; now it was time to rebuild whatever was destroyed and start all over again. And they were all looking to him once more to lead them back into the life they knew before all of this.

Yet, after all that was done and everything that had taken place, Daniel still felt uncomfortable and ill equipped to stand before an entire kingdom and tell them what they needed to hear. He might be the Great Lord, but he still felt like he was just Daniel, an ordinary city boy who had just been through an extraordinary experience. Still, he had already accepted this responsibility and honour, and he would not shy away from it now.

Trying to come up with words appropriate for this moment, he looked at the crowds before him and began to speak.

'People of Endërland, wingmen, and mermaids, my brothers and sisters; today we rejoice, for we have claimed back our kingdom, our lives, our freedom. Evil has been conquered and we are free once again; though the price we paid for this is indeed high, for we lost many of our loved ones. Do not hold back your tears, we will miss them all dearly; but as we say goodbye, let us celebrate the life they gave so that we may continue to live. We owe it to them to make the most out of it and live it to the fullest.'

Daniel stopped for a moment, an idea already forming in his mind. Looking at Heli and all the celestial warriors before him, he now knew the best way to honour the fallen ones.

'As we welcome the start of the new season, and the Silver Sceptre is now passed on to Spring, we will honour our fallen heroes by lifting them up into the sky, where they will continue to watch over us, just like our brothers and sisters here always have. And each time this day comes, we will gather in this place to celebrate and remember them, and I promise you that on that day, they will all come down and celebrate with us.'

With everyone wondering what he meant by this, Daniel raised both his hands over his head, with his palms up and eyes closed. In his mind, he imagined the bodies of every single one of the fallen heroes levitate from the ground and rise slowly towards the sky. As they continued to ascend, they began to transform into radiant light that kept growing brighter and more powerful as they joined together.

Sounds of awe echoed throughout all of Arba, as Daniel opened his eyes and found that this was exactly what was happening. The two wingmen covering the body of the Sky-Queen, were still sitting in the same position, looking up with their mouths and eyes wide open. He watched as her body slowly ascended and joined with the rest of the fallen, flesh and bone scintillating out of existence before the stunned eyes of the entire congregation. Slowly, thousands of beams of light rising up from the ground came together, ultimately forming a single heavenly structure. Once it finally reached the roof of the sky, it flickered, stopped, and became a permanent member of the celestial family. Daniel smiled; a bigger and brighter version of the Milky Way now stretched all across the visible sky.

Applauds and cheers erupted from everyone around him, with tears freely falling as goodbyes were said. From somewhere behind him, among the mermaids of the sea, a very clear and powerful voice arose above the noise of the waves and the exclamations of everyone else. It was a voice that defied all other voices with a beautiful song of bravery and strength, gratitude, and love.

From the seashell where he was sitting next to his mother, Nemo turned around to see the mermaid to whom that voice belonged. It was Agnes, the older mermaid he had met before. He understood now why they called her, "the loud one". Smiling, it dawned on him that she was very likely the legendary mermaid of the well, and he could not wait to share this little fact with Daniel.

Soon, the old mermaid was joined by her sisters and then everyone else, and thus the song grew louder, echoing throughout all of Endërland.

As the singing continued, with everyone's eyes glued to the sky, Daniel spotted Heli approaching him, accompanied by another striking young man, with a look just as jolly as his.

'My lord, may I introduce you to a very good friend of mine; you know him as the Northern Star.'

The young man flew closer to Daniel and bowed in respect.

'We are all very happy you have returned, my lord. It was about time you called on us; we were getting quite a bit restless up there. If it weren't for this guy,' he motioned at Heli, 'some of us would have come down here on our own.

But he insisted on waiting on your call; he knew you'd come through.'

'Thank you,' Daniel said, smiling fondly at Heli who returned the gesture. Then, he remembered something and turned to the man again. 'Hey, you're the funny one, right? The one with all the jokes?' Right then he wished he hadn't said anything.

'I see my reputation precedes me,' the young man said, looking at Heli. 'Well, I haven't prepared anything for the occasion, but here, maybe you haven't heard this one.' He then proceeded to tell a joke before Daniel could stop him.

'Guy meets girl at a feast, you know; guy tells girl: "Did it hurt?" Girl says: "Did what hurt?" Guy says: "When you fell down from heaven?" Girl starts going: "Aww...," but guy continues: "Because your face is all messed up..." Ha ha...'

The celestial ended the joke there, laughing hysterically as if it was the funniest thing he had ever heard or told. Daniel could not help but laugh along, more at him than at his joke. For a while there, he'd thought they'd never laugh this way again. But this felt good, really really good.

When they were done laughing, the young man bowed once again.

'It really was an honour, my lord; you know where to find us, should you ever need us again.'

Smiling, he put his beautiful fiery wings to use, and signalled the rest of his friends to follow him back up towards the sky. People continued to thank them and wave them goodbye, while thousands of singing voices still soared above them.

Only Heli stayed behind, and now it was just the two of them. Daniel looked into the eyes of his big friend with indescribable longing and a little sadness.

'I'm sorry I couldn't save you, Hel. You've no idea how much we've missed you.'

481

'I'm not,' Heli said, the smile never fading from his handsome face. His blonde hair seemed to have been set ablaze like his fiery wings, and contrasted beautifully with his big black eyes, which, as far as Daniel was concerned, were no longer the only thing he had in common with Hëna. 'I would do it all over again, if it meant helping you find your way.'

'But how did you know?' Daniel asked. He had always wondered why Heli had believed in him from the start. Heli kept smiling but did not answer. Instead, he looked behind Daniel, where Hëna and his parents could be seen anxiously approaching. Daniel saw them as well and knew it was now their time. He stretched his hand out to Heli, who extended his in return.

'Until next time, my friend.'

'Until next time,' Heli replied and flew in the direction of his family.

Daniel watched them from a distance. Hëna's gushing tears at the joy of holding her brother in her embrace once again somehow gave him closure, and he felt happy for her, for all of them. But then, for a single moment their eyes met, and he felt uneasy, so he turned and headed towards his own family. He found his mother holding Damien in her arms, and the two of them watched the stars taking their place back into the night sky. Daniel threw his arms around both of them, and they continued watching together. He wished he could freeze this amazing moment in time, and they could stay like this forever.

Diane seemed to be feeling the same way. She smiled and kissed both of them on the side of their heads.

'I love you, boys; I'm so proud of both of you. If only daddy was here to see you now.'

'Dad,' Daniel said, remembering. And just as if on cue, the Oracle appeared by his side.

'Alfie, where did you disappear to? I haven't seen you since the battle ended.'

'I was minding some other business, which I need to talk to you about.'

'What is it?' Daniel asked. The Oracle glanced at Diane and Damien, not sure if he should speak in front of them.

'Alfie,' Daniel insisted.

'I have news from your world, and it's not all good, I'm afraid.'

'Are dad and Sam alright?' Daniel asked right away.

'They're fine. They managed to get to you in time, before Butler could kill you, and they've taken your body to the hospital.'

'What's the bad news?'

The Oracle paused for a moment, not too eager to be the bearer of bad news, but he knew there was no way around this. So, he finally answered.

'Butler is dead.'

Daniel looked at him with horror in his eyes. He knew what this meant; his brother would never be able to return to his own body and the life he was robbed of so long ago. He would remain here forever and would never get to see their dad again. He looked at Damien, who lowered his head in despair, while Diane tried to comfort him.

'I'm so sorry,' the Oracle continued. 'That's not all, however. Your body has grown very week, and if you do not return now, you might never get a chance to. You need to go back, Daniel, now.'

Daniel slowly turned away and looked at everything and everyone around him. The people were now safe, but there was still a lot that he had to do here. Would they judge him, if he left them now, even if only for a little while?

He turned to his mother.

'I guess I have to go back, mom. I don't know how long I've been gone for, or if my body can survive any longer.'

'The portal,' Diane said, 'we have to go right now.'

'But mom, what about everything here? There's still so much we need to do.'

'It will all be here when you get back, sweetheart. Right now, you have to go and take care of yourself, Sam, and your dad.'

Sam.

Thinking of her inadvertently led his thoughts to Hëna, and now he knew that, whatever happened between him and the moon girl, he and Sam could only ever be friends.

He looked over to where Hëna was, and saw Heli rise up and take his place once again as the brightest star above Arba. She looked peaceful, almost happy. He felt relieved, seeing her like that. He still heard her words in his ear, telling her that she didn't want him, and it still hurt, but he knew that time would heal that wound too. She was alright, and that was all that mattered.

He headed towards the three of them, with Diane and Damien following him. He stopped in front of Autumn and his wife, making every effort not to look at Hëna.

'My Lord Autumn, I'm afraid I have to go away for a little while; there is something very important I must see to before I can do anything else here. May I ask you and your sisters to look after everything in my absence?'

Autumn appeared puzzled, but he did not ask.

'Of course, my lord. As always, we are here to serve.'

Hëna looked at Daniel, but he did not meet her gaze.

'Thank you,' he replied. 'I will be back soon.'

He bowed his head in respect and turned away from them, while Hëna's eyes followed him, wondering. For a moment, he thought she would chase after him and stop him, and part of him really wanted her to, but she didn't. So, he just kept walking away, leaving her and everything else behind.

With the help of Séraphin and his wingmen, Daniel arranged for all three of them to be airlifted to his mother's castle in the shortest time possible. The journey didn't last long - the wingmen flew fast - and the sight was definitely an improvement from the battle worn site of Arba and the surrounding areas. Snow and ice seemed to be melting quickly in the kingdom, and the land was once again regaining its colourful face. Seeing this, Daniel finally felt signs of relief kicking in; they had done it, they had actually saved Endërland.

Once at the castle, they thanked the wingmen and made their way up to his bedroom without delay. There were signs of pillaging and sacking all over the place, but these were more evident as they entered his bedroom. With a trembling heart, Daniel headed towards the secret room, which he had never visited a second time. As the door opened to let them in, he was relieved to find that it had not been discovered, and thus the portal had remained hidden.

He gave his mother a thankful look and stepped inside. Gazing over the bed he had slept in, the portal appeared in the form of an image of the room he was being kept in back in London. He recognized right away the two people he saw through the image. Sitting on the far end of the bed where he was resting, was his dad. He had one hand holding his.

'Dad,' Daniel whispered, a lump forming in his throat. His dad looked tired and sad.

'You can see dad?' he heard Damien from behind him. Turning around, Daniel looked at the longing faces of his mother and brother and knew that they missed him just as much as he did, if not more.

'Come,' he said and stretched out both arms, taking their hands. As their fingers touched, the image from the other world became visible to all three of them, allowing Diane and Damien to see David for the first time in a very long time.

'That's dad,' Damien kept repeating and crying. 'Mom, look, it's dad.'

'I see him, my love. I see him,' Diane replied, too overwhelmed by emotion to hold her own tears back. 'Oh, thank you, Daniel; I never thought I would get to see him again.'

They stood there for an endless moment, looking through the portal and crying. In a weird way, this family had been made whole once again and that was more than they could have ever hoped for.

After a little while, Damien asked.

'Is that Sam?'

Daniel nodded with his head, smiling. She was sitting on a chair right next to his bed, and to his surprise, she seemed to be sleeping, tucked under a hospital blanket.

'She's alive,' he said and couldn't stop smiling.

A few more moments passed, after which Diane dried her eyes and said.

'You need to go, sweetheart; they're clearly very worried about you. You've risked your health for far too long; it's time.'

Daniel looked at her and then shifted his gaze to his brother. He thought of the evening before his first dream, and how he had complained that he couldn't even remember their faces. Now, they were both here, he had found them again; he could see them, touch them, and hold them close. He knew that he would be back with them soon enough, but Damien would be stuck here forever, and he and their dad might never meet again.

He shook his brother's right hand, which he was still holding in his, and looked at him straight in his sorrowful eyes.

'Would *you* like to go? That is, if you don't mind living in my body.'

Damien gasped, staring back at him, not sure what to say.

'Daniel, what are you doing?' Diane asked.

'It's ok, mom; my place is here, I know that now. But I want Damien to have a chance to live the life he was deprived of, to be with dad. We will see him again, I promise you.'

He turned to Damien again.

'So, what do you say, big brother, wanna get back to the real world?'

'Are you sure, Dan?' Damien managed to ask, clearly wanting this. Daniel nodded again, smiling.

'Yes,' Damien almost jumped from joy, 'yes, I'd like that very much.'

'Very well, then.' Daniel took something out of his pocket and placed it in his hand, closing his fingers around it. He then let go of his hand and stepped away from him. Damien opened his hand and found a small white plastic watch, old and worn out. It seemed to have stopped working a long time ago. His face grew brighter as he recognized the item.

'This was mine,' he said, barely believing it. 'You've had it all this time?'

'It's mine too,' Daniel replied, 'it was all I had of you. Now, look over the bed; can you see the portal?'

Damien turned and nodded with his head.

'I see it.'

'Great. Now go; all you have to do is walk through it and you'll awake on the other side.'

Damien took them both in his arms one more time, before heading towards the portal.

'Tell dad that we miss him, and we love him,' Daniel said for both himself and his mother who affirmed through teary eyes.

'I will,' Damien said and climbed on the bed. 'See you soon. I love you.'

Those were the last words he said as he went through the invisible portal and over to the other side.

Opening his eyes, Damien found that they hurt. His eyelids felt heavy, and at first, he struggled to keep them open. He shifted his gaze away from the ceiling light that felt too bright for him and tried to look down at the end of the bed, where he knew his father was sitting. David was still holding his hand but seemed to have dozed off, his head hanging down on his chest. Damien looked at him for a moment, barely believing it. His dad had changed so much over the years.

He tried to move but felt too weak and found his whole body and even his arms to be too heavy. So, he gave that up and tried instead to squeeze his father's hand. That proved much easier to do; his fingers obeyed his control and the sensation caused David to wake up.

'Hi, dad,' he managed to whisper, as the stunned David looked into the open eyes of his loving son.

In a heartbeat, David leaned over and embraced him, careful not to pull out any of the tubes connected to him.

'Danny, you're awake. Oh, thank God, I was beginning to lose hope. I love you so much, son; I will never let you go again; do you hear me? Never.'

'Love you too, dad,' Damien replied, happy to be in his father's arms once again. 'I've missed you so much, dad.'

'I've missed you too, Danny, so much. How're you feeling, son?'

'A little week,' Damien answered, as his father released him from his embrace. 'I..., I can't move, dad.'

'I know, son; you've been asleep for over a month now and have been in a coma for the past week. The doctors said it was your body's way of protecting itself by shutting down. They could do nothing else but keep you well fed and exercised, and hope that you'd wake up eventually. But now that you're awake everything will be alright; with a little therapy, you will be up and out of here in no time.

'Oh, Danny, I was so afraid you'd never come back to me.'

'I'm sorry you've had to go through all that, dad,' Damien said, looking at his father much clearly now that his eyes had adjusted to the light in the room. 'You're so much older than I remember.'

'What are you talking about, Danny? It's only been three months, son; I couldn't have gotten that old.'

Damien knew he had to tell him; he couldn't hide the truth from his dad, not after being apart from him for so long.

'Actually dad, it's been almost 16 years; well, for you at least.'

David looked puzzled.

'What do you mean?'

'Daniel stayed behind with mom, dad; he let me come back instead.'

It took David more than a moment to understand what he was hearing. His eyes filled up once again, as his fingers reached for the face of his son.

'Damien?' he asked unsure.

'Yes, dad, it's me,' Damien answered, now crying a river.

'But how could this be? How is this possible? Where have you been all this time?'

'It's a very long story, dad, but I will tell you everything in due time.'

'I cannot believe this. What about Daniel? Is he alright?'

'He's fine, dad. He and mom send their love and want you to know that they miss you very much.'

David felt this was all too surreal.

'Mom is there with him?'

'Yes, dad. You should see her now; she is even more strong and beautiful than when she was here with us. And she has a mean throwing arm, too;' Damien chuckled through the tears. 'You would be so proud of her.'

David leaned back, not knowing what to make of all of this. Every human sense told him that the boy before him was his youngest, Daniel. But he had learned enough by now to doubt his son's words. He did not get how this whole dreamworld thing worked, but he didn't have to; he knew in his heart it was all true. He looked at his son again and smiled.

'I cannot believe this, you're back, and now I have both my sons here with me. Damien,' he repeated his name, as if trying to get used to it again. 'This is all so weird.'

'I know, dad,' Damien smiled again, 'don't worry, we'll get there.'

From the corner of his eye he saw Sam move and turn in her chair.

'She's still here,' he said, not really asking.

'She never leaves.' David looked fondly at the blonde girl. 'She eats here, she sleeps here, she even takes showers here. She keeps waiting for you to wake up. She saved both our lives, Dan..., Damien. Without her, none of us would be alive today.'

As if sensing that they were talking about her, Sam woke up and her blue eyes met straight away with Damien's.

'You're awake,' she almost yelled, throwing away the blanket and being by his side in an instant. David got up and gave her some space.

"Why didn't you wake me?' she rebuked him.

'I'm going to get the doctor,' David simply said, winking at her, and then leaving the room.

Damien looked at Sam's beautiful face hovering a bit too close above his but did not feel uncomfortable. He remembered her from that night in Endërland; she was the same proud and beautiful girl, yet there was something different about her now.

'Hi, Sam,' he whispered, happiness brightening up his smile. 'Did you sleep well?'

Sam kept staring at him as if trying to convince herself that he was real. He was finally back, awake, and now she would be able to do this again.

'Like a baby,' she answered and reached down with her lips, kissing him passionately.

She smelled so nice, and her lips felt so good and soft against his, that Damien did not protest. Something deep inside of him told him that he wanted this apparently just as much as she did. So, he kissed her back, and he kissed her again that day, and the next day, and the day after...

The days that followed were all about restoring Endërland to its former glory. The first thing that Daniel had to do, was appoint replacements for Heli and Hëna in the sky. Summer volunteered her own son and daughter for the job, and he gladly accepted. He held no grudge for the part she had played during the council meeting; her heart had been in the right place.

Next one to be replaced was Winter. The position of the White Lord had to be filled, if things were to return to normal as much as possible. Daniel offered it to Andrés, Ari's eldest son and firstborn in this world. He had proven invaluable during the battle and had earned Daniel's and everyone else's respect from day one. Andrés graciously accepted the position and took over the role of the Lord of winter. Together with his family he moved into Winter's tower and helped rebuild Arba with the rest of the Lords.

It took no time for Spring to restore the garden and make it even more stunning than it was before. The surrounding sequoia trees were as healthy as ever, and with Summer's help, the healing water was once again springing all over the city.

Under Autumn's supervision, all weapons in the kingdom were destroyed, including Winter's gifts to the three queens, until no trace or even a memory of them was left. There was no image of them recorded in the Chronicles, nor instructions on how to make them.

As for the new Lord of winter, he decided to dedicate his gift not to the city, but to the Great Lord himself. Out of ice that would never melt, he sculpted a life-size replica of Lightning, the bravest stallion the kingdom had ever known. This was then placed on top of the grave where Lightning was buried. Daniel wept the first time he saw it, feeling forever grateful for this.

Things changed in the sea world as well. Eleanor finally decided that time had come for her to leave, and thus her successor was elected. However, unlike tradition required, this time there was no competition to determine which one of the candidates would replace her.

To everyone's surprise, Vanessa herself had withdrawn her candidacy, declaring in front of everyone that Nemo had proven to be the wisest, strongest, and most courageous of them all. Thus, he was unanimously crowned King of the Seas in front of all the mer-people. Daniel couldn't be prouder and happier for his friend. In time, Eleanor said her goodbyes and took her last journey into the open sea, never to be seen again.

As for the sky-people, they had lost more than half of their wingmen during the battle, including their beloved queen. In their own tradition, they mourned their loss for forty days and nights, after which the crown was passed on to Séraphin in a great ceremony. Daniel welcomed the decision, knowing this was the right choice, and gave the new Sky-King his blessing.

Gabriel's position as Chieftain of the Northern tribe would be filled by his young wife, until their unborn child would grow old enough to take over, as agreed by both Séraphin and Daniel.

With the Lords' help, the Shadow Forest was transformed from a dark and desolate place, into a forest filled with life and all manner of living creatures. Abundant sunshine and moonlight fell on it all the time, and soon the old name was forgotten and stricken from the record. It was now called, Brightwood.

As all of these changes took place, life in Endërland gradually returned to normal, without much excitement or anything out of the ordinary happening. Ari's sons returned to New Sotira and continued their life there, much like before. The Oracle returned to his little house in Tálas, where Veronica waited for him. Diane continued to serve as

Queen of Endër, while Damien returned to visit them every day, always bringing news from the other world.

For some reason, Sam never came back to Endërland, and Daniel never saw her again. He was very happy for her and Damien though, knowing that in a weird way, she got together with the man she loved, and his brother found the best girl there ever was.

Feeling that everything was as perfect as it could be in the kingdom, Daniel eventually found himself with very little to do. Everyone had their own place in either world, only he felt like he did not belong anywhere. He loved to live in the castle with his mom, just like he loved spending time in Arba with the Lords. But as the seasons passed, there weren't that many things that required his attention, and the castle was his mother's place, not his. So, he decided to go to the one place he knew he would never tire of, the seaside.

With Garret and Sarah's help, he built a small house, not too far from theirs, so that he could live next to the sea and his best friend. He spent a lot of time under the sea with the new king, whenever his royal duties and the lovely Íro would spare him. And he could never get enough of it. At nights, he would still stay up until late and stare at the big and beautiful moon traveling through the sky, lighting up the entire kingdom. Even the stars seemed to shine brighter than before, as if they were happy that the moon was back amongst them. To Daniel, however, it no longer felt the same; this was not his moon. But it was the next best thing, and it was all he had.

* * *

On a late summer's day, almost two seasons after the war ended, he was sitting on the beach just outside his little house, like he did every afternoon. The sun was on the last

494

mile of its journey for that day, and was preparing to kiss the sky goodnight. The air was still hot outside, despite a cool breeze blowing in from the ocean.

Daniel relished in the warm lovely feeling of the sand under his feet, his mind as always going to the usual topics, like waves running towards the same old rock. He thought of the first night he spent on this beach and smiled to himself. He had been convinced then that this was all nothing but a dream. To this day, he still wasn't sure that he was wrong; he half expected to wake up at any moment and find himself back in his bedroom, at his London flat with his dad. He missed home and his dad, but he had fallen in love with this place, and knew that this was now his home.

The sound of light footsteps approaching behind him claimed his attention, and he turned to see who it was. Hëna walked towards him, wearing a simple white dress and hair loose much like the first time he had seen her. Her big black eyes were focused on him, full of light, while her beautiful red lips formed the loveliest smile he had ever seen on her. Her bare feet stepped gracefully on the dry sand, causing his heart to beat in sync with the rhythm they kept. The rays of sunshine bounced off her perfect white skin, coming away even brighter than before. It seemed she still had some light left in her.

Daniel was so surprised to see her that he failed to even get up, as was the polite thing to do.

'Hi,' she simply said as she sat beside him on the warm sand. The breeze blowing in from the sea played with her long black hair, carrying her enticing scent over to him. Daniel inhaled inconspicuously, cherishing it like he would never get another chance.

'Your mother told me I would find you here,' she said. Her voice was as melodious as he remembered it.

'Yes, I live here now,' he answered, all the while trying

to control the crazy pounding of his heart, which had never obeyed to him before. 'I've always loved the sea; plus, I get to hang out with Nemo a lot.'

Hëna smiled but did not ask of Nemo like he thought she might. Instead, she cast her gaze at the horizon before her, far where the sky met the ocean, and allowed herself to take it all in.

'I can see why; It's so beautiful here, so peaceful. I understand why you like it so much. I should come out here more often.'

Daniel said nothing; this wasn't really a conversation, more like an icebreaker. He sensed that she was simply stalling and would soon say whatever she had come to say, so he just waited.

'My father says "hello",' she continued, still biding her time. 'He wonders when you'll be visiting Arba again; he says he's got a couple of ideas he'd like to run by you.'

This wasn't news to Daniel; he'd already received this message from Autumn through his mother. And he'd already replied that Damien would be the one to deal with these things from now on. Ever since his brother had taken over his life back in the real world, they now both shared in the responsibility of being the Great Lord over Endërland. Daniel much preferred it this way. He wasn't cut out to lead an entire kingdom, or maybe just wasn't ready for that yet. So, he was more than happy to delegate this part to Damien instead.

'Thank you,' he decided to reply to her, nonetheless. 'I will go and visit soon, though it's really Damien he should talk to about these things now.'

'That's right,' she said, though she didn't seem as intrigued as she sounded. 'You're both Great Lords now. How does that work?'

'I don't think I even know myself,' Daniel answered.

'I let him go through my portal, giving him possession of my body along with the right to the lordship of Endërland, I guess.'

'And you're okay with that?' she asked, though what she really wanted to know was why he had decided to stay in the first place.

'I would give it all away if I could; it was never what I wanted. I was happy being just Daniel and wouldn't really mind going back to that.'

Hëna understood. She'd been a lightbringer for so long that she had forgotten what life actually was like. And now that she was no longer in charge of the night, she could be herself again and experience everything that she had put aside in favour of her duty. If only Heli were there with her too.

She continued to stare at the horizon ahead, all the while playing with the sand between her fingers. For the first time ever since he'd met her, Daniel realized that she was nervous.

She took a little more time, during which he just sat there, waiting, and then, without looking at him, she finally spoke again.

'Why didn't you come to me? For a long time after the battle I waited for you to come and find me, but you never did.'

Finally, she'd said it. Daniel felt like smiling.

'I didn't think you wanted to see me again,' he replied, not knowing what else to say. Deep inside his chest, however, his heart was doing a little dance. It was about time they had this conversation, and the fact that she started it was a good sign.

She looked at him only for a moment and smiled feebly.

'I guess I must have been very convincing,' she said

and then looked down and away from him, as if feeling guilty. 'I did not really want you to leave, Daniel; I didn't mean any of what I said that day. I just..., when I heard the White Lord threaten to kill you, I panicked. I thought, convincing you to go back, was the only way to save you. I knew there was no hope for the rest of us here, but there was still a chance for you. I guess, I didn't have enough faith in you; I'm sorry.'

Daniel felt like he wouldn't be able to stop his own lips from widening without his permission. A part of him had always known it had been an act, but he couldn't allow himself to actually believe it.

'Don't be,' he said, 'I doubted myself for a very long time before that day, and until the very last moment, I never really believed I was the Great Lord.'

'Still, I should not have doubted you. Heli always knew, and for a while, his faith became mine. But my fear got the better of me.'

'That's funny, I never thought you were afraid of anything.'

'Me neither, until I met you.' She now turned again to look at him in the eyes and held his gaze. 'I was afraid I would lose you forever and I couldn't live with that. I thought, as long as you were safe, I could deal with anything.'

Daniel's heart began to race even faster now, as he realized what she was actually saying. He reached for her hands, drawing closer to her, and this time she did not push him away.

'Well, you didn't lose me, though I must admit, you came pretty close; I almost left.'

'I'm glad you didn't,' she said, and he knew she meant it. They sat like that for a while, still looking at each other, not really knowing what to do next.

Then Hëna spoke again.

'I've been meaning to ask you something. Did you

know Heli would return that night with the rest of them?'

'No,' Daniel replied, smiling as he thought back on that night. He had been as surprised as everyone else to see his big friend again. 'I didn't. But I think I wanted him too.'

Hëna smiled that lovely smile again and said,

'I had a feeling you might have. Thank you.'

They were too close now, and her eyes suddenly sparkled with that mischievous look he knew all too well.

'You know, there's something I've been dying to do since the first day I saw you.'

'Oh yeah? And what's that?' Daniel asked, thoughts running wild in his head. Hëna drew closer as if to kiss him, and at the very last moment raised her hands and dipped her fingers in his hair, messing it all up.

She laughed heartily, as did Daniel, lifting his hands instinctively to fix his hair again. She then leaned even closer and placed her lips on top of his, kissing him softly. Daniel ignored his hair then, and held her face with both his hands, kissing her back.

'I love you, Daniel,' she whispered, taking her lips back for a moment, 'I always have.'

Hearing her say those three simple words, he knew that it was true. He knew that she was the reason why he would always choose this world; he knew that with her was where he belonged. He drew back, looked into her beautiful bright eyes again and answered.

'And I love you.'

(End of Volume I)

The ENDËRLAND Chronicles

Volume II

'BOOK OF SERENA'

(Preview)

Ed Marishta

Chapter 1

THE OTHER WORLD

he moon was high up in the middle of the sky as Serena watched it from her bedroom window. She loved looking at the moon every night; it was big, and round, and it always shone so bright. It made her feel like she could reach up, climb on it and ride in the sky all through the night, looking at the world below. But she knew that wasn't possible. She envied Élena, the daughter of Summer, who had taken over the job after the Dark Winter.

When she was little, she would ask her mom to tell her all about it; what it was like to be among the stars and shine down all over Endërland, when it used to be her up there. And her mom would talk for hours and hours, until she'd fall asleep. Sometimes her dad would sit down with them and join in the stories, telling her how the two of them had met and how they had fought in the Big War and won. She used to love listening to those stories.

She was too old now to waste time with that stuff; tomorrow would be the eighteenth autumn since she had been born. She did not want to spend her life indoors; she wanted to get out there, experience the whole world and travel to the farthest reaches of the kingdom. But everyone kept telling her that there was nowhere to go. There *had* to be something beyond the ocean, or on the other side of the Northern Mountains; the world did not just end there, did it?

Moving away from the window and leaving it open so she could watch the moon from her bed, she got ready for sleep. Her parents had already turned in for the night.

She wasn't really looking forward to tomorrow. Yes, her dad was sure to have prepared some special surprise for her, like he always did, but other than that, she knew it would be just another day in Endërland. And she felt like something was really missing, like she had yet to uncover her purpose in life.

Determined to do something about it, she slipped into bed and closed her eyes. Tomorrow would be a new day; she would make sure of it. It took her a while, but eventually her body relaxed, and she fell asleep.

When next she opened her eyes, she had to close and open them again, unable to believe what she saw. She did that a few more times, but every time she opened them, she saw the same thing; a cloudy sky above her, instead of the familiar ceiling of her bedroom. She felt a chill run through her body and realized she was lying down on a very cold and hard surface. She stood up, barefoot as she was, and looked around. She did not recognize this place.

She appeared to be standing on top of a very tall castle, built with large flat stones and mirrors. She almost felt dizzy from being so high up. All around her she saw many other similar buildings, but most of them were smaller, pretty much like usual houses. There were so many streets between them, with so many weird coaches that moved really fast and without any horses dragging them. Pillars of smoke rose up from several places in the city, while in the sky, giant metallic birds flew very high, leaving behind a long white trail.

Fear gripped her now, not knowing where she was or how she got here. How would she go back home? What would mom and dad think when they would not find her in her room in the morning?

Stepping back from the edge of the terrace she was on, she heard a door creak open behind her, and a voice calling her name.

'Serena?'

She turned around and saw a young man approaching with careful steps. He had short brown wavy hair, wearing strange clothes and a silly smile on his face. He was slightly taller than her, with broad shoulders and an athletic body, and didn't seem to be that much older than she was. He stopped halfway from the door to her and said.

'Hi. I'm Freddie. I'm here to help you.'

(Continue reading in Volume II, "Book of Serena")

ABOUT THE
AUTHOR

Ed Marishta was born in the winter of 1976, in the small town of Gramsh, Albania. Like most of his fellow countrymen in that time period, he grew up in a country with challenging economic conditions and political upheaval. A renowned geologist in his area, his father was away with work much of the time, therefore the task of raising, educating, and caring for their five children fell mostly upon his mother.

Ed's writing inclinations and rich imagination manifested at a very young age. As early as 10 years old, he tried to write his first "masterpiece", a story about a little boy with psychic powers, which he titled "The Adventures of Ren". Sadly, that manuscript was lost, and he never got to show the world his "genius" until many years later, when he picked up writing again.

The changing of the political climate in the 1990s, followed by the mass immigration of Albanian people in search of a better life, also prompted Ed and his siblings to immigrate to neighbouring Greece for several years, and later on to the UK and USA. Ed constantly worked on projects and ideas for novels, as well as translation works, which helped with his language skills, up to the point where he felt confident enough to write in English.

In January 2014, he finally self-published his first novel, "The Endërland Chronicles: Book of Daniel", with the second revised edition coming a year later. He has now also published the second and third volumes in the trilogy, titled "Book of Serena", and "Book of Joshua".

If you enjoyed reading about Daniel and his friends, and would like to see how their story ends, as well as stay informed with any other news or information, visit the book's page at: https://www.facebook.com/EnderlandBook.

Ed would also greatly appreciate any reviews posted on iTunes, Amazon, Goodreads, Smashwords and elsewhere. This is a great encouragement for him to keep writing.

Thank you!